Red Rain

Red Rain

PATRICK J. O'BRIAN

ISBN: 978-1-60414-275-4

This is for Erie County Sheriff Tim Howard, who goes above and beyond for me on these projects. Congratulations on being reelected to serve the fortunate people of Erie County for another term.

Thanks to Brad Wiemer, Carol Pyle,
Nannette Bell, Chris Myers, Barb Caster,
Dave Blackford, Tim Howard, Rick Donovan,
Jim Hathaway, Wayne Huff, Danny Bayer,
Jeff Geesaman, Brian Tolbert, Joy Winslow,
Juddy Plumb, Mike Summers,
Marty Bronisz, and Bryan Lockerby for their
contributions. Also a big thank you to everyone
who works for the Erie County Sheriff's
Department for their assistance.

Special thanks to Kendrick
Shadoan at KLS Digital for creating
the cover, handling photography, and
doing a great job as always.

Visit www.klsdigital.com

Other novels by Patrick J. O'Brian include:

The Fallen

Reaper: Book One of the West Baden Murders Series

The Brotherhood

Retribution: Book Two of the West Baden Murders Series

Stolen Time

Sins of the Father: Book Three of the West Baden Murders Series

Six Days

Dysfunction

The Sleeping Phoenix

Snowbound: Book Four of the West Baden Murders Series

Sawmill Road

Ghosts of West Baden: Book Five of the West Baden Murders Series

Sin Killer

The Doomsday Clock: Book Six of the West Baden Murders Series

Hallowed Grounds

Non-fiction projects by Patrick J. O'Brian include:

Risen from the Ashes: The History of the West Baden Springs Hotel

Pluto in the Valley: The History of the French Lick Springs Hotel

Check out the author's other projects at

www.pjobooks.com

or look him up on Facebook.

CHAPTER 1

Saturday, April 12
Buffalo, New York

Winter finally broke its stranglehold on the second largest city in the state of New York, only after it dumped a final mountain of snow for remembrance. An early April snowstorm left the street department nearly five feet of snow to clear with their depleted supplies of salt and sand.

Aided by two days of thunderstorms, the workers did their best as the streets transformed into a slushy mess. The wave of warmer weather freed residents from their homes and apartments, now starved for entertainment with spring fever infecting them like a virus.

Like clockwork, the criminal element also fell into the streets, creating more headaches for law enforcement, the fire department, and medical personnel alike. Officer Tom Covington and his partner, Marty Renz, patrolled the city during the midnight tour, finding their shift more eventful than planned.

"Must be a full moon," Renz commented from the passenger's seat as Covington turned onto Otto Street in the industrial south side.

"It's something."

Covington identified with the working class people living in the Old First Ward. A historically strong Irish neighborhood, the Ward provided an interesting mix of residences and the businesses that once prospered in South Buffalo. While much of the industry moved or died off completely, the neighborhood remained, and with it, a few mainstay taverns, local eateries, and empty factories.

Covered in mud and slush, their patrol car's white exterior looked more like a drab eggshell color, trying in vain to shed its new coating by constantly hitting puddles. Covington surveyed the government housing area for activity, taking it slowly, as the activity of Interstate 190 buzzed overhead. The revving of motors came and went with the headlights as truckers and commuters traveled just past the midnight hour.

Barely an hour into their shift, the pair already had two reports to fill out, but they decided to wait because their night was far from over. Renz typically entered their reports into the computer near the end of their shift, having attended college and typed numerous papers. Too smart to be a cop, Renz decided against entering the family business, a successful one at that, to join the city police force after graduating with a business degree from New York University.

His parents never seemed to understand his decision, though they respected his wishes. Renz kept his upscale family a secret from most of his colleagues on the Buffalo Police Department. He and Covington had partnered for the better part of a year, so few secrets remained between them.

In some ways the partners were polar opposites. While Renz remained faithfully married, with two beautiful daughters, Covington was twice divorced with a ten-year-old son he seldom saw, except occasionally on holidays and weekends. Renz had a knack for using technology, constantly on his cell phone, text messaging friends, or downloading music for his iPod. Covington came from a lineage of factory workers, much more blue collar than his partner. Like his brother, a captain on the Erie County Sheriff's Department, he broke away from the declining factory profession.

He had purchased a used computer two months prior, after Renz nagged him incessantly for months to join the modern world.

With his fiftieth birthday less than a year away, Covington felt too old for change. He had watched Buffalo's decline from a powerful industrial powerhouse to a city barely clinging to life from an economic standpoint. Steel and grain mills once lined the waterfront, a potent display of the city's major exports. Now health care providers and banks topped the list of employers within city limits while the old mill buildings faded and deteriorated, too expensive to convert or demolish.

In the past few years the city he loved had seen an upswing in employment, but he wondered how a tougher national economy might slow the progress to a crawl.

"You given any more thought to changing shifts?" Renz asked, checking something on their car's computer terminal.

"What? And leave all this scenery behind?"

Covington's girlfriend of five months didn't like the idea of him working midnights. He personally liked keeping busy all night, hating the morning shifts with all of the front office brass roaming around their old police headquarters. He preferred heading home as most of them were commuting to work, knowing his pension checks were drawing closer by the day.

His girlfriend worked mornings at the hospital, which drastically limited their time together, particularly since she had a teenage daughter.

"This is the weirdest thing I've ever seen," Renz commented as lightning flashed, illuminating the city streets around them. "Who ever heard of thunderstorms with snow on the ground?"

"Stick around here long enough and you'll see everything."

Covington experienced the days when beating suspects with flashlights and knocking out a few teeth wasn't a national news event. Those were the good old days when cops were nicer to drunk drivers, giving them a lift home or calling a friend for them, when a moderate beating served as a substitute for jail time. Both parties ended up content, and a lesson was learned. While Covington seldom participated in the rough stuff, he watched the judicial system slowly break down over the years, making him wonder which method proved more effective.

"Where you want to stop tonight?" Renz inquired about their inevitable dinner plans.

Covington had a feeling their shift was going to provide barely enough time for a meal on the run. Working in the middle of the night limited their options for quality fast meals.

He was about to make a few suggestions when a call came across their radio regarding shots fired in the vicinity of O'Connell and Fitzgerald, about five blocks southeast of their present location. The dispatcher quickly added information about the caller phoning from a cellular phone, thinking the shots originated inside a nearby building.

"Giddie-up," Renz said before responding that they would take the call, while Covington flipped on the master switch for their patrol car's lights, and another switch for their wailing siren.

Renz savored the action, along with the thought of unforeseen danger, though Covington's love affair with perilous calls ended years earlier, like the magic lost in marriages over time. Still, he wanted to be the first on the scene, like any good cop, so he floored the gas pedal, slowing only for a few stop signs before reaching a row of large older houses in an area where houses often stood only a few feet apart. Strangely, Fitzgerald Street, which stretched about three city blocks before dead ending on either side, was the exception to the rule with just a few houses and several grassy lots. Many of the houses had been demolished in years past, with no new buildings to take their places.

Renz radioed in that they were in the area, no one was visible from their position, and that they were about to check the area on foot.

"This place is abandoned," Covington noted as they stepped from the car, looking up to an old two story house with darkened windows and a faded tan exterior.

Every other building in the working class neighborhood appeared occupied, some with lights on following the shooting disturbance. Only one other house on Fitzgerald Street faced toward the street, with the neighbors standing on their front porch, curious about the police sirens in their neighborhood. Condemned by the city, soon to be a vacant grassy lot, or perhaps someone's new parking spot, the building had suffered fire damage inside the upper level the year before.

Covington noticed the old house was converted into two separate apartments, one on the ground floor, and the other accessible only from an exterior staircase that led up the side of the building. From what he observed, the building hadn't been occupied for quite some time, and the stairs along the side didn't look particularly safe. Despite the rainfall, mounds of snow still dotted the yard and collected around the curb where the rain washed small chunks toward the street corners. Based on paperwork tacked to the door and stuffed into the mailboxes, the house had been repossessed by a local bank at some point, which partially explained the stalemate on the condition.

The front door required little more than a gentle push to open, which Covington expected. Occasionally used for drug deals, prostitution quickies, and other nefarious activities, the building had suffered poor ownership. Now it awaited its death sentence to be carried out, or a saving grace to transform it into something useful, which seemed unlikely.

Other officers pulled up to the scene as the partners stepped inside the foyer. Covington took a moment to radio that the incoming units should check the alleys and the other houses since they had found nothing yet. Calls of shots fired draw police officers to a scene faster than moths flutter toward open flames, so the veteran officer wanted to make certain his colleagues remained cautious while doing their jobs.

He motioned for Renz to remain silent as they crept through the ground floor. When the outside lights ceased to provide assistance in the deeper reaches of the lower apartment, Covington turned on his flashlight, letting it guide them through the foyer, the kitchen, and the living room on the ground level.

Covington used another hand signal to his young partner, indicating they were going to check the bedrooms together. One of the doors was wide open, and the other barely ajar, which set off warning bells inside his mind.

Holding his firearm in a ready position, he stepped into the open room, which revealed nothing except a naked bedroom. Only the various stains on the beige carpeting showed any signs of recent visitation. The pair swept through the bedroom completely, clearing the closet and checking the window for damage.

Moving on, they returned to the hallway where Covington cautiously gave the door a gentle push. It sluggishly opened as he peered into the second bedroom, slowly letting his flashlight's beam create a path into the room. It followed the warped and water-damaged hardwood floor inside until it reached a shiny pool that appeared black in color at the other end of the bedroom. A chill ran through his spine because although he had seen everything from accidental drowning victims to savage murders with slit throats, he had never encountered something so cryptic and evil as what lie before him.

"Shit," he said, immediately knowing what he had found before his light revealed the entire twisted scenario to him.

"What is it?" Renz asked, not readily able to see inside from his position outside the door.

He started to step inside, but Covington stopped him with his left arm before radioing dispatchers to request detectives and crime scene technicians.

Renz used his own flashlight to illuminate the opposite end of the apartment, seeing for himself what might normally have been termed an ordinary shooting if not for the strange symbol looming over the corpse.

"What the hell is that?"

"Your guess is as good as mine. Get the scene tape, Marty, and no one steps foot inside the building until the investigators get here."

Renz nodded before departing to carry out his orders, while Covington relayed information over the radio that they had a gunshot victim and the shooter might still be in the area. Though not a supervisor, his knowledge and experience were well-respected by the other officers. It occurred to him that the shooter might potentially be inside the building, though he seriously doubted it. If he or she was on the second level, there was no means of escape from the old building short of jumping.

Although the victim appeared quite dead, based on the bullet wound in the center of her forehead and the small pool of blood around the area, Covington stepped carefully inside for a cursory check of vital signs. Finding none, he retreated the same way he entered, trying to preserve evidence as he replaced his firearm to its holster.

Giving a sigh, Covington leaned against the doorway, folded his arms, and prepared for a long night culminating with his partner doing lots of paperwork.

CHAPTER 2

Detective Sergeant Lee Harris received the call about a murder victim at 12:21 a.m. at his desk. As the homicide division supervisor during the late shift, he caught most of the firearm investigations within city limits.

He threw on his sport coat, then drove to the address his dispatchers gave him over the phone in his unmarked car. When he arrived, he found the scene secured by a patrol lieutenant who stepped forward to meet him.

"What have we got, Jim?"

Jim Teagle had enough years on the job to retire, but with his two youngest children in college, he had no immediate plans to call it quits.

"Covington and Renz found a body inside the apartment building on the first floor. They secured the scene and we've had our guys comb the area out here."

"Anyone see anything?"

Teagle walked him toward the front door where Renz stood just outside the crime scene tape. Several patrol cars remained in the area as most of the officers fanned out to look for the shooter beyond the local perimeter. Harris noticed the crime scene technicians parked nearby, probably examining the murder scene already.

"No one saw anything," Teagle stated. "We've checked all the nearby buildings, and the caller apparently didn't stick around."

"The coroners here yet?"

"One of them is inside with our people. Anderson sound familiar?"

"Mike Anderson? He's one of the better ones."

The blatting of a train whistle echoed in the distance as a locomotive approached on tracks a short distance from where they stood. Several patrolmen continued to direct their flashlights toward the other side of the tracks, searching for any sign of the killer's presence, including a vehicle or tire tracks.

Harris decided to start with Renz, since he was nearby and the first officer on the scene. Some of the officers thought Renz was soft because he went to college and carried about twenty pounds of extra weight on him at such a young age. Harris didn't much care about what they thought, or about the reputation of the young officer.

He just wanted some answers.

"What's the kid's first name?" Harris whispered to Teagle.

"Marty."

"Thanks."

Harris walked up to Renz, quickly shaking his hand.

"Tell me what you saw, Marty."

Renz quickly walked him through the call and the discovery of the dead body inside the room.

"Let's go inside," Harris suggested. "Show me step by step where you two went."

Renz led him through the first floor, Harris memorizing the path for evidence elimination purposes later. When they finally got to the last bedroom, they found Covington standing on the opposite side of the hallway as the forensic team worked inside. Harris spoke with Mike Anderson and his department's investigators a moment at the door, discovering they were still examining the apartment for trace evidence. He couldn't readily see the body because two technicians blocked his view as they photographed the area and swabbed the floor for clues. Two portable generators lit the room with attached halogen bulbs, providing the only useful lighting for the investigators. Windows and doors were left open throughout the building so the carbon monoxide put off by the generators wafted harmlessly outside.

Harris trusted Covington more than most officers. For some reason the man stayed on midnights and never chose to test for promotions, but Harris chalked that up to him nearing retirement.

"I stepped into the bedroom just long enough to check for vitals," Covington assured the detective immediately when Harris approached him.

"I know, Tom."

Covington's hair had grayed somewhat over the past few years, now a peppery mix of black and gray he often buzzed, then let grow out a few weeks before repeating the process. He always kept his mustache trimmed to what looked like a week's growth, somewhat militaristic in appearance. Considering the man spent four years in the Army before joining the force, he might have brought his grooming habits with him.

"Did you see anything that might help us?" Harris asked.

"No. The shooter had a head start on us. We did a door to door and found the body in the last room."

From what Harris had gathered, the uniform division quickly closed off the area and searched for the shooter, but they found no one on the streets. Though a few other houses and factories stood nearby, no viable witnesses came forward. Indeed, no one from inside the buildings even heard a gunshot, which caused Harris to wonder if the shooter himself had called in the crime.

"What the hell *is* that?" Covington asked, referring to the strange artwork on the wall above the body.

For the first time since he stepped inside the apartment, Harris looked at the red symbol above the dead black woman's body. A full circle was drawn in what appeared to be the victim's own blood with an upside down "Y" inside of it, somewhat like a peace symbol, with a number inside each of the three spaces.

The number within the top left area was 36, with a 14 drawn to the right, and the number 242 beneath both of them. Harris stepped a bit closer, seeing drips of blood still clinging to the finger-drawn artwork on the wall. Jesus, he thought, not daring to express any emotion in front of the uniform division. A number of possibilities immediately ran through his head, including a possible jilted former love, a disgruntled pimp, or a john who couldn't risk being identified later.

Her head and a bit of her upper torso rested against the wall while the remainder of her body remained flat on the floor. A form of pink sparkle lipstick twinkled like a star against the bright artificial lighting. Her fingernails displayed a similar color, confirming Harris' thoughts that she worked a profession where getting noticed was mandatory.

The victim's legs were left straight, though her arms were left by their appropriate sides with the palms facing upward. Her eyes were closed, the remainder of her face a blank canvas void of expression. Harris wanted to know her identity so his team could question her pimp, if she indeed had one, and any working girls who might know her habits and clients.

"Recognize her?" Harris asked Covington of the victim.

When the veteran officer stepped closer, he took a few seconds to study the black woman's corpse, looking her clothing up and down, before answering.

"They call her Vee, but I can't remember her real name. We've run her in a couple times for prostitution."

Renz nodded in agreement.

"She's young, maybe twenty. Veronica Lee might be her name."

"Sounds right," Covington agreed.

"Who brings a prostitute over here to kill her?" Harris wondered aloud.

"Maybe no one," one of the technicians answered. "We don't have any signs of blood spatter anywhere in this apartment."

Harris looked to Covington, who raised a suspicious eyebrow.

"What are you thinking, Tom?"

"The guy left us a calling card in blood, so maybe he wanted to make sure he got our attention in the first place."

"If there really was a shot fired, a slug might still be around here somewhere."

Renz stepped forward cautiously, seeing something the others might have overlooked. He stared at the body a moment, a hole centered within the dead prostitute's forehead. While he looked at the wound initially, he cocked his head slightly to observe the wall directly behind her.

"What if the second slug is in the same place as the first one?" he questioned, pointing to a tiny streak of blood that trailed from the back of her head down the wall.

No one had moved the head from the wall yet, but one of the technicians did so now, finding a limited spatter pattern against the wall, while some of the blood stuck to the locks of her hair. Harris knelt down, examining the pool of blood near the body, finding no source where the blood originated. Morbid as it sounded, the killer might have collected the blood, brought it along, then used it as paint for his artwork after dumping it on the floor.

"Has anyone found a shell casing?" he asked, receiving negative head shakes in return.

A smart killer, he surmised.

Each of the cops exchanged exasperated looks, knowing their long night was about to take some unexpectedly strange turns. The individual responsible for the murder was going to cause the investigators fits for some time to come if they didn't find a witness or receive a tip very soon.

CHAPTER 3

L ately, things had gone rather well for Terry Levine, an investigator with the New York State Police. Timing and luck placed several opportunities in his lap within the past two months, taking him off the road and back to his natural niche of investigations.

The investigator covering his district moved south following a divorce, leaving Terry to assume his position a week before taking the sergeant's exam. His ten years as an investigator made him a perfect fit for the position, though Canton proved significantly quieter than his previous assignments. Unofficially he had more than ten years of investigation experience because he was continually called to assist on cases while a trooper assigned to road patrol, now drawing close to his nineteenth year with the state police.

After spending Sunday morning at church and the afternoon with his parents at their house, Terry's evening brought an unexpected call from his dispatchers. Minutes before midnight, he received a call at his rural home to investigate a homicide just outside the Canton town limits, almost half an hour away.

Dragging himself out of bed, he put on a shirt, tie, and slacks, then drove his unmarked police car toward Canton.

Violent crimes were unheard of during his childhood in St. Lawrence County. Investigative stints in New York City, near Buffalo, and Albany scarred him enough that he eventually returned home. His kids hated the move to the northern tip of the state since rural New York bored them compared to city life.

In the end, it seemed as though violence and murders followed him home. His once cherished hometown area succumbed to the same newsworthy crimes every big city saw on a regular basis.

Shortly after leaving his house, Terry phoned a familiar judge in Canton to get the paperwork started on a search warrant. His agency's standard procedure called for warrants during homicide investigations, contradicting the glamorous cases seen on scripted television where evidence and bodies were manhandled with little regard about contamination.

During the half hour drive to the scene, Terry found time to reflect on his career and all of the homicides he'd investigated. His unfortunate lot in life was to match wits with serial killers, which led to arrests on several occasions. He possessed the uncanny ability to think on their level, despite being a married father of three nearing his mid-forties.

When he pulled up to the scene, Terry found a marked state police car with red flashing lights illuminating the area, blocking one lane of traffic. Terry shook hands with his two fellow troopers, remaining outside of the secured scene. He looked around, finding no technicians in the area, knowing it was going to take them longer to arrive because they lived further from the crime scene.

"What do we have, guys?" he asked both men, already knowing them the way all small town folks in the North Country know one another.

"Someone reported an abandoned car beside the highway," the senior trooper began. "I came to check on it and found a flat tire, then some footsteps leading away from the car."

Bill Campbell was a twenty-one year veteran of the department, having carried out most of his tenure on the road. He worked briefly with the narcotics group a few summer seasons, finding that he preferred keeping it simple on patrol.

"Where have you been?" Terry asked him, surveying the area.

"I followed the trail to the body, checked for a pulse, and found he was shot in the back of the head."

"So you touched him?"

"I had to, to see if he was alive. I put gloves on when I saw he wasn't moving in case I had to start CPR."

"Okay," Terry said with a nod, glad Campbell did the right thing. "Did you sweep the area for any other victims?"

"We both did, but we didn't find anyone else."

Terry saw a brand new sedan parked beside State Highway 11, stepping closer to see the flat tire for himself. Thinking it looked intentional because of a noteworthy gash along the side, he followed the footsteps from the car, tracing his colleague's path so he didn't disrupt any evidence. Spring arrived late, leaving tan, flattened grass and mud in the long winter's wake. Terry wore a windbreaker over his shirt and tie to brace himself against the biting wind.

Deciding to buck standard procedure, which meant waiting for more investigators and the search warrant, Terry wanted a jumpstart. He half expected to find a victim of a botched carjacking or robbery attempt, though such things were unheard of in his district.

Instead, he discovered something slightly more disturbing.

"Stay back, Kyle," he told the rookie trooper, who had followed him as though he might require some consolation from the initial shock.

On the department less than a year, Kyle Gregory didn't know Terry's reputation very well. A young, blond-haired kid just a year or two removed from college, Gregory had an uncle who commanded several barracks in the Syracuse area. Despite the family background, he constantly stared at new scenarios with curious green eyes that would keep him from ever being a successful poker player. All road troopers drove in pairs after eleven o'clock for safety reasons, and less experienced troopers benefitted from the wisdom of men like Campbell.

The body of a well-dressed Caucasian man in a tan suit was posed at the base of an abandoned building which Terry believed once served as an independent convenience store at the edge of town limits. Now overgrown with weeds and shrubs, a short walk from the road, the building appeared faded and on the verge of collapse.

While the building was in terrible shape, the dead man fared much worse. With his arms outstretched to his sides, the black shoes on his feet touching one another, and his head arched somewhat upward, he looked like most renditions of Christ on the crucifix in Christian artwork. Terry shined his flashlight beam over the body, not daring to step closer or touch anything before the forensic team arrived.

Spying gray hair atop the man's head, Terry wondered exactly what events led to his death. Above the man, he found a strange symbol drawn in what appeared to be blood. Still fresh, some droplets of the blood had crawled down the worn wall like tears, or maybe red rain drops. Within the red circle, Terry found the same emblem seen in Buffalo a few weeks prior. The left side contained the number 6, the right side 5, and the bottom glistened a 97 at him.

His worst fears about confronting another serial killer were staring him in the face. Taking a deep breath, he stood mesmerized at the scene, not mortified like most officers because dealing with scenes like this was his specialty. Though Terry hated using the word hardened to describe his reaction, he supposed there was no better definition. He seldom saw murders in person, and certainly not fresh like this, because he typically consulted on bizarre murders, often after the fact through photographs and case files.

He recalled receiving a computerized memo from Buffalo about a similar case that had local investigators stumped. The state police database would provide him with more answers and contact information later, but for now he wanted to know more about the victim in front of him. Hearing a vehicle stop beside the road, Terry figured one of the forensic technicians had arrived. He decided to give the victim's car a quick examination, pulling latex gloves from the pockets of his slacks as he retraced his steps toward the disabled vehicle.

Without stepping on the side of the road, Terry glanced for tracks behind the car, not seeing anything in the pea gravel and mud mixture. He appreciated the two troopers parking in the road, apparently sensible enough to avoid contaminating the scene.

"Have any witnesses come forward?" he called to Campbell.

"No. Dispatch said the call came from a passerby on a cell phone who didn't bother stopping."

Considering the late hour in a small town, he didn't particularly expect to find any witnesses to the crime. The next day kids were going to be in school while their parents worked, so it made sense that most people were already in bed.

"Can you two canvas the area for anyone who might have heard or seen anything?" Terry asked, receiving affirmative nods before the troopers left on foot.

Sean Morris stepped from his departmental van with a discouraged look on his face as he pulled two bins from the vehicle by their handles. Younger than Terry by about ten years, Morris knew his job better than most technicians because he spent about a month of his work year training. Only a few FIU (Forensic Investigation Unit) members worked in their area, so Terry knew all of them by name, rank, and reputation.

Being the only forensic investigator living on the Canton side of his post, Morris arrived first. Terry didn't expect the other FIU members to show up for at least another hour.

Morris tended to be a bit more territorial than most of the technicians, but Terry wasn't going to tiptoe around someone with less than half of his investigative experience. Because Morris worked out of the Ray Brook headquarters, Terry decided to break the ice before he went digging inside the car since they were potentially going to be working more cases together.

"Did they get you out of bed?"

"No," Morris answered as he pulled his camera equipment from the van. "I was at the hospital with my little girl."

"What happened?"

"She fell off her friend's pony and broke her wrist. I think she was tickled about the idea of getting a cast so her friends could sign it at school."

Terry chuckled, having been through a few similar incidents with his own children.

"Who else have we got coming?" he asked a few seconds later.

"I'm afraid we're it for a while, *Investigator* Levine. The team's all been notified. Congratulations by the way, on getting the spot."

"Thanks. If there's no cavalry, I'm going to start with the car and let you play with the body."

"What do we have?"

Terry spent a few minutes explaining his finds to the young investigator, then showed him the path leading to the body. This time he brought his flashlight, which illuminated a wet, somewhat muddy path deviating from the original trail.

"Looks like our guy may have been killed a little further down the road, Sean."

Morris knelt beside the weathered blades of grass, taking note of the pattern.

"Looks like we might have some footprints. Might have been a chase of some sort, maybe even a carjacking gone wrong."

Terry cleared his throat.

"Once you see the body you'll probably revise your theory."

After giving a suspicious look, Morris walked over toward the body, careful to follow the same repeated path. When he looked from the body to the inscription above it, his expression changed to one of utter confusion.

"What the holy fuck is that?"

"I'm not sure, but that's what we need to find out. The same thing happened in Buffalo about two weeks ago."

"All right. Let's get to it, then."

Terry asked Morris to photograph and sweep the car first so he could follow with the hope of identifying the victim. When Morris finished an initial check, he gave Terry an okay to go ahead. By this time the other forensic team members began showing up to help in the search for evidence. Knowing they were going to be hours, perhaps even a day or two at the scene, they exercised caution.

From radio traffic, Terry knew his Bureau of Criminal Investigations (BCI) lieutenant was en route, possibly another fifteen minutes out. Terry's job consisted of assisting the evidence technicians without interfering or contaminating evidence. He started toward the car, hoping to ascertain the victim's identity and some information that he might run with while the technicians gathered their evidence.

"Just be careful not to rub anything inside because they might vacuum for fibers," Morris warned him before briefing his team members on the situation.

Terry found the doors unlocked and the keys inside exactly as it was when he rolled up to the scene. He still wondered what flattened the tire as he searched the inside of the car without leaning or rubbing against any part of the seats or floorboards. He carefully dug inside the glove compartment, finding a registration belonging to Harold James Mitchell and nothing else of value. The back seat revealed a briefcase which Terry ignored long enough to examine a leather-covered Bible and a small stack of business cards bound by a rubber band.

The contents of the briefcase and business cards revealed Mitchell was a pastor, and apparently a popular evangelist of some sort with a radio talk show and several television spots in Rochester. Billing paperwork confirmed this much, leading Terry to wonder what he was doing so far from home. The Canton area was no Mecca for Christian gatherings or conferences, and certainly not on the way to anywhere special, except maybe Canada.

He found some receipts inside the briefcase for gas, hotels, and several other travel needs. It appeared Mitchell stayed the weekend in Montreal on business, which might require involving international police agencies. Terry finished searching the vehicle, then checked in with the two troopers, who did little more than shrug their shoulders at the lack of results.

"There aren't any houses around here, and no one stuck around if they saw anything," Campbell reported.

Terry surveyed the area, finding two rusting vehicles in a nearby field, a small deteriorating barn across the highway, and a few locally-owned businesses closed for the night down the road. Barely a car had passed the scene since Terry first arrived, leading him to think he needed to move fast if he planned to catch the shooter.

He finally turned to watch Morris, who had a full night ahead of him until more FIU members arrived. Photographing the body, combing the vehicle and area for trace fibers, and figuring out exactly where Mitchell died were just the appetizers in a full course investigative meal.

Terry briefly considered having the state police monitor traffic on both ends of Highway 11, but the trail was already growing cold because the murder was a minimum of forty minutes old. Realistically, it was closer to two hours, meaning the killer was long gone, and Terry had no idea what kind of vehicle the killer was driving.

Sighing to himself, he realized his night wasn't going much better than his colleague's, but he hoped to leave with some answers.

CHAPTER 4

The investigation went well into the morning once the FIU team arrived in force. No one questioned Terry and Morris about starting before the warrant cleared, though their effort made little difference. Terry found out more about the similar crime in Buffalo by accessing the state database that linked various police agencies.

Senior Investigator Walter McBride took charge of the scene when he arrived, assisted by the man in charge of the Ray Brook Violent Crimes Investigations Team (VCIT). Now at a suitable retirement age, McBride made no secret about the fact that he planned to retire the following year, then move to Florida.

Terry sat behind his desk inside the building the St. Lawrence Sheriff's Department and the state police shared as a centralized law enforcement center in Canton. Under normal circumstances the man sitting across from him might be considered his boss, but McBride had incredible respect for Terry's accomplishments. No slouch as an investigator himself, McBride helped crack a serial rapist case the previous decade.

Physically fit for a man nearing retirement, McBride knew how to control an interrogation like few police officers. Not always an easy man to read, he shielded his emotions from his fellow troopers. Only a horseshoe of gray hair remained around his head, giving him a grandfatherlike appearance, though his actions seldom depicted a gentle, compassionate side.

"I don't like this one bit," McBride said with a thoughtful cupping of his chin. "This guy travels halfway across the state to kill people and leaves us a calling card in the process."

"And very little evidence," Terry added. "This guy is smart, whoever he is."

"Could be a transient, or maybe a trucker. We need to check homeless shelters and local shippers."

"And see if anything like this has popped up in other states," Terry suggested.

"I'm getting the troops together at eleven for a meeting. Can you bring us up to speed on the Buffalo angle?"

"I was just about to call their lead investigator. Anything specific you want me to ask?"

"You know what you're doing, Terry. We need to swap information with them for comparison's sake, but I'd like their lab results if they have any."

Terry nodded.

"I'll find out. That calling card still has me perplexed, Walt."

"What about it?"

"According to Buffalo PD's report, the thing was written in the victim's own blood. The numbers didn't match what we found last night, but I'll lay down money that was our victim's blood written above him."

"Do you have a theory?"

"Could be a code of some sort."

"Is he trying to make us look bad?" McBride asked, rising from his seat.

"If he wanted that, he'd probably go public. He gives us the option of censoring him by leaving his notes at the scenes. Buffalo didn't go public with the code, Walt. Is it time to let the cat out of the bag?"

McBride folded his arms thoughtfully a moment.

"Not yet. Let's give our people a crack at it first. I'm going to talk with the FIU guys, but I'll check back with you before the meeting."

Terry nodded before the Senior Investigator left the room.

It took him several minutes after calling the Buffalo Police Department to reach Detective Sergeant Lee Harris.

"Trooper Levine?" Harris asked when he picked up the phone. "Sorry to keep you waiting. How can I help you?"

"You had a homicide a few weeks back that mirrors one we had last night."

"Oh? Where are we talking about?"

"Upstate. Canton town limits."

A momentary pause informed Terry that Harris didn't recall where Canton was located.

"About five hours northeast of you, Sergeant Harris. I'd like to compare notes on our cases."

"I can send you my complete case report and scene photos, but we don't have all of the lab results."

"Please send me whatever you have."

"Certainly," Harris replied before clearing his throat.

"Who was your victim?"

"A local prostitute we'd run in four times since this time last year."

"So much for three strikes."

"Blame our courts, brother. Anyway, we didn't pick up much in the way of trace evidence and the shooter made certain our uniform guys trampled over everything in their search for the body."

"Sounds very familiar. We didn't find any casings, either."

"Same here," Harris stated with moderate dejection. "You know, if he'd never left the bloody numbers, we might have written the thing off as a trick gone bad."

"Maybe that's exactly why he left us messages. There's something about these victims he wants us to know about. Have you sent the code anywhere for analysis?"

"I gave it to a buddy of mine in the Bureau. He said his people and the military might be able to crack it."

"You'll see ours in the scene photos. Is it possible that this code needs a key? Three numbers doesn't sound like much of a sampling."

A momentary silence crossed the line again. Terry stared at the digital photograph printouts from what felt like a day prior, though they were only hours old. His mind felt numbed from a lack of sleep, struggling to concentrate on the pictures and his conversation with Harris.

"Something tells me our guy isn't going to be forthcoming with any hints, Trooper Levine."

"Call me Terry. Maybe it's a sequential code, or it could be gibberish. I'm just considering possibilities."

"Or it could be a locker combination. Get me your contact info and I'll send you what we've got."

"Thanks, Sergeant Harris."

"Lee."

"I hate to rush you, but we have a task force meeting at eleven. Is it possible to get me something to show the guys by then?"

"Should be. I'll e-mail the important stuff."

Terry swapped information with the detective, then stared at the photos a few minutes longer, wondering what significance a minister and a hooker shared for a murderer. Terry knew serial killers typically singled out a particular type of victim for their crimes, assuming this person was indeed a serial killer and not a hired gun or thrill killer.

Background checks were still underway for Mitchell through state police in the Rochester area. Terry suspected McBride might have some developments during their meeting regarding the minister's finances and dealings, but he was more concerned about the bloody messages at each crime scene.

Cracking the killer's psyche might depend upon him figuring out their meaning, so he sat back, giving them his full attention.

Even when the time came for the meeting a few hours later, he found himself perplexed by the codes. He learned a few things about the first crime scene and its victim from Harris' reports and photographs, sharing them with the rest of the group. Without a completed background check on Mitchell, a comparison proved impossible. Any link between the two victims was significant, considering they appeared to live on opposite ends of life's spectrum.

Terry needed to understand the killer's motive, and for that, he needed to know why someone targeted those specific individuals. Unfortunately he believed it might take more crime scenes to find the answers he needed.

***

When his shift ended in the middle of the afternoon, Terry virtually stumbled through his front door after being up all night. He wanted nothing more than to go straight to bed, but his three children were just getting home from school and his wife, Sherri, had yet to get home from work.

She had always worked whatever flexible jobs she could find that kept her home with the kids when necessary, but in Terry's eyes, she could do just about anything. He felt lucky to have such a devoted wife who followed him wherever his career took him. Stops in Albany, near Buffalo, and in the Big Apple kept the couple on the move with their kids in tow like Army brats over the years.

His oldest daughter was now a senior in high school, destined to attend college in the fall, though nowhere near far enough away from her parents and the small town atmosphere she detested, in her own words.

He had just thrown his sport coat over a kitchen chair when his kids began filing in through the front door of his rural farmhouse.

"Hello, Britney," he said, giving her a quick kiss as she passed him.

"Hi, Daddy," she replied, hurrying upstairs to her room.

She was always too busy to stay home these days, always finding something to do in a town she claimed had nothing to offer. Terry considered her far too beautiful to be on the dating scene, constantly worried that he was going to be a grandfather before he knew it. With his forty-fourth birthday around the corner, he simply wanted to get his three kids raised first.

He kissed his younger daughter, Jessica, on her way through, inquiring about her homework and getting a shrug in return as she went to watch television. His pride and joy, Corbin, came running through the kitchen to give him a hug. Barely nine, Terry's son shared a connection with him that couldn't be described. Maybe because he had given up hope of ever having a son before Corbin's unexpected arrival came his way, Terry felt especially bonded to his youngest child.

His brothers both had sons, and he would have felt left out without one of his own to raise. Corbin adored him, and loved that Terry was a police officer. When they were alone, Terry tended to spoil him a bit more than the girls, because it was a guy thing. They kept it between them, never telling Sherri or the girls.

Throughout his career, Terry had dealt with blood and guts, the worst of criminals, and some of the most twisted minds on the opposite side of the law, but returning home always seemed to wash away the red stains in his mind. He was able to separate the man who thought like devious killers from the family man determined to raise his kids correctly by the laws of man and God.

Terry was looking through the refrigerator when his wife arrived home almost half an hour later. He found it remarkably barren considering Sherri had just been to the store on Friday.

"Looking for something?" she asked as he rose to give her a kiss.

"I was going to start dinner, but there's nothing in there."

Sherri motioned toward the table where two brown bags were overflowing with groceries and a fresh meal.

"I bought fried chicken and the fixings at Kenny's store."

While Terry's younger brother didn't own the store and deli combination in nearby Norfolk, he did manage the place. They patronized the store whenever possible, despite cheaper prices at some of the larger chain stores.

"Was my little brother there?"

"He was on his way out. Said something about a Bible study meeting."

Terry grunted to himself. He attended church and feared God as much as the next man, but his brother had gone to extremes since his near-death experience a few years ago. In some ways, he wasn't the man Terry grew up with, though the eight years difference between them made certain they never totally understood one another.

Kenny had left the Catholic Church for a parish that held more meetings and services, virtually throwing himself into religion. He began taking classes to become a minister, giving up his search for a better job with benefits.

"It's hard to talk to him anymore," Terry admitted. "Even Pete thinks he's acting kind of weird."

Pete was the middle of the three brothers, working for the county highway department when he wasn't carrying out his duties as the local volunteer fire chief. Pete and Kenny had always been close, distanced from Terry who was older and more mature in their younger days. He loved them enough that he had returned home to spend the rest of his career around them and his parents.

"So what kept you out all night?"

"Caught a new homicide. The techs were still scouring for evidence when I left the barracks."

"Welcome back to investigations," Sherri said sarcastically, knowing her husband's magnetism for bizarre cases. "I saw something on the news about it."

"It was hard to miss if you were driving down the road."

"Who was it?" Sherri asked, planting a kiss on his cheek as she passed him to unload the groceries.

"Some minister from Rochester. We still don't know much about it yet."

Terry neglected to talk about the bloody message, or how the portion of the wall was removed to keep the press from spotting it. It was one of the few secrets being kept from everyone outside of the investigative team because the Buffalo police chose not to reveal similar evidence.

"Are you happy?" Sherri asked.

"About what?"

"Don't be coy, dear. About being an investigator again."

Terry scoffed at the notion with a wave of his hand.

"I wasn't miserable on the road. This is a better schedule for all of us. You know that."

"And I know you've always had that itch to solve cases."

She drew close to him, throwing her arms around his solid shoulders, looking into the blue eyes encased within his handsome features.

"You were never one to chase down speeders with lights flashing and your ticket book nestled in your dashboard."

"You sure do know a lot about me," he replied, drawing closer to her lips. "You been stalking me or something?"

"Maybe a little."

He drew her into a kiss, trying to escape his day which proved to be a mixed blessing. On one hand he liked the steady hours and bringing closure to a murder case, but he hated the details between the beginning and the end. Informing families of deceased relatives was never an easy task, but the satisfaction of seeing their faces when a murderer was convicted made the journey worthwhile.

"Get a room," Britney said when she saw them kissing as she passed through the kitchen.

"Not a bad idea," Terry said with a smirk.

"Later," Sherri said, pressing her finger to his lips.

Terry appreciated the offer, though he suspected fatigue would get to him before Sherri had the chance.

CHAPTER 5

Steven Paulson left a cabin almost ten miles from Buffalo just before midnight, having concluded his meeting with his fellow Ku Klux Klan members in secret. Forced to lurk in the shadows like thieves in the night, his group no longer carried out regular acts of violence on minority groups. Cross burnings, beatings, lynching, and torture gave way to more intellectual forms of racism through parade marches, web sites, conventions, and strategic recruitment.

Being more old-school in his approach, Paulson preferred to batter his victims, or at the very least verbally assault them. He had participated in over two dozen beatings, burned one body when a beating went too far, lynched a man in front of his family, burned crosses in yards, and shot two people to death based on their skin color. With the exception of a few minor infractions, Paulson remained under the police radar.

The message spread, particularly in a declining city like Buffalo where people were quick to blame someone else for their problems. Paulson and his group solicited anyone who would listen, speaking of how politicians solved nothing and economic downturns could be traced to blacks and illegal immigrants.

Driving home through a turbulent thunderstorm, Paulson felt overdue to mimic a random violent crime in order to beat a black man senseless, or lure an illegal into a false job opportunity only to leave him bloody and near death. He hated that so many of his group's messages required veiling, but he often made certain the victims knew they weren't wanted in his city.

He also hated gay people with a passion, but they would have to wait their turn. His group prioritized their targets, and right now gay people were little more than a nuisance.

Tonight's meeting simply allowed the group to plan their next few strategies. Paulson was allowed into the standard meetings, but not those exclusive to the Klan leadership. Though they never said as much, they regarded him as their best muscle to get the job done, considering him too hotheaded and irrational to assist in major planning.

Paulson felt wronged, particularly since he did jail time for the cause, but he did what they asked of him. Someday they would see his value and move him up through the ranks.

Finally reaching his apartment on the south end of Buffalo, Paulson hesitated before stepping into the downpour. He didn't own an umbrella because it seemed the city was more often covered in snow than hit with rain. Gathering his notes, he protected them as he stepped from his old truck. Making a dash for the front door, Paulson stepped inside, then unlocked the security door before heading up the stairs to his second floor apartment.

Though the building was showing its age after thirty years, it was maintained decently enough that a working man like Paulson could afford it. He spent most days working at a plastics factory as a quality control team member. Four people with less seniority had made supervisor ahead of him with management giving him a different excuse each time. Paulson's annual reviews typically showed unfavorable numbers and comments, often noting his issues with minority workers and a lack of tolerance toward others in general.

Dripping wet, he walked past several doors until he reached his own, finding a short stack of colorful brochures on the floor. He scooped them up with an angry hand, irritated that solicitors always seemed to find their way inside his building.

He studied the pamphlets momentarily, realizing they were all for black scholarships or minority churches. Crumpling them in his hand, he placed his key in the lock, turning it so he could get on with enjoying his weekend, beginning with a few beers.

"Mother fuckers," he muttered to himself as he stepped inside, hurling the brochures toward the floor.

Paulson reached for the light switch as the door shut behind him, discovering too late that he wasn't alone in his own apartment for him to react. Though a stout man himself, Paulson found himself grasped by a powerful right arm that trapped his own right arm to his chest while the forearm pressed against his windpipe. His assailant pressed him against a wall, similar to how cops position suspects before searching them. Paulson felt himself pinned against the wall by his assailant's shoulder, which freed the right hands of both men. He immediately struggled to free himself, about to scream for a neighbor's assistance, when a hand clad in a leather glove clasped his mouth as hard metal pressed against his back.

Inaudible groans barely escaped the leather glove as Paulson struggled to free himself, realizing an angry, bull-strong person had a gun jabbing his shoulder blade. He couldn't break the assailant's grip, so he tried pushing his way backward toward another wall, hoping to slam the person hard enough to break free.

Apparently threatened by the move, or fearing Paulson might be able to call for help, the killer stood his ground, refusing to budge, before firing the silenced weapon. Blood droplets splattered against the ceiling as the bullet ripped through Paulson's heart, ending his struggle immediately. He exhaled a final gurgle before slumping downward, his descent slowed only by the killer's supporting hands before hitting the floor, leaving him beside the brochures he despised so much.

CHAPTER 6

Erie County Sheriff's Department investigator Randy Gosser looked over a crime scene flooded with powerful spotlights shortly after nine p.m. A local farmer owned the land southeast of Buffalo near the edge of Erie County, finding a body near one of his fields while tilling the ground. Gosser spent the better part of an hour talking with the farmer while forensic technicians from his department collected evidence.

Not regularly on duty during weekend evenings, Gosser wore a shirt and tie virtually snagged from a chair on his way out the door. Not quite warm enough for departmental polo shirts, he wore a dark jacket over his clothing, watching his breath form in the night air. Standing beside his unmarked car, Gosser caught a glimpse of himself in the window momentarily.

His slightly thinning hair, a light red color with graying temples, put his mixed Scottish, Irish, and German heritage on display. Even at forty-three years of age, a few childhood freckles dotted his upper cheeks, just below his hazel eyes. His blue-green eye color shifted toward one shade or the other sometimes, almost like the seasons, during the ups and downs in his life and career.

The victim, Steven Paulson, was known by local police, though the farmer didn't admit any acquaintance. Gosser wasn't sold on such a statement, considering the farm served as a Klan meeting place from time to time. In fact, Paulson's body was found a few feet away from a large wooden cross, blackened from fuel and fire. Whether the cross was already there, or placed there by the killer, Gosser didn't yet know. The grass surrounding the cross appeared worn, possibly from group outings on this end of the farm property.

Gosser watched the technicians do their work, photographing the body and the area, as he studied along with them. He stood as close as he dared without treading on evidence, already wearing disposable covers on his feet and latex gloves. Based on personal experience, he figured Paulson had been dead at least twelve hours. Still clothed, the body exhibited very little color because all of the blood had pooled toward the soil, following gravitational laws. Paulson was found on his back, hands by his sides, not positioned in any particular fashion.

Paulson's work boots had traces of mud on them and the cause of death looked readily apparent around the left side of the chest where cloth from the man's shirt and jacket were ripped outward. Based on the small exit wound, Gosser surmised the man was shot at close range from behind. It would require incredible strength to stab someone through the heart in one stroke from any direction.

Set back several feet from the body was the one standing wall from an otherwise fallen storage barn. The remains of the other three walls and the roof were lying in the foundation's center, as though the building had been professionally demolished. It was along the one standing wall, however, that the most striking piece of evidence glistened in the moonlight for Gosser and the technicians to see.

In what he assumed was blood, inside a circle divided by three uneven lines, he found the number 2 on the left, the number 4 on the right, and the number 105 beneath them both. The killer's cryptic message both disturbed and perplexed him as it had every other investigator who laid eyes on the strange symbol.

As one of two Senior Investigators on his department, Gosser knew to have his dispatchers contact the sheriff. On most homicides, the sheriff didn't need to be contacted immediately. He trusted his personnel to investigate the case thoroughly and professionally, but this was no ordinary case. Gosser knew about two other cases similar to this one, and the symbol drawn in blood above Paulson's body changed everything about how he approached the murder.

Following that call, he made some additional calls to legally check out the victim's residence in Buffalo. It didn't appear Paulson was killed where he was found, and though he may or may not have been killed at home, his residence might shed some light on why he was killed or his known associates. Feeling somewhat like a secretary, Gosser needed to make a courtesy call to the Buffalo Police Department so he could investigate on their turf, and to discover who caught the dead hooker homicide. Gosser had every reason to believe the two murders were committed by the same individual.

Every minute counted when it came to tracking down a killer who might strike again at any given time. Gosser watched the technicians comb the crime scene momentarily before receiving word that his dispatchers had reached the sheriff and Gaffney was en route.

Sheriff Paul Gaffney had recently won his second term as sheriff after helping solve a rather major case the previous fall. A retired state police investigator who eventually made captain, he brought credentials to his new job, finding most of his deputies liked and respected him during his tenure. Gosser appreciated Gaffney because the man was hands-on with almost everything, not content to sit behind his desk, or in meetings, all day long.

"What have we got?" the sheriff asked when he arrived, finding the technicians too busy to report.

Gosser briefed his boss on the body and Paulson's history with the law.

"Not exactly a friend of the department, eh?" Gaffney asked with a smirk.

Still a good-looking, physically fit man nearing his mid-fifties, Gaffney's dark brown hair and mustache showed more peppery gray than ever. He worked out often, spent time with his SWAT team on the range, and made himself accessible to the media when necessary. Not one to hog the spotlight, he preferred recognition for his deputies and investigators instead.

His shrewd blue eyes missed very little on the field, and they continued to scan the area like an eagle as Gosser informed him about Paulson's murder. Though he typically donned a suit at work, Gaffney opted for his formal uniform tonight in case he needed to host an impromptu press conference.

"Are you going to let the press know this is connected to the other murders?" Gosser asked. "Assuming, of course, it's not a copycat."

"Considering the bloody circles aren't public knowledge, I'd say this is genuine, Randy. And, no, I'm not going to let them know until we have to."

"Thanks, Sheriff."

"The techs are going to be a while," Gaffney thought aloud. "What else have we got?"

"I was about to head over to his apartment."

Gaffney observed the technicians a moment, then looked at his watch.

"Want some company?"

Gosser raised an eyebrow.

"Sir?"

"Let's go," Gaffney said without hesitation, leading his detective toward his black, unmarked SUV.

Neither man spoke more than a few sentences on the trip over to the apartment. Gosser found a superintendent on the first floor, talking the man into letting them inside Paulson's apartment since the resident wasn't going to be needing it anytime soon.

"Paulson's a weird one," the man informed them as they climbed the stairs. "Not much of a people person, you could say."

"We kind of figured," Gosser replied. "Did you see anyone unusual around here earlier this evening?"

"I just got back from Rochester a few hours ago. Mrs. Thompson is our local snoop if you want to talk to her. She sees everyone and everything around here."

"That would be great," Gosser said evenly as their three sets of footsteps clomped along the old wooden stairs.

A moment later they were atop the stairs before the super led them past two apartments on either side before reaching the one in question.

"Here you go," he said, removing his key ring from his belt, finding the correct master key with expert precision.

As soon as the door was unlocked, Gosser took a look inside, spying blood spatter along the two entry walls. His eyes drew upward toward the ceiling, an otherwise eggshell finish with hundreds of red specks dotting the textured finish. Both men knew this was the place where

Paulson was murdered, meaning it was a threshold they dared not cross. In an investigation already hampered by time, they had just encountered another hurdle.

"Well, well," Gosser muttered, noticing the sheriff staring upward as well.

Gaffney gave an unsettling groan.

"Let's call for the city forensic team," he said, knowing his own people were going to be preoccupied for hours where Paulson's body was dumped.

Gosser felt a bit surprised that Gaffney didn't want to call the department from which he retired, but it was in city jurisdiction and the state police were miles away.

"They're already involved, so we're looking at a joint investigation anyway," Gaffney stated as they stepped into the hallway, shutting the door to keep the superintendent from peeking inside. "I don't like this being in our backyard, Randy. Not one bit."

"It's not just us, sir. What about the other murder up north?"

A gleam seemed to reach the sheriff's eye.

"I know someone who's an expert when it comes to sick bastards like this one."

"That trooper who helped with the Toomey investigation last year?"

"One and the same. Maybe it's time we give him a call."

CHAPTER 7

Terry had more answers about his murder scene and his victim, but no results to show for his efforts. Sitting in the Canton barracks, he read the various interviews forwarded to him by E Troop from the Rochester area. The interviews with friends, family, and church patrons seemed favorable, as though Mitchell never made one enemy.

Former business partners and ex-patrons, however, told a much different story. It seemed Mitchell led two lives, or simply kept some of his dealings out of the public eye and away from his family. He went from an acting pastor at a Rochester church to spreading his word across national television after his local Sunday sermons were spotted by network executives on local television.

Shown only on Sunday mornings, and typically on public service channels, Mitchell's live services reached a growing number of people, bringing his congregation fan support and financial gain. His marketing plan included web sites, hotlines, online offerings, and other multimedia outlets that generated thousands of extra dollars monthly, if not weekly. His problems, and potential enemies, seemed to stem from the money and some of the contacts he used to make him more influential.

While Mitchell may have angered some people, Terry found little incentive to murder the man, particularly half a state from his residence.

Still, someone traveled the distance from Buffalo to Canton, or vice versa. Even more troubling than that, he left undefined messages behind.

"What do you want from us?" Terry questioned a photograph of the first bloody symbol. "What makes you take lives?"

Considering the killer didn't touch the victims meant he was either extraordinarily cautious, or harbored physical contact issues. Intimacy or contact issues might be signs of childhood abuse, particularly of a sexual nature. Such issues might also explain why the killer left symbols instead of being brash and arrogant in his advances toward the police. More direct taunts could be left in the mail, or phoned to officers or dispatchers.

Terry continued flipping through the crime scene photographs, thinking something about this killer didn't fit a pattern or any psychological profile. They all had a past, something that transformed them into cold-blooded murderers with a primitive underlying need. He needed to know more about the person behind the gun if he wanted to catch *this* killer.

While he often dealt with routine cases, including murders and rapes, Terry found himself pulled into high profile cases across the state by his superiors or other departments requesting his input. Some agencies asked for his input before calling the FBI. While he was flattered by the confidence these agencies placed in his abilities, Terry didn't always like the headaches that came with tracking hardened killers.

He hated failing to solve any mystery even more though.

Walt McBride scurried toward Terry from a centralized hub within the barracks.

"Come here," he said urgently enough that Terry bolted to his feet and followed his supervisor to the closest television.

A channel out of Watertown was showing breaking news about a murder near Buffalo, particularly since the sheriff was conducting a press conference. Terry immediately wondered why Gaffney was speaking with reporters before conferring with other agencies about the murder. The words streaming along the bottom readily informed viewers that the murder appeared to be the work of the same killer who took a life in Buffalo, and another in Canton.

"Son-of-a-bitch," McBride muttered. "Gaffney was one of us. He knows better than to pull this shit."

"Let's just watch and see."

Over the next five minutes Gaffney avoided several questions and answered several more with vague replies. He didn't let out any details, including the symbol written in blood which Terry felt positive was at their scene. A reporter appeared to wrap up the segment, stating they had inside information about the slaying that prompted the press conference. If they indeed had information, it never surfaced, or Gaffney shot down their source during the interview.

"When did the murder take place?" Terry inquired.

"They found the body last night."

"Our guy gets around, doesn't he?"

Terry wandered from the television to think a moment.

"What's going on inside that brain of yours?" McBride questioned, tailing him down the hallway.

"This isn't the work of a serial killer, Walt."

"Hell if it's not! The guy's killed three people we know of so far."

"That's not what I meant. A true serial killer doesn't just drive around the state bumping off three people in a month's time. They take their time and plan it out, pick their victims carefully, relive the crime until the new wears off."

McBride leaned against a doorway, folding his arms with a crooked grin.

"This guy is leaving us messages in blood, Terry. Call me crazy, but I think he's doing some pre-planning."

"It's not just that, though. A true serial killer has to touch his victims in some capacity. He doesn't shoot them at a distance or make them kneel down for a mafia hit. This guy has something else going on inside his head."

"If anyone can figure out what, it's you."

"That's what I'm afraid of, Walt. This guy just isn't the same breed."

Terry's cell phone rang at his side, prompting McBride to find another task while he answered.

"Levine."

"Terry, it's Paul Gaffney from Erie County."

"It's hard to forget you, Paul, especially since you've been on every news channel the past hour."

Gaffney chuckled briefly.

"Not by choice. The news people kept saying they had information about a message left by the killer."

"So you decided to confront them publicly?"

"No. I decided to confront that individual beforehand and learn what she knew, which was nothing, then I held the press conference to make certain our information stayed with us."

Terry walked with the phone into a more private area, snatching a pad of paper on the way.

"So what do you have?"

Gaffney spent the next ten minutes relaying information to him about the murder.

"We've had two of these, Terry. I know this is your thing, so I'm asking you to analyze this guy and give me your thoughts."

"I'm already knee-deep in this case, Paul."

"What do you mean?"

"I'm the one who caught the investigation of the victim up here. I've already been working with BPD on their case."

Terry heard a disgruntled sigh over the line.

"We've got to get our shit together and get a task force formed on this. God only knows how much we might be letting slip through the cracks."

"That's all well and good, but I'm still waiting for lots of lab results, and I think Buffalo is, too."

"What do you make of the messages?"

"I'm really not sure yet. I think they're for our benefit, or he would have made certain they went public."

"Think he's taunting us?"

"I don't know, but he wants us to work to find the answers."

"I'm going to send you what I have, Terry, but I think we're going to need to get everyone together on this."

Terry sensed where this was going, much as it had the previous fall when his old state police partner wanted him to see some crime scenes in person.

"You better not be trying to drag me down there, Sheriff. I've got my hands full up here with this case and about two dozen others since I moved back to investigations."

"I wouldn't dream of it until we get some more information back from the lab," Gaffney replied in a somewhat mischievous tone that told Terry to have a contingency suitcase packed within the next few days.

"I'll send you our crime scene files within the hour. How is Deputy Hardegen doing these days?"

Terry referred to the deputy he worked with during the Toomey investigation. Hardegen was left wrapping up the case in a permanent way after Terry and the other investigators were unable to bring him into custody.

"John's doing well. He quit the drug task force and went back on the road after the holidays."

"Good for him. Take care, Paul, and let me know if anything comes up."

"Will do."

Terry ended the call with the push of a button as he tossed the blank pad of paper aside. Deciding he wanted to see all of the facts before developing a profile for the killer, it seemed prudent to send his information to Gaffney right away. He didn't want to waste a second when he received the information about the latest murder.

"What's going on?" McBride asked when he saw Terry calling up the case information on the computer.

"Gaffney called to send his regards. He wants to swap information, and I think he might want you to go down to Buffalo."

"*Me?*"

"Yep. You."

CHAPTER 8

Monday, May 5

Buffalo, New York

Later in the morning Gaffney was informed his nephew was waiting for him downstairs. It took an elevator trip to reach the second story where the sheriff's offices were housed in the old building. The Erie County Sheriff's Department Holding Center was originally built in 1938, in Art Deco style, serving as the nucleus for several additions over the years. Downtown Buffalo was built over the course of four distinctive periods, beginning in 1815 when the original village was rebuilt after damage sustained during the War of 1812. The current jail was first constructed during the last of the four eras. Construction essentially ended in the downtown area when World War II began, receiving little attention until the 1960s. What began as a facility built to accommodate 156 prisoners now held 680 when necessary, making it the second largest detention center in the state outside of New York City.

Gaffney was buffered by a secretary outside of his large office and another assistant downstairs who directed visitors to various parts of the building, or answered general questions. If he didn't want to see someone, they weren't getting into his office very easily.

Ben Belinski was his older sister's son, looking little like Gaffney except for the deep blue eyes. An investigative reporter for the *Buffalo News*, Belinski had a weekly radio spot, television time with the local NBC affiliate, and a national award for at least one of his written pieces. Because he carried some extra weight and didn't have striking good looks, Belinski was overlooked for elevated status in the television world.

When he stepped into Gaffney's office, the two shook hands, then exchanged a quick hug. Belinski had recently let his flattop haircut grow out to freshen his appearance on the news. He looked as though he had dropped a few pounds, possibly taking his uncle's advice to start working out.

"Good to see you, Ben."

"Likewise, Uncle Paul. Thanks for making the time."

Gaffney waved off the notion.

"I always have time for you. You know that."

For the sake of their separate professions, they kept their family status out of the limelight, though they sometimes helped one another solve problems. Gaffney occasionally asked his nephew to make certain particular pieces of information were inserted, or kept out of the newspaper. In turn, he sometimes fed his nephew exclusive pieces of information to get the scoop on other reporters once a case was due to be public information.

"Things have been hectic with this new case," Gaffney admitted as he took a seat at the nearby conference table. "We're working with a few other agencies and waiting for some lab results."

Belinski took another of the eight seats, looking his uncle in the eye.

"Any leads yet?"

Gaffney had no hesitation about being open and honest with his nephew. Not once had Belinski ever printed anything "off the record" from their conversations.

"So far it's been a dead-end wherever this guy's struck."

"This case is actually what I'm here about, Uncle Paul."

"I'll give you whatever I can, Ben. You know that."

"I know," Belinski said with an appreciative nod, "but I want what you can't give me, too."

Gaffney returned a puzzled look.

"Two reasons," Belinski said quickly before his uncle could conjure up an excuse. "One, I've heard this guy is leaving you clues at the scenes. If that's true, I might be able to help you figure out what they mean. Some people are more willing to talk to reporters than cops."

"You're getting a bit ahead of yourself, Ben. No one said there were any clues left at any scenes."

"That's not what a little birdie told me," Belinski said as he flashed a quick smile.

"One of your friends mentioned something to me before my press conference."

Belinski let a sly grin slip.

"You put him up to it? That's pure evil, nephew."

"But your body language in the press conference told me you were lying when you denied my buddy's rumor."

Gaffney chuckled because Belinski had skills equal to most of his investigators. The only reason he wasn't an officer was because he set his sights too high after college. The state police turned him down once because Gaffney was still a member of the force and the powers in charge of hiring new officers were on a nepotism kick. Belinski passed the written test and the physical agility test but the interview process knocked him out of contention when they realized his uncle was a captain. The interview process was the one area where personal judgment entered into the testing process.

A second testing process ended before it truly began when Belinski shattered his right ankle in a hockey mishap with his friends on a Sunday afternoon. He was rendered unable to complete the physical portion of the testing by an injury that hampered his ability to run or play sports for two years after the fateful incident.

Belinski worked as a police reserve officer in communities near Buffalo until he landed a job with the newspaper as a crime beat reporter.

From there his relationship with Gaffney helped him skyrocket to new heights at the paper, enough so that other avenues presented themselves. Between his three jobs Belinski found himself earning enough money to buy a nice house just outside of Buffalo and a sports car that turned heads whenever he drove it within city limits. At thirty-eight-years old, Belinski had his entire life ahead of him. He also landed a wife Gaffney considered a super model. The sheriff had to virtually pry his eyes away from the woman at family gatherings, wondering how his nephew got so lucky.

"My body language, huh?" Gaffney finally brought himself to ask.

His nephew flipped open a blank pad, already holding a personalized pen Gaffney had bought for him one Christmas.

"Off the record, Uncle Paul."

"Everything I'm about to tell you is off the record, Ben. Go against your word, and compromise this investigation, and you'll be next door."

Basically a continuation of the sheriff's administrative offices, the jail towered over the sheriff's building about a stone's throw away.

"And I'll order a full body cavity search," Gaffney threatened. "You never got to your second point either."

"My second point is that I want a detailed account of this crime, because if he's leaving you clues, this guy is book worthy. I want to write a true crime book with every gory detail in it and give you due credit after you catch the guy."

Gaffney looked toward his ceiling, unsure of how to take such a proposal.

"Generous as that sounds, I think you're looking for your nest egg above all else, Ben."

"Maybe I am, but I'm thinking this is going to be a big case, Paul. *Big.* And like I said before, I might be able to help you piece together some of the puzzle. You know I'm very good at digging things up."

"Yeah. I know you also get a lot of people pissed off at you, too. Ben, I trust you completely, and I'm willing to give you what I've got, but you can't go John Wayne on me and get yourself hurt. This guy, whoever he is, is incredibly dangerous."

"Obviously. This is important to me, Paul, or I wouldn't be asking you for the details. I've never asked for anything like this before and I'll owe you big time."

"Bet your ass you will. The road runs both ways, you know? I want to know anything you find out that we don't have."

Belinski gave a wide smile, knowing he had accessed the vault of one of the most potentially prolific cases to hit New York State in a long time.

"Fantastic. Can we start with whatever clues he's leaving you at the scenes?"

Gaffney reached for some files behind him. If he didn't trust his nephew as a reliable asset, he would never have agreed to share the information.

If Belinski printed one wrong word it potentially damned both of their careers.

***

Though Terry spent much of his day following up on several local burglaries, his mind kept wandering to Harold James Mitchell and the two victims near Buffalo. He had Gaffney's information as well as the images and files Lee Harris sent him. Considering the victims were a known prostitute, a preacher, and a construction worker who moon-lighted as a racist, the dots didn't connect. Serial killers worked in patterns, even routines that drove them to murder particular people. The more he thought about it, the more this case left him uneasy.

After conducting some interviews, he returned to the barracks to check in with McBride about any new leads. Distracted by a phone call, his boss basically shrugged at him, indicating nothing new had come their way. At this point, lab results might provide a DNA link or some crucial information to them, but Terry suspected it would also serve to confirm some of his theories.

It was almost a given that the blood used to draw the symbols came from the victims themselves. Forensic teams might determine the height of the killer, or which hand was his dominant hand from the results, but Terry wanted a name, and to find that, he needed to know the man's psychological makeup more than his physical traits.

After looking at his notes from state police in the Rochester area, he decided he wanted to follow up with one particular interviewee who had left Mitchell's parish rather disgruntled. A former associate pastor at the Rochester First Church of God, Albert Nichols took a position as a youth minister with another parish after he and Mitchell had a falling out over allocation of church funds.

Nichols didn't give many details about specific issues regarding the money, possibly thinking he was a suspect in the murder, so the troopers made notes to check Mitchell's personal accounts and the distribution of parish funds. Considering the nature of the murder, and others related to it, Terry felt the state police would act quickly to secure warrants and check all of Mitchell's finances in Rochester. Depending on the organization and availability of record books, the process could already be finished, or might require several more days.

Terry picked up the phone, deciding to call Brian Hargrove at E Troop before trying Nichols. Having some numbers and information before interviewing the youth pastor sounded prudent, so he hoped for the best as a dispatcher put him through to Hargrove.

"Hargrove," a voice came over the line a few minutes later.

"Brian, this is Terry Levine from Canton."

"Hi, Terry. What can I do for you?"

"Just wondering if you had time to dig through Harold Mitchell's finances yet."

A pause came over the line, followed by the sound of rustling paperwork.

"We're in the middle of it, and believe me when I say it's complex. This guy had more bank accounts and hidden funds than most dogs have buried bones."

"Can you give me some ideas why he was hiding his cash?"

"Seems Mitchell started making a lot more money once he got his television deal, and I do mean a *lot*. Also seems he didn't have a whole lot of interest in sharing it with the people who got him to the big time."

"Sounds like motive."

"That's what I thought, but the list keeps growing."

"Obviously his parishioners bought into what he was selling, so who are our prime suspects?"

Hargrove took a few seconds before he answered, probably conferring with a list.

"Looks like mostly old business partners and a good number of people at his old church. His church had a board of directors who kept track of the money at his local parish, but when Mitchell took the next step they were all left behind. There doesn't seem to be much of a checks and balances system in place."

"But wasn't he still affiliated with his old church?"

"Sure. He was using the property for his extra services on Sunday mornings, but not paying them anything extra from all of his new revenue. He did, however, put some serious funding into expanding the church, mainly to make it more television friendly. Seems some of the people wanted him gone, but he was still good for their business even if he wasn't paying them extra revenue."

"Plus he was making money doing conventions and traveling across the country."

"He had a couple of books out, too. Nothing great, but he spent time at bookstores and religious conventions selling and signing."

Terry looked at the three files sitting before him. While the unofficial task force had to examine every possibility, he thought it unlikely someone killed two other people to simply distract them from the Mitchell murder. It occurred to him Mitchell wasn't a preacher in the sense most people thought of, which lumped him in a category much closer to that of a hooker and a racist.

"Brian, I appreciate your work on this. Please give me a ring if you get any developments."

"You got it. I've had a few guys from the Erie County area call me too. Aren't you guys coordinated on this yet?"

"We're working on it," Terry answered ambiguously. "Hey, have you made contact with Albert Nichols yet?"

"Who's he?"

"One of the associate pastors who worked with Mitchell."

"I didn't personally, no."

"Okay. I'm about to give him a call to follow up on what your guys asked him."

"You're not stepping on my toes. Let me know if you need anything else."

"Thanks. I'll be in touch."

Terry hung up the phone as Walt McBride stopped in his doorway.

"Anything new?"

"Not much. I'm in the middle of contacting some people in Rochester. Sounds like Harold Mitchell wasn't exactly up for a nomination to sainthood."

"Oh?"

"Let's just say Jimmy Bakker isn't the only one who's sinned against Thee my Lord."

"He was banging prostitutes?"

"Wrong televangelist. Bakker was the one who went down for fraud and tax evasion, though he had a thing for the young ladies as well."

"So Mitchell wasn't the saint he appeared to be?"

"No. He used some influential people to get to the top then stepped on them. He started making serious money, giving little or nothing back to the ones who helped him make it big."

McBride leaned on the doorway, a skeptical look crossing his face.

"We're talking about Rochester, Terry. How rich could the guy have been?"

"He apparently expanded his church to make it more television friendly and he had a solid deal with network television. Everyone on television has to get a start somewhere."

"I suppose," McBride grumbled. "Oh, by the way, I talked with Gaffney today and he said he would love for you to come down when they get an official task force together."

Terry couldn't help but smile, remembering the white lie he told his direct supervisor about possibly being summoned to Buffalo.

"Nice try, Terry."

"Thanks, Walt. I'm expecting a call from my good buddy in Albany any day now, ordering me to assist in Buffalo."

"And I'll gladly sign whatever forms he requests," McBride said with a smirk as he rubbed his hands together in a sinister fashion.

"I bet you will," Terry sighed before staring at the three case files on his desk.

He knew going to Buffalo, or wherever the joint task force met, was in his near future. The fact that his good friend in the state police administration hadn't called yet worried him, but his bags had been packed on short notice before.

Aside from calling Nichols, he still had several other cases to work on while he waited for news from Buffalo or the state forensics lab. Tapping a pen upside his head, he leafed through the crime scene photos from all three scenes, looking for something familiar that tied three completely different scenes, completely different people, together somehow. He felt certain some common aspect continued to elude him, finding no fault in the work of the photographers.

Taking a deep breath, he picked up the phone to call Sherri, deciding to keep his mind off work for a few minutes before refocusing his attention on the details.

CHAPTER 9

"I'm so glad you're here," Martha Tillman said when Officer Jared Bowman walked into her shop.

"How can I help you?" Bowman asked the older woman who owned a flower store in an otherwise vacated strip mall.

"There's a smell coming from one of the other shops."

Martha's store was located on the west end of a central Syracuse strip mall nowhere close to the highway or other essential landmarks that modern stores required for success. Bowman supposed she clung to the old days when her shop flourished, or perhaps patrons actually visited the store for friendly, personal service.

She seemed like a nice old lady to Bowman, probably less hardened than she believed she was to remain in such a decaying neighborhood. Her gray hair appeared dyed, possibly to a darker shade of gray than its natural state. Dressed casually, because no one expected a small shop owner to wear business attire, she walked around the counter to direct him to the source of her problem as he opened the door for her.

A fire department pumper pulled beside his squad car, as Bowman walked down the line of vacant shops, staring at each of their deteriorated fronts. Martha followed, remaining several cautious steps behind him as she took baby steps compared to his rigid walk. He wasn't sure if she was curious about the smell, or acting like a protective grandparent to make sure he didn't wander into trouble.

"Ma'am, shouldn't you stay with your store?" he asked, stopping to briefly turn around.

"Oh, I never get any business anyway. This is the most excitement I've had in years."

Bowman waited until he turned around before rolling his eyes, prepared to carry on with his search until he noticed the fire department crew approaching him.

"What have we got?" asked the company lieutenant, a man of about fifty with a bushy salt and pepper mustache, who wore his helmet and protective pants with their suspenders.

"Not sure yet. I was just walking the front to see if anything was out of place."

A few of the firefighters sniffed the air, one making a sour face.

"I just got a whiff of whatever it is."

"Probably a dog crawled into one of the buildings and died," his buddy offered.

The lieutenant cleared his throat to silence his men before addressing Bowman.

"How can we help?"

"You might check around back, but be careful. We get homeless people and crackheads staying in places like this all the time."

"That's not very reassuring," Martha said as the firefighters walked the other way.

"Ma'am, that's just how it is. I would suggest you find a new landlord."

"I might. This one's a prick."

Bowman smirked as he continued down the line, passing a former comic book store and a beauty salon that looked anything but beautiful. Both put forth faded white paint dotted with dirt and green fungus, the salon's windows tinted with years of dirty rain on the exterior and layers of dust inside. Its sign, now covered with graffiti and severely faded, clung to life on one nail as it swung slowly, squeaking in the gentle breeze that rocked it.

Near the end of the row the officer found a former BINGO hall with its door slightly ajar. The smell, which had come and gone with the wind, seemed stronger now, piercing his nostrils. Fearing the pungent smell could only mean one thing, he motioned for Martha to stand behind him as he cautiously approached the door, hand already positioned on his firearm.

Stepping inside, he found the large room engulfed in darkness because the only two windows were covered by musty drapes. Pulling out his flashlight, Bowman shined the beam across the room, finding several chairs overturned beside a few remaining broken tables. For the most part the room looked long since cleared of anything useful. No BINGO equipment remained, writing lined the walls, and flipping a light switch was certainly a futile gesture. He found a set of footprints starting at the door that ended abruptly about halfway into the room. Bowman carefully stepped to the side of the footprints, using his flashlight beam to guide him further inside.

"Find anything?" Martha called from the doorway, startling him.

"Ma'am, please!" he shouted, turning around just long enough to shoot her an irritated expression.

Bowman walked slowly, panning the floor to his left, then the right, with the flashlight's beam. The odor soon became overwhelming, informing him the answer to his inquiry was somewhere in the mammoth room. He doubted the landlord ever visited the property because Martha probably mailed her rent promptly every month, never requesting his presence for anything.

The lack of visitation also meant a lack of witnesses to what he figured he was about to find. Bowman knew the smell of death from his hunting days, but a dead deer's smell was fractional compared to that of a human being. Unfortunately he had experienced the latter several times over the years when residents called his dispatchers, wanting to check on the welfare of an elderly or recently unseen neighbor.

Bowman had cleared most of the room within two minutes, now approaching the farthest corner from the door, which proved to be the darkest. He surrendered his right hand from the firearm to cover his mouth and nose with his forearm. Too late, the odor had already embedded itself within his nostrils, so he shined his flashlight around the last overturned table, finding the source of his troubles wrapped neatly in a plastic drop cloth with a circular symbol above the body on a wall.

"Holy shit," he muttered, fumbling for the microphone attached to his portable radio.

CHAPTER 10

Apparently word of the serial murders had spread within the New York State Police organization because McBride received a call from the Syracuse Police Department about the latest murder an hour after it was discovered. In turn, Terry found himself making the three hour drive to Syracuse upon McBride's request, which became an order the second he questioned it.

He only questioned why his supervisor wasn't going, which prompted McBride to answer that he knew Terry was better suited to analyze the killer and his methods. As though a peace offering of sorts, McBride called the police in Buffalo to see if they had an interest in comparing facts in Syracuse. Terry felt a joint task force was overdue, because e-mails, photographs, and documentation packed more of a punch when their creators were able to elaborate.

Though he didn't like McBride shirking his duties as a Senior Investigator, Terry knew he was more capable of dissecting a serial killer's methods than his boss. Terry felt a bit excited about observing the crime scene, mainly because he felt it might do some good. Preliminary finds indicated the body had been there for some time before someone broke into the building and left it open, after finding the body. Terry had a hunch this was the killer's first victim, and first victim scenes often held more clues because the killer wasn't yet refined in his or her methods.

Terry made good time because he used an unmarked car from his barracks that was obviously a police vehicle. Even if a young trooper pulled him over he would soon be on his way after explaining the situation. Being friends with an administrator had perks he never used for his own benefit, mainly because he never needed to.

When he finally pulled into the edge of the parking lot just short of the yellow tape, Terry flashed his credentials to an officer and signed a log sheet before stepping inside the crime scene area. He saw a few forensic technicians scouring the grounds for evidence with the aid of some uniformed officers. At this point they weren't concerned with trampling over evidence because months had passed since the murder. Any lingering evidence would have to be large enough to weather the past few months of snow and rain.

Fortunately any preserved evidence remained inside the building because the overcast sky began to cut loose with some drizzle. Terry looked skyward, wondering when the rain might cut loose and drench the parking lot and everyone within its confines.

It took a few minutes for someone to approach him since most of the officers occupied themselves with the search. A detective wearing a tie and sport coat offered his hand with a crooked grin. Terry looked down to shake his hand, noticing the man's shoes were covered with dust and some grime.

"Brian Hathaway," the young blond-haired detective said as they shook hands. "And you must be Trooper Levine."

"That would be me."

"I've heard quite a bit about you, even before today, so it's an honor to meet you."

"Thanks."

Hathaway wore his badge clipped to his belt, which Terry recognized as that of the Syracuse Police Department. While he certainly didn't know everyone in his own department, Terry knew a fair number of investigators statewide from working cases with them or attending seminars and classes over the years. He guessed Hathaway had recently made the grade of detective, considering he was Terry's junior by about ten years.

"How did you even know to contact me?" Terry inquired.

"One of our guys remembered the memo you sent out about the murders with a symbol near the bodies. We just called your barracks and asked if our scene sounded like the same thing."

"And the rest is history. So what exactly do you have?"

Hathaway led the way toward the former BINGO hall, speaking as Terry followed.

"Our guys have swept most of the building. They didn't find very much because most of the stores have been abandoned for a year or two. I think our people are done with the body, but they held off with the coroner's office until you had a look at it. Your supervisor said you might be able to pick out some details when you saw it."

Terry grunted doubtfully to himself.

"I'd hate to make a liar of him."

When they entered the large room Terry found several portable lights illuminating the room. Generators might have been used if not for fear of carbon monoxide poisoning, so smaller battery-powered lights took their place. Most of the lighting was concentrated on the far wall where equipment and a few technicians occupied the space around the body. Terry immediately saw the body with plastic wrap around it, replaced as close to its original state as possible because the evidence technicians had cut the covering for their photographs.

They had cut a single line up the length of the plastic along the center of the torso, which remained on its back, one side angled slightly higher than the other. Whoever killed the man within the plastic cocoon had done so very efficiently before wrapping the body tidily for long-term storage. A lack of heat within the building had maintained the body through the spring months, and a time line had been loosely established by the investigators. Terry suspected this was the earliest documented kill by his serial killer, and he verified his theory when he spied writing in blood above the deceased male.

The number 34 occupied the left spot, the number 1 in the right, and below them, the number 20 displayed a dried droplet of blood frozen in time along the dingy wall.

A familiar odor entered his nostrils, though nowhere near overpowering enough for him to take measures against it. He knelt beside the body, donning latex gloves before removing the plastic from over the body like one might peel aluminum foil from a baked potato, laying it to the sides.

"Interesting," he said to himself, examining the corpse from head to toe.

"What's that?" Hathaway asked.

"Figured the body would be more decomposed than this. Your people sure this is a few months old?"

"That's a guesstimate. The landlord said he was last in this building at the end of February, so that puts us between early March and today, but this door would have been reported by someone before today. The shop owner down the way says she drives by this entire strip every day."

"Any possible witnesses?"

Hathaway shook his head negatively.

"Truckers sometimes park their rigs down here, but they're asleep the minute they shut their trucks down."

Terry noticed the dead man wore blue jeans, biker boots, and a tattered black leather jacket over a gray hooded sweatshirt.

"Dressed for winter," Terry commented to himself.

The dead man also wore a blue and black cloth striped bandana stained with blood on the right side where a bullet entered the man's skull weeks or months earlier. The blood had long since dried to the cloth, which also held skull fragments like macaroni pasted to a paper plate. His eyes, though swollen, were half open, indicating he might have been conscious when the bullet entered his skull. An untrimmed beard occupied much of the man's face, while the skin around it appeared crimson and purple from the onset of decomposition due to warmer weather arriving.

When the body thawed like the weather outside, it began to decompose rapidly, explaining the odor escaping the old BINGO hall. Around the neck the skin appeared loose, showing signs of slippage from the bones and muscles that once held it together. Terry figured the dead man's clothing was the only thing from keeping his body from melting down like a wax figurine to a semisolid puddle.

No evidence of struggle presented itself as Terry examined the knuckles, fingernails, and forearms, possibly indicating the man was taken by surprise. Since no blood, except for the printed word, existed on the wall or floor near the man, the murder likely took place somewhere else.

"If this guy's a biker, where's his bike?" Terry questioned aloud. "Or any vehicle for that matter?"

He fished through the man's pockets for identification, finding none in the jeans or the jacket. Running his hands through the insides of the boots, he found no paperwork or useful information.

"You might look for any motorcycles or vehicles found abandoned since the end of February. I can't imagine this guy was out riding during the winter. Maybe we can find some tattoos or match some dental records with missing persons."

"He looks like a good Samaritan, so I'm sure someone misses him," Hathaway mused. "I'll keep you posted on the coroner's finds once we get our boy to the morgue."

"I appreciate it," Terry said. "Sounds like we're going to be seeing lots of each other the next couple days."

"So I've heard. Who's going to be heading up this little operation?"

Terry shrugged.

"Not me if I can help it."

"Any ideas who our killer might be?"

"You gave me an idea when you said truckers like to sleep down here. Maybe it's someone who travels the state on a regular basis. Trucker, salesman, maybe another biker. With the exception of maybe this one, all of these murders could have happened in riding weather."

"What about days of the week?" Hathaway asked. "Any patterns?"

"Not really. About the only similarity I'm finding is the artwork. These people come from all walks of life."

"For all we know, this guy could be from out-of-state."

"I don't think so, Brian. This guy seems to know his victims, even if they might not know him."

Hathaway placed his forefinger near the blood symbol on the wall, tracing the air an inch away from it.

"He's trying to tell us something, isn't he?"

"Us and us alone," Terry noted. "He's letting us decide how far the information goes. And right now we're a ragtag band two steps behind his every move."

Terry milled around the crime scene with Hathaway nearly ten minutes longer before stepping outside to let the technicians and the coroner's office complete their work before transporting the body.

"Where do we go from here?" Hathaway asked, leading Terry toward the yellow police tape boundary.

"It sounds like the boys from Buffalo are heading up this thing since they have two bodies to our one each. I need to find a hotel and get the details about the task force."

"I think my deputy chief is getting us a location for tomorrow. Get me your cell phone number and I'll call you later with the specifics."

Terry handed him a business card after jotting down the number. He was ready to get a hotel room and study the new information from the crime scene. Though he didn't necessarily expect to see familiar faces from his days in the Buffalo area, he wanted to meet the investigators who were merely voices on the phone.

"I'll put a rush on the evidence and the body," Hathaway informed him. "I'm curious to see the notes from the other cases."

Terry nodded, suddenly taking notice of a silver BMW convertible atop a hill overlooking the plaza parking lot. Without the benefit of tinted windows, the driver was plainly visible to Terry, whose keen eye noticed the man staring intently at the crime scene. He wasn't certain, but thought the man might be holding a camera just below the window.

"What's wrong?" Hathaway asked.

"Recognize that car?"

"Can't say I do. Looks like a nice ride, though."

"Maybe it's time I see why he's so interested in our crime scene."

"Want some backup?"

"Thanks, but no. I'm going to play this cool and catch him by surprise. Just act like you never saw him, Brian."

"Will do," Hathaway said with a sly smile before turning toward his fellow officers.

Terry signed the log to state he was leaving the scene, then drove his car in a roundabout way to the road above the plaza. He didn't want to alert the man in the BMW that he was sneaking up on him by requesting marked patrol units for assistance. For all he knew the man was a curious onlooker, or a reporter, but people driving expensive cars weren't typically the types who stopped to observe police activity.

Considering Terry brought a state-owned car, he was able to do a traffic stop if he deemed it necessary, but he opted to pull in front of the

BMW to make certain the driver couldn't maneuver away from him. As he pulled to a stop, Terry peered into his rearview mirror, noticing the driver reaching into the passenger's seat. Stepping from his car, Terry observed the driver without blinking as his right hand rested on his firearm.

"Problem?" the man asked, automatically rolling down his window to greet Terry as the investigator presented his credentials.

Allowing his eyes to scan the seat beside the man in less than a second, Terry saw no camera, though he did find a crumpled Burger King bag in the passenger's seat and a Styrofoam coffee cup in the beverage holder.

It appeared the man was traveling, perhaps on business.

"Any particular reason you're parked up here?" Terry asked, deciding not to sound accusatory.

"I used to own one of the businesses down there, so I was just being nibby."

Terry took a second to think of his next question while studying the man. He wore a beige dress shirt and tie, covered by a black leather jacket. Considering the cool nature of the overcast day, outerwear didn't seem the least bit inappropriate. The man carried a few extra pounds, possibly compensating for his appearance through nice clothes and vehicles.

"What did you own here?" Terry inquired.

"A dollar store," the man said without hesitation. "I took my business to Buffalo a few years back."

"Buffalo, huh?"

The man nodded, though a lump traveled down his throat. He didn't seem to have any characteristics that set off serial killer warnings in Terry's mind. Still, the Buffalo connection had the investigator wondering how this man was connected to the case, because he was connected regardless of what he said.

"What brought you to town, sir?"

"I'm selling some property."

"This one?"

"No. I leased this one."

Terry wanted to catch him in a lie if at all possible, but so far the man knew the right answers. Still, he wasn't letting the man go without somehow identifying him. Asking for his identification didn't seemed fair, considering the man hadn't technically done anything wrong, so he decided to be subtle. He didn't want this traveler to leave with any doubts or worries that the police were observing him.

"So what happened down there?" the man asked, giving Terry an appropriate opening to act upon.

"Nothing for you to worry about, sir. Could you move it along before someone runs into us?"

"Sure," the man answered with an untrusting look, rolling up his window before merging into traffic.

Though Terry casually strolled toward his vehicle, he memorized the front license plate on the car as the man pulled away. Because of the car's make, he had serious doubts about it being a rental. If his hunch played out correctly, he would have the man's identification within minutes by running the plates by local dispatchers.

Hathaway approached him with a smirk when he returned to the crime scene area.

"You let him get away."

"I don't think that was our guy," Terry replied, ignoring the joke. "Still, I have something I want you to check for me."

He held up the slip of paper with the license plate number scribbled on it.

"I knew you wouldn't be convinced that easily."

"Our mystery man said he lives in Buffalo."

"Could be a coincidence. It *is* only two hours from here."

"I'd like to know before we have a meet and greet with everyone tomorrow."

Hathaway nodded.

"Let me get right on that."

After stepping away for a few minutes, the detective returned, phone in hand, with a sheet of information in the other.

"Your new friend is Ben Belinski, who is indeed from the greater Buffalo area."

"There's still something he wasn't telling me," Terry thought aloud, "but at least now we know who he is. Thanks for doing that."

"You're welcome. Maybe our guys will find something inside that'll point us toward the killer."

"We need something. Anything. Otherwise we're meeting tomorrow to talk about a lot of what ifs."

***

Later that evening Terry milled around his hotel room, trying to figure out new angles on the case. He had already called the family between sessions of studying the photographs and information on all of the crimes. The Syracuse murder *had* to be the first of the four confirmed deaths by the same man, and the medical examiners would confirm that soon.

Because the scene was so old, the police forensic team found little useful evidence inside the room, and none of it was confirmed as useful when Terry last talked to Hathaway. Hair samples, fingerprints, and blood evidence were common at crime scenes, but they didn't always belong to the killer. Based on how this killer operated, Terry wasn't optimistic about the team finding anything matching him. The elements had destroyed or contaminated much of the evidence anyhow, leaving much of it inadmissible for courtroom purposes.

At this point, however, the team hoped for any kind of clue to point them in the right direction. Terry followed the rules whenever possible, but he was willing to circumvent some regulations if his work could identify the man he was pursuing.

Falling onto his bed, he took up the case files from the first three cases, and the photographs of the Syracuse case that Hathaway had delivered to him once they were printed. Though Terry had his laptop computer with him, he wanted hard copies of the images to compare side by side with the others.

He had just started laying out the photos atop the bed when his cell phone rang from a nearby end table. Hoping it was Hathaway with good news, he snatched it up, finding a higher power calling him.

His former major.

Now an assistant deputy superintendent, Dave Duggan had the means to get things done quickly and effectively. He often called upon his former protégés, which included Terry, to check on high profile cases and make certain adequate, quality people were assigned to the case. He trusted Terry to no end, which was appreciated, but sometimes Duggan intruded like a nosy parent on prom night.

As Terry answered the phone, he hoped this wasn't one of those times.

"Hello, Assistant Deputy Superintendent Duggan."

"My, aren't we formal tonight, Terrence."

"If this is anything other than official business, I'll take back my earlier formality."

"It's official business."

"I figured," Terry said, stepping into the small bathroom to organize the things he needed for his impending shower.

"I want you to head up this investigation, Terry."

"You know that's not my thing."

"No, but you're going to be a Senior Investigator soon, so it will be your thing. I know you're content doing your analysis in the background, but this way you'll have access to everything and everyone involved."

"Won't this step on Walt McBride's toes?"

"I'll make sure he understands. The fact that you're in Syracuse and he's not tells me what I need to know."

Terry didn't like the idea of Duggan causing McBride any trouble. Troopers already talked about Terry's relationship with the ADS. Though the two seldom spoke, and saw one another even more rarely, people seemed to think Duggan constantly did Terry favors like helping him through the promotional process. Unfounded, untrue rumors constantly drifted through the workplace like gnats swarming around rotting food.

"Anything else I need to do before tomorrow, boss?"

"No. I've already cleared this with my boss and everyone you'll be working with tomorrow. They're relieved you're taking the lead on this."

"I'm sure they're thrilled," Terry said sarcastically, hating it when Duggan buttered him up needlessly. "I'll do it, Dave, but I can't promise any miracles. So far we don't know the first thing about the guy behind all of this."

"Anything you need to crack this, you've got it. The brass are taking a lot of heat over this guy crisscrossing the state and shooting people at will. How much longer do you plan on keeping the bloody writing under wraps?"

"As long as I can. I think there's more to be lost than gained if we make that information public. God forbid we get more crank calls or a copycat killer."

"True, but you might figure out what it means if more people see it."

"I'll get it figured out. This guy wants us to know what it means, but he's not going to make it easy. Maybe tomorrow when everyone compares the scenes we'll get some answers."

"Like I said, anything you need, you got it."

Duggan paused before making his next statement.

"I know you get self-conscious about what people say about you, and about us."

"You make it sound like we're gay, Dave."

Duggan chuckled.

"That might be the next rumor, but you've got to shrug it off, Terry. You've overcome everything thrown your way so far and I'm proud of you. This is going to be another feather in your cap when you nail this guy."

"Again with the gay references. You deserve some credit for showing me the ropes, ADS Duggan. If I find our killer, you deserve half the credit."

"And you can best believe I'll take a bow, but first things first. Keep me posted on what you find, but don't let me be an anchor that slows you down, either."

"Will do. I appreciate the vote of confidence."

"I'm not greasing your wheels when I tell you I want you on this case because I think you're the best goddamn investigator I've ever seen. That's the truth, and no matter how fucked up this agency gets, know that you made a difference when you get old and gray like me."

"I'll try. Thanks, Dave."

Terry hung up the phone after a goodbye, took a quick shower, then laid out all of the photographs, searching for a clue he felt certain was staring back at him.

He concentrated on one scene at a time, examining the newest scene first because he felt certain it was the oldest. Strange, he thought, that the killer basically hid the first body, then left the next three on display for police to find. Luckily the cryptic messages left at each scene were quickly photographed and removed to keep the public from knowing about their existence. It was almost as though the killer wanted the police to be the first people laying eyes on the bodies and the messages.

Perhaps his messages weren't reaching the right people, so he made the crimes more public, Terry thought. Strangely, he wrapped the initial victim in plastic, but made no attempt to cover or preserve the later victims. If the biker was killed in March, as the team speculated, the killer might have expected the body to be discovered sooner.

"We weren't getting your message, were we?" Terry questioned aloud, looking from the unidentified biker to the next victim.

Veronica Lee was found by police after shots fired, apparently by the killer's design, though she was killed in a still unknown location. He examined the posture of her corpse, because the killer certainly had time enough to position her however he wanted before making a hasty exit. Except for being slumped against the wall, she appeared to be almost peaceful at rest. Her hands were positioned with the palms facing upward, which reminded Terry of something. Images flashed through his mind of pictures, paintings, and familiar death scenes, but nothing clicked with Veronica Lee.

Despite originally catching the Harold James Mitchell case, Terry stared at the man's body once again, finding it painfully obvious the man was posed like Christ on the cross. The easy answer for this action was Mitchell's indiscretions against the church and its members alike. Because it was so distinct from the other posed bodies, Terry never gave it a second thought.

Until now.

He quickly skimmed through the images of the Paulson murder to see how the alleged racist was posed near a farming field. Unlike the other victims, Paulson's body looked as though it had been dumped onto the ground unceremoniously. While the body was on its back, the image showed it tilted slightly to one side with one arm tucked near the chest and the other limp by Paulson's side. Both knees were buckled slightly, giving the impression of anything but a premeditated pose.

"There has to be something," Terry muttered, flipping through the remainder of Paulson's death photos.

Most of the photos concentrated on the details on and around the body, including the entry and exit wounds, stains, and superficial wounds on the skin. Terry studied the dirt and grass around the body, searching for any sort of hidden or subliminal message beyond the body itself. He remembered them finding no distinct footprints, despite the ground being wet from recent rain, indicating the killer might have used some kind of foot padding to prevent leaving evidence.

"Smart," Terry reasoned. "Almost like he knows what it is we do."

By "we" he meant sworn police officers and forensic technicians.

Undaunted, he studied the photographs one by one until he found an image taken a few feet away from Paulson's boots, covering the length of the body. Something behind the body caught his attention, discreet as it was from the lack of natural or artificial lighting.

Setting down the images, he picked up the case report, skimming it for details about the crime scene. Though he had read it through several times over, nothing significant stood out from the wording or the description of the scene, thorough as it proved to be.

This time, however, he wanted to know about the landscape around the body. Trees, barns, and tilled dirt probably didn't sound interesting the first time through, but this time Terry wanted confirmation of something stuck in the recesses of his mind.

"A burned crucifix," he read the words aloud as his eyes glanced over them. "A few feet from the body."

Suddenly the pieces fell into place. Subtle as the clues might have been, Terry believed he knew the message the killer was sending through the staged crime scenes. Scooping up his cell phone from his bed, he found the speed dial number for the one person he felt was most qualified to help him prove or dismiss his theory.

The phone rang twice before his youngest brother answered.

"Hello?"

"Kenny, I need a huge favor from you."

"Okay."

"You've probably heard that I've got some unsolved homicides between Canton and Buffalo, right?"

"Sure. You want my help with *that*?"

"I think my killer is leaving me religious clues. I can't think of anyone more hooked on Biblical stuff than you."

Kenny remained silent a moment. Their relationship, even as brothers, became somewhat strained when Kenny turned to religion after his near death experience several years prior. When Kenny left the Catholic Church for another parish, even their parents didn't know what to think, though they continued showing him support.

"You're treating me like some kind of idiot savant who knows nothing except religion," Kenny finally said.

"I just know you're well-versed on the Bible, little brother. If there's any chance I'm right about this, you could help save countless lives."

"What exactly do you need?"

Terry explained the case to him briefly, wanting to keep the classified parts to himself, but realizing if he left anything out, Kenny wouldn't have a fair shot at deciphering the bloody numbers. Kenny wrote down each set of numbers, along with the corresponding case and its circumstances.

"What finally made you think these messages were religious?" Kenny asked once apprised of the situation.

"The way he posed the last few bodies looked familiar to me. He posed one near a crucifix, posed another one like Christ on the cross, and the last one threw me, but he had the last one leaned against the wall with arms outstretched."

"Kind of like the statues of Jesus and Mary that scared the crap out of us as kids?"

"Exactly. You know, you're the only one outside of law enforcement who knows about these messages, Ken. You've got to keep that to yourself, no matter what."

"That won't be a problem. It would help if I could get pictures of the bodies, though."

"I can get you copies. Again, they're for your eyes only."

"Understood. I can start with the numbers and see if the sets have Biblical implications."

"So you're in?"

"When have I ever said no to you?" Kenny sighed. "I'm only at the store a half day tomorrow, so I'll take a look at it after that."

"If I'm lucky I'll get home tomorrow night and I'll get those files to you."

"Maybe you'll crack the case and you won't even need me."

Terry gave a troubled chuckle.

"I wouldn't bet the farm on it, little brother."

CHAPTER 11

Thursday, May 8

Syracuse, New York

Hathaway called Terry the next morning with directions to a closed library branch where the city police chief decided to place the task force. Reasonably close to police headquarters, the location made it easy to transport needed equipment while giving officers easy access to records and resources.

Terry caught a break when the Syracuse chief had SPD's media officer speak with the television and newspaper hounds. He knew when he took a lead position over the task force he would become the spokesperson for the group unless he found someone who actually liked talking to the press. At least when he got home to the Canton area, they wouldn't track him down so incessantly.

When he stepped inside the small building, he found himself surrounded by more officers and detectives than he expected. Nearly two dozen men from at least six organizations sat or stood around a makeshift table compiled of individual desks. He noticed one woman standing behind the already seated men, dressed in a tan business suit complete with a brown blouse. She held a notepad as her curious hazel eyes locked onto Terry the moment he stepped into the room.

"I've got all of the slides together," Hathaway informed Terry as the two men quickly shook hands. "I put them together like you asked."

"Thanks, Brian. Hopefully they shake something loose from this crowd."

Hathaway nodded before leaving to find a seat as the well-dressed woman approached Terry.

"Amanda Perry," she said, offering her hand as she shuffled the notepad aside.

Her name struck Terry as familiar, though he couldn't immediately place it.

"I work in Albany with ADS Duggan."

"Now I remember. Did David send you to keep tabs on me?"

Amanda laughed easily, giving Terry a moment to study her features. She had full lips and large eyes that seemed to stare straight through him, as though they could read his soul. Her face was thin, the remainder of her body conditioned like an athlete beneath the dress clothes. Her light brown hair was clipped behind her head, giving her a professional air that reeked of NYSP headquarters in Albany.

Despite this, Terry immediately felt he could trust her, mainly because Duggan sent her. And though he had heard her name through the grapevine, it didn't come attached with speculation and vicious rumors that often accompanied anyone from headquarters that troopers didn't like.

Besides, he just had a good first impression that came from years of reading people on sight alone.

"David said you might need someone to help you organize things and take care of your public relations," Amanda revealed. "He said you hated being in front of cameras."

"He does know me well. You'll get a quick education from the next couple hours as we stand up and dictate our cases to one another. I take it you have investigations experience?"

"About five years," Amanda revealed.

Terry suspected she was in her late thirties, probably finding herself in positions other than road patrol rather early in her career. He had nothing against anyone leaving road duty because Duggan took time to mentor him early in his career, grooming him for investigations. Like a professional baseball scout, Duggan knew which people fit best in available NYSP positions.

Paul Gaffney approached them, wearing a suit rather than his dress uniform.

"Amanda, Terry," he said.

"Paul," they simultaneously returned the greeting.

"You two know each other?" Terry inquired.

"I may be retired, but I stay close to the important people," Gaffney replied.

Amanda gave a brief, amused laugh.

"I didn't realize my position carried so much clout."

Gaffney gave a sly grin in response.

"You're Duggan's go-to gal. I'd be a fool not to stay in your good graces."

"Be that as it may, I'm merely Terry's media person while he takes charge of the investigation."

"Congratulations, by the way," Gaffney said, offering his hand to Terry.

"I'm not sure this situation warrants congratulations, Sheriff."

"I was actually referring to your investigative spot. Heard you're going to be making sergeant before long, too."

"We'll see what happens."

"You could always come back to Buffalo if things don't work out."

"Is that a job offer?"

"I could do a lot worse than gain a deputy who tracks serial killers and rapists."

Terry gave an uneasy smile.

"You'll probably have to bribe me heavily to get my wife to move again, Paul."

He checked his watch, noticing most of the officers and investigators were occupying the available seats.

"We should probably get this show on the road. This may not be the prettiest conference we've ever put on, but the important thing is that we all get on the same page."

"Have you got any developments?" Amanda inquired. "On a personal level, that is."

Terry returned a perplexed look instead of answering.

"David told me you had an inside edge when it came to cases like this. You have quite a reputation within our department."

"But it took Duggan telling you about me to learn of my reputation?"

Gaffney smirked at their banter, though he put forth no comment.

"All right, I've heard about your exploits and they are quite impressive. I'm looking forward to seeing you crack this case."

"You say that as though it's a foregone conclusion. Duggan tends to overestimate my abilities, so don't buy into his hype."

"He says you have a sixth sense about these things, so I'm looking forward to your analysis on the situation."

"Unless there's some new information I haven't seen, my analysis may be very general."

Once everyone settled in, Terry started the meeting with a quick introduction of everyone present and their represented department. While he wanted to keep it informal, he knew the importance of every case being viewed and scrutinized by everyone present. Each officer in charge of his specific case used Hathaway's computerized slide show and their own materials to present facts and photographs from each murder.

Between them, the departments had nearly two-hundred leads that failed to pan out in any way. Most of the leads were unsubstantiated, often angry neighbors reporting one another, wasting investigators' time and the public's tax dollars. Some were the usual nut jobs wanting their fifteen minutes of fame without earning it. Chasing down empty leads kept investigators from focusing on the facts and studying what was sometimes right before their very eyes.

An hour and a half passed quickly as everyone presented their particular case to the group. No one requested a break, and all eyes remained focused on the photographs and information projected on the wall before them.

"Keep in mind the public hasn't been made aware of certain facts," Terry said after Lee Harris from Buffalo covered the prostitute's murder last. "We've kept the bloody handwriting and numbers from the public, so let's keep it that way."

"Do you have theories about what they mean?" Gaffney asked from his seat.

The decision of whether or not to tell the group of his own theory plagued him after calling his brother the previous evening. He didn't want the group developing tunnel-vision if they believed his theory as accurate without looking at other possibilities. At the same time he didn't want the fate of future victims lying solely in the hands of his younger brother if his notion eventually proved correct.

Ultimately he found some middle ground.

"I have an idea what they might be, but I'm not positive," Terry revealed. "Last night I was thumbing through the photos when it struck me that some of the victims were posed like or near religious icons. I passed this on to an expert I know in the field of religion, and I plan on telling our contacts at the FBI who are already analyzing the numbers."

One of the investigators asked Terry to show them what he meant by the religious implications at the death scenes, so he took time to show them each of the three photographs he believed were subtle hints from the killer.

"The murder here in Syracuse was his first that we're aware of. Because the body wasn't found, or he figured we weren't taking the hint, I believe the killer started leaving us clues."

"So he's killing in the name of God?" Randy Gosser questioned.

"It's a possibility," Terry replied. "None of the victims were squeaky clean by any means, but I'm not sure they qualified as devil's advocates, either. We don't know who our first victim is, but we have one confirmed prostitute, a racist, and a dirty preacher. While certainly not pillars of the community, they aren't the worst of offenders by any means."

"Actually we know our fourth victim," Hathaway said, waving several freshly faxed sheets from a nearby door. "Michael Gregory Allen, twice accused, once convicted of rape. Seems he became a local resident here in Syracuse once he served his time, joining a group of bikers with similar, um, interests."

"Sounds like we may be paying a certain biker gang a visit."

"They prefer to be called a club," Hathaway stated. "More politically correct so they can lay low while carrying out their nefarious activities."

Terry decided to wrap up the meeting with the information everyone wanted to hear, which was his personal take on who the killer was and what made him tick.

"Look, everyone, our killer isn't a touchy-feely type of person. He uses a gun instead of getting close, which may make him more of a vigilante than a standard serial killer. There's a strong possibility he has knowledge of how we work, or God forbid, he could be a cop. There's also a chance he might be someone who tested for a police department and didn't make it. We need to be looking at failed psych tests in particular."

Terry cleared his throat before continuing.

"None of the scenes have left us any trace evidence. No fingerprints, no distinct footprints, and no DNA thus far. We know his shoe size is somewhere between a ten-and-a-half and an eleven, but he's always worn foot coverings so we don't have a shoe print. He also uses his left hand to trace the bloody symbols, so he's probably a lefty. The lab folks think he's just over six feet tall based on some consistencies of bullet trajectories. We have a .38 weapon killing two, possibly three of our victims, and a silenced .22 on the Paulson murder, but no matches to anything in the databases."

Terry cleared his throat, noticing all eyes on him.

"We know he travels across the state to carry out his crimes but we've had no luck at gas stations, restaurants, or rest stops. He could drive a truck or run his own business, which would provide him time and money to travel around the state. I've been checking national and state databases with no luck, so he may be native to New York. Considering two of his crimes have taken place in Erie County, I'd say there's a fair chance he lives in or near Buffalo."

He looked to Gaffney.

"Sheriff, your department and Buffalo PD may have to take a hard look at trucking companies and business owners who travel in your area."

"Easier said than done," Gaffney retorted, "but we'll get to it."

Terry addressed the entire room once more.

"Our killer isn't discriminating very much already, so chances are he's going to get more violent with his kills and the victims may become innocent victims. He's bound to slip up eventually, but we can't wait for that. Keep reviewing your cases and looking for any possible witnesses. Something has to eventually break loose."

Now a lot of questioning eyes were directed his way, along with some incoherent grumbles throughout the room.

"I know you want me to paint a picture for you based on my experience," Terry said, taking the hint. "The truth is this guy is a blank slate to me so far. He's meticulous, possibly obsessive compulsive in nature.

Probably the standard Caucasian in his middle thirties, but I can't say what turned him to killing. Serial killers usually have some glitch from childhood, often stemming from mental or physical abuse. That's possible with this guy. Maybe he was mistreated at a young age and everyone he kills is a manifestation of the person who wronged him."

"We're not expecting miracles from you, Terry," Gaffney said, speaking boldly enough that the crowd followed his lead. "We know you're doing the best you can."

"Our guy isn't leaving very much at the crime scenes for me...for us, to analyze," Terry admitted. "I already have contact information for everyone here, so we need to stay in touch. The most important thing is that we all know about any further murders by this guy. We absolutely cannot let the bloody symbols go public or the media will be in our way twenty-four hours a day."

He looked toward Hathaway, who nodded that he was ready to go conduct some tricky interviews.

"Thanks, everyone, for making the trip. If we're lucky we won't be doing this again in the near future."

Some of the investigators left immediately to embark on their trips home, but a few stuck around to ask questions of Terry and one another.

"How can this guy know all of the victims and their backgrounds?" Lee Harris asked Terry once everyone else had broken off from the group.

"Even as cops we don't have access to every criminal across the state unless we do some inquiries," Terry answered. "I've been checking on that, but so far nothing comes back from databases or the departments I've called. It's possible he just checks newspapers and assumes the people he murders are guilty of their accused crimes. It'll take some time, but we need to cross-reference anyone who gets papers from different cities."

"It just seems too convenient, like he has the pulse of every crime in the state or something."

"That thought crossed my mind, but that's a dark place even I don't want to go just yet. Investigating one of our own would be incredibly tough, but someone with clout or authority would be about impossible."

"I guess we just go where the evidence leads us."

"I guess we do."

***

Hathaway drove Terry toward one of the three known locations where Michael Gregory Allen's associates spent their time. He thought the task force meeting had gone rather well, particularly since everyone now knew every case like it was their own.

"Tell me all about Mr. Allen and his charming friends, Brian."

Hathaway grinned, keeping his eyes on the road.

"From what I read, Allen moved often, doing odd jobs for different biker chapters in New York, Vermont, and Pennsylvania."

"Odd jobs, eh?"

"Mostly drug runs and prostitution bookings. He thought he was going to move up the ladder, but he kept making mistakes and getting caught."

"So rape wasn't his only goof?"

"No," Hathaway said matter-of-factly. "He was arrested for theft, battery, and disturbing the peace. Nothing that put him on the radar until the rape charge, though."

Terry watched the scenery change around them as the business district blurred into a seedier part of town with rundown houses, overgrown yards, and deteriorated streets. Gray and tan coloration dominated this part of the town like a western filmed with a sepia filter. Even the sky appeared bleak behind so much neglect and disrepair.

"And what about his friends?"

"I asked around and some of our local drug task force guys said these guys think their place in the scheme of things is inflated. They'll probably put up a front, but we can get some answers if we play our cards right."

"You plan on busting some heads or something?"

Hathaway intentionally laughed maniacally, indicating he had something devious in mind without getting physical.

"These guys aren't rocket scientists, Terry. They're very gullible and they don't have the money to be connected. Or afford good lawyers."

"I'd say I like where you're going with this, but I have a feeling the less I know, the better."

"Yeah, I'd agree with that statement."

A few minutes later Hathaway pulled into the remains of a parking lot now lined with sparse gravel and numerous potholes. The small tavern at the far end of the lot had seen better days, with no visible windows remaining because boards and sheets of wood covered them. The primarily black paint scheme covering the building had faded from years of direct sunlight. The messages in the few remaining signs served as ghostly shadows left from the former ownership.

"I'm almost certain I saw this place in one of those places to visit before you die books," Terry commented sarcastically.

"And we haven't even seen the inside," Hathaway added with mock cheerfulness.

He put the car into park, staring at the building for only a few seconds.

"Stay here, Terry, and I'll bring one of them outside. Away from their buddies they're more likely to say something."

"Sure you don't want backup?"

"Nah. I got it. Just play along with whatever I say once I bring our unfortunate victim out here."

As Hathaway flipped through a few tattered sheets for information about Allen's acquaintances, Terry counted the motorcycles in the parking lot, finding eight. Not bad odds, he thought, though he wasn't going to wait very long for Hathaway to emerge with an unsuspecting informant.

Next, the detective riffled through the Allen case file, searching for a few key photographs and facts about the case. He put some of the items near the top of the file for easy access, then opened his car door.

"Wish me luck," he said without giving Terry a chance to answer or change his mind.

Instead, Terry sighed to himself, hoping he didn't have to see the inside of the bar. He watched as Hathaway tried the door, finding it unlocked, then let himself in as though he owned the place. Terry almost expected gunfire to erupt when the gang spied an intruder in their building, but nothing happened.

He waited a few minutes, growing more nervous for Hathaway's safety with each passing second. Letting himself out of the car, Terry cautiously approached the bar as he listened for activity inside. Hearing nothing, he tried the door and stepped inside.

Expecting to find Hathaway laid out, or tied to a chair in the back of the bar, Terry was slightly surprised to discover seven men, all passed out at the bar or surrounding tables. The entire place reeked of stale tobacco, as though the odor had embedded itself in every crevice over the years. None of the slumbering figures looked especially dapper, most wearing faded clothing that looked like items picked up at a rummage sale.

Apparently Hathaway's plan hadn't unfolded quite as the detective expected, or he altered it the second he walked through the door, because he stood at the far end of the bar talking to a gray-haired man. Obviously a biker himself, the man wore tattered black jeans and a leather vest over a faded black t-shirt. His arms were practically sleeved with tattoos, some of which looked like the prison variety with very dark ink and jagged, untidy edges. Surprising, Terry figured, that he hadn't paid to have them redone. Perhaps this biker was proud of the chapters that comprised his life, not wanting to delete a single one.

Before him Hathaway had laid out the most gruesome photographs from the Allen murder. While the man didn't appear happy about the images, he certainly wasn't broken up at the thought of Allen being dead.

"Terry, this is Jerry Wenger, leader of the notorious biker gang you see sleeping around us."

Wenger openly disagreed with Hathaway's comment, like a man caught between two undisclosed truths now coming to light. His biker gang wasn't very respectable in any sense, particularly following their association with the now deceased Allen. The man's death only served to cast a negative light on his gang's image and reputation, which meant less illegal business coming their way.

"Mr. Wenger, this is Terry Levine from the state police. He's investigating the death of your colleague, and he has a few questions for you about your association with Michael Allen."

Wenger grimaced.

"Like I told you, I ain't got nothin' to say."

"We can keep this between us, or we can invite a whole lot of our friends in here," Terry offered. "Be like a little party of sorts, but not like your slumber party last night."

By the steely look in Wenger's eyes, a random stranger might have thought his mother was severely insulted. He contemplated his situation, realizing he had no backup of his own, and so far, no witnesses who knew he was speaking with the police.

"Maybe we should talk in the back."

When the man turned to lead the way, Terry looked to Hathaway for an explanation of why the plan changed, receiving a shrug and a mischievous grin in return.

"Just roll with it," he whispered.

Terry glanced behind him, finding every biker still passed out, a few snorting or groaning with their heads placed near the remnants of beverages and food from the past evening. He followed Wenger and Hathaway into the business office, which looked as though a tornado had sucked up files and forms, then dropped them randomly atop desks and shelves.

"Nice place," Hathaway commented, apparently not one to let up once he held the advantage.

"Get to your point," Wenger said, taking a seat behind his desk, though the investigators dared not occupy the filthy chairs available to them.

"We know you were affiliated with Allen," Hathaway began. "We can handle this one of two ways. Either we can consider you a person of interest in his murder, which will undoubtedly bring you lots of unwanted attention over the coming weeks and months, virtually crippling your business ventures..."

"Or?"

"You can put me on the right track without feeding me bullshit when I ask you some questions."

Wenger folded his hands atop the desk, pondering his situation momentarily. He undoubtedly had run-ins with the police, which likely slowed his already questionable business.

"We barely knew that son-of-a-bitch," he stated.

"That why he wore your club's patch on his gear?" Hathaway countered. "I was under the impression those had to be earned, but apparently you give them out like candy at Halloween."

"Fuck you."

Hathaway smirked.

"That's about what I expected you to say. This is your one chance to separate yourself from Allen before the shit hits the fan."

Wenger weighed his options. Terry studied his eyes and facial expressions, seeing the man didn't want to talk, probably from the embarrassment of ever keeping company with the dead biker.

"Keep your questions strictly about Allen and I'll give you whatever the fuck you want. He's already dead, so what's the harm?"

"Exactly," Hathaway agreed. "I would think he carried some baggage that even you didn't want coming back on you. Did anyone in your group have cause to go after him?"

"We found out he raped a high school girl," Wenger stated coldly. "After that, we didn't have *nothin'* to do with that mother fucker."

The statement caught Terry a bit off-guard, considering he hadn't read the facsimile sheets like Hathaway. He maintained a straight face to play along as his task force colleague asked of him.

"The fact that the girl was eighteen was his only saving grace," Hathaway stated more for Terry's benefit than to recount facts. "He came here to start over, and your group is the one he landed with, under false pretenses I assume. Didn't that piss you off just a little bit when you found out?"

Wenger's eyebrows narrowed.

"Look, *Detective* Hathaway, we weren't happy, but Allen had only been here a month or two. We kicked him out, and that was it. After that we never seen him again."

"No one was especially pissed at him?"

"We was more disgusted than pissed. He lied to us until we found out from one of the other chapters that he violated that girl. None of us here are hitmen. And we can't afford to hire something like that done even if we wanted to."

"I can tell," Hathaway said, his eyes panning around the office.

"Do you have any other questions, or you gonna keep wastin' my time by insultin' me all morning?"

Hathaway crossed his arms, a smug look crossing his face.

"I can always insult you by writing a review about your establishment, so let's continue with the questions."

"This is a private establishment," Wenger said sourly. "We don't want the likes of cops or pussy drinkers here."

"The world will never know what it's missing. So, *Jerry*, in the few weeks you and Mr. Allen were intimate, did he tell you about any enemies he had? Anyone following him?"

Wenger shot Hathaway a look that told the detective to go fuck himself with his tone of questioning, then pondered the answer.

"He never mentioned nothing like that. Didn't have a steady girl that we knew of, and mostly kept to himself except when we sent him on errands."

"Errands?"

Wenger rolled his eyes, realizing he had stepped into a dung pile by mentioning any part of his business.

"Little things. Nothin' that would get him in any trouble."

Terry knew, as he suspected from the moment they arrived, they were barking up the wrong tree and Wenger had nothing to offer them. The chances that Allen ever saw his killer before his death were minuscule because the killer researched, roved, then killed without warning, all while remaining unseen.

"When was the last time you saw Allen?" Terry asked.

"Middle of February, because it was a few days after V-Day that we found out."

"And none of your buddies had a bond with Allen? None of them said anything about Allen after he disappeared?"

"We never knew he disappeared," Wenger reaffirmed his earlier statement. "We figured he moved on to the next city."

A thought occurred to Terry.

"Did he store his bike somewhere during the winter?"

"He never said."

"Where did he stay?" Hathaway asked, following up Terry's inquiry.

"Where do any of us stay?" Wenger answered, waving his arm toward the barroom behind them.

Hathaway folded his arms with a skeptical expression.

"Everyone crashes somewhere other than a bar. Did he live with one of your guys out there?"

Wenger shook his head negatively, but his expression told the investigators he wasn't being forthcoming.

"We can ask each of them," Hathaway offered. "We'll just tell them their boss is assisting us in the murder investigation of his good friend and known rapist, Mike Allen, and I'm sure they'll be happy to oblige."

"That is fucked up," Wenger growled. "I've done nothin' *but* assist you and you're rolling me like some fucking crack whore."

"Just tell us where he stayed," Terry pressed.

"He stayed in one of my apartments. I own a few buildings south of the city."

"What's at that apartment that you don't want us to see?" Hathaway inquired, folding his arms like an imposing statue.

"They're all being lived in," Wenger volunteered too eagerly for Terry's taste.

"There was something in his apartment after he left, wasn't there?"

"What do you mean?" Wenger asked warily.

"Was he killed in there? What did you see that you're hiding?"

Hathaway raised an eyebrow at the accusation, then returned his penetrating stare to Wenger.

"We can do this here or publically," the detective threatened.

"There was a little blood on the walls, like maybe he got in a fight or something."

"Did you clean it?" Terry asked, already knowing the answer.

"I had to. I had people moving in the next week."

Terry exchanged disgruntled looks with Hathaway. Even if they found evidence in the apartment it was surely going to be compromised for court purposes. His desperation for any clue, however, made some kind of search necessary.

"We need you to take us there," he said.

Wenger started to object, but Hathaway stopped him short by pointing his finger.

"I don't care who you have to kick out of there, that place is ours for the rest of the day, maybe two, with your blessing."

"Then you'll both be out of my hair?"

"That depends on what we find."

CHAPTER 12

Practically under orders from his parents, Terry brought his family to his parents' house for an afternoon cookout. His father manned the grill, cooking up hotdogs, burgers, and chicken breasts until Pete insisted on taking over grill duty. Though overcast, the day proved barely warm enough for the kids to play outside until lunch was served.

Terry's brothers each had two children, and with Kenny and Pete both bringing their entire clans, the country home felt stuffed when everyone came inside to eat. Most of the kids ran inside with dirt and mud on their clothes, prompting their mothers and grandmother to take up towel duty before they sat down to eat.

Most everyone at the adult dinner table had little to say. Terry's mother tried making small talk, but he retreated into his thoughts mere seconds after filling his plate. Searching Wenger's apartment didn't reveal anything immediately useful, though tests were being run on hair and fiber evidence left behind. Considering Wenger had new tenants virtually every week, sorting out DNA evidence was going to be an almost certain waste of time, and a tedious process at that.

After returning from Syracuse, Terry gave his youngest brother photographs from the crime scenes, particularly the bloody numbers, along with complete profiles for each of the victims. He had given Kenny some time and space, but now he shot his brother questioning looks, knowing neither of them could talk about it over dinner. Kenny refused to look at him for the longest time until they had finished eating. Only when the kids ran outside and everyone else began clearing the table and doing dishes did they retreat to the upstairs.

Terry sometimes felt bad for his youngest brother because Kenny had the worst luck of the three brothers. His hair had virtually receded to a fringe by his mid-twenties, and he put on weight shortly after marrying Erika which he couldn't seem to shed. During his near death experience his heart actually stopped, prompting fellow volunteer firefighters to start the CPR that brought him back.

He kept a full goatee the same color as his remaining dark brown hair, which went against recommended firefighting procedures when wearing masks with bottled air. Pete had recently grown out his goatee from just a mustache as well, while Terry kept his usual clean-shaved look. He had enough issues with people comparing him to his brothers without him looking like them.

Inside Kenny's old bedroom they took seats on the covered mattress while posters from Kenny's teenage years still clung to the walls.

"Funny how they never cleaned this room," Kenny commented. "It's like they expect me to come home someday."

"Or take the initiative to clean it yourself."

Kenny forced a half-grin.

"I like my theory better."

"Speaking of theories, how goes the search for my killer?"

"He's a tricky one. I've been searching through religious texts for the use of numbers, particularly in those combinations. It's complicated because some of the numbers are used repeatedly with one another in the Bible, but I couldn't find any of the combinations of three used together, even using the internet."

"Did you get to look at the profiles?"

"I looked, but most of them had more than a few things wrong in their lives. I'm not sure there's a common theme except they broke a few laws and sinned a few times. Everyone sins, Terry."

"Yeah. Even you."

"Not as much as I used to."

"Thanks for researching the numbers. I can drop by and look them over with you sometime."

"Not necessary. I just need some library time so I can get some more resources in front of me."

"The university might be your best bet."

Kenny stood, glancing at the posters across the closest wall, touching a trophy on his old dresser top. In high school he had been a fairly good hockey player, helping his team win a regional tournament. Terry suddenly found it amazing that all three brothers still lived in the area, considering how many of their fellow high school graduates moved away for work and college, never to return.

After living in three of the largest cities New York had to offer, Terry grew to enjoy some of the benefits of city life. His brothers had never experienced city life long-term and he envied them for never getting caught up in the impersonal side of urban life. Having more to do wasn't always a great thing when he had less time for his family and leisure. Nothing quite compared to sitting on the front porch, staring at the woods or farmland around his house. He always missed clean air and scenery when caught in traffic or stuck in a cubicle all day at work.

"You work tomorrow?" Terry asked his brother.

"I open the store, yeah."

"You know, Pete and I can probably get you a job with the county or the state."

"Sure, but those kinds of jobs won't work around my church time."

Terry sighed.

His brother went overboard with church, but other aspects of his life had changed as well. He decided to get religious tattoos on each of his upper arms and one on the back of his shoulder. He had considered getting a few more on his forearm, but Terry and Pete both spent time dissuading him from taking such action in case he interviewed for a new job. Terry also didn't like the idea of his brother looking like some kind of religious biker when that didn't fit Kenny's personality in any way.

"You've got a wife and two kids to think about, Ken."

"I'm not on welfare, Terry, and Erika works, too."

"I don't want to start this argument with you again, but I want what's best for you. Mom and Dad are worried that you're sacrificing your family for your new church."

"That's a crock and you know it. I passed on college and all kinds of jobs to be responsible for my firstborn, did I not? I make fairly good money at the store, you know."

Kenny's high school girlfriend got pregnant right around his graduation, which threw his life plans into a downward spiral. He sacrificed everything into making it work with her, but their daughter died less than a month after being born and his girlfriend left him with nothing except a pile of medical bills. Luckily his father's insurance took care of some of the bills, since Kenny was young enough to remain included on the plan.

"I swear I'm not giving you a hard time, Ken. I'm just saying if we can get you a good job *with* benefits, you might want to give it some thought. Half of your church stuff is at night anyway."

"I'll think about it," Kenny said, though somewhat dismissive like he wanted the conversation to take a different direction.

Footsteps could be heard from the stairway, meaning their talk was nearly over anyway.

"I'll keep working the numbers," Kenny promised.

"Thanks."

Terry was about to add something to his statement when Pete walked through the door. Like Kenny, their fire chief brother was somewhat burly, and beginning to lose his hair in the front. He lived and breathed fire department life when he wasn't paving or plowing roads for the county.

"Am I breaking up a tender moment?" Pete asked in his usual brash way.

Of the three of them, only he possessed the distinctive New England accent that many New Yorkers used when speaking.

"A little trip down memory lane," Terry said before Kenny could accidentally blurt something inappropriate.

Terry had always envied their relationship because they were close in age, making him feel more like an uncle than a brother sometimes. They shared the same interests, looked somewhat alike, and ran around together a lot more than they spent time with him. He knew he could count on them for anything, but they simply had a bond he couldn't fully understand.

"What are you two up to?" Pete prodded, a suspicious look crossing his face.

"You worried we're planning something for Mom and Dad without you?" Terry asked in reply.

"Not really. You two are probably plottin' to give me a wedgie, aren't ya?"

All three of them laughed, easing the tension slightly.

"Ken, can you help me move a table for Mom?"

Kenny nodded, then followed Pete downstairs, leaving Terry out of the loop once again.

A few minutes later Terry took a seat on the front porch beside his father with nothing except a few Victorian posts between them and the great outdoors. Terry rocked in his chair momentarily, recounting all of the recent events in his life, particularly the series of murders that befuddled him like none before them. He popped open a beer from his father's basement stash, though he seldom drank alcohol.

"Penny for your thoughts," Daniel Levine stated from his rocking chair, looking to his oldest son.

"They're pretty dark, Dad."

"You're putting a lot of pressure on yourself for one murder, son."

"It's four, actually."

"But only one around here, son. You can't always solve the world's problems by yourself. This guy moves like a ghost across the state."

Instead of feeling more relaxed, Terry tensed at the thought of his own family monitoring his case through the news and him being powerless to catch the man responsible.

"Tell me something, Dad. What drives a man to kill fellow human beings?"

His father chuckled briefly.

"You're asking me? That's your area, isn't it?"

"I know, but you've seen a lot of things over the years. What makes a man forego religion and all rationality to start killing people he's never even met?"

"Sickness I suppose, Terry. Our minds are fragile things that can be set wayward by our environment." He paused momentarily to analyze his own words. "Shit, I sound like you now."

"And that's not what I was looking for. Hell, I don't know what I'm looking for, Dad."

They both rocked in silence momentarily as a deer crossed the county road in the distance.

"This killer you're after seems purposeful. He may be sick, but it's almost like he's out making hits. You know, business instead of pleasure."

"But there is some pleasure for him. He moves the bodies and leaves us a clue with each one. You're right, though he shoots them instead of getting close and personal. And we know he's a very strong individual based on one of the murders."

"I saw you and Kenny acting like two kids with a secret at the table."

"You're reading a little too much into it."

"I have seven grandchildren, son. And I think I know my own three hooligans well enough to know when you're hiding something."

Terry watched a car slowly drive by, both he and his father waving to the driver who waved first. Things like that never happened inside city limits because people simply weren't neighborly. In the country, during Terry's childhood and now, simple friendly acts like waving had never changed.

"I asked Kenny to look at the religious aspect of the case for me."

"You're not going to drag him into something dangerous, are you?"

"Dad!" Terry retorted, finding it incredulous that his father would ever think such a thing, much less ask it. "I know he's your baby, and you're worried after what happened to him, but he's not glass. He's still a fireman for Christ's sake. He's not going to fall apart."

"I know, but I worry about him. Sometimes I feel like you and Pete don't watch after him enough."

"He's an adult with two kids of his own, Dad. You can't keep him in the nest forever."

Kenny had clinically died after a fire rescue a few years prior. No one knew why his heart stopped, but it simply did. In the days following his resuscitation Kenny remained in a coma, while questions about brain damage and whether or not he would ever regain consciousness plagued his family.

Terry's father never forgot those lingering days with his youngest son on the brink of death. Ever since the day Kenny left the hospital his parents had covered him with a figurative blanket of protection with daily phone calls and continual monitoring.

"Kenny needs to live his life, Dad," Terry stated, looking to his father. "Maybe helping me with this case is a welcome diversion for him. And he might be able to save some lives."

Daniel Levine said nothing for a moment, pensively staring at his grandchildren in the distance, playing in the tree house he had built at the edge of his property.

"He needs to live life all right, but he can't when he's at that church all the time."

"So he found God. You can't hold that against him."

"No, but I don't think the Lord above wants him to sacrifice his family."

Before the conversation could grow more awkward, Pete and Kenny both stepped onto the porch as though sent from above. Pete seemed to sense he was interrupting something once again, probably thinking both conversations centered around him. Very proud of his job and his position on the fire department, he hated the possibility of anyone speaking one negative word about him.

No one in the family criticized Pete, though he felt a need to measure up to Terry in the eyes of his parents. Life with brothers was nothing if not competitive from birth until the bitter end.

"You never built us a tree house," Pete kidded his father.

"You never asked for one. Besides, you three always had chores to keep you busy."

"And we enjoyed every chore you gave us," Kenny said, rolling his eyes.

Terry rocked a little in the chair, recalling a busy childhood of farm work and schooling. It was a wonder they hadn't gotten into more trouble escaping sheer boredom on the farm.

"We didn't turn out too badly, did we, Dad?"

"Not bad at all. I'm proud of all three of you. Maybe all those chores gave you good work ethics."

All three laughed at the notion, remembering how much they hated chopping wood, feeding animals, and cleaning stalls. Now Pete and Kenny had their children doing similar chores on Pete's farm.

Sherri took care of most chore assignments at Terry's house because they didn't own a working farm, despite the big red barn behind their house. She often had the kids clean their rooms or help with dinner and cleanup. More times than not, they knew their roles when Terry was the only adult at home.

One moment all of the Levine men were standing or sitting comfortably on the porch, then the silence was broken by Pete and Kenny's fire department pagers beeping simultaneously. Instructions from a dispatcher informed them two callers had confirmed a house fire just east of Norfolk town limits.

"Time ta go," Pete said for both of them. "We can take the wife's car."

"We'll make sure everyone gets home," Terry volunteered to expedite their departure in the already fading hope they might save someone's house.

Sometimes false alarms took up his brothers' time, but this didn't sound like one of those incidents. Two separate callers providing the same information would have to be a well-planned ruse or, more than likely, the real thing.

"Thanks," Pete said before he and Kenny stepped down from the porch.

"Be careful," their father called uncharacteristically, possibly worried about a repeat of his youngest son's deadly incident.

Terry watched his brothers dash into action momentarily, wondering where they stowed their gear, or if anyone else would show up at the fire scene. Though he didn't admit it, he admired what they did, particularly since they didn't expect any pay for doing it.

Once they pulled away in Pete's second vehicle, Terry stepped inside to begin making travel arrangements for everyone to get home safely, hoping his brothers followed suit.

CHAPTER 13

Kenny Levine unlocked his store the next morning, then found himself working in the pizza and sub shop portion of the building because his cook called off work with a sick child. He had one other employee coming in around noon to help with any potential lunch rush, leaving him a little time to study some texts during the morning hours after getting the shop ready for business.

Because the shop was technically separate from the store, he inspected it before turning on the lights, the grill, and the fryer. He barely found time to drop off his wife and kids at home after church, still wearing a shirt and tie, along with his black lizard-skin cowboy boots. On Sundays he preferred to wear blue jeans at work, typically allowing his deli employees to dress casually, but today black dress slacks would have to do.

He reeked of burned wood from the previous day's house fire despite a morning shower. Only a small miracle kept the house from burning to the ground when a door between the family's study and living room slammed shut as the family fled the house. Without a rich oxygen supply the fire burned itself out, and Pete's decisive thinking, despite a lack of adequate manpower, kept the damage contained to the study.

Since the day he could crawl Kenny had always looked up to his two brothers. While Terry built a reputation for catching serial killers, Pete was quietly becoming a fire chief of legend among volunteer firefighters. Though he wasn't the most physically gifted individual, Pete studied how fires worked, and after commanding so many scenes, he knew the limitations of his equipment and his men.

Only Kenny and two other firemen made the initial response with Pete, one of whom had to man the pumper truck. Pete always wanted his brother to drive the pumper, stating he felt Kenny was an excellent driver and operator. Kenny knew the real reason was that Pete wanted to keep him safe after the incident a few years back. His parents might have requested Pete keep him safe at all costs, but Kenny refused to abide by any of their advice while he felt perfectly fine.

Disregarding his brother's request, Kenny went into the house with the other firefighter and sprayed some water on the embers and few remaining flames. Kenny didn't have any hero syndrome, but he wasn't going to stand on the sidelines and watch everyone else do the work.

After he and Pete kept the house from burning to the ground, Kenny found time to visit the campus library in Potsdam and check out some books. Fortunately Terry had spared him the more grotesque photos from the crime scenes, though he provided valuable information in the reports and personal analysis.

It wasn't that Kenny hadn't seen gruesome scenes during his lifetime that worried him. During rescue runs he had seen the sides of people's heads shaved to the brain matter and limbs reduced to broken bones and mangled muscle that resembled raw sausage.

He tried recalling facts he'd read from the Bible that resembled the seedier deeds of the victims, but he had only read the book from cover to cover twice. Only certain stories from the ancient text stood out, and he knew very few by theme and teller. It frustrated him that he wasn't the expert Terry touted him to be in front of his police buddies, but at least no one was breathing down his neck to find the answer to the killer's riddle. Terry had requested his friends at the state lab and FBI check the numbers, but they were focused on looking for numeric codes, not Biblical messages. Unfortunately this made him the sole individual examining such an angle.

When his first customer walked into the sub shop just after eleven, Kenny fixed a turkey sub with bacon, mushrooms, tomatoes, lettuce, and a ranch sauce that some said was unrivaled by even the chain stores. He even took the time to sauté the mushrooms upon the customer's request, giving the sandwich an added zing.

He welcomed the distraction because his brain felt overwhelmed by all of the information being force-fed into it. When he stared at the numbers, Kenny decided to simply focus on the top two numbers from each crime scene, because they were always smaller, like passages from the Bible. Some of the bottom numbers were simply too large to be passage labels. It was possible they were numbers from within given texts. With hundreds of passages, however, he knew combing through them was going to take some time.

Saying a little prayer that his memory might serve him well, Kenny flipped open a copy of the King James Bible to start at the beginning.

Genesis.

***

Ben Belinski found himself secluded in his study instead of partaking in his usual Sunday activities like driving his BMW convertible or playing golf. Sometimes he traveled with his wife to different parts of the state on the weekends or did special reports for the television station. He enjoyed spending time with the wealthier locals, trying to elevate his own status without being labeled a hack.

Today, however, he voluntarily locked himself in his study on the third floor of his suburban house just outside the town of Orchard Park, a suburb southeast of Buffalo. Only a full bathroom and a walk-in attic shared the remainder of the space on the top floor. His study was larger than some small town libraries, housing books on three walls surrounding him, while two desks, a filing cabinet, and several cozy chairs were placed accordingly throughout the room. A small bar island, complete with a mini-fridge, rounded out the furniture ensemble.

Light streamed in through the fourth wall, which mostly consisted of floor to ceiling glass from the large picture window overlooking the body of water known as Lake Louise that preceded the housing addition. Occasionally the sun peeked through the clouds dominating the overcast sky, which suited Belinski just fine. He wasn't in a bright and cheery mood, despite his uncle providing him with updates about the task force's findings.

Right now he had his mind set on helping solve one of the most intriguing crimes to hit his home state in years before writing the definitive book about it. His uncle was taking a chance by sharing the case information with him, and Belinski didn't plan on letting him down.

The close call in Syracuse with Terry Levine was unexpected, and a reasonably bold move by the investigator. From what he knew about Levine, he didn't expect the investigator to make such a forward move. The trooper wasn't known for being physical or confrontational, though he was no slouch physically.

Belinski started his search by running down the list of arrests or suspicions related to the murder victims. With files spread across one of his desks, he turned on the computer, skimming through his information while it booted up. He soon began cross-referencing keywords with the numbers on an online search engine, coming up with nothing solid.

"Maybe I'm being too literal," he muttered to himself, trying synonyms and abbreviated versions of some of the crime words.

He quickly discovered he needed to modify his search, which might require hours of concentration, so he stood to pour himself a full glass of Grand Marnier Cent Cinquantenaire. Belinski had discovered the orange-flavored cognac during a trip to Cincinnati about five years earlier. Both sweet and dry, the liquor had a great flavor that came at a high price. He ordered it by the case, seldom drinking it except on special occasions.

Taking a strong swig from the glass, he set it down beside his computer before scrolling down the list of Steven Paulson's crimes. He typed in 'battery' with the three numbers from his crime scene, finding no results in return.

"Shit."

He added the word 'Bible' into the mix, still getting no concrete results. It took him nearly fifteen minutes of adding and rearranging words with possible crimes before he got to racism, then typed it in with the numbers. Most of the hits came up with bookstore sites that had the keywords jumbled in various sentences. Again, no concrete hits, so he changed 'racism' to 'racist' without finding any difference.

After awhile he switched to his favorite beer instead of wasting his expensive stash once he reached a preliminary buzz. Still able to think clearly, but now much more comfortable as he worked, Belinski continued to stumble through various words and numbers with no new leads. He even tried putting the numbers together to see if they formed some kind of pattern on a website, but they resulted in useless hits.

Exasperated, he decided to take a break by leaving the room and walking through the house. Carrying his beer with him, he took the stairs down from the third floor. After descending the second floor to his kitchen, Belinski warmed a bowl of chili from the night before, glancing over the morning paper.

Since gaining his uncle's complete trust, he had tossed around some ideas for naming the killer, but nothing quite fit yet. If the killer had a theme and he named the man, that made for great press and a personal touch to the book he planned to write. He wanted to take the lead among journalists covering the story, but that meant walking a fine line while protecting his uncle.

"Are you drunk?" Belinski's wife asked when she walked into the kitchen to return an empty plate.

Jennifer Belinski possessed observational powers equal to that of a reporter, though she worked in a much different field. She ran a tourism company that catered to businessmen and wealthy tourists by bus, boat, or helicopter. While she didn't own the company, Jennifer made excellent money carrying out the duties as its manager.

"I'm working on it," her husband answered, belching slightly as he cupped his mouth with his fist.

"Making any headway?"

"No. It's just dead ends."

Maybe he felt more aroused because of the alcohol, but he found his wife exceptionally attractive at the moment. She was gorgeous in the eyes of everyone who knew her, and Belinski certainly grew tired of comments saying he was damn lucky to have such a hot wife, but he felt fortunate to have her every waking day. At times their lives felt like two trains passing in the night, but they were still remarkably happy when they had time together.

He drew behind her, suddenly wanting a larger distraction than a few minutes. Caressing her neck, he kissed the soft skin from her right shoulder up to the underside of her jaw.

"You can't be serious," she said, though moaning. "You're drunk."

He ran his fingers gently through her strawberry-blond hair, now kissing her cheeks, moving toward her lips.

"I'm only half-drunk. I can perform flawlessly."

"For the usual two minutes?" Jennifer kidded, letting him begin to undo her blouse from behind, which she had only half-buttoned in the comfort of her own home that morning.

"I'll give you three."

Jennifer acted as though swooning from his advances, hand to her head.

"Carry me."

Belinski swept her off her feet like they were honeymooning in some Hallmark Channel movie and carried her to their bedroom.

***

Kenny rubbed his head in frustration as he reviewed the numbers again. It was now after noon and he felt like he had read half of the Bible in some twisted search by numbers game. Being a layman, he still couldn't understand every word in the book because it had been translated numerous times over the centuries. He felt certain he had missed something due to altered wording between previous generations who worked on the ancient scrolls.

His noon help had arrived on time, though very few customers walked in to keep them busy. Sundays were typically slow at the store, especially in the sub shop, until suppertime. Kenny needed to stock items in the store, do payroll, and order products from his vendors, but he was too engrossed in the mystery to quit now.

His duties could wait another day.

Referring to several Biblical study books beside him, Kenny picked out a newer Bible, translated from the older versions for the modern reader. He started from the beginning all over again, with the first two numbers in each of the four sets. Reading the passages was tedious, only because he was looking for certain words that might relate to the murder scenes.

He breezed through the first two entries in Genesis, finding no words that appeared relevant to the search, then he stumbled upon 34:1 which laid it out in plain words that Shechem had raped Dinah shortly into the story. Confused and wondering how he had missed such a stark clue earlier, Kenny returned to a traditional Bible, finding the wording slightly different.

Kenny read the passage aloud.

"And Dinah the daughter of Leah, which she bare unto Jacob, went out to see the daughters of the land. And when Shechem the son of Hamor the Hivite, prince of the country, saw her, he took her, and lay with her, and defiled her."

"What was that, boss?" Kenny's cook, Jillian, asked from behind the counter.

"Nothing," Kenny answered quickly, realizing he needed to read more silently.

He looked at the text, realizing his mistake because 'defile' had a different literal meaning in modern times. Now knowing that Genesis 34:1 through the next few paragraphs dealt with the rape of a woman, and Michael Gregory Allen was an alleged rapist connected the dots for Kenny.

Growing rather excited at the find, he refrained from jumping up to call Terry before he verified he was on the right track. Using the modern Bible as his guide, he checked out the rest of the numbers, spending the next forty-five minutes finding that Job 36:14 made reference to prostitutes being unclean, which was Veronica Lee's known vocation. He then found Timothy 6:5 and the text before and after it speaking of a servant of God losing his way and not practicing what he preached. Harold James Mitchell seemed to be just such a man.

"Dear God," Kenny muttered, beginning to realize this serial killer was possibly killing in the name of God, which in and of itself was utter sin.

With trembling fingers he found James 2:4 speaking of judgmental thinking, making reference to hatred and dislike of those different from one's self. Racism, Kenny concluded, thinking of Steven Paulson.

He was partway to unraveling the mystery, but the third number in each set eluded him.

Stealing another look at the four sets of numbers, he let his mind speculate about the possibilities.

36:14:242

6:5:97

2:4:105

34:1:20

The last number couldn't mark the end of the chapter because none of the books in the Bible had 242 chapters. He doubted any of them reached the century mark. The Bible was nothing if not broken up into succinct segments.

Kenny skimmed the page before him for the number twenty, finding it used in two separate instances, neither of which made sense compared to the meat of the story. His eye glanced up to the top of the page, where the page number was twenty-seven. Struck with inspiration, he opened another Bible to the same passage, finding the page number at twenty-three. The print was slightly different in size and spacing than the other book, and of course the book was printed by a different press.

Considering the Bible was the most printed book of all time, by thousands of different publishers, variations were natural. Kenny owned a pocket version, a leather bound copy, and everything in between.

"Is it really that simple?" he questioned aloud, jumping up to grab the phone.

He dialed Terry's home number, getting Britney who used the phone more than anyone else in the house since her cell phone reception wasn't often good at Terry's country home.

"Is your dad home?" Kenny asked quickly.

"Yeah. Just a sec."

Terry was outside doing something, so it took him the longest minute of Kenny's life to reach the phone.

"Hello."

"Terry, I think I figured it out."

"You're kidding!" Terry asked with unrestrained excitement, an unusual reaction for the normally stoic state trooper.

"We need to get to Potsdam so I can look something up. Can you pick me up?"

"Sure. I'll be there in five."

"Okay. I'll explain everything on the way, but I think I know what the killer's trying to tell us."

***

After Belinski's extended break, he returned to the study, opting for bottled water to go with his reheated chili. He tried entering several various combinations into the computer without luck before he studied the numbers once again. He noticed the last of the three numbers in the four sets were typically large compared to the other numbers, as though possibly a marker rather than part of the message.

He typed in *36:14 Bible* into his computer's online search engine, his eyes widening as some surprising results appeared before him.

While the first three and the bottom three results seemed practically worthless to him, he found a title in the middle article that caught his attention due to one word.

Prostitutes.

More specifically *Job 36:14 They die in their youth, among male prostitutes of...*

"You've got to be kidding me," he said, flipping through his uncle's files, discovering that the first victim in Buffalo was indeed a prostitute, her body discovered with the 36:14:242 number combination above her head.

Rising from the desk, Belinski darted over to the section where he kept the books on Biblical studies and religion. He kept his study organized much like a library so he knew where books of various topics could be found. Otherwise he would waste hours looking for references in his collection containing thousands of books.

Finding the title he wanted, Belinski pulled the book from the shelf, then flipped through the alphabetical listings as he returned to his desk. He cursed himself for not thinking of it sooner, because the book was basically a reference of where to find any particular topic in the Bible. It had been out-of-print for several years, so Belinski counted himself lucky to have snagged a copy at a used bookstore in Rochester a few years prior.

As he looked up the alleged crimes of the four victims, he began finding numeric references that matched keywords from the Bible. He now knew the killer was sending a message that he was taking out the unclean people of the world. Gaffney had told him Terry Levine thought the killer might be more of a vigilante than a serial killer, but the thought of a Christian vigilante seemed almost absurd.

Belinski took time to read the passages thoroughly, searching for further hidden messages. He discovered the tales in the scriptures didn't exactly match up with the murder scenarios. Instead, he decided, the killer was simply providing a theme, an explanation of how he chose his victims.

"But how do you find them?" the reporter questioned aloud.

He typed in the victims' names into his computer, finding return articles that had nothing to do with any of them because people across the country shared the same or similar names. He narrowed the search by putting in a name with a city, beginning with Allen.

Within five minutes he discovered that only Mitchell had any kind of stature within the internet. The other three could have been found during arrest logs, Belinski deduced, but why wouldn't the killer simply stick to his home turf? Transient killers were harder to find and catch, but vigilantes typically wanted their own cities free of crime.

"What a quandary you present me with, my friend," Belinski thought aloud, wondering if the killer did indeed work for a police or state agency that had access to criminal databases.

He jotted down a reminder to check on what agencies entered and accessed criminal arrest information.

Satisfied he had discovered the killer's messages to the police, Belinski leaned back in his chair, pondering how to approach his first major article about the mysterious enigma. He planned to confer with his uncle before printing anything, to ensure he didn't give away any secret police clues that might anger Gaffney's peers.

His mind began churning creatively as it sometimes did with the combination of discovery and alcohol. The thought of scooping everyone else on the story exhilarated him, and suddenly, as though heaven sent, a perfect sensational identity for the killer came to him.

"I'll call you the Sin Killer," Belinski said, smirking with self-indulgence at the thought of what glory the killer might bring him.

Not that Belinski wanted to see anyone hurt, but he wasn't going to pass on the once-in-a-lifetime offer laid before him. He had covered the Toomey killings around Buffalo the previous year, but that was a brief period of time and a limited circle of targeted individuals. Belinski suspected this killer might last years before stumbling and getting himself caught.

"And to think, I might have just accidentally expedited the investigation," he said to himself, picking up his cell phone to call his uncle.

He still had enough pride and good upbringing to put civic duty above money and prestige.

***

Terry found himself at Willow's Used Books with his brother, thankful they opened at noon, after Kenny had explained his finds to him.

"So why are we visiting a used book store?" he questioned in return.

"A couple reasons. One, they have the largest selection of Bibles around, and two, they carry a lot of out-of-print versions that aren't on regular store shelves."

"I guess you would know," Terry sighed, following his brother to the religious section.

Kenny found them a small table with a few chairs where people could test out books before buying. The owners of the bookstore were very friendly people, and highly religious, so they loved seeing Kenny visit. He knew the ins and outs of the store as though *he* owned it.

"I think the last number of each sequence is the page number," Kenny explained a second time, "so we need to figure out which Bible he's using in case there's a deeper meaning."

The wheels in Terry's mind began to turn. If they knew which Bible was used, they had a chance at tracing it to a seller, or finding out if any churches had bought the publication in bulk. New possibilities opened to the task force if he found out what version the killer was using to provide his messages.

Terry looked at the shelf before him, realizing it wrapped around the other side of the wall, though the section didn't continue very far. Possibly hundreds of Bibles were shelved before him, most of which had no duplicates in sight.

"I had no idea," Terry muttered, his eyes locked onto the colorful array of Bibles.

"The campus bookstore would have a fraction of this," Kenny stated, already pulling the books from the top shelf, trying to keep them in order.

He began opening them, flipping the pages in search of a certain chapter, then closed them one by one.

"I can help," Terry volunteered. "What are you looking for?"

"The book that has Genesis 34:1 on page twenty."

Terry joined in the search, finding it reasonably easy considering Genesis was the first story told in the Bible. With so many different books, however, it was going to take time to get through them all unless they got lucky.

"What if we don't find the book at all?" he questioned.

"This is only a fraction of the Bibles published. It could be anywhere. Hell, it might be in a different language for all we know."

Terry felt somewhat deflated after his brother's statement, but Kenny readily knew things he might have to look up otherwise. If there was a best-seller that spanned worldwide, the Bible was that book.

"You've done the hard part, Kenny. Even if we don't find the specific book, we know his reason for killing these people, insane as it may be."

"I've come this far. I'd like to see it through."

"The store's open another four hours. We should be able to knock it out by then."

The brothers searched the entire inventory over the next two hours before Kenny came across a soft-cover paperback book with a plain brown color and golden lettering. It was a King James edition, out of circulation for almost a decade by a company he hadn't heard of from

New York City. He discovered all of this information only after finding Genesis 34:1 on page 20 of the first section in the book.

"This is it," he blurted, thumbing through the pages to verify the other three entries.

It took several minutes, but he found them on their appropriate page numbers.

"I forgot it starts over," Terry said as Kenny skipped through the Old Testament into the New Testament where two of the entries were found.

"Each book gets its own treatment," Kenny explained with a somewhat scolding look.

"I know," Terry said testily, remembering his church school studies more clearly. "So this *has* to be the book."

Kenny nodded.

"Should I tell Karen you want to make a purchase?"

"Definitely. And we need to see if they have any more copies."

While Kenny left to speak with the owners, Terry cleaned up their mess, shelving the dozens of Bibles, hoping there might be more Bibles in a storeroom. He felt a step closer to discovering the killer's identity, though he felt certain the killer *wanted* the police to understand his messages.

Kenny returned, reporting that the store only had the one copy, but Terry felt confident he could find more online. He wanted everyone in the task force to have one in case another murder came across their desks. They might also be able to check around and see if individuals or businesses had purchased copies when they were new. It felt like a long shot, but he needed to try anything at this point.

CHAPTER 14

After a week of FBI schooling in Quantico, Virginia, the last thing Sheriff Lynn Stover wanted was to report to her office on a Sunday evening. The drive from the Great Falls International Airport took an hour after her flight landed and she felt desperate for a hot shower and some sleep. Though Teton County saw little action requiring police assistance, she needed to catch up on her mail and messages before reporting to work the next morning.

Lynn hated being surprised by anything, and with spring weather finally arriving throughout the state, people were starting to get frisky. Traffic accidents were already on the rise, criminal activity would become more frequent, and more truckers typically crossed the state on their coast-to-coast runs.

She let herself into the station, finding only the dispatcher in his centralized room as she turned on the rest of the lights. Though it wasn't always unlocked, the building was manned at all hours by a dispatcher, even when deputies weren't on patrol in the overnight hours. Lynn felt strange when she attended conventions with urban officers because city life rendered more frequent and violent crime. Lynn dealt with neighborly disputes, the occasional intentionally cut fence, and farm accidents far more often than stabbing victims, shootings, or the ever rare murder.

Homicides occurred in Montana, though seldom in or near her county. Lynn served as a deputy almost eleven years, the last of those as undersheriff, before taking the helm in Teton County when the previous sheriff left on disability. Much to the chagrin of her deputies, Lynn fell into the role of sheriff upon her approval through the county commission. Of course the rumors flew abound that she had slept with her predecessor, or found unflattering information about him that she used for blackmail purposes to rise through the ranks.

It angered and insulted her that some of them couldn't believe she was actually qualified for the job. Female sheriffs weren't common in Montana, so she found herself working extra to prove herself to her subordinates and pave the way for other women to advance in law enforcement.

"Hi, Dan," she said as she passed the dispatcher, who returned a courteous nod because he was on the phone with someone.

As she took a seat at her desk, Lynn started at the top of the short stack of paperwork awaiting her. She found a handful of messages jotted on paper, along with a dozen on her machine. With a push of the play button, she paid loose attention to the succession of messages as she looked through the notes, finding little of importance.

Only a few of the messages proved important, so she moved from departmental business to the notes and fliers delivered by other agencies, or faxed from states as far away as Florida. Some were memos about missing children, or reminders of memorial golf or softball tournaments coming later that summer. Lynn leafed through them until a National Crime Information Center (NCIC) memo came to her from the state police in New York sent out to every dispatch center in the country. Luckily one of her dispatchers discovered and printed it, possibly recognizing the significance of the message.

The memo originated from an investigator by the name of Terry Levine, who stated he had caught a case in upstate New York. He found a rather unusual aspect of the case and wanted to know if anyone else had seen a similarity with any homicides in their area. Though the information seemed veiled and guarded, Lynn found something interesting within its content.

I'm interested in any homicides in which the killer has left any kind of message scribed in blood.

She immediately thought back to an area case that was never officially solved where two similar homicides occurred in Teton County and two others in neighboring counties. In both cases the killer left something inscribed on the wall above the victims. Unofficially, the task force working the case believed the case was closed when one of the two prime suspects died in a car accident and the murders ceased entirely.

Lynn found contact information atop the printout, deciding she could call Trooper Levine in the morning. She wanted to speak with the lead investigator on the Montana homicides to see if he could shed more light on the subject, or possibly lend a hand to authorities in New York personally.

Before she did anything, Lynn needed some sleep, so she took up the printout and waved goodbye to the dispatcher before locking the office behind her.

CHAPTER 15

It took longer than usual for winter to release its stranglehold on one of the state's most beautiful counties, finally providing green grass and fertile soil for planting. Joe Taggart lived and once worked in the scenic county he called home. Though the morning hadn't proven comfortable for riding horseback or tending to his small group of cattle, he couldn't wait any longer. Wearing a gray Stetson and a yellow slicker, Taggart battled the drizzling rain and cool morning as he checked his fence line.

Even his thick, brown beard provided only limited protection against the elements, so he sometimes wore a kerchief to keep the wind and debris from irritating his face.

Living in the sparsely populated county suited him because he knew many of the people in the surrounding towns, and they were the only people he cared to know. Living alone on his ranch, Taggart had little need for big cities or the people who inhabited them. Most of his visitors came in the form of coyotes or deer, though once or twice a year he spotted a bear wandering through his fields.

Keeping his head down to shield his face from the wind and rain, Taggart checked the fence for any breaks or damage as he did once a week during tolerable weather. A day without wind east of the Rocky Mountains never happened, so he tried picking otherwise reasonable weather when riding. Though forty-five years old, he considered himself retired from everything except work on his land. As he rode at a leisurely pace, his mind wandered back through time to his former life.

Once the county sheriff, Taggart left his position after five years in office because a particular call rendered him unable to carry out his duties as he saw fit. His career as sheriff was plagued by two looming shadows that seemed to follow him like rain clouds wherever he went. While one was a physical scar, the other ate through him like bone cancer because two county residents died under his watch and their families never received answers or peace of mind.

Taggart wasn't expected to be wherever danger lurked like some superhero, but he wanted more closure for the residents who elected him and paid his salary. In a state where many children learned how to ride a horse shortly after they took their first steps, he wasn't a native. A job opportunity brought his father to Montana when Taggart was only three, but the entire family immediately took to the most laid-back of the fifty states.

After Taggart graduated high school, his parents returned to their home state of Wyoming when his father took a promotion within his company. With no other prospects lined up, Taggart joined the Air Force, staying close to home at Malmstrom Air Force Base once he completed training for the Security Forces.

Deciding he liked police work, he studied every course that came his way, including investigations, until his discharge ten years later. He found work as a deputy for ten years before discovering the sheriff of Teton County planned on retiring when his term expired. While the work wasn't glamorous and Taggart was overly qualified for the position, he ran anyway and won by a landslide because so many local residents liked and respected him.

Back in the present, he picked up the pace, ready to be out of the elements for the day. The circle around his vast acreage led him back to the front gate, where two wooden posts were intersected by a large sign some twenty feet off the ground that welcomed visitors. The hand-crafted wooden sign preceded the lengthy driveway, letting visitors know they had arrived at the *Brown Quarter Ranch*. Beneath the title, which belonged to a previous owner, now buried on the property with his family, read *Joseph A. Taggart*, which stated the current ownership.

Not one to disrespect the dead, or their memory, Taggart left the name unchanged when he purchased the property. With a cemetery half a mile away, plainly in view from the house beneath a large Ponderosa Pine, Taggart somehow felt bonded with Edmund Brown, who might have never left the property after his death. Taggart didn't need angry spirits badgering him, so he tended to the property and altered little. Brown, buried beside his wife, daughter, and a brother, was long since gone, though local people knew his name well.

Most of the property was fenced with wooden posts and barbed wire, but anywhere the property was visible from the road, the driveway, or the house, it was done completely in natural wooden posts and beams. The previous owner spared little expense having the place appear as expensive as the larger ranches in Teton and neighboring counties, with moderate success.

The house, built sometime in the 1960s, accommodated a family of five, plus a guest or two, rather easily. Two stories tall, the residence twice underwent renovations and modernization before Taggart purchased it. While Taggart preferred the idea of living in a cabin, he found the Victorian look of his current house grew on him with each passing day. The barn, however, was the selling point for him.

Equipped with five stalls, a ventilation system, and climate controls that kept it above freezing during the harsh winter months and reasonably cool during the summers, the barn was a dream come true. Painted traditional red with white trim, the barn was the first thing immediately visible from the entrance nearly a quarter of a mile away. Every part of his ranch, including the Rocky Mountains to the west, made every morning like waking up to a living picture from some travel brochure.

Now into the middle of the morning, Taggart considered frying up bacon and eggs with some toast for a late breakfast after simply grabbing a granola bar on his way out the door nearly four hours earlier. His plans changed, however, when he spied a white truck with sheriff's department markings and a cab covering the back as he neared the end of his driveway.

Seeing no one inside the vehicle, he knew who had driven miles outside of town to pay him a visit. He removed the saddle from his horse before turning it loose in a nearby field to run freely and graze. Taking up the walking stick he had leaned against a wall inside his barn while he rode, Taggart limped toward his house with its ever necessary assistance.

Inside his large farmhouse the aromas of breakfast reached his nostrils as he heard bacon sizzling atop his gas stove. He found a shapely uniform in front of his stove, filled by his replacement as sheriff. Lynn Stover was his former undersheriff, current girlfriend, and virtually a perfect match for him. Based on his recommendation, before they ever shared a personal relationship, she was easily voted in as sheriff of Teton County.

Lynn possessed farm girl good looks, carrying herself very well in any rural setting. Taggart felt lucky to have her, though most men avoided her because she was in law enforcement and put many of them to shame on a working farm. Her brown hair was pulled back in a ponytail much of the time, which dulled her appearance, though she said it gave her a look of authority.

"Good morning," Taggart said, putting his hands around her waist from behind, gently kissing her neck.

"You smell like manure," she commented, though not rejecting his advances.

"I've been busy. And I thought you liked my musky odor."

Lynn chuckled.

"Are you here to help me pass the day in bed?" he dared ask.

She responded with a raised eyebrow.

"I'm here on official business, Joseph. And I'm going to buy you a new cane by the way. That thing looks like the dog chewed on it."

"I hate it when you call it that," he said, breaking away to have a seat at the kitchen table. "It's a walking stick, and the dog *did* chew on it."

Taggart believed canes were something with curved handles that the elderly used to get around. He preferred a walking stick, like the decorative type used in the early Twentieth Century by the wealthy who toured the country and stayed at resorts. His pride sometimes cost him dearly when his hand grew sore from cupping the wooden stick's gold-colored metal top, or the stick didn't provide enough balance for him to maintain a steady course while limping around.

"How do you feel about traveling?" Lynn asked as she cracked a few eggs and dropped them into the pan.

"You know I hate going into town once a week for food. Why would you ask that?"

"Because you might have a chance to catch your killer."

Taggart looked at her as though awaiting the punch line to a joke.

"Donnie Childress died in a car accident two years ago."

"Donnie Childress was only one of your suspects, Joe."

Lynn brought over a plate of food with a glass of orange juice as he took a look at the sheet of paper already resting on the table.

"You've got to agree that's compelling," Lynn said when he finished reading the memo.

"Could be a copycat."

"You never let out those kinds of details, Joe. No one could know our killer's signature."

"Signature? Just because they both write something in blood doesn't make them the same person. And the things they're writing aren't even the same."

Lynn sat beside him, looking him squarely in the eyes.

"They have four murders across the state of New York, all tied to the same person. Based on what this man is saying, and asking for, I think you should at least make a call."

Taggart hadn't touched his breakfast, and based on where the conversation was heading, he wasn't sure he planned to.

"Why don't *you* call him?" he asked, refusing to give in easily.

He detested the idea of being drawn into an investigation once again, particularly given his physical condition.

"You're the authority on what happened here, Joe. Only you can tell this guy if he's on the right track."

"I ain't the authority no more, Lynn."

"You need to swallow that damn pride of yours, Taggart, and call this trooper."

"Hell, I don't even have a phone."

They both knew he owned a cell phone, but the reception at his ranch was terrible at best on most days.

"Now you're just being difficult."

He sighed, forking some eggs into his mouth.

"Can I at least eat before you drag me into town?"

"Sure."

Taggart had kept a copied set of the case files at home when he was working the case actively. They were stowed away in a file cabinet drawer he hadn't opened in almost two years because he thought the case was closed forever. A nagging feeling always ate away at him, though, that a man intelligent enough to avoid leaving *any* clues at four different crime scenes was careless enough to die in a car crash.

Before he reached any rash conclusions, Taggart would have to speak with the man in charge of the New York investigation and see if there were any similarities beyond bloody writing.

He enjoyed his privacy, but deep down he wanted redemption for never being able to tell four families he knew who had killed their loved ones and that individual was going to pay. To attain internal peace, he might indeed swallow his pride and help with the investigation. Within the hour the former sheriff would know whether his killer was six feet beneath an unattended grave marker or assuming a new life half a country away.

***

From Taggart's home to Choteau, the small town where the Teton County Sheriff's Office was located, the drive took just under an hour. He preferred being away from town, like much of the state population that remained rural despite a push for city life everywhere else in the country. He lived closer to town when he worked as a deputy, then as sheriff, because sometimes the unforgiving winters stopped even the stoutest of vehicles from reaching their destinations and he hated missing work.

Taggart felt like an alien being as he walked into the sheriff's office with Lynn when all eyes locked on him. Three deputies were biding their time by getting coffee or walking through the building while a dispatcher sat in her chair beside the phones and computer system. Each of them stopped what they were doing the instant he stepped through the door, all of them having worked for him a few short years ago.

He hated giving any of them ammunition for the vicious rumors about Lynn obtaining the sheriff's office by sleeping with him, even though she didn't seem to care. While they had a perfectly valid reason for being seen together, new speculation would start the minute they left.

"You're all looking at me like I was back from the dead," Taggart said.

On the few occasions he saw them when he was in town, the conversations were brief. He was no longer on the job, and they thought of him as a crippled recluse who wanted to be left alone.

At least some of their information was accurate.

Without letting another moment of awkward silence pass, Taggart hobbled behind Lynn toward her office through the common work area for the deputies. The sights and smells all returned to him because he reported to the office daily after seeing it built toward the end of his first term when the old sheriff's office was deemed a condemned building.

Like a parallel to Taggart, the old office stood beside the new one in disrepair and neglect because it was a registered historical building. It served for storage and little else.

Lynn closed the door behind them, wasting little time as she picked up the phone and dialed the contact number before handing the phone to Taggart. He only waited one ring before someone on the other end answered.

"State Police, Trooper Hinkle."

"I'm trying to reach Terry Levine."

"May I ask who is calling?"

"Sheriff Joe Taggart from Teton County, Montana."

He gave Lynn a wink after his partial indiscretion, since he didn't really have any authority as a law enforcer, or a title, since leaving office.

"Let me see if he's in."

Taggart waited less than a minute before someone came back on the line.

"Sir, he's out of the building at the moment. Can I take a message?"

For a fleeting moment Taggart considered simply leaving a number with the trooper and calling it a day, but he knew a returned call would never reach his farm and he didn't want to stay in town all day.

"Look, it's important I speak with him right away. I may have information about the murders he's investigating."

Taggart heard nothing for a few seconds, speculating the trooper was deciding if he was the real thing or some kind of sneaky newspaper person wanting access to Levine.

"Let me put you through to his cell phone," Hinkle finally said.

This time two rings passed before someone answered.

"Levine."

"Trooper Levine, my name is Joe Taggart. I'm calling about the memo you sent out with information about bloody writing at a crime scene."

"I sent that out over two weeks ago. Any particular reason you're just now calling?"

"It just came to my attention last night."

Taggart gave Lynn a look that indicated he thought he was wasting his time. She simply held up a finger, indicating for him to be on his best behavior.

"What kind of information do you have?" Levine asked, cutting to the chase.

"I had four murders about three years ago, two of which occurred in my own county, where the killer left bloody numbers above each of the victims."

"You have my attention, Mr. Taggart. What can you tell me about these murders?"

"Well, in each case the killer left a single number written above the victim in the victim's own blood. The first homicide was the only one in which he used a gun. He used a knife in the other three. Victims were all local residents, all white, middle-class women."

"Any trace evidence?"

"No. This guy was smart."

"Did you have any suspects?"

"I had two. One died in a car crash and the murders stopped after that. I kept an eye on the other suspect, but I think he moved away within the year. The locals didn't take to him too well once we brought him in for questioning a few times. I lost track of him after he moved."

"Lost track?"

"I'm no longer in the police business, Trooper Levine. An accident forced me out a few years ago."

"I'm sorry to hear that," Levine replied sincerely enough that Taggart believed him.

Taggart looked beyond Lynn's closed door, seeing strange looks from the deputies when they walked into their common area. They had to be wondering if something from Taggart's era had drawn him into the office, possibly suspecting the murders had somehow bubbled to the surface in someone else's swamp. Most of them felt partially responsible for never catching the man behind the killings, because everyone suspected it was someone local.

"Would it be possible for you to forward me some of your case files?" Levine asked.

"Does this mean you think all of this could be connected?"

"I'm not convinced, but I'd probably know once I saw your files."

"Can I ask what you've got up there?"

Levine hesitated a few seconds before answering. Taggart understood the sensitivity surrounding the case because he had endured keeping certain secrets during his investigation.

"I have four homicides, so far, that have all been shootings. The killer seems to be preying on criminals, not waiting for the judicial system to decide their fate. In all four cases he has left a set of numbers written in blood beside the bodies and it seems to have religious sentiment. That little nugget is just between us."

"Understood. Sounds kind of like a vigilante to me."

"That's what I'm starting to think. I don't want to talk myself out of anything, though, because you're the only person who's called me back so far."

Taggart was surprised more people didn't leave creative crime scenes for cops to examine, though he doubted many serial killers took the time to decorate their scenes at all.

"I'll have the local office forward the files to you in Canton."

"Where can I reach you if I have any questions?"

Taggart supplied his cell phone number, then gave Lynn's office and cell phone number after explaining that reception on his farm was terrible.

"I appreciate the call," Levine said. "I'll get in touch with you either way and let you know if it seems like a match. Is there anyone still actively pursuing the case on your end?"

"It's still officially open, but there haven't been any new leads in almost two years."

"Okay. Thanks again. I'm looking forward to seeing the files."

"I'll get to work on sending them over."

After a cordial goodbye, Taggart hung up the phone, looking to his girlfriend.

"I guess we need to fax and e-mail everything we can to New York."

Lynn gave him a pensive stare, having heard the entire conversation while reading his body language.

"Do you think it's the same killer?"

"Based on what he told me, no I don't."

"I think you should travel there and find out," Lynn joked.

"Sounds like you're trying to get rid of me. Besides, you're the representative for our department now. I'm old and washed up."

Standing up, Lynn gently moved her hand across his lap.

"If we weren't in this office right now, I'd give you the biggest kiss, then undress you before you could put up a fight."

Taggart smiled at the offer, then cautiously looked behind him as though the deputies were going to walk in on their conversation at any moment.

"I could lower the blinds if you wanted to take me right now," Lynn said mischievously.

With wide eyes, Taggart turned to find her laughing.

"I'm kidding, Joseph. Let's get these files sent so we can get you home."

"Where you're sure to take advantage of me because I can't run away."

"Exactly."

***

By that evening Terry had the files from Montana, curious about the man he had spoken with that afternoon. Taggart didn't sound very old for someone already retired from law enforcement. Terry questioned every-thing about the task force investigation in Montana because he wanted to make absolutely certain they had covered every aspect he dealt with in his case. He had met investigators from Montana in seminars, and the only thing they lacked was some of the technology and communications that many investigators took for granted.

Thanks to Kenny's research, the entire task force had copies of the exact King James Bible the killer was using. They also knew what the messages meant, though Terry kept them sworn to secrecy, despite the press hounding the investigators for developments.

Sitting out back in a collapsible lounging chair, Terry kept a glass of iced tea on one side and the stack of files on the other. In a month the kids would be splashing in the pool, but for now he had only an hour of daylight left and the air around him continued to cool as the pinkish sun faded away beneath the horizon.

"Getting anywhere?" Sherri asked as she took a seat at the nearby picnic table.

"It's an interesting read, but I'm starting to think the sheriff had it right. Their perp was messy with a knife and he numbered his victims one through four as he killed them."

"I know I'm beating my head against the wall telling you this, but this case isn't your life."

"I'll be done in an hour or two, I promise."

Sherri stood up, then squatted beside him, taking his hand.

"It's not this in particular. You've been coming home every day lately and fretting about this case. You get so obsessed when you go after these killers."

"Are you worried about me?" he asked, grinning before he pulled her in for a kiss.

"No," Sherri answered between lip contact. "I'm worried the kids are going to think you're ignoring them."

Terry set the paperwork beside him, taking a deep breath as he looked into his wife's loving eyes. She wouldn't admit her concern for him because that was a battle they had waged several times over with no resolution. He knew his reason for being put on God's green Earth was to track the worst of the psychotic criminals.

Sherri knew this as well, accepting the fact though she hated it when he wasn't an ideal family man.

"Do we need a family night out?" he suggested.

"We don't have to go anywhere," Sherri said on the verge of exasperation. "The kids just need you to ask them how school went, or what they want to do this weekend. You don't have to fly in and be Superdad."

"They hate it when we ask about school."

"They say they hate it, but we have to stay involved, Terry. Our oldest leaves for college this fall and she already makes comments about how cool it is that Uncle Pete drinks whenever he wants."

"Uncle Pete is a borderline alcoholic with his own issues. I'll have a long talk with Britney before she leaves for school this fall."

Sherri gave him a sour look.

"And I'll go hug and kiss my kids before they call protective services," he said, propping himself to a standing position.

"I ask you to spend time with them and you want to send them fleeing in terror."

"How about some quality time then?" Terry asked, scooping up the files. "I can look at these after they go to bed."

Sherri drew close to him.

"Maybe I need some TLC too."

"Woman, you don't like to make it easy on me, do you?"

"Never."

She ran her finger along the bottom of his chin.

"Only a lunatic would refuse the advances of a neglected wife."

"I wouldn't want to be labeled a lunatic, so I guess I'll be seeing you in a little bit, Mrs. Levine."

Terry grabbed his glass before toting the paperwork inside with him. Sherri tried to avoid being a nag, but there came a time when he slipped into his work and forgot about everything around him. His kids were the most important thing to him, so he never wanted them to think they took a backseat to the degenerates he pursued daily.

***

Playing the part of a dutiful father, Terry spent time with his three kids, receiving gratuitous sex from Sherri once they were all in bed. Despite fulfilling his family obligations, his conscience nagged at him to know whether the murders in Montana were related to the four across his home state.

At three in the morning he found himself in the living room lying on the couch with the photographs and paperwork spread across the floor and the coffee table in a somewhat organized manner. His large black lab, which he had owned since he first brought it home as a puppy, had long since given up vying for his attention. It found a comfortable corner, then plopped itself down in a ball before falling asleep.

Each of the Montana victims was a local resident, meaning the killer didn't travel far to carry out his dirty work. While the first had been shot, the three following were stabbed repeatedly with a large military style knife. The same make of knife was used for all three killings, rammed through the rib cage or to the side of the sternum in each murder.

The forensic people deduced that the killer was left-handed based on the way the numbers were drawn, which Terry found interesting. No matter how hard he wanted to make a connection, to know his killer had a background, Terry couldn't find enough concrete evidence to make an official conclusion.

In Montana all four victims were female, and authorities believed there had been physical contact from the killer in each case, including the shooting. He made certain to wear latex gloves when touching the bodies, particularly in the vaginal areas. He also seemed to spend some time with the bodies, probably acting out some sort of fantasy with them present.

Nothing like a vigilante might do.

No full footprints were ever found, but the technicians estimated the shoe size of partial prints to be around ten-and-a-half, a reasonably common size. No fingerprints or unverified DNA evidence were ever found, implying the killer was intelligent. Terry couldn't totally dismiss the Montana killer based on what he found, but few serial killers ever changed their modus operandi, even when they changed locations.

He planned to continue studying the information while forming questions to ask Taggart as they came to mind. Based on the evidence gathered from his own four cases, Terry knew it would take more murders to give him a realistic chance of catching the killer. Eventually they all slipped up, whether a witness saw their heinous acts or they accidentally left hair or skin fibers behind that provided authorities with a direct link. Occasionally a neighbor snooped and stumbled upon a killer's activities, though they often hesitated to call the police until it was too late.

Somewhat dejected, he shuffled the files and pictures together before setting them on the coffee table. Deciding not to disturb his wife, Terry pulled a blanket over him. Tossing and turning on the couch for about ten minutes, Terry finally drifted into a restless sleep that kept him dreaming about murder scenes all night.

CHAPTER 16

Sunday, June 1
Buffalo, New York

When Gaffney picked up the Sunday edition of the Buffalo News he felt his face flush red, almost positive he could detect his blood pressure rising to dangerous levels. He didn't live far from his nephew, the reason for his anxiety and agitation, so he calmly collected himself, got dressed, then drove to Belinski's house.

Weeks had passed without new developments on the case except for Terry Levine's brother discovering the Biblical connection the same day Belinski found the same link. When called about the development, Gaffney asked his nephew to keep quiet about the discovery and let Kenny Levine take the credit. Either way, the task force couldn't go public with the information, and Belinski had his uncle as a witness if he wanted to take credit when he wrote his book.

As he parked in his nephew's driveway, Gaffney snatched up the paper, staring at the headline as though trying to decide if what he read was really the handiwork of his nephew.

Sin Killer Claims Four Across New York State.

He got out of his unmarked departmental SUV, walked up to Belinski's front door, then commenced to pound on the door until Jennifer answered.

"Uncle Paul," she said, because she had taken to calling him that when she married Belinski.

"Jennifer. Is my former favorite nephew here?"

"Sure," she said, the look on her face telling that she had seen this coming without the benefit of psychic abilities. "He's in his study."

"Good. There won't be any witnesses."

Gaffney brushed past Jennifer, heading directly for the staircase. He barged into the room without knocking first, barely surprising his nephew with his actions or his angry stare. Belinski sat at his primary desk, simply turning from his computer to face his uncle.

"What the *fuck* were you thinking, Ben? I trusted you and this is the thanks I get?"

"It's covered, Uncle Paul. If you had bothered reading the story you would see how I deduced the facts based on the murder victims and testimony from friends and family."

Both men knew the truth. Anyone with police experience wasn't going to believe Belinski deduced the facts alone. The best case scenario was none of the task force members got wind of the article, which seemed highly unlikely with Harris working in Buffalo. The worst case scenario placed Belinski and Gaffney in cahoots, or worse, made Belinski a major suspect in the murders.

"Paul, I didn't make any mention of the numbers or your sensitive information. I thought long and hard about all of that stuff before I wrote it."

"Ben, we're walking a fine line already with me giving you classified information."

"I'm not going to rat you out, Sheriff," Belinski said with a confident smile. "I made a separate set of notes to show how I reached my conclusions and I have sources who gave me information about all four victims. There's no way this is going to bite you in the ass."

Gaffney folded his arms.

"Says the snake to the mongoose. And you had to name the guy? What kind of name is Sin Killer?"

"It's what he does, Paul. We both know it."

"You just made yourself a target, Ben."

Belinski dismissed the notion with a quick chuckle and a wave of his hand.

"This guy isn't going to come after me. I just made him famous."

"No, he won't come after you, but my colleagues will, and your fellow reporters will be questioning your tactics."

"This is exactly why I didn't talk to you before printing this. I knew you'd overreact and say the sky was falling."

"The sky is going to fall if you don't handle this perfectly, nephew of mine."

Giving a sigh, Belinski suddenly appeared a bit more perturbed at his uncle's lack of faith.

"Paul, I would go to prison before I would ever let on that you helped me in any way. Don't worry, I put a lot of thought into this before I wrote it."

Gaffney didn't feel convinced, but badgering Belinski all morning wasn't going to change the fact that thousands of people were going to read the article. The newspapers and television news channels were going to be abuzz by that evening and Gaffney knew his nephew had what he wanted. For the investigation, however, things were about to take a negative turn when the press hounded them about either being incompetent because a reporter scooped them, or being secretive like big government.

Threatening Belinski with withdrawing his help wasn't a realistic option because they were in this together. Gaffney doubted he could ever trust his nephew fully again, but the next twenty-four hours would prove whether or not Belinski had truly planned for the onslaught about to hit his front door.

He was still furious, though he started to question whether he had overreacted.

"I'm going to be getting calls about this, Benjamin."

"Tell them you don't know me."

"I can't tell them that," Gaffney replied sternly. "The truth is going to come out sooner or later."

Belinski held up a folder stacked an inch thick with paperwork.

"Paul, I'll handle it. I promise."

"You'd better, or we're both finished."

"Believe me, I'm not done yet. I'm finding out all kinds of things about some of your victims."

"We've already checked their backgrounds thoroughly. You're not going to leverage me into trading information."

Belinski grinned slyly.

"After the dust from this article clears we'll do lunch and I'll tell you what I've got. Believe it or not, I haven't been riding your coattails this whole time."

"Then maybe you should have a copy of your files on my desk by this afternoon. If it's useful maybe I'll forgive you and maybe I can distract the task force from putting your head on a fencepost."

The reporter hesitated only a second, realizing the importance of keeping his uncle in his corner.

"Done. This afternoon."

"And bring that wife of yours, too."

"You *are* a dirty old man, you know that?"

"I may be sheriff, but I'm still human."

***

Gaffney started receiving calls well before the afternoon, demanding how such an article ever made it to print. He told white lies that kept him safe for the moment, knowing all along he was going to be linked to Belinski in a matter of days, maybe weeks if his luck held out. His nephew's article was sure to bring out the media bloodhounds. While Belinski didn't advertise his relationship with the sheriff, someone had to know.

Someone with a mouth and some ambition who would share that information for a piece of the pie.

After fending off a call from Lee Harris, Gaffney's wife handed him the phone with her hand cupped over the mouthpiece.

"Terry Levine."

Gaffney rolled his eyes, knowing he had to speak to the task force leader. He motioned for the phone, taking a deep breath before speaking.

"Hi, Terry."

"Hello, Sheriff. I hear we've been scooped."

"Word travels fast."

"Lee Harris called me. He wasn't very happy."

"None of us are. Look, this guy did his homework and started talking to people associated with the victims. I didn't see anything in there that could compromise our investigation."

Gaffney stepped into the next room to ensure his conversation wasn't monitored by his wife. He hadn't told her the truth about Belinski using his information. Not another living soul knew the truth behind his nephew's project except for the sheriff and the reporter.

"But he named our perp and let people know his motive."

"It was bound to happen, Terry. He guessed and got lucky."

"I'm not convinced luck had much to do with it. We can't afford a leak on this, Paul."

"And we can't be wasting time and effort hounding this guy when we still have a maniac on the loose. I've already talked to the reporter and he doesn't seem to have much of anything. I called a few of his sources and he *did* talk to them."

"Lee Harris told me his name and that has to be the same guy who showed up at the Syracuse crime scene."

Gaffney stiffened, beginning to wonder when the investigator would put the facts together and accuse him of being in cahoots with Belinski.

"What exactly are you getting at, Terry?"

"There's no way he could have known about that crime scene so quickly unless someone was helping him or he stumbled upon it by accident. I'm doubting he was in the right place at the right time."

"I don't know what to tell you, but he's been talking to the right people. Who knows what contacts he's made."

Gaffney had called a few of Belinski's sources, mainly to protect his own good name when the task force inevitably questioned him later. He clung to a dying hope that no one discovered he and Belinski were related.

"Look, Terry, it's no secret that these people weren't pillars of society. He put two and two together and figured it out."

"That's in your backyard, Paul. We can't be letting this guy print whatever he wants just to sell papers."

"I know. I'll handle it."

"Good. I got a call from authorities in Montana this week."

Gaffney welcomed the update from Levine, if only to change the subject. He listened intently to the trooper's experience and judgment about how the murders in Montana didn't seem to tie in with their four cases.

"One thing I noticed was the killer kept everything within the same state," Gaffney noted after Levine finished.

"I thought of that, too, but the differences seem to outweigh the similarities. Without any DNA evidence I'm not sure how we'd link any of the murders short of a confession."

"If you want a second opinion on the files I'd be happy to give them a look. And I won't even forward them on to the reporter."

Gaffney intended his last statement to be humorous, to help lessen the tension, but he barely registered a chuckle from Levine.

"I'll forward copies your way, Paul. And please make sure your reporter doesn't get wind of them."

CHAPTER 17

While most local residents stayed in for the night, preparing for working weekends or family trips, the younger generation found other ways to pass the night. Tonya LaShomb wasn't sure she wanted to lose her virginity to her boyfriend of two months, though Tony Cirillo claimed he was a changed man.

Practically beyond the point of no return, Tonya found herself in a parking lot beside an entry point for the local hiking and biking trail. Not particularly known as a spot for making out, on a Friday night it was the best possible spot to avoid police and nosy parents. Tonya was fresh out of high school, still living with her parents who disapproved of her seeing Cirillo. She had to lie every time she left the house, having friends cover for her or pick her up.

While the nearby hamlet of Clarence Center provided a number of suburban activities and stores, Tonya found herself being more inventive with each passing week to keep from dying of boredom. Locals knew the area as the Four Corners because a business occupied each intersection of the downtown area, making it the busiest place in the town of Clarence.

Music played from the stereo in the old Pontiac Bonneville as Cirillo rubbed his hands along Tonya's thighs in the backseat. She couldn't get comfortable because the thought of getting caught had embedded itself in her mind too deeply to shake. Instead of taking in his kisses, she wanted to scout like a prairie dog for predators outside the car's steam-covered windows.

"This just doesn't feel right," Tonya finally said as her boyfriend's fingers began unzipping her pants for better access.

"You're just being paranoid."

"No, I'm not," she insisted, pushing him away from her body. "We're going to get caught."

Cirillo shook his head, looking at the dashboard.

"It's almost midnight. No one comes out here after dark."

He made advances once more, but she shoved him back.

"It's not just that."

"What then?"

"I don't know. I guess I expected my first time to be more, well... romantic."

Something else had Tonya worried, though she knew he would say she was making up excuses if she said anything. A car had followed them partway to the trail, turning off at a point where someone might suspect exactly where they were going. She kept looking for headlights, afraid her parents had asked a family friend, or the police, to monitor her actions.

"Babe, we can't do anything romantic because your parents will find out, remember?"

While his point was valid, Tonya thought back to the reasons her parents didn't want her dating Cirillo. At twenty-three years of age, he had dropped out of high school, been incarcerated three times, twice for the same crime, and never held a job for longer than a month. After burning so many bridges, there weren't any local employers willing to hire him.

As her parents said, he was trouble, but she still found something fascinating about him that kept them together. Even if their relationship was secretive, Tonya used it to rebel against her parents who had laid out her entire life for her.

Cirillo started to cup her breasts with his hands, probably prepared to take her shirt off for a closer look, when the sound of crunching gravel reached Tonya's ears. No headlights reflected from Cirillo's car, but the distinct sound caught them both by surprise.

"Fucking cops," Cirillo muttered, fumbling to zip and button his pants which he had yet to remove. "Sons of bitches turn off their lights to trick ya."

"I don't know," Tonya said almost subconsciously. "Someone was behind us on the way here."

"Thanks for telling me now," Cirillo hissed as he finished with his pants, attempting to sit up straight in his seat as a car door slammed behind the couple.

Footsteps crunched, drawing closer to the car, while Cirillo attempted to roll down the window. An intense flashlight beam kept both of them from seeing the person stopping at the driver's side door. A few seconds passed without words from either party, giving Tonya the creeps as she tried peering around the open window.

"Miss, I need you to step out of the car," the voice finally came.

She couldn't place the region, but there was definitely some kind of Southern drawl in the voice. When Tonya tried to look at the man, he raised the flashlight, keeping her from getting a good look at him. He was tall, dressed in dark clothes based on his outline, but a complete mystery otherwise. She had little doubt he was a cop based on how he conducted himself and the authority in his voice.

Tonya reluctantly opened the door, then stepped outside, all the while trying to further analyze the situation.

"Hand me the keys, son," the shadowy man said.

Cirillo hesitated, as though doubting the authenticity of the figure standing beside his car, then reluctantly handed over the keys. If this person had a flashlight, he could just as easily pull a gun, Tonya decided. She looked for a police car behind her, but found no vehicle whatsoever. A cluster of nearby trees and shrubs likely hid the car behind them, setting off warning bells inside Tonya's mind.

The person holding the flashlight was definitely no cop.

She wanted to warn Cirillo, but there was no telling where the mysterious man's attention was focused behind the flashlight. Her boyfriend seemed to suspect something wasn't right as well, because he looked toward her, then out his window, trying to get a better look at the man.

"Get on your knees," the man said, returning his attention to Tonya, who froze in complete fear.

Cirillo started to speak up at this point.

"Hey, you can't-"

He never finished his sentence because a fist crossed his jaw with a pistol of some sort gripped tightly in its grasp. Tonya noticed the hand was white, though it seemed ghostly in color despite the low lighting around the bike trail. It moved and retracted quickly, then the light was shining on her again before she could look more closely at Cirillo's assailant. Her boyfriend remained in the car, appearing loopy as though on the verge of blacking out.

"On your knees," the voice commanded Tonya more forcefully this time as the gun pointed directly at her for the first time.

Realizing this wasn't a prank, or a scared straight tactic set up by her parents, Tonya quivered with terror as the figure stalked around the back of the car toward her. Restraining a shriek as he drew closer, she dropped to her knees, complying even though she felt the action condemned her to certain death.

She dared not look up or behind her as he approached. Before her mind conjured up any ideas of escape or postponing her death sentence, Tonya felt a strong hand shove her to the ground. Now lying on her belly, she was helpless as the figure handcuffed her hands behind her back, then cuffed her ankles together. Ensured she wasn't escaping, the figure skulked around the back of the car once again, catching Cirillo as he stepped out, clubbing him with the gun across the chin.

From her position, Tonya found herself able to see slightly above the car and around ankle level, but little else. Her only feasible movement was rolling to one side or the other, and that wasn't enough to escape. She watched her boyfriend get thrown roughly to the ground as the assailant tucked the gun behind his dark sweatshirt, then produced a long knife from some kind of extra pocket. He nearly fumbled it as he searched for a good grip on the handle, almost as though he had second thoughts about carrying out his intended plan.

Tonya gasped as the man raised the knife high above his head, then plunged it toward Cirillo's upper back. Able to avoid the first strike, Cirillo rolled to one side but the assailant had already reared his foot back for a punt that connected with his victim's ribs, cracking or breaking at least a few of them. Tonya saw the figure was wearing black boots that looked as though they might have steel toes.

Cirillo withdrew to a fetal position to block further attacks, but the killer wasted no motion as he plunged the knife downward again, catching Cirillo in the shoulder. Blood spurted upward as the young man cried in pain, leaving Tonya to wonder what her brief future held. She wanted to run, but the restraints kept her in place and she was a captive audience to the torture enacted upon her boyfriend.

She screamed, hoping someone at the nearby chicken farm heard. A working farm, it looked dark and deserted in the nighttime hours because she saw no house on the property. If such a house existed, it sat behind the barn, which emitted enough noise through two large ventilation fans to drown out her screams. Adding to her fears, the killer didn't appear fazed by her cries as he continued to punish Cirillo. Uncertain whether her boyfriend was even alive at this point, Tonya immediately regretted her decision to draw attention to herself, catching glimpses of his bloodied and battered form.

After providing Cirillo with another swift kick to the head, the mysterious man stalked toward Tonya once again. After watching the brutality Cirillo endured, seeing the bloody end of the knife, she now feared for her life.

"No, please!" she pleaded when he returned, never standing still long enough for her to get a good look at his figure or his face.

He grabbed her by the arms, pulling her to a standing position before half-dragging her toward the back of the car. Tonya closed her eyes, now sobbing as she wet herself from a fear she was about to be murdered then tossed inside the trunk like a sack of potatoes. She opened her eyes to find the trunk lid up, barely able to see through her tears as she was thrust inside the cavernous area.

Despite being roughly tossed into the trunk, Tonya found courage enough to look upward, hoping to identify the man if she survived the ordeal. His entire body was silhouetted against a bike trail light behind him, but for the briefest of seconds, his flashlight pointed upward, illuminating his blue eyes. She couldn't see anything else except those cold orbs that seemed as unfeeling as the oceans are deep. Sea blue, she thought to help her remember. The solid lid slammed down, trapping her like a fly within a Venus Flytrap just waiting for the end.

Sobbing as she cried seemed about the only way to drown out the painful screams emitted by her boyfriend over the next five minutes until the ordeal ended rather suddenly. She heard every strike pierce his flesh, sounding like a slab of meat being hammered upon, causing her to cringe and withdraw further into a corner of the trunk.

She waited for the trunk to pop open, for someone's evil eyes to undress her, then do unspeakable things to her body, which might include sex, brutality, or both. As the minutes passed, her crying ebbed and her breathing slowed, but the trunk never opened, altering Tonya's thoughts regarding her fate. Now she remained stuck in a tiny space with her boyfriend likely dead beside the car, and no help on the horizon.

Tense moments passed with the night as she realized how many hours were left until daylight when someone might stumble upon the potentially gruesome scene just outside the old Bonneville. Even if the assailant dragged Cirillo away from the general area there was certainly going to be blood. Tonya prayed for someone to drive up to the bike trail parking area so she could call for help and see another day of life.

***

Randy Gosser couldn't believe his eyes when he arrived on the scene later that morning. He had just left for work when he heard radio traffic from a deputy responding to a call that someone had found a car beside the Newstead bike trail along Davison Road and someone was screaming from the trunk of that car. It took assistance from a local fire department to free the woman from a trunk while more officers arrived, finding a pool of blood near the car.

Based on what the young woman reported, her boyfriend was attacked and stabbed by an unknown assailant outside the car while she was locked inside the trunk. He learned she was unharmed, so he wanted to know the vital facts quickly in order to determine what might have happened to her boyfriend.

He pulled one of the interviewing deputies aside for a debriefing.

"What's the deal?"

"She and the boyfriend were making out, a car pulls up behind the shrubs, then some guy walks up with a gun and orders her out of the car. He binds her then goes to work on the boyfriend, hitting him with the gun and stabbing him. Puts her in the trunk then keeps working the boyfriend over with the knife."

"Where's the boyfriend?"

The deputy shrugged helplessly.

"We did a quick search of the area but we didn't see anything. It took forever just getting the fire department out here and getting her out. Then we didn't want to screw up any evidence by tromping around."

"I appreciate that," Gosser said as he started toward the bike trail, scouring the ground as he went.

He passed a barricaded entrance to the trail which provided bike path rules and safety precautions on two white signs. A park bench stood beside the entrance, covering part of the metal barrier's bland appearance. As though the barricade might not be foreboding enough, a sign warned motorized traffic against entering the trail, so Gosser passed the reflective strips, examining every inch of the area with scrutinizing eyes.

Dense with shrubs and young trees as far as the eye could see, the trail was actually paved in asphalt, wide enough for bicycles and pedestrians to travel with ease. The sides were lined with loose gravel, providing just enough room for someone to rest if he or she stepped off the solid surface.

Following a cautious step behind, the deputy seemed unsure about following the investigator to see if a body turned up, or continuing the interview with Tonya LaShomb. Gosser didn't say anything because he didn't care either way. They had left Jeff Davis, a veteran deputy, to conduct the interview with a female deputy by his side.

Gosser couldn't spot anything useful along the grass and dirt leading up to the trail, but when he reached some decorative pebbles near the trail itself, the investigator spotted blood droplets. He knelt down, picking up the direction in which they traveled, a knot forming in his stomach because he sensed something bad was lying ahead of him.

Intersected by the occasional road, the bike trail felt like it went on forever sometimes, particularly on a warm, muggy morning such as this one. He already felt sweat beads forming along his chest and armpits as the morning sun beat down on the black surface and those who dared tread it.

Less than a quarter of a mile up the trail Gosser found an obvious symbol meant for him or whomever came along the path first that morning. In the center of the path, drawn in blood, a symbol virtually looked Gosser in the eye with three numbers inside a circle. Glistening from the sunny day, the blood adopted the color of its asphalt host, looking both dried and fresh at the same time. He knew exactly what he was about to find, though he didn't see readily apparent signs of a body nearby.

"Stay there," Gosser told the deputy, moving slowly toward the bloody symbol as he reached instinctively for the firearm at his side.

His mind told him the killer was long gone, having no interest in a confrontation with the police, but his training told him to err on the side of caution. He looked along the ground for more blood or a body, his eyes finally locking upon a small pool of blood along one side of the trail. If not for the morning sun hitting it just right, the glimmer from blood might never have caught his eye because it had soaked partway into the dark soil and rocks beside the gray concrete path.

Gosser circled the blood like a cat uncertain if it wanted to attack its prey or observe it a bit longer. He decided waiting wasn't in anyone's best interest so he knelt beside the blood, still looking for a body nearby. He found nothing except trees lining the path, and a small open area just ahead, so he looked to the deputy who shrugged once again. At this point, Gosser stepped from the path, following the sporadic droplet trail toward the open, flat area flanked by two taller trees.

He stopped almost directly beneath one of the trees, finding the thinning trail ceased beside another small pool of crimson liquid mostly devoured by the loose, dark soil.

Since he hadn't put on his sport coat yet, Gosser felt a wet droplet tap his shoulder through his light green dress shirt. Thinking little of the morning dew falling from the leaves above, he continued looking around the area, standing up for a better view. It wasn't until another wet drop hit the back of his shoulder that he took notice of the red dot staining his new shirt. His gaze went from the red rain falling on his shoulder to the leafy tree above.

"Oh, Jesus."

The body above him was awkwardly positioned with the hands cuffed behind the back, around the tree, keeping it in place as the feet dangled downward. Handcuffs kept the hands hooked to a branch that supported the weight of the victim's body. Blood dripped from the chest area, soaked completely through the shirt the victim wore while dying. Gosser suddenly felt disgusted and a bit nauseous that the same blood now soiled his shirt, which he wanted to change immediately. The leaves seemed to embrace the body, which made it difficult to find until Gosser stood directly beneath it.

Death appeared certain as Cirillo's eyes, half open, were already showing the glaze of the dead over the pupils. His mouth remained awkwardly agape as though trying to tell someone his dying wish, or to reveal who attacked him. Gosser performed a cursory examination of the body from below, finding minor injuries along the arms, hands, and neck, while the face appeared heavily bruised.

How in the world the killer placed Cirillo almost ten feet above ground level eluded Gosser, but he knew it was time to call in the forensic people. One look to the deputy let him know the man was equally surprised to see the body suspended in the tree. Gosser inspected the area quickly for signs of how the killer hoisted Cirillo into the tree, though he didn't see any indentations left by a ladder, or any distinct footprints.

"This is bad," Gosser muttered, stepping back from the tree, careful not to leave his own footprints in the soil.

He plucked his cell phone from the clip on his belt, prepared to call in a team to scour the area for any forensic clues. Taking out a notepad, he jotted down the numbers within the bloody circle for reference, now ready to hear what Tonya LaShomb had to say. He wondered why she was left practically untouched while her boyfriend was stabbed repeatedly. Surely the killer had the means to kill Cirillo by himself without risking a witness to the crime.

Tonya was the only person to have seen or heard the killer in any way, making her the most important person to the task force at the moment.

8:1:315.

Gosser committed the three numbers to his notepad, finding the 8 on the left, the 1 on the right, and the 315 below the other two numbers. He sucked in a deep breath, wondering when the madness surrounding his county, and the state of New York for that matter, might end.

CHAPTER 18

By noon Terry knew of the homicide in Erie County with limited details because Gosser took the time to call him during the investigation. Terry requested the bloody symbol be washed away as soon as investigators photographed and documented it to keep the press from getting wind of the killer's motives. On open scenes such as that, they often did helicopter flybys for television news footage during their breaking news segments.

He found it strange that the killer left a victim alive when it seemed a jobless man could have been taken at any time. Perhaps the killer didn't have time to spare, possibly in the area for a short time on business or vacation. Considering he ensured Tonya LaShomb didn't see his face or any details about him, perhaps the killer simply felt complete confidence in his planning. Despite the killer's caution, a few new details emerged from the crime scene and the witness he left behind.

Stepping outside of his house, he found the cell phone number for his former major within his contacts list.

Exhaling in a huff, he called Dave Duggan, suspecting he was sentencing himself to more commitment within the case than he wanted to give. The ADS answered his phone on the second ring as though expecting the call since that morning.

"Please have good news for me, Terry."

"We have some new clues, but no breaks. That comes from Gaffney's top investigator."

"What the hell happened?"

Terry spent a few minutes explaining the murder and the surviving witness's account, stating that he was waiting for more details.

"I want you down there," Duggan stated. "Three of the five murders took place in Erie County, so the guy probably lives down there."

"It's quite possible," Terry agreed.

"If I have to rent you a fucking house, I want you down there, Terry."

"You're the boss."

"Ultimately Sherri's the boss. She going to be okay with this?"

Terry chuckled briefly.

"No. That was a rhetorical question, right?"

"I suppose it was. Still, I want you down there pronto."

Terry stared out at one of the fields beside his house, suspecting he might not see it again for quite some time.

"Are you keeping me hostage until I solve the case?"

"I just want you down there beating the streets to make sure we're doing everything possible."

"Not to sound disrespectful, Dave, but Buffalo and Erie County are capable of checking on leads. What you want me for is that weird thing I do that I can only do in person."

"You're like a bloodhound when you see those crime scenes first-hand. I've seen you in action, so you can't deny it."

Terry knew Duggan wasn't lying, and he wasn't forcing him to do anything unusual. There were times that Terry found important clues in the subtle things other investigators ignored where the murders took place. He had worked in the Batavia barracks near Buffalo for a number of years and he had worked with Gaffney on previous cases, so the temporary move to Buffalo fit like a glove.

"What do you need from me?" Duggan offered.

"A car for starters. I might also want a roommate while I'm there."

"Won't Sherri be jealous?"

"The person I have in mind is a former sheriff from Montana."

"You've gotten kinky in your advanced age."

"Funny. Based on what happened last night, I think this guy was investigating our killer in Montana a few years back. I want him flown to Buffalo to help me track our guy."

Terry's black lab came running toward him from across the road. He went to pet the dog before realizing it had been swimming in the algae-covered swamp behind his mailbox.

"Not a chance, dog," he said, cupping the phone's mouthpiece.

"We can pay for the flight and put him up. You can charge the other local expenses as you see fit."

"Sounds good. The hard part is going to be convincing him to make the trip."

"Why's that?"

"Long story. Let me call him and get back to you."

"I'll make a call to your barracks and get everything squared away for you. Can you leave by tonight?"

Terry took in the country scene around him, wondering how he was going to tell his wife his job was taking him away from her again. He always took comfort knowing his farmhouse, barn, and open fields awaited his return and didn't judge him for leaving his family to save innocent people he would never meet.

"I'll leave within the hour so I can see that crime scene while there's still daylight."

"And the Montana angle?"

"I'll call them on the way. If this guy knows what I think he knows, I'll drag him to Buffalo myself if I have to."

"Sounds like a hostile witness to me."

"He's a curmudgeon, kind of like some people in the State Police brass that I know."

"I like the guy already. Get him to Buffalo."

"Yes, sir."

Terry clipped his phone to his belt, ready to break the news to his wife, turning to find her standing at the threshold.

"You're leaving, aren't you?" she asked, fighting to keep from looking completely irritated with the inconveniences that accompanied his occupation.

"Buffalo. Today."

"Kenny's on the phone for you," Sherri said before returning inside.

Terry sometimes considered his gift a curse. Being a tracker of serial killers kept him away from home more than most officers. It wasn't fair to Sherri, considering how hard she worked, to leave her with three kids so often.

He stepped inside, picking up the cordless phone from the kitchen counter, hoping Kenny had news regarding the numbers found at the latest crime scene.

"Good news?" he asked without any verbal salutation.

"The literal translation speaks of the victorious Babylonians planning to desecrate the grave of Judah, digging up him, his family, and his servants. My guess is your victim either dug up some bodies or messed with some tombstones. Grave robbery isn't real common these days, but look for something about cemeteries in his past."

"I'm sure the Erie County penal system will be familiar with the dearly departed."

"Hope that helps."

"It'll steer us in the right direction. At least we have a ready ID on this one."

"You going to Mom and Dad's tomorrow?"

Terry sighed, looking outside where his son was playing with the family dog. He was going to miss the quiet life he returned to after fifteen years in the big city.

"No. I'm heading to Buffalo today. Duggan's orders."

"That guy either has total confidence in you, or hates your guts."

"Thanks, I think. He sends me to catch them for a good reason. I would think you'd know something about that firsthand."

Kevin Alan Kimmerling continued to elude a finalized life sentence after murdering at least four people in New York State because of questions regarding his sanity in the courtroom. Kenny might have been one of his victims if not for a combination of good and bad luck that left him hospitalized at the time the murderer was looking to abduct him.

To this day, Terry's youngest brother wondered why Kimmerling targeted him as the perfect father figure for his warped perception of an ideal family. Kimmerling spent months studying his victims, so something in Kenny's church or family life caught the man's attention. It disturbed Kenny deeply, not so much that the man was alive, but how he reached his conclusion that Kenny was the best candidate possible.

Terry regretted making the statement referring to Kimmerling immediately, because he knew it ate at his brother.

"When will you be back?" Kenny asked, trying to shake off the comment.

"Hopefully soon, but Duggan's offering to put me up in a house, so it could be a fairly long-term thing. I think he's trying to light a fire under me to get this solved."

"As though you're putting off catching him?" Kenny asked with a chuckle.

"Something like that. Well, I better get off here and pack. Thanks again for the help."

"You're welcome. Hope you catch him soon, but anyone schooled in the Bible is probably a worthy adversary."

Terry looked outside to the quiet country road where an Amish horse and buggy slowly made its way down the road, reminding him of the serene and quiet life he was about to leave.

"Take care, little brother. I'll see you soon."

CHAPTER 19

Taggart returned from a morning ride to find the sheriff's truck parked beside his barn once again, wondering why Lynn decided to pay him a visit so early in the morning when they had dinner reservations for that evening. He hobbled into his house, leaning heavily on his walking stick to find her sitting at his table without any breakfast cooked.

"I'm in trouble, ain't I?"

"You're going to New York."

"Ah, hell. I ain't up for travelin' an' you know it."

Lynn simply shook her head.

"You're more stubborn than a mule sometimes."

"What happened that I have to go up there all the sudden?"

"Someone was murdered near Buffalo with a knife. The killer left a bloody symbol near the body."

Taggart said nothing, his blue eyes shifting from Lynn a bit more thoughtfully toward the kitchen window illuminated with morning sun.

"How did I know the right son-of-a-bitch didn't die that day?"

"You did everything you could, Joe. The murders stopped after Childress died."

"But Daryl Swanson slipped through the cracks, Lynn."

She took a seat, cupping his hand between both of hers.

"You had your own problems, remember?"

Taggart bobbed his head slowly in acknowledgment.

"I can't just leave the animals behind, you know."

"I can take care of things around here," Lynn volunteered. "I practically live here anyway."

"You sure they want a broken down old cop like me hangin' around?"

"Trooper Levine requested you personally. He thinks the latest murder has some similarities to what happened down here. He also said the killer spoke with an accent, a drawl of some sort."

"Swanson had a drawl. He was from Texas."

"Exactly."

Lynn opened a shipping envelope that contained several documents. She slid one of them toward Taggart after removing it from the brown envelope. He examined the gruesome, bloody crime scene photograph of a man suspended from a tree, his arms bound behind him. Taggart's memory immediately went back to the second of his local victims, hanging from a tree after being stabbed repeatedly nearby. He recalled the rope creaking as the woman's body swayed in the morning breeze when he approached it. The smell of defecation, urine, and the unique odor that accompanied death touched him like a ghostly finger reaching through the years.

Lynn took note of his surprise, which she expected when she handed him the photograph.

"Similar, isn't it?"

"Yeah," he said absently, understanding the need for him to travel east.

Both of them sat silently a moment, Taggart fiddling with his walking stick momentarily as though wondering what he should do.

"Joe, you were the first legitimate sheriff this county had in a long time. I spend every day just trying to live up to the standards you set."

"Now you're just buttering me up."

"That's partly true, but you were a lot better than you give yourself credit for. We can head upstairs and pack your things whenever you're ready."

Taggart gave a sly smirk in return.

"I can think of some other things to do while we're up there."

"*After* you get back."

Despite the severe injury to his right leg, Taggart chose to keep his bedroom upstairs, despite two readily available bedrooms on the lower level. Though it sometimes anguished him to limp upstairs, he made the trek at least once or twice a day, hobbling all the way.

"If you don't make this trip to New York, you'll be spending a lot more nights alone up there, Joe," Lynn warned.

"I'm going, woman," he said, propping himself to a standing position with help from the decorative wooden stick.

She followed him to the stairs.

"You could've at least cooked breakfast, ya know," he muttered without turning around.

"And spoil your appetite for airline food? I'm sure the State Police spared no expense to fly you up there."

"I'm sure," he added sarcastically.

Though he wouldn't admit it, the thought of being completely alone, without Lynn, worried him. One of life's few remaining pleasures was having a warm body beside him during the cold Montana evenings.

"Everything is taken care of, Joe. Your ticket is waiting for you at the airport, and I'm going to drive you there. Trooper Levine wants to meet with you personally once you land."

Taggart planned on bringing all of his files with him, especially those concerning Daryl Swanson, along with clothes enough for a few days. He didn't plan on staying more than a week, particularly since his cooperation was voluntary and he doubted he could add much to their investigation. Until he spoke with Levine, he wasn't certain this killer was the same person. The possibility of a copycat or someone thinking they were creating original murder sites existed within his mind, though he caught himself hoping Swanson wasn't responsible. That possibility haunted Taggart, because it meant he hadn't completed the task of arresting the man two years earlier.

Either way, he hoped to have closure soon, though he didn't expect it based on the fact a larger task force failed to produce more results than he and his task force had two years prior. Carrying the burden of an unsolved case after his injury weighed on his conscience because the families of four Montana victims hadn't forgotten about their loves ones. His injury didn't force him from the office of sheriff, because doctrines in Montana mandated no physical requirements for those voted into office.

When he left, however, Taggart believed everything was in order after the death of Donnie Childress.

He reached the top of the stairs, feeling some pain in his injured leg. Despite five separate surgeries he still walked with a limp and pain that came and went like someone turning the volume control on a stereo. On good days he really didn't need the walking stick, but he always kept it nearby in case his leg became fatigued. Since he spent a lot of his time on horseback, the leg normally didn't throb too badly.

Flying in a post 9/11 America was sure to cause him some trouble because of airport security and the fact that his right leg still had metal pins holding some of the bones together. He wouldn't be able to bring a firearm, which he typically kept by his side on the ranch, and he was about to be a fish out of water in a state he had visited only once in his life.

Walking into his bedroom, with Lynn behind him, Taggart decided to make the most of the trip. His investigative instincts kicked in for the first time in years, fueling his desire to find answers, whether they led him to Swanson or some other culprit. He took off his Stetson, examining it briefly before setting it on the bed.

"You plan on looking like a city slicker, Joe?"

"Hardly," Taggart replied, limping to a nearby wardrobe before opening its doors. "I may get some funny stares, but I'm going as myself."

One of the few things Taggart changed after receiving settlement money was part of his wardrobe. He bought more expensive boots, western sport coats, and hats which he seldom wore unless he and Lynn traveled to the big city for dinner or a night on the town. He examined the clothes momentarily, trying to decide what to take when he turned to Lynn instead.

"Thank you."

"For what?"

"For gettin' me out of my comfort zone. I think I needed this."

"You're welcome. Now get a move on so we don't miss your flight."

He loved her because she knew what he needed, even when he didn't always recognize the voids in his life. If not for her support, a trip to

New York would be impossible for him because he was about to miss the remaining comforts in his life.

Catching a serial killer brought satisfaction to any investigator, Taggart included, so he looked forward to contributing to an investigation, if only for a short time.

CHAPTER 20

Terry's original plan fell through when construction held him up and he discovered Taggart caught an earlier flight than expected. It seemed Lynn Stover's confidence in her influence over the former sheriff proved well-founded. She called Terry personally once he boarded the plane, which provided the state trooper with some hope that new, genuine help was coming his way.

Unfortunately their timetables were now completely different regarding their individual arrivals to Buffalo. Terry requested Gaffney send someone to pick up Taggart at the airport because he was over an hour away from Buffalo when the plane neared the runway. When traveling across the state with Duggan's blessing, Terry often requested a marked car from his barracks to avoid being pulled over while making good driving time.

When he parked near the bike trail where the murder took place he discovered one other marked car, a few forensic vehicles, and several unmarked cars. It appeared the trail had been closed for several hundred yards on either end of the scene to keep bicyclists and runners from snooping. Terry stepped from his car, removing his sunglasses with one hand as he stepped toward the crime scene, looking for any familiar face.

He quickly recognized Randy Gosser, shaking hands with the red-headed detective before looking to a man dressed in cowboy boots, a western sport coat, and a tan cowboy hat. Taggart also sported a round belt buckle, though it was nowhere near the size of those worn by rodeo champions. Like some kind of gimmick character from a television police show, the man cupped a walking stick beneath one palm, though it didn't seem to support the brunt of his weight. Dark walnut in color, the stick appeared traditional, without a handle or any supportive legs on the bottom.

"Terry, this is Joe Taggart, your man from Montana."

Taggart removed his hat as the two shook hands, revealing a head of parted brown hair to accompany his full beard. His blue eyes seemed very observant and penetrating, almost hardened to some extent. Terry decided he wasn't entirely dependent on the walking stick because he let go of it momentarily to shake hands.

"Good to meet you, Joe."

Taggart flashed a quick smile.

"Wasn't quite what you expected?"

"I guess I expected you to be older since you said you were retired."

"I'm not sure 'retired' was the word I used when we spoke."

"My mistake."

Gosser cleared his throat to change the subject.

"We've been going over the scene, Terry."

"And the body?"

"At the morgue. We couldn't leave it out with the media and their choppers coming around."

"Did they see the symbol?"

"No. We covered it, photographed it when we could, took swabs, then washed it off the path."

Terry walked toward the yellow tape still surrounding the clearing where the body was found. By now the forensic people were combing the area for any trace evidence along the ground near the Bonneville, where the body was found, and where Tonya LaShomb believed the car was parked behind some shrubbery.

Their search focused on those three areas, though it stemmed across the entire parking area. The chances of finding useful evidence grew slimmer with every passing minute, and now half a day had passed since the discovery of Cirillo's body. While it took labs to confirm whether or not DNA evidence belonged to the victim or another individual, the people gathering the evidence didn't appear confident they had broken the case wide open.

"What do we have on the victim?" Terry inquired.

"His rap sheet indicates he was arrested for the same crime twice in the last year. He desecrated tombstones in two different cemeteries. Your brother guessed right about the symbol's meaning."

"He didn't have to guess. Once he got the modern translation he knew it was right."

Terry walked over to the ground below the tree where Cirillo was found, finding the grass and dirt barely moist from the original bloody pool. He looked up to the tree, wondering why the killer bothered to place the victim above ground level. While the other bodies had all been moved to some extent, little effort was placed in transporting or displaying them.

"Wasn't one of your victims strung up?" he asked Taggart.

"Yeah, but she was hung by the neck after being stabbed once in the chest."

"Does this feel the same to you in any way?"

"A little. It's just different enough that I don't think it's the same guy."

"How so?" Gosser asked.

"It's like he read about the murders and wanted to copy them without knowing the real facts. While things are similar, they ain't exact."

Terry thought momentarily, looking to the wet bike path where the diluted blood still lingered along its edges.

"Did you ever have the FBI or any outside agencies help you out?" he asked Taggart.

"We only had one task force meeting before the killings stopped, but they were there."

Gosser looked at Terry suspiciously, getting the idea.

"That's a dark place you're heading to, Terry."

"I know, but if there's a possibility one of our own is behind this, we need to see if any FBI people have transferred from Montana to New York the past few years."

Taggart didn't appear convinced.

"We don't have any FBI people near my county," he stated. "Based on where the bodies were found and who the victims were, we had the impression a local person did the killing."

"For elimination's sake I'm still going to check."

Terry walked over to the tree where Cirillo was hung, circling it carefully so he didn't step in any blood.

"What are these?" he asked, pointing to some chips in the tree's surface that appeared man-made.

"The techs think our perp used boots with spikes to climb the tree and hang the victim," Gosser answered.

"Great. Now we're looking for a lumberjack. And I believe they're called crampons by the way."

Taggart looked at the tree for himself, touching one of the indentations, then finding one close in proximity.

"This guy probably didn't have much experience with climbing," he noted. "These chips are close together, like he had trouble getting his footing."

"True, but he was carrying a body up with him," Gosser added. "That can't be easy for anyone."

"I've seen guys from the phone company and electrical workers climb poles like that," Terry said. "We can't rule out cable installers, either. The other thing that bugs me is what kind of person plans to hang a victim from a tree as though they know exactly where the victim is going?"

"What are you getting at?" Gosser asked.

"Either this guy knew without a doubt he was going to be near some trees where he could publically display the body, or he has that footwear with him at all times. And if he's carrying that footwear with him, that probably means he's a local who finally found an opportunity to get Cirillo."

Terry wondered why the killer chose an opportunity with a witness that he intentionally left alive. Witnesses were sometimes problematic for criminals because they might run away, interfere, or remember details valuable to authorities. So far their witness hadn't revealed anything earth shattering, but one detail plagued Terry about the killer.

"Tell me about Daryl Swanson," he requested of Taggart.

"He was one of the two suspects I had based on very sketchy witness accounts. Our killer wasn't as careful as yours. He liked to talk, and he wasn't as careful about keeping his appearance secret."

"Why were the witness accounts sketchy?" Gosser asked.

"Because they were always from a distance. There was a lot of leeway between two accounts I received, but they led me to Swanson and Donnie Childress, the one who died a few years back."

Taggart shifted his legs and feet to a more comfortable position.

"Want a seat?" Terry offered.

"No. I'm fine."

Taggart seemed to think they were exhibiting pity, his response indicating he didn't need or want anyone's sympathy.

"We narrowed it down, or so we thought, to people who were hanging out at a certain bar in my county. Childress and Swanson both had issues with alibis when we questioned them. Neither had a job at the time and they both harbored resentment toward women that turned to violence at some point."

"But then Childress died," Terry said, wanting the focus to turn to Swanson.

"I never had much on either of them," Taggart admitted, "but practically everyone else around had an alibi and no reason to kill four women. When Childress died the killing stopped, so we figured that was it."

"How exactly did Childress meet his end?" Gosser inquired.

"He got drunk, took a turn at high speed, and met up with a very large rock face first. We checked for foul play because a lot of locals thought he was our killer, but nothing turned up. After he died, we kept tabs on Swanson but the man got a job, went to work, and went home. I kept looking for ways to put him at the murder sites, but the evidence just wasn't there."

Terry looked the tree up and down, pondering the similarities between both sets of cases.

"And one day he just up and left?"

"Shortly after Childress died I had the accident that left me in my current condition."

Naturally, Terry wanted to ask what happened to Taggart's leg, but decided it wasn't professional or courteous to do so.

"Things fell apart after that," Taggart revealed. "I was in and out of the hospital while my people tried to do my job and theirs. Swanson disappeared during all of this. We tried to find him but he was long gone. My people tossed his trailer but he didn't leave anything behind. He cleaned the thing top to bottom so we couldn't link anything to him."

"Convenient," Terry said. "I asked the FBI to run a check on him after Sheriff Stover told me he was your last remaining suspect. Not only did they not find him in New York, but they couldn't find a solid match for Daryl Swanson anywhere in the United States."

"So he's changed his identity, or he's living in Canada or Mexico," Taggart offered.

"I've got Canadian authorities doing their own search, but so far they haven't found anything."

Again he looked to Taggart.

"What kind of work did the man do?"

"He was a jack-of-all-trades. Construction, truck driving, you name it. Mostly made a career out of keeping a barstool warm."

"Doesn't sound like a criminal mastermind," Gosser said, observing the scene around him. "Then again, alcoholics can do amazing things when they set their minds to it."

"Nonetheless, we might start looking at businesses that send their employees out of town, particularly in the blue collar fields," Terry suggested. "Our killer either has time to travel on his own, or he's doing his work on company time. Chances are he lives around here, though, because he seems to know Buffalo and Erie County well. He basically dumped the body in my territory and any fool could figure out the strip mall in Syracuse isn't in business these days."

"You're telling me you never found trace evidence or footprints in your cases?" Gosser asked Taggart.

"None that ever matched anyone we tested. Our guy was smart enough to keep from driving over dirt and he wore some kind of foot covers to mask his shoe treads."

"Sounds familiar."

"We only found hair fibers at one scene. They didn't match the victim, our suspects, or any of our officers. It always made me wonder if we had a fifth victim somewhere."

Every development seemed to further compound the complexity of the case. Terry wanted a defining clue that connected the Montana cases with the five victims in New York. The number of victims in his state alone seemed staggering, bordering some of the major serial killer tallies Hollywood made films and documentaries about.

He found Taggart a bit like his horseman brothers, though he had yet to establish the man's legitimacy as an investigator. Gaffney had over twenty years as a state trooper before he ever ran for sheriff. Terry didn't know if Taggart had any experience as a police officer, or if he simply ran for sheriff in a town like Mayberry and won because folks liked him.

"Randy, can you let me know when we get some results?"

"Sure. You taking off?"

"The sheriff and I have to get some rooms reserved and compare notes before we meet with your people."

"Former sheriff," Taggart corrected.

"I'm just showing due respect."

"I'm glad, because if you came to Montana they'd probably only pay for one room," Taggart added before he hobbled toward Terry's car.

Gosser grinned mischievously.

"I'm starting to like him already."

Terry grunted before turning to follow Taggart's lead.

***

Once Terry paid for adjoining rooms he took a quick shower, then spread the case files across his bed for comparison. The ride from the crime scene to the hotel proved rather unsettling because Taggart spoke a total of four words, all of which came as one-word answers to Terry's inquiries.

Terry refrained from asking about the injured leg, partially because Taggart acted cold about answering any questions in detail. Lynn had warned him about the man's tendencies, stating he might act distantly because he lived alone and didn't trust people easily. Though she never said as much, Terry guessed they were more than former colleagues. Lynn knew details about Taggart and his lifestyle that casual coworkers simply never learned on the job.

Changing into blue jeans and a polo shirt, Terry made certain all of the files were laid out on the bed before knocking on the door between his room and Taggart's. It took nearly a minute for the former lawman to answer, wearing the same clothes as before with the exception of his boots and the sport coat. Terry noticed a rounded container of chewing tobacco jutting from his shirt pocket and a pinch already between Taggart's gums and lower lip.

"Ready to compare notes?" Terry asked.

"Sure."

Taggart snagged his files and an empty Pepsi bottle from a nearby dresser, bringing them into Terry's room without a sound as his gray socks took awkward steps across the floor. Terry noticed him struggling without the walking stick, though he refrained from staring. Since the room had two beds, Taggart tossed his files on the bed, haphazardly spreading them out by case number. He unscrewed the bottle top, spit tobacco juice into the bottle, then replaced the cap.

"Bet you're wondering what happened to my leg," Taggart said almost casually.

"The thought had crossed my mind."

Taggart grunted, obviously not prepared to tell the story behind his injured leg just yet. Several forms of regret entered Terry's mind as he wondered why he was initially excited about bringing a man into the fold that he obviously knew very little about. Lynn Stover wasn't at fault, because her description of the man proved forthcoming and accurate. Terry simply hoped Taggart only behaved uncivilly around people in Teton County when he formally requested the man's presence.

"I get the feeling we started off on the wrong foot," Terry stated.

Taggart supported himself with the back of a chair, locking eyes with his new partner.

"Are you referring to your refusal to pick me up at the airport, or how you practically ignored me at the crime scene? You step out of your car and whip off your shades like you're some sort of crime show detective, then you look at me like I'm some hick from the hills who's barely in your league."

"I didn't realize-"

"No, you didn't. I ain't the smartest detective in the world, but you barely said two words to me at that crime scene back there. I'm no social butterfly, but you're not doing much to bring out my best."

Terry took in the words, then hung his head, realizing he had done exactly as Taggart stated, though he never meant any ill will.

"I apologize, Joe. I never meant to treat you like a third wheel."

"For what it's worth, I've probably been a horse's ass so far. Truth be told, I'm not excited about being here."

"Truth be told, I absolutely wanted you here to help me confirm or eliminate your four murders as the work of my serial killer. Sorry if I judged you based on your condition. It just wasn't what I was expecting."

Taggart grinned, then stepped outside the door long enough to discard his chewing tobacco.

"Let's stop feeling sorry for ourselves and get to work, shall we, Trooper Levine?"

"Sounds good."

The pair spent the next hour leafing through one another's case files, trying to find similarities that linked them or major differences that proved without a doubt they possessed no links. Terry finally gave a sigh, putting down the files because his eyes found it difficult to focus on the print after staring intently for an hour straight.

"I can't get over the fact that Swanson had an accent and the guy doing these murders spoke with one as well," he admitted to Taggart.

"But he let a witness hear him without harming her in the least. My killer didn't let any women live to tell."

"There aren't too many people in New York State who speak with a drawl. Could be a coincidence, but there are too many similarities. How many people in your area knew the details about the murders?"

Taggart gave him a look that indicated he knew where Terry was going with this particular line of questioning.

"About a dozen of us. Like you, we never let it slip that we had bloody numbers at the scenes. I really can't imagine any of my team letting the details get out, much less doing copycat murders."

"I really wasn't thinking about your people killing anyone, but is there any chance someone got a sneak peek at the files?"

Taggart shrugged.

"You know how it goes. Everyone has a copy of every single document. With a dozen or so copies out there, anything is possible. You telling me your wife has never rifled through one of your case files?"

Terry chuckled.

"She tries to distance herself from my work, but I see what you're saying. If it's not Swanson committing these murders, we're looking at a family friend, family member, or a cop of some sort. Can you have Lynn quietly check for a Montana, New York connection amongst your task force members and their families?"

Plucking his cell phone from his side, Taggart held it up.

"I can get reception around here."

He set to calling Lynn as Terry thought more about the case. The obvious answer seemed that Swanson had moved, evolved his skills and messages, then carried on with his work. Terry wanted to find the man, but every check so far led to a dead end. Canadian authorities had nothing useful so far, and Mexican authorities took what seemed like forever to get anything accomplished, especially for Americans. The only reason Mexico entered the picture was because Swanson previously resided in Texas, and Mexico allowed anyone to become a shadow for the right price.

Terry couldn't help but think the bloody numbers and the fact both killers used their left hands to draw the symbols pointed to Swanson. Of course anyone who investigated the crimes also knew about the same similarities. The fact that Swanson had quickly left Montana, likely changing his identity in the process, also alarmed the investigator.

When Taggart returned from his call, Terry looked up from the paperwork strewn across the bed.

"I think it's time we start looking for Daryl Swanson in Erie County."

"The guy can do absolutely anything for a living. Where do you s'pose we should start?"

"Somewhere with low hiring standards, that won't ask many questions."

Taggart took a seat to rest his bad leg, perplexed in thought as he did so.

"What if he got paperwork and actually changed his name?"

"Then we may be fucked. I really don't want to plaster his picture across the news channels because it'll scare him away, but we need to find him one way or another."

"I've got pictures of him that we took when we questioned him."

Taggart struggled to his feet, sifting through his own files to locate the images.

"Of course he could have changed his looks. The man ain't no dummy, which is why he made the top of my list."

A few minutes later he handed Terry two photographs of Daryl Swanson, who looked reasonably average with short, dark hair, a five o'clock shadow, and green eyes. He didn't look the least bit pleased in either photograph, wearing the same flannel shirt in each of the images.

"Tomorrow we're going to make copies of these and get the task force looking in businesses where Swanson might apply for work, legitimate or otherwise. I'll have Gaffney and his people get us a list of construction and blue-collar jobs in the area."

"I want to be there when we find him," Taggart admitted. "If he's responsible, I'll know it when I see his face."

"You got it. I'll give Gosser a call and we'll start first thing tomorrow."

CHAPTER 21

Ben Belinski took a chance going to Bill and Sheila LaShomb's residence to speak with their daughter, using his local celebrity status to gain their trust. He informed them her ordeal might bring media networks, writers, and directors their way, which he might be able to expedite if they wanted some monetary reward for the trauma their daughter suffered.

Belinski presented his case tactfully, ensuring them it was only fair that they and Tonya receive something for her pain and suffering. He felt like a cheap lawyer in one respect, planning his own version of the entire saga which seemed incomplete without details of the killer's latest slaying. Talking to the only surviving witness over the course of five murders made the top of his research list, no matter what sacrifices he needed to make.

His ethics were among the good qualities being cast aside at the moment.

"Some coffee or tea, Mr. Belinski?" Sheila offered.

"No, thank you."

He took a seat across from Tonya's father, feeling a bit awkward because he never really expected to get invited inside. Now that he was, Belinski felt certain he was going to be whacked with a baseball bat from behind for daring to intrude upon their daughter's traumatic ordeal, like a scene from some backwoods horror movie.

Instead, they actually seemed enthralled about having him approach them personally. Bill LaShomb softened a bit, tapping his foot nervously as he looked from the reporter to the clock sitting atop the fireplace mantle. He looked a bit guilty as he finally looked to Belinski and asked a question.

"Do they want to put us on the news?"

"I know we could get you on locally," Belinski replied cautiously, "but it's possible the Today Show might want to interview the family, too."

"Really?"

LaShomb's face lit up, though he quickly appeared guilty over receiving his fifteen minutes of fame. Belinski suspected the family could use the money, though they weren't excited about dragging Tonya's name through a media minefield to obtain any reward. When he first arrived, Belinski had taken time to analyze the house before knocking on the front door.

Based on the condition of the roof and the vintage appearance of the aluminum siding, he determined the LaShomb family probably didn't have much in their savings account. He hated preying on anyone's weaknesses, but he needed answers for his forthcoming articles and novel. Sometimes reporters learned extra information because police were too sensitive, or harsh, toward victims, or parents trusted celebrity reporters just a little bit more than abrasive cops.

Belinski wasn't feeding the father a lie about the Today Show because their station had an excellent relationship with the national NBC news center. Picking up anything related to a serial killer was a juicy morsel the national affiliate would hastily devour. He didn't want to give false hope or promises because his immediate objective was to learn about Tonya's ordeal. Gaffney refused to share any information with him, despite him deciphering the cryptic messages left by the killer. The fact that Kenny Levine accomplished the same feat at the same time gave his uncle an excuse to keep him out of the loop.

Gaffney promised to keep good notes that he would give to his nephew, only when the case was officially solved and closed. Belinski was not impressed or amused by his uncle's dry humor.

Sheila brought their daughter into the living room a few minutes later, guiding her gently to a chair across from Belinski. Tonya had obviously been briefed on why the reporter was there, and though she appeared slightly apprehensive about recalling her ordeal, Belinski had to believe she liked the idea of going public with her saga.

"How are you holding up?" Belinski asked the girl before her parents could interject or change their minds.

"Okay," she answered shyly, though he detected Tonya was acting coy to avoid being overly forthcoming.

"Can you tell me what happened a few nights ago?"

Again there was hesitation, but this time Belinski felt positive it was for show. He prided himself on making a living by bullshitting people, and he wasn't about to fall victim to an amateur acting job.

It took about fifteen minutes for Tonya to tell the story in detail, with Belinski interrupting a few times to ask supplemental questions. For someone who could just as easily be lying in a morgue, she seemed reasonably calm about the experience. He didn't sense she had anything to do with the crime, though perhaps she knew something about violence, either from her deceased boyfriend or her family.

The condition of the house's interior reflected a reasonably normal family atmosphere with photographs lining the walls, clean, though not elaborate living room and kitchen areas, and a golden retriever puppy running around the downstairs. Bill took the puppy outside halfway through Tonya's tale, not the least bit rough with the dog as he took it to the doghouse outside. Belinski tried piecing together the elements of the tale with those of the teller, wanting to sort the truth from embellishment.

"Was there a point where you believed he wasn't going to kill you?" Belinski inquired, wanting her instinctive, unrehearsed response.

"After being in the trunk about ten minutes, I knew Tony was dead and I figured this man wasn't going to hang around."

A genuine tear finally came to Tonya's eye as she relived the horror of waiting to die inside an area no larger than her bedroom closet. Belinski believed her thoughts had finally caught up with her words and the images and sensations of being stuffed inside a locked area with no hope of escape.

"It's okay," Belinski assured her, creating a buffer for his next line of questioning. "If we're going to get the word out there and keep this from happening to someone else, I need to know what you remember about this man."

She hesitated, wiping the teardrop from her eye.

"How tall was he, hon?"

"Hard to say. At least six foot."

"I know you said he had an accent. A Southern drawl from the sounds of it."

She nodded.

"Did he speak proper English?"

"Come again?"

"Did he sound educated, or did he sound like a hick?"

"Um, he didn't speak badly."

"Was he articulate? Did he use long words?"

Belinski could tell her parents didn't like him prodding so deeply, possibly because the police had already put her through the wringer with their questions.

"Just a few more questions," he promised, looking them both in the eyes.

He directed his attention to Tonya, flashing her a reassuring grin.

"Did he mention anything about the Bible, or doing God's work?"

"No."

"Did he touch you other than to put you in the trunk?"

"Yes. He shoved me to the ground."

"But nothing else?"

"No."

Belinski had one last thing to ask, then he figured he would know about as much as the police.

"You said he had a gun and a knife. Can you identify the gun at all?"

Tonya thought a moment before answering.

"It looked a little bit like a police gun. Stainless steel with a clip."

"Did he handle it like he knew what he was doing?"

"Yeah. He was rigid, like my Uncle Dan."

Belinski looked to the parents for further explanation.

"Dan, my brother, was in the military," Bill elaborated. "He's a police reserve and kind of a gun nut."

"I worked as a police reserve until my schedule got too hectic," Belinski said casually to ease any escalating tension. "What about the knife, Tonya? Was he proficient with that, too?"

Belinski's hunch was the killer might have been a military person, possibly suffering from delusions brought about by post traumatic stress disorder. It didn't explain some of the police tendencies or knowledge the killer displayed, but police work and soldiering were cousin job descriptions.

"It took him a minute to get a good grip on the knife," Tonya revealed.

"How so?"

"It was like he wasn't sure what to do with it, or maybe having second thoughts."

Belinski doubted the man had second thoughts after murdering four other people. If he was uneasy with a knife, or the blood that such a weapon produced, then he likely wasn't the person who knifed three people to death in Montana. A reliable source he knew with the media there had spoken with the families of the two victims, picking up many interesting clues in a case that eventually stalled with the death of one of the suspects. The killer there left bloody clues, though much simpler in nature.

He began the process of excusing himself by stating he would check with the television network about a local interview, which he would. Depending on how the local interview went, the national affiliate might choose to air it during their morning show or the evening news. The media was already abuzz around the homicides, even though they didn't have the details linking the five murders.

Tonya's eyewitness account put him even with the information generated by his uncle's task force. He knew the general area where the killer had drawn the bloody symbol on Friday evening, based on areas of heavier foot traffic along the trail, so he visited the area equipped with luminol and a black light. He had acquired the luminol, a chemical used for blood and semen searches, during his time as a police reserve when the department technician wasn't looking. Knowledge of how to use it came easily from the internet and some practice, which led him to writing down the numbers from the blood residue soaked into the concrete.

Washing down any surface that blood or semen touched wasn't enough to eliminate every trace of the byproducts unless bleach or chemical detergent was used in large doses.

Once he stepped outside, Belinski wondered what to do with his newfound information. He could threaten to go public unless his uncle let him back into the fold, or simply continue informing the public of the Sin Killer's motives. Compelled to look at the bigger picture, Belinski wanted current, accurate information compiled for his future book. The thought of upstaging the entire task force and solving the killer's identity crossed his mind occasionally, though that was bad for business. Being a step behind the task force certainly didn't help his chances, so maybe he needed to visit his uncle.

As he opened his car door, Belinski thought about taking in a round of golf that afternoon, then talking to the network about doing a story on Tonya LaShomb. He wanted to play that card slowly to make certain he conducted the interview and remained in control of the information released to the public.

Life is good, he thought as he backed his car out of the driveway, prepared to head home for a few hours.

CHAPTER 22

Checking businesses over the weekend proved less than fruitful for the task force, because many of them were closed. It gave Terry a chance to remember the city from his days assigned to the nearby Batavia barracks. It also provided him with time to learn about Taggart, though the former sheriff wasn't very forthcoming with personal information.

Terry wasn't the most talkative partner in the world, but he preferred conversation to dead silence. For the better part of two days the humming of the marked car's motor was about the only noise around them because Taggart milled through the files, constantly on the lookout for a common thread between their sets of murders.

Despite seeing the man in obvious pain several times while using the walking stick, Terry refrained from inquiring about the injury. Taggart seemed stubborn and proud to the extent that he didn't speak about anything law enforcement related. Surely a former sheriff, a deputy before that, and a soldier before that, had some interesting stories to tell. Terry pictured Montana as a vast, flat, green state with people so sparsely populated they didn't even know their neighbors. Taggart said nothing that dispelled his theory, based on what he told about his farm and its closest community.

"Who is this Ben Belinski?" Taggart finally asked, leafing through the file from the Allen murder in Syracuse.

"A reporter here in Buffalo."

"And he was at your scene in Syracuse? Isn't that a little bit out of his jurisdiction?"

"Maybe. The guy is a crime beat reporter. He probably got wind of the murder and hightailed it to Syracuse. These news guys are like an evil syndicate with their communication."

Taggart didn't seem thoroughly convinced.

"Have you questioned him yet?"

"We spoke at the Allen scene. He didn't strike me as a potential suspect. When he wrote the story a few weeks later I just figured he'd been digging for a scoop in Syracuse."

"What if he's creating his own sensational story?"

Terry continued driving toward the next workplace on their list. He felt certain Belinski wasn't a valid suspect. The man had access to phenomenal information, but that probably meant he had talkative police contacts. Taggart had a point, but Terry hadn't found time to check on the man's background, or ask a task force member to do so. Belinski hadn't warranted further review based on his hunches, and Terry's intuition usually served him well.

"We can check on him later," Terry said to appease his temporary partner. "He wore a wedding band, so maybe we can have a chat with the wife to scope him out."

He wondered if Taggart held some kind of grudge against reporters based on the way he immediately deemed Belinski as a threat. A few minutes passed as Terry stopped at red lights, seeing people on the south side going about their business. Kids shot basketballs into tattered nets, adults conversed on corners about things Terry doubted he wanted to know about, and he found himself seated beside a complete paradox of city life.

"You seem at home around here," Taggart commented.

"Just because I know my way around this city doesn't make me a city slicker."

"You're not wearing boots, so you're not country."

Terry grunted to himself.

"You remind me a lot of my brothers. They ride horses and don't give two shits what people think about the way they dress."

"You ain't worried about how people perceive you, are you?"

"It's nothing I dwell on, if that's what you mean."

Terry watched the dull gray of sidewalks and old buildings blur past him momentarily, wishing for the green of trees and the red of freshly painted barns instead. He was country at heart, even if he didn't wear it on his sleeves.

"So why is it you're so different from your brothers?" Taggart inquired.

"You're not getting Freudian on me, are you?"

Taggart laughed.

"I'm not that complex. It sounds like you strive to be different from them."

"It's the other way around. Pete's a few years younger and he wanted to be anything but me. Kenny just followed Pete's lead because I was so much older. It was kind of like being an uncle to Kenny instead of a big brother."

"I'm sure he looked up to you."

"He probably did to some extent. We aren't real big on expressing our feelings to one another."

"Ain't we all a little like that?" Taggart pondered aloud as Terry pulled into the driveway of a local construction yard.

Terry had just put the car into park when his cell phone rang. He looked, finding the call was from Randy Gosser, who typically only communicated when something newsworthy came his way.

"Levine," Terry answered.

"Terry, we got a phone tip about a possible suspect."

Siphoning through the dozens of new tips each and every day irritated investigators to no end. Terry personally hated dealing with obvious dead ends, but the job required every lead to be checked by a qualified investigator. He doubted Gosser as one to fall prey to a misleading tip, though he wasn't ready to close the case file until he heard the details.

"Guy threatens his girlfriend and says he'll do to her what he's done to the other five victims," Gosser explained. "I didn't think much of it until she said he drives a truck in the tri-state area and spends a lot of time on the computer."

"Doesn't sound too farfetched," Terry reasoned aloud. "Where do we find him?"

"He lives in the Marine Drive Apartments. We're getting a SWAT team together to raid the place."

"Isn't that a bit excessive for an interview?"

"Turns out this guy and his girlfriend are both a little off their rockers, so she told him what she told us and now he's holed up in their apartment."

"That sounds like our standard luck."

"Just inviting you to the fireworks show. I'm heading there right now."

"Fine. I'm on my way."

Terry started the car.

"Just follow the trail of flashing blue lights," Gosser chuckled.

Terry groaned, then put the car in reverse. He remembered the Marine Drive Apartments because they were difficult to forget. Standing twelve stories tall, the seven adjacent buildings once served as government housing before being renovated as standard apartment buildings for working class adults.

Luckily the construction yard wasn't across town from the apartments. In fact, it took only ten minutes for Terry to reach the seven buildings along the waterfront, debriefing Taggart as he drove. Over a dozen police cars crowded along the northeast side of the seven brick buildings. On the other side of the apartment complex stood two large military ships, long since decommissioned for use as a maritime museum.

"Looks like they're surrounding the building on the end," Terry noted as he pulled beside a city police cruiser. "The buildings all have names like The Gulfstream and The Admiral, but I can't remember what that one's called."

Taggart shot him a quizzical look.

"You know, they have waterfront names," Terry added quickly.

"I'm just surprised you'd know something so trivial."

"Let's just say I've done a few stakeouts in this area."

Buffalo officers and Erie County deputies were trying to keep people from entering the building, while encouraging those who exited to stand a safe distance away. Terry caught sight of the SWAT team around the building, preparing to enter and find the apartment provided by the girlfriend. He had a bad feeling about the situation, not that he thought someone was necessarily going to die, but rather that this man was too much of a loose cannon to be the killer. He doubted the man behind the five murders maintained *any* kind of relationship, especially one with a quarreling girlfriend.

"Joe, I'm afraid the locals won't know who you are, so you can either stay close to me, or hang back. I don't plan on playing hero and following the SWAT guys inside, but they're probably going to ask for my input, so who really knows."

Taggart simply smacked his lips as he weighed the decision, taking less than two seconds to reply.

"You know, I think I'll just stay back here and watch this powder keg explode."

"And explode I'm sure it will," Terry said before shutting the door and heading toward the group of cops clustered closer to the building.

***

Taggart observed the scene from the passenger seat of the marked car a moment, seeing Terry talk with Gosser and several uniformed officers. No one paid any attention to him or the marked car, so Taggart stepped out, pulling his chewing tobacco canister from the pocket of his blue jeans before putting a pinch between his teeth and gums. As a guest he showed Levine the courtesy of not chewing or spitting within the confines of the car.

As he observed the scene, figuring the local authorities had everything under control, the song *Meet Me in Montana* ran through his head. Despite living in Montana he hated the song, even as the voices of Dan Seals and Marie Osmond rang through his head. He supposed at one time he liked the song just fine, but after hearing it what seemed like a million times, it wore thin. Levine had put a country station on the radio, probably out of kindness to his guest, and the song followed a classic Toby Keith hit.

Growing more homesick by the day, Taggart tried to avoid thinking about his residence as he focused on the task at hand.

Spitting a bit of tobacco juice on the ground, he observed the SWAT team marching orderly toward the entrance. He reached inside the car to grab his walking stick in case he decided to move more than a few feet from the patrol car. He suddenly realized how much he missed police work, especially the simple things like helping someone in trouble and the freedom to carry a firearm at any time without question.

Unfortunately the job he loved took away his ability to carry out his duties effectively, so he settled for a life less glamorous.

A uniformed officer guarding the nearby perimeter turned around and saw him, tensing defensively at the thought of a civilian endangering his post.

"Sir, please step back."

"I'm with the state trooper up there," Taggart countered testily, nodding toward Levine.

The officer seemed unsure of how to proceed. He appeared young, like he wanted to do the right thing without question, perhaps in fear of his shift supervisor reprimanding him.

"Sir, if you could just step back."

Taggart stepped back, slamming the marked car's door shut, trying to show the officer he had indeed been riding with Levine. This action didn't seem to faze the officer, who shifted his attention between Taggart and the action near the apartment complex.

Giving up the fight, the former sheriff hobbled closer to a group of people who were watching and speculating about the scene. He looked up to the third story of the closest building, seeing a woman sticking her head and shoulders outside where a screen should have been. She began yelling toward the crowd about threats made against her.

Taggart barely caught the first few sentences because he stood so far away from the complex. He paid less attention to her rambling than the fact that no one appeared behind her. If she were truly in mortal danger, the boyfriend would have her subdued somewhere, or at least pull her away from the window.

Something clicked inside his mind as he spat once more, removing his eyes from the scene for less than a second. He seriously doubted this woman was putting on a show for the benefit of those on the ground below.

Instead, it was for *one* person below her.

Taggart made his way through the crowd, trying to avoid feet and legs with his walking stick. The growing crowd made movement difficult, and tracking one particular person almost impossible. He looked up to the woman, monitoring her eye movement, tracing where she focused her attention the most.

It took mere seconds for Taggart to find a man locking eyes with her, euphoric smile on his face, as his right hand remained near his groin. Too many people nearby kept him from simply sticking his hand down his pants. While Taggart realized this entire lead was nothing more than a scam by two mentally deranged people for their own enjoyment, he didn't want to see the man get away.

Knowing he couldn't realistically walk, talk, and defend himself at the same time, Taggart stopped to use his cell phone. He used the contact list to find Levine's number, then clicked a button to call.

"Levine," came the voice after two rings.

"I think I've got your perp in the crowd near me. He and his lady friend are making lots of googly eyes at each other."

"He's not in the building at all?"

"No. Look four o'clock from your position."

"Too many people, Joe. I can't make him out."

Taggart saw Levine making his way toward the crowd, his cell phone still up to his ear.

"How will I know which one is him?"

"He'll be the one getting tackled."

Taggart clicked the phone shut, then approached the man in question, who had just spotted Levine making his way toward the crowd. He suddenly appeared a bit more apprehensive, particularly since his girlfriend had left the window. Perhaps the SWAT team had distracted her or kicked in the door, but Taggart's attention remained focused on the man, who made the mistake of trying to slice through the crowd in his direction without looking ahead. Chances were the man thought he'd have a clear shot of making it to his car in the parking lot, but a simple movement of the walking stick tripped the suspect to a sprawled position beside Taggart.

Planting his left hand in the center of the man's spine, Taggart put all of his weight down, pinning the suspect into place. Though he squirmed to escape, Taggart wasn't letting him get away as the adrenaline coursed through him for the first time in years.

"Hey! Get off me!" the man protested.

"Citizen's arrest," Taggart replied calmly, not overstepping his bounds.

Terry finally made his way through the crowd, taking out his handcuffs.

"Zach Snyder?" he asked the man on the ground.

Instead of answering, the man simply growled to himself, which gave Taggart and Terry all the reply they needed. Terry knelt down, slapping the cuffs on Snyder as Taggart stepped aside.

"You have the right to remain silent," he began without hesitation into the Miranda Rights.

Taggart fought his way back to his feet, using the walking stick to steady himself. For the first time in two years he felt as though he had accomplished something worthwhile. He somehow doubted Snyder had anything to do with the murders, probably using what he saw on the news to obtain his fifteen minutes of fame.

Finding an equally disturbed girlfriend likely took him years, meaning she was a keeper. Taggart heard over a radio that she was now in custody with no sign of the boyfriend in the apartment or the building. He felt absolutely confident he had done a good thing by tackling Snyder.

The right thing.

Half of his trip to New York was over, and so far their visits to local businesses had given them even more false leads. He felt certain Swanson would get word of their search and flee the city, and possibly the state, before they ever laid eyes on him. Leaving Montana wasn't easy for Taggart because it meant abandoning the only comfort zone he knew. What most people considered boring and mundane gave his existence meaning at his ranch.

"Nice work," Terry said as he stood, yanking Snyder to his feet.

"Thanks," Taggart replied, helping him lead the prisoner toward the young officer whose expression fixated somewhere between disbelief and nausea.

CHAPTER 23

Terry went to the airport with Taggart to see him off, despite the fact he wanted to get home to see his own family. Their week went from promising to miserable once they started inquiring about Swanson at businesses. Owners, supervisors, and foremen apparently couldn't be trusted to keep their mouths shut despite their verbal promises.

"I'm sorry this turned out so bad," Taggart apologized, sitting across from Terry at a small table inside one of the airport lounges.

"Good idea, poor cooperation."

Wearing his brown cowboy boots, beige Stetson, and a tan and brown western blazer, Taggart seemed to have no issues with showing everyone exactly what he was about. Terry had traveled across the country for seminars and cases, knowing Taggart would fit perfectly with the crowd in any Missouri airport. While airports in general served as a melting pot of nationalities and personalities, Taggart was a unique find amongst the traveling crowd.

Just outside the Anchor Bar people streamed by on the way to flights, phone booths, or the other various airport eateries. Terry bought Taggart a beer, settling for a Coke because he had a long drive ahead of him in a marked state police car. Since Taggart had already been screened by security they had some time to talk before his flight departed. Terry used his credentials to enter the zone otherwise occupied by only screened passengers with tickets.

"You don't have to babysit me," Taggart said. "Your family is waiting for you."

"I have a few things to clear up around here before I head home. One of them is Zach Snyder and his girlfriend, the other being an informal background check on our favorite local reporter."

Taggart shook his head.

"Where did the time go? It feels like we didn't get anything accomplished."

"Too many false leads."

Snyder and his girlfriend indeed wanted quick and easy fame, receiving a total of about five minutes of air time on each station the day of the occurrence and about another three the following day. The payoff hardly seemed worth it, compared to the weeks they were going to spend in the county jail before their court hearings. Months or years were sure to follow in prison if the judge overseeing their cases possessed minimal common sense.

Better yet, Terry thought, he might toss them both in the loony bin and throw away the key.

"You know we're not going to give up," he told Taggart.

"I know. And if you find the son-of-a-bitch I want to be there for the interview."

Terry raised his Coke bottle.

"I'll make sure it doesn't start without you."

Staring out at the crowd, Terry listened to what sounded like incomprehensible buzzing from a nearby beehive. The sounds of people talking in murmurs or feet gently clopping along the tiled concrete reached the lounge whenever there was a lull in overall conversation. A television sports show rattled off baseball scores behind them as businessmen and couples killed time before their flights.

"You're not going to tell me what happened to your leg, are you?" Terry pried.

Taggart smirked.

"Tell you what, if you get Swanson in custody and save the interview for me, I just might tell you what happened to me."

"Fair enough."

Terry took a swig of Coke, barely acknowledging the voices over the intercom calling for flights and passengers with flight or luggage issues.

"Did you have to give up your position after the accident?"

"As sheriff?" Taggart asked with a raised eyebrow. "No. State law would have let me stay on, but I doubt the guys would have respected an invalid sheriff."

"If you were a good sheriff they wouldn't have cared."

"It's a different world out there, Terry. You have to ride horses and drive up and down hills and mountains that don't have wheelchair ramps. I could have kept my job title, but I couldn't really do the job with one good leg."

"If you don't mind my asking, how do you get by?"

"There was a lawsuit. It ties into the story I might tell you someday."

A passenger jet roared as it took off less than half a mile from the terminal. While the walls and bar noise muffled some of the sound, the high-pitched revving of the engines was unmistakable. The time for Taggart's departure from New York drew closer by the minute.

"Wish we could have accomplished more this week," Taggart said dismally as he finished his beer.

"If word of mouth hasn't gotten to him, we'll find Swanson. He can't hide forever, even under an assumed name."

"Maybe me and Lynn can talk to some people who worked with him."

"Something tells me you covered all the bases before he left town."

"I focused on him heavily until Childress died. To be honest, I spent a lot of time on both of them, but there's always some clue hidden somewhere. After all this time maybe someone will talk."

Taggart looked at his watch, obviously thinking of returning to the home he loved.

"I'm going to have a little talk with our reporter friend," Terry said as he stood. "Trouble is going to be catching him by surprise."

"I'm sure a resourceful man like yourself can handle it."

"I want to get home soon. Believe me, I'll track him down."

The two shook hands, then Terry walked out of the bar without looking back. Somehow he sensed he would find Swanson and see the former sheriff again when they conducted the interview. Like a fisherman dangling a baited hook, Taggart had laid out the promise of a back story to his mysterious injury. Terry supposed if he dug deep enough he could learn the story himself, like he was about to do with regard to Ben Belinski. The reporter had some kind of secret, possibly an inside connection, and Terry suspected he knew the answer.

He planned on knowing if his hunch proved correct within the hour.

***

It required only two calls for Terry to deduce where the reporter might be around noon on a Friday. He had done a television news segment that morning, and the newspaper said he seldom visited their offices, often e-mailing his articles from home. Fortunately for Terry the newspaper secretary enjoyed gossip, revealing he might be golfing or enjoying time at home with his wife. She said they often ate lunch together in town on Fridays and weekends, wishing her own husband might be so good to her.

Orchard Park, a small town loosely considered a suburb of Buffalo, hosted some of the most beautiful housing additions and residences in the county. In a newer, rather lavish addition just outside the town itself, Terry found a beautiful three-story gray stone house towering above the other luxurious homes on Birdsong Parkway. Overlooking a nice pond, the house appeared to have lots of square footage, enough for a local reporter to kick back and enjoy life a little when he wasn't printing potentially damning information about murder cases.

Terry pulled into the driveway, which led to a garage on one side of the house, finding no vehicles parked outside. He stepped from the marked police car, taking a look around the house and property, discovering a nice in-ground pool out back, and windows as tall as a grown man along the upper two stories. After sizing up the house, Terry stepped around front to knock on the door, figuring he would have to wait for Belinski or his wife to return home from their jobs or lunch.

When he knocked, however, he found a beautiful woman with blond hair opening the door to him. He caught himself staring at her nearly flawless face, trying to avoid eye contact with her breasts, which remained cupped within a red cachet twist front organza top. She wore loose-fitting black jeans, completing a reasonably formal look except for the tennis shoes on her feet. She was either primping herself to go somewhere, or between engagements, deciding to kick back for a little while before leaving.

"Can I help you?" she asked, reasonably calm and accommodating for someone confronted by an officer of the law.

Perhaps her husband dealt with the police quite often, or knew lots of cops personally. It might explain his inside knowledge of the investigation, which still didn't make it right.

"Is your husband home?"

"No, but he will be shortly. You're welcome to come inside if you like."

Terry stepped inside, greeted by a foyer that took up two levels, partly to house a six-foot wide fireplace of stone that matched the house's exterior. The chimney, as wide as the fireplace itself until it disappeared through the second level's ceiling, impressed Terry in craftsmanship and obvious expense. Strangely, the fireplace provided a double-sided centerpiece for the ground floor that divided the living room from a smaller family room on the other side with open space all the way around.

The home's square footage alone proved awe-striking, but the open concept, lavish furniture, and overall design provided a ballpark figure for the investigator to surmise what kind of incomes the couple drew.

"I'm Jennifer," she said, quickly shaking his hand once Terry finished eyeing the arched ceilings above.

"Terry Levine. I work with the state police."

"I could tell by your badge. Ben works with lots of police agencies, and I get to meet some of his buddies."

She led the way into the living room, offering him a seat.

"Should I take off my shoes?" he asked, trying to be polite.

"No," she scoffed, taking a seat across from him. "How do you know Ben?"

"We met in Syracuse a while back. He never mentioned what you do for a living."

"I do high end tours for businessmen and celebrities. You'd be amazed how many football players, singers, and politicians want to kill a day when they're in Buffalo."

Jennifer's cell phone beeped as she received a text message. She quickly apologized as she took time to open it. Terry seized the opportunity to examine the house further, wondering why a reporter living the good life even cared about making a name for himself by sensationalizing the murders.

"It's Ben," Jennifer revealed after closing her phone. "He's on his way home."

"Great. I'm only in town for a little while longer, so I wanted to surprise him."

"Would you like the grand tour while we wait?"

"Sure."

Jennifer took him through the extensive kitchen area, then the immense master bedroom with a Jacuzzi tub, then the other three bedrooms on the second floor, two of which contained their own bathrooms. A detached bathroom and a study complete with computer filled out the remainder of the second level. She took him to the third story, accessible only by a single staircase that seemed out of the way compared to the rest of the house's features. Terry felt as though he were being allowed access to Area 51 by a carefree military guard.

What he found on the other side of the door impressed him, partly because of the view overlooking the small lake, but equally in the fact that thousands of books surrounded him within the ideal man cave. Terry had a workroom within his house, complete with a desk, organized shelving, and a fireplace that warmed him during the colder months, but it paled in comparison to this room.

Terry studied the room only a few seconds more before a door shut three stories below them, causing them both to glance down the staircase. There, they found Ben Belinski setting his car keys on an end table before looking upward. The color drained from his face when he saw who was standing beside his wife and while Terry never made any claims about reading lips, he felt certain he knew the words uttered by the investigative reporter.

"Oh, shit."

***

It took some maneuvering by both men to keep Jennifer from discovering they knew one another, though not in the friendliest of ways. Belinski took her up on an offer to make them iced tea, giving Terry an opportunity to explain the situation as they stood outside the third floor study.

"She thinks we're buddies who met in Syracuse."

"No she doesn't," Belinski said with a perfectly serious face. "She knows who you are and she's playing along so she can torment me later."

"How would she know who *I* am?"

"You've been on the news as the face of a state-wide task force. We watched the news last night and she asked if I knew you. I can't lie to her."

Now Terry put on a stoic face as they strolled inside the study.

"No, but you apparently *can* lie to me."

"Look, this whole thing is going to be epic, and I just want to be the guy to write the definitive book on the Sin Killer."

"The guy you named yourself? Sounds like you're scripting your own movie, too."

Belinski hung his head, but only for a second or two.

"I know you're a hotshot, but this could linger on for years. It only took me a few dead bodies to realize what this guy was capable of doing."

"But you have someone helping you. You can tell me now or run the risk of me making your life a living hell when I find out from someone else."

"His uncle," Jennifer said from the doorway, holding a tray containing two glasses of iced tea. "I guess I'll just leave these here for you two boys while you get your stories straight."

"I can see why you love her," Terry said after Jennifer shut the door behind her.

Belinski grinned.

"She's far more charming once you get to know her."

"Your uncle, huh?" Terry asked, not allowing them to get off the subject. "It's Gaffney, isn't it?"

A flicker of surprise showed in the reporter's eyes, then disappeared as quickly as he blinked.

"He wasn't very forthcoming when I talked to him," Terry revealed. "You were a sore subject for him."

"Apparently I still am. Look, before you crucify the sheriff, I've got to-"

"I'm not doing anything to Paul, and I'm not going to speculate about your involvement any further than this conversation. He obviously trusts you or finds you useful in some way to make you privy to the investigation. I'm willing to extend you a similar courtesy if we can use your media outlets and you promise not to write any more stories unless guided by us."

Belinski narrowed his eyes cautiously.

"I definitely want whatever information I can get once the case is closed. Hard to write a book otherwise."

"You're not in much of a position to negotiate with me, Ben. If you keep your word and assist us, rather than hinder us, I might be inclined to give you access to the information when the case is officially closed."

Terry wasn't sure he could keep that promise, or if he even wanted to. If he didn't think Belinski might be an asset, he would have thrown Gaffney to the mercy of the task force, or at the very least given the sheriff a tongue lashing. Of course he wasn't much better about going by the book after granting his brother access to the most secretive part of the case. Perhaps Gaffney saw something similarly useful from his nephew, which was exactly why Terry decided to follow the same path, rather than divide the task force when they needed unity the most.

"Did you interview Tonya LaShomb personally?" Belinski dared ask.

"No. Why?"

"I don't think your killer is the same person from Montana."

Now Terry grew suspicious.

"How exactly do you know anything about Montana?"

"I have contacts," Belinski answered. "Very good contacts across the country."

Terry grunted doubtfully.

"You talked to the family?"

"You'd be surprised what people will do for a chance to get on TV."

Terry rolled his eyes.

"I'm pretty sure I *don't*, considering I'm one who hates publicity."

"You'd make a great interview someday, but we can talk about that later."

"Your information?" Terry pressed, growing impatient.

"Tonya said the guy didn't seem comfortable handling a knife. The suspect from Montana killed most of his victims with a blade, didn't he?"

"Yes, and you didn't just say that."

Belinski grinned.

"You're right. I have no idea about any murders in the state of Montana or the greater Buffalo area."

"Or Syracuse. Say it."

Belinski hesitated, sighing with a resigned chuckle.

"Or Syracuse."

Terry spent a few minutes longer with the reporter, swapping contact information and simply learning a little bit about the man. Knowing he was Gaffney's nephew, Terry completely eliminated him as a suspect, officially leaving him with one. The suspects generated from phone and online tips all seemed temporary, dispelled one by one as the task force ruled them out.

He was only heading home for a day or two to see his family, because he could call the shots from there if necessary. The task force had no new leads, and forensic evidence was nonexistent thus far. Investigators continued to follow leads while checking various workplaces for signs of Daryl Swanson.

"So we're not speaking to my uncle about this?" Belinski inquired once they both stood outside the front door.

"No. Better my task force doesn't have any blemishes."

"You know, I actually figured out the killer's messages the same day as your brother," the reporter added, as though he needed someone other than his wife and uncle to know.

"Oh?"

Belinski provided an abbreviated version of how he used internet research to discover the Biblical messages, surprising Terry that it could be so simple with the correct logic. He gave details that made his claim difficult to refute, including a self-reference that he once served as a reserve police officer.

"Now you're making me feel stupid for not having found the solution myself."

"Don't. It was your tip to my uncle that put me on the right track. Once I heard you were thinking Old Testament type stuff, I tinkered with the numbers until my computer hit something."

"Must be the former cop in you. Too bad you turned to the dark side."

"It came down to money and lifestyle in the end. I couldn't golf every day if I had to shake down suspects. No offense."

"None taken. I may need your services when I get back if we don't get any leads regarding the Montana suspect."

"No problem," Belinski said as they shook hands. "Have a safe trip."

CHAPTER 24

The word quaint accurately described the small town of Pittsford, best known for its access to the Erie Canal. Lots of old, charming buildings lined the waterway, most well-kept and varying in color. Some called Pittsford a "Dickens" town because it looked like something out of a storybook or Norman Rockwell painting.

When business at the Canal died off from the advent of the New York State Thruway and the St. Lawrence Seaway, many of the old barns and work buildings found new life as cafes, shops, and restaurants. Tourism became the driving force of the scenic town lining the man-made waterway.

Carmen Loretta Sanchez found herself closing down her floral gift shop on Pittsford Victor Road shortly after seven o'clock, ready to grab a bite to eat before heading home for the evening. She took one last look inside the shop, assuring herself the lights were turned off as several dolls stared back at her. In addition to flowers and accessories, Carmen carried quilts, stuffed bears, candies and fudge, baskets, candles, and wreathes.

As she locked the door, an overhead security light allowed her to view the parking lot beside her. A large semicircle, the lot was shared by three roadside shops, including Carmen's. She had bought the store less than a year after her husband's death to bide her time. A couple wishing to move to the greater Tampa area in Florida gladly sold her the store, which she transformed to meet her vision. Less than a month from her forty-fourth birthday, she finally felt content in life now that she was past the grand opening spectacle, and tourist business brought her some income.

The overhead light, one of two in the large drive, hummed as it flickered, as though it might burn out at any given moment. She walked toward her car, hearing a branch snap in the small tree grove behind the shop that shielded travelers from seeing the Erie Canal directly behind her shop. Trees deadened the canal's noise, though the water wasn't at all like the roar of a rushing river, or a waterfall. Stopping just long enough to put her work keys into her purse and retrieve her car keys, Carmen sighed as the thought of a long jasmine-scented bubble bath entered her mind.

Carmen allowed herself only a momentary distraction when the snapping branch reached her ears, because she saw nothing except darkness between the trees. When she returned her attention to her car, however, she saw the silhouette of a man standing at the back of her vehicle. She hesitated momentarily, seeing no other vehicles in the semicircular drive, wondering how he had materialized beside her only means of egress.

"Can I help you?" she asked for assessment purposes more than a genuine desire to assist the creepy man standing in the darkness.

Instead of answering, he produced a knife from behind his back, holding it in a taunting manner before running his forefinger and thumb together across the blade. Carmen shrieked, instinctively running for the road, but he quickly cut her off, forcing her to dart toward the trees and the canal beyond them. A gravel path ran along the canal for miles on end, which led into town, or further into the county where help was certain to be more scarce.

As she entered the small grove, Carmen debated whether to scream for help or use a combination of running and hiding like a rabbit attempting to outwit a fox. She quickly opted for stealth, doubting anyone was taking an evening walk along the canal in the cold fall weather. She could see her breath in the low light provided by overhead lamps across the waterway, trying not to exhale so the deadly stalker couldn't spot her.

After a few seconds passed without the sound of crunching leaves or snapping branches, she darted toward the water, figuring he would guess incorrectly that she might dash for traffic or a phone. Though she kept her wits enough not to drop her purse, her cell phone emitted a light that would rival some lighthouses when opened. Running felt like her safest option until she reached some form of safety or solitude.

Along either side of the canal ran an old pull path, used by horses to tug barges before the modern highway came to Pittsford. The side closest to her business had been transformed into a bike path for cyclists and joggers. Carmen stayed along the side of it, trying to avoid making detectable noises in her escape.

Thankfully she chose to wear comfortable shoes that morning instead of heels or something that might have slowed her. She dared not trick herself into thinking she could outrun her potential assailant on physical attributes alone. Her only advantage was knowledge of the terrain, gained primarily by short walks along the canal while she talked on her cell phone during breaks from the store. Familiarity with her surroundings lasted only about a hundred yards, though the light from artificial sources grew more intense as she drew closer to the heart of town.

No houses lined the canal beyond the several lumped in her own plaza, and businesses were sporadic at best, and likely closed for the evening. Having no real means with which to defend herself, Carmen stopped long enough to pick up a large branch, fallen from a towering elm tree likely planted decades ago. She surveyed her surroundings, defensively holding the branch in front of her as she remained beneath the tree for cover. This was no early Halloween prank, because the people she associated with did no such things.

No, the man she found beside her car meant business.

When the sound of a snapping branch finally met her eardrums, she whirled with the stick, intending to club him and run the opposite way. Her plan met a dead end immediately when a gloved hand caught the branch, using it to pull Carmen into his powerful grasp with one swift tug. She felt completely helpless, beneath the pale moonlight, as he whirled her around while looping something over her neck.

Carmen fought and clawed at his arms and neck, trying to find any accessible exposed flesh to scratch or injure. He was covered in thick clothing, wearing leather gloves, making him virtually impervious to her countermeasures. Even his neck was protected by a scarf or some other form of cloth. She found herself able to struggle only a few seconds before the cord wrapped around her neck drew taut, cutting off her airway.

Gasping for breath, she looked desperately for anyone or anything that might save her from unspeakable acts being performed upon her body, followed by certain death. He lessened the grip on the cord momentarily, as though toying with her, before pulling it tight again. Carmen saw nothing of use to her, and she couldn't reach the ground if she wanted to. Yelling for assistance was certainly beyond her current capabilities as the lights of her eyes faded like the night surrounding her.

She kicked swiftly behind her several times, like a disobedient mule, connecting twice with the man's shin. He grunted painfully, then tightened his pull on the cord, sending her toward unconsciousness or death. Carmen considered either option a reprieve from whatever form of torture the sadistic man had in store for her. Painfully aware of her croaking gasps for oxygen, which sounded uncouth even at death's doorstep, she continued to struggle until her body abandoned her. Carmen's eyes blinked several times before the lack of oxygen sent them rolling back into her head.

CHAPTER 25

Randy Gosser felt relieved that Terry Levine trusted him enough to represent the task force until he arrived, but the detective felt a bit out of his element traveling to the Rochester area. Granted, he was much closer to the crime scene than Levine, who had split time between Canton and Buffalo the past few months until the task force exhausted every available lead. Only a week prior, Levine packed up and went home for good, then the killer struck, as though on cue.

State troopers were accustomed to traveling around the state while Gosser had never initially investigated any crime outside of his county, despite his years on the job. Traveling for extradition wasn't foreign to him, nor was comparing notes with investigators in other states or countries. As he stepped from his unmarked car, readily showing his identification to the officers securing the scene just outside the yellow tape, Gosser squinted in the early afternoon sun. He wondered why it took more than three months for the Sin Killer to strike again.

Grunting to himself, Gosser decided he hated the killer's given name. Most serial killer names were corny, though often partially truthful in their descriptions.

"Detective Gosser?" a man dressed in slacks and a tie asked as they shook hands. "John Broughton."

Broughton seemed a bit young to be a police detective, but Gosser figured Pittsford didn't maintain a very large police force.

"As soon as we saw the symbol near the body we called your dispatchers."

Gosser found himself amazed that word of the bloody symbols hadn't reached the press. It seemed as though every officer in the state knew exactly what they meant, and who to call the moment they spotted them. Levine was carefully vague in his memos across the state regarding the cryptic messages, never revealing the blood itself or any details. Then again, Gosser supposed there weren't an abundant number of serial killers in New York at the moment.

"It's over here," Broughton said, leading him toward a grove of trees directly behind a parking lot that served three shops.

Gosser followed him through the various trees, finding leaves and twigs on the ground all around them. Several forensic technicians combed the area, searching for clues on and around the body. In the variety of orange, tan, and yellow leaves, finding evidence was going to be time consuming and tedious. As he laid eyes on the body itself for the first time, he wondered how anyone had found her.

Leaves rustled in the wind above, while rolling like tumbleweeds on the ground near the investigator's black shoes. Lying face up, the dead woman stared lifelessly into the slightly overcast sky above through hazel brown eyes. Her neck appeared visibly reddened from some form of cord or wire used to cut off her airway. Gosser had seen strangulation homicides before, but seldom were the wounds so glaring. Once or twice he investigated particularly sadistic killers who had taken their victims to the edge of unconsciousness repeatedly for the thrill of empowerment. Based on the multiple pressure points along the neck, he wondered if the Sin Killer was exploring new ground.

Her throat was cut, though not deeply. The lack of blood surrounding the wound indicated the wound was likely postmortem, simply providing an access point from which to draw ink for the killer's artwork. Gosser ignored the nearby symbol momentarily, choosing to focus on the deceased.

"Carmen Loretta Sanchez," Broughton stated her name, as though reading from a cue card. "She owned one of the shops directly behind us."

"Have your people gone inside?"

"We were just about to. There's an active alarm system, so we wanted to shut it down before we made entry."

"So based on that information, we can probably assume he jumped her once she closed shop last night."

"Her car is still on the lot."

"Who found her?"

"One of the neighboring business owners came in early to do some inventory and saw her car here so he went looking and found the body."

Gosser made his way toward the body, careful where he stepped to preserve evidence. Kneeling down beside her, he looked at the large tree closest to her body, finding a bloody symbol, drawn with one finger, just like the others.

"Okay, Carmen," he said under his breath, "what was your sin?"

He read the red ink on the tree, finding the number 17 on the left, 11 on the right, and 319 below the other two numbers. Gosser, having read through the case files what seemed like thousands of times, recalled the last murder's page inscription was 316, only a few Biblical pages away from the current page number.

"You quoting Jeremiah again?" he asked himself thoughtfully, wondering if the killer had some kind of pattern to offer after all.

"What was that?" Broughton inquired.

"Nothing."

Gosser stood and looked around him. He studied the ground for indications of a struggle, but found nothing because of the leaves. Taking a stroll toward the car, he scoured the soft ground for drag marks or penetration into the fading grass. Finding no indications near the car, he wondered if she had seen him and ran. He doubted a killer who never left fingerprints, footprints, or DNA behind would suddenly develop stupidity enough to be seen by his victim unless he chose to be seen.

He walked a line from the car back to the body, which was almost directly behind her shop, though set back closer to the canal. Staring at her features a moment, he realized Ms. Sanchez had been an attractive woman, perhaps a cougar, given her age. After two failed marriages of his own, Gosser wished he understood sexual intricacies between men and women, but he was a deviant when it came to bedroom activities.

If it was exotic or kinky, he liked it.

His ex-wives did not.

Love on the go left him a lonely man, perhaps like the woman lying before him, but he wasn't about to judge her. His fellow officers and detectives judged him, knowing about some of his past indiscretions with women outside of his marriages, including a few mistakes with women of the night. Gosser never justified his actions, or argued the accusations, though he found being single kept his lifestyle more private than before.

Occasionally Gosser walked into work to find cartoons drawn by his coworkers posted in the common areas, or lying on his desk. They typically resembled the explicit cartoons from the Playboy Magazine with Gosser in some precarious position and a one-liner beneath the illustration. He tended to say little or nothing about the chiding because the situation would only escalate to the point that the sheriff might step in and make it worse.

With a ten-year-old daughter from his first marriage, he questioned how he was going to give her the sex talk. Gosser hoped Casey's mother took care of the situation, because he wasn't sure if he could provide a conventional lesson without cracking. God only knew what his ex-wife, or others for that matter, said about his extracurricular activities. He saw Casey on some weekends and holidays, trying to make extra time a few times a year for her.

"We may have to rake these leaves," Gosser finally said as Broughton approached from behind.

"I'm sure we will. What are you looking for?"

"Footprints, maybe drag marks. I don't think she was killed right here."

Gosser carefully surveyed the scene around him, then walked purposefully toward the canal, looking for clues of a struggle. He finally discovered some broken branches and foot impressions beneath a tree, though no distinctive prints other than those made by a woman's shoe. The ground was soft, easily giving away the clues the killer allowed himself to leave.

He found more indentations circling around a neighboring tree as though someone had stopped and stood there momentarily. Again, no distinctive prints, just shoe-sized impressions.

"She knew to run," Gosser decided aloud. "He was playing a cat and mouse game with her. Have you gotten anywhere with the neighboring businesses?"

"Not yet. All the businesses were closed except hers. We're canvassing the area for witnesses, but there isn't much around here. Traffic just drives on past."

Gosser considered the fact that she hadn't called 911 from her cell phone, which most people in distress found time to do.

"Where is her purse?" he inquired.

"We haven't found one."

"Surely she had a purse," Gosser said more impatiently than he intended to sound.

"Maybe her killer took it."

"He's not into souvenirs. I've got to assume her purse held her keys, phone, wallet, and everything she needed with her."

Breaking off from the group once again, Gosser wondered if the purse had been discarded into the canal. It made perfect sense for the killer to dispose of evidence, but it seemed unnecessary unless the item held something damning. If the cell phone was inside, the signal might be used to trace Carmen Sanchez's whereabouts if and when she was reported missing.

Suddenly he hit a brick wall driving at full speed, even doubting his earlier assessments. For a moment Gosser had felt like Terry Levine, pulling unseen clues from the air, knowing how the killer thought, but now his confidence drained like fuel leaking from an overturned tanker. As the wind picked up, he stuffed his hands inside the pockets of his jacket with a shiver. He wondered how Levine seemed so sure of himself, as though he psychically envisioned the crimes happening before his very eyes. If that were the case, however, someone would already be inside the Erie County Jail awaiting trial.

Though he took the time to throw on a tie and slacks before leaving the house, Gosser suspected he looked like a wino from the classic black and white movies, minus the tattered felt hat. No one shot him strange looks when he approached the scene, or questioned his identification, so he probably didn't look as disheveled as he envisioned himself.

He scoured the area a moment longer before finally giving up hope that the purse was anywhere to be found. Technicians continued to comb over the grounds while photographing the body, and specifically the wounds. Trace evidence, if any existed in the first place, had surely blown away or become contaminated in the overnight moisture.

"Fuck," Gosser cursed under his breath, irate that such a sick bastard could roam freely throughout the state to murder at will and never slip up one time.

Standing safely away from the body so the technicians could work, he looked over to Broughton, who spoke with an older woman who had pulled up outside of the crime scene. Her gray hair was pulled up and she wore a conservative dress, as though heading to church and stopping to inquire about the nice young woman who ran the gift shop.

As Gosser slowly made his way toward the conversation, he noticed Broughton's expression change several times in various degrees of surprise until the local detective finally looked in Gosser's direction with wide eyes. Hurrying his pace a bit more, Gosser threw the yellow tape over his head as he ducked it, joining the pair beside a police cruiser.

"What is it?"

"Mrs. Tucker here says she saw a white delivery truck parked in the back of the parking lot last night on her way to BINGO."

"Parked in the lot or turning around?" Gosser questioned.

"Maneuvering in the lot as though he was backing into a spot," Broughton answered for the witness.

"Did it have any logos on the side?"

"A blue and red logo," Mrs. Smith answered for herself this time. "It wasn't a symbol like Pepsi, but a company name. I just can't remember what it said."

"A semi, or more like a box truck?"

"Oh, a box truck. Probably about the size of a larger moving truck."

"Would you remember if you saw it again?" Gosser asked.

"I think so."

Broughton looked to him with a sudden hope.

"You have an idea?"

"There are a couple of shipping companies in Buffalo that might use trucks like that," Gosser said, plucking his cell phone from his side. "I can get some people checking on it right away. See if she can remember any other details, or maybe a partial plate."

"Will do."

Gosser stepped aside, finding refuge under some trees away from the crime scene where he could call Terry Levine and have some connections check the local shipping companies around the Buffalo area. Strangely, he couldn't recall the names of any company names using trucks like that, but he felt positive he'd seen trucks with those colors on a regular basis when he patrolled, and even occasionally as a detective.

Based on that line of thinking, the company, or companies, had been in the Buffalo area for years and hopefully someone would remember seeing those trucks recently.

Gosser fished a cigarette from inside his jacket, lighting it as he dialed the number for one of his road patrol buddies on the sheriff's department. Though he didn't have the loyalty of everyone on his department, he still had enough contacts to make his job feasible. With Levine already on the road, he could be briefed later, especially if more revelations surfaced regarding the box truck.

Taking a deep drag on the cigarette, Gosser exhaled upward as he waited for his buddy to answer, praying for a rare easy break in the case.

CHAPTER 26

Things gained momentum in a hurry, like a boulder rolling down a hill without a single tree or bump in its way. Gosser's buddy immediately recalled the blue and red symbol as that of the Erie Wholesale Shipping Company located in Tonawanda, just north of Buffalo, along Sawyer Avenue. When their trucks traveled through Buffalo it was likely to provide local delivery, because the old factory converted to a warehouse was located beside several major highways and interstates.

When Terry Levine arrived at the facility, he found Gosser standing outside the warehouse's entrance door, finishing a cigarette as the sky grayed above them.

"What do we have?" he asked the detective.

"One of the processing agents identified Daryl Swanson as a driver here, so we know the guy worked here as recently as yesterday. He goes by Daryl Johnson here, so he might have forged documentation. The worker phoned one of the distribution managers so we'll have access to everything in about ten minutes. The manager was Swanson's direct supervisor, which is great news."

"What the hell's a processing agent?"

"The guy who loads the palates onto the trucks."

"Sounds like a term used to make employees feel better about themselves."

Gosser shrugged.

"He seemed happy enough about getting some overtime."

Gosser looked elated compared to his normal stoic nature. He wasn't giddy, but he seemed bound with nervous energy like a kid on Christmas Eve. His clothes appeared moderately wrinkled, indicative of his rough day. With the time close to three in the afternoon, they were fortunate to find anyone working at the shipping facility.

"What does this place do?" Terry asked curiously.

"They ship bulk canned goods to schools and universities around the tri-state area and Canada."

"Sounds like someone could get around all of New York that way."

"My thoughts exactly."

"What did you find at the murder scene earlier?" Terry asked, not having found time to visit personally with the new developments.

Gosser took only a second to recall the details before speaking.

"She was strangled, like I told you on the phone, but he cut her throat after she was dead to access the blood. Not only that, but it looked like he strangled her multiple times, possibly in and out of consciousness based on the number of ligature marks on her neck."

"He's upping his game by getting closer to the victims. Maybe we can find trace evidence on the victim."

"Here's hoping."

"He's getting away from the knives, though, which has me curious. He's changing his choice of weapons without rhyme or reason."

Gosser gave a curious, narrow look through his bluish eyes.

"You said it yourself. He's escalating the thrill."

"Maybe, but this doesn't sound like our guy from Montana. These guys tend to stick with the tried and true."

"If we're lucky, we can ask him ourselves in an hour or two," Gosser said with a hopeful grin.

"Hopefully. Why are we standing outside anyway? It's fucking cold."

"Sorry. I came out to burn one after talking to the shipping guy."

Terry stepped inside as Gosser held the door for him, immediately seeing more activity than he expected on a weekend. Forklifts moved palates wrapped in plastic with inventory sheets taped to them to staging areas or down the long concrete path that led to the trucks parked along the building's two loading sides. The steady hum of the forklifts cruising along the surfaced concrete floor seemed to echo in the vast space of the former factory.

Industrial shelves stood across the aisle from the two investigators stacked top to bottom with various bulk canned supplies. Everything from pudding and soup to pickles awaited transport in one-gallon cans or five-gallon buckets. Practically anything a school or college cafeteria might need was readily available from one shipping company. What had Terry's mind stirring was how Swanson found employment here under a name similar to his own without raising flags when the task force searched him in a multitude of databases. Even worse, no one from the task force apparently visited the company when they were passing out fliers with the man's picture on it.

One display of the composite to a single employee provided Gosser with immediate verification he worked there. Granted, Tonawanda wasn't within Buffalo city limits, but it didn't require much thinking out-side of the box to visit factories and construction businesses outside of Buffalo, particularly when it came to its suburbs.

"One busy place," Gosser commented.

"Perfect place to come in and never be noticed, especially if you're out driving all the time."

Terry heard a door shut behind them, then turned to find a man a few inches taller than himself with cropped black hair and a five o'clock shadow. He was dressed in blue jeans and a red button-up shirt beneath a dirty canvas work jacket. He appeared to be younger than either inves-tigator, which nearly caused Terry to dismiss him as a manager of any sort.

"Nick Vaughn," the man introduced himself, shaking hands with both investigators. "I'm one of the distribution managers around here."

"One of your packers said you're Daryl Swanson's supervisor?" Gosser asked, raising his voice over the droning hums.

"Let's find an office," Vaughn suggested, finding it difficult to hear the question.

Minutes later he shut the door after they entered a small conference room, cutting off the industrial sounds behind them.

"Did you say Daryl Swanson?" Vaughn asked for clarification, his face wrinkling in confusion.

"Sorry," Gosser said, "I guess you know him as Daryl Johnson."

Vaughn nodded slowly, apparently trying to understand the situation.

"I deal with a lot of Daryl's routes," he answered. "Eight drivers are assigned to me and we run daily to three different states and sometimes up to Canada. Can I ask what this is about?"

Terry fielded the question before Gosser complicated the answer needlessly.

"We have reason to suspect he may be involved in some criminal activities throughout the state. We've got some particular dates and places to cross-reference with your records if you don't mind."

"I'm not sure he strikes me as the type who would engage in anything illegal," Vaughn stated. "Our drivers follow a strict delivery schedule or they fall behind. That's when I take disciplinary action against them."

"Do they ever do layovers?"

"Occasionally. They're given a company card for meals and hotel expenses."

Terry looked to Gosser, who seemed to be thinking the same thing. Daryl Swanson, or whatever he chose to call himself, had opportunity with his travel, and self-made motive to kill six different people across the state of New York. Despite his desire for more information and proof, Terry decided it more important to pay Swanson a visit and get him into custody before someone tipped him off about the authorities visiting his workplace.

"Can we get the address he has on file with your company?"

Vaughn hesitated in thought.

"I'd have to call in our human resources person. She's the only one with the key to her office."

"How long?" Gosser asked.

"Half an hour or so. She lives outside of Buffalo."

Possibly sensing their urgency, Vaughn made a suggestion.

"He goes out drinking with a few of the guys here who might know where he lives. I can call Grace while you question the guys if you like?"

"Sure," Terry said, looking to Gosser. "Can you handle that for a minute without me?"

The detective nodded before pushing his way through the door in search of unwitting victims. Terry turned to Vaughn with an idea in mind.

"Do you keep contact numbers handy for your drivers?"

Vaughn snapped his fingers as though he should have thought of checking before asked, then walked briskly to a laminated sheet of paper taped above a workstation.

"Here," he said after writing down a home and mobile phone number for Daryl Johnson.

Terry planned on tracking the cell phone number the second they received confirmation a search warrant was signed. Finding Swanson wasn't going to be difficult unless he knew the police were searching for him. Of course, being a weekend, he might have left town or begun tracking a victim elsewhere. Sometimes bringing in murder suspects was as easy as pulling up to their house and knocking, and others dragged out for months.

He preferred the knocking option.

***

Terry and Gosser waited for Grace Ellington to arrive with nervous excitement, but she quickly got them the records they required and the two investigators quickly made their way to the apartment building without benefit of a search warrant or backup. Though they drove separately, the two kept in contact with their cell phones the entire way, breaking a law they were sworn to uphold by doing so.

Only city police typically enforced the laws regarding driving while sending text messages or making calls. It generated funds for the city, but state and county officers constantly broke the law, feeling guilty if they wrote citations.

"Ready for this?" Gosser asked as he donned a Kevlar vest in the parking lot adjacent to the apartment building where Swanson reportedly resided.

"I just hope it pans out," Terry said, not giving himself false hope about any aspect of the investigation.

Once he had Daryl Swanson seated at a table with handcuffs on, then he might breathe a sigh of relief. Right now they had nothing except strong circumstantial evidence, meaning no SWAT team raid, and no search warrant. The best they could expect was to find Swanson at home, then bring him in for questioning. With that done, the task force could get a search warrant and begin compiling real evidence.

Or so Terry hoped.

"How can it not pan out?" Gosser asked with a cautious smile, putting his jacket on over the protective vest. "The guy changed his identity and lived on the lam for the better part of two years."

Terry secured his own vest, then zipped his generic black nylon jacket with the wording "POLICE" across the back. His continued use of a marked car paid off, because he was able to keep virtually every necessary tool and article of clothing within arm's reach at all times.

Both men checked their firearms, replaced them at their sides, then retrieved the paperwork provided by the shipping company where Swanson worked. While their primary goal was to find Swanson, both men considered him dangerous enough to protect themselves in case he proved hostile.

"Apartment 229," Terry said without enthusiasm. "We don't want to be skulking around the complex any longer than necessary. Let's go talk to the manager to avoid making a scene."

Making an effort to conceal their vests and firearms, the pair walked inside the complex to the office and knocked. Terry expected the manager to be out for the weekend, which he was, but they found a super living on the ground floor near the building entrance. The complex was secured, so they had to buzz the man's apartment, then identified themselves when he answered in a gruff voice.

Looking as though he had dressed down for the weekend, the man wore brown work pants and a wrinkled red shirt that probably resided atop a dirty laundry pile until the man snagged it to greet his visitors. When he opened the door, he eyed the two detectives suspiciously as Terry held up his credentials while Gosser simply pointed to his belt where his badge was clipped.

It took very little convincing for the super to lead them up a flight of stairs toward the apartment. Before heading up, he gave the investigators a quizzical stare.

"You know, some other cop was here yesterday asking about Johnson."

Terry and Gosser exchanged concerned glances.

"Who exactly was here?" Gosser asked first.

"Some guy waving a badge around like you two. Said he was with the FBI, I think, and wanted Johnson to call him. He left a card."

"Still got it?" Terry asked.

"No, I gave it to Johnson like he asked."

Terry wondered if another cop or agent suspected something about Swanson. Perhaps the matter wasn't related and the inquiring party knew nothing about Swanson's past in Montana. Regardless of what anyone knew, or didn't know, a card from any law enforcer was likely enough to send him back into hiding.

"Let's get up there," he said to the super.

"You got it."

"What was the name on the card?" Gosser pressed as they ascended the stairs.

"Don't remember."

When they reached the door, Gosser requested the key from the super. After safely tucking the super behind him, Gosser stood beside the door, then proceeded to knock three times. No sounds came from inside the apartment, so he carefully placed the key into the lock. Terry had already drawn his firearm, assuming the opposite position beside the door. When Gosser turned the knob, Terry entered first with his duty weapon in a ready position.

He immediately decided Swanson had split town, because the apartment was in shambles, with items overturned and strewn throughout the living quarters. It wasn't the type of chaos left by a home invasion or burglary, but more of an organized chaos that came with sorting and sifting through items quickly to decide imperative versus nonessential travel items.

Without touching anything, Terry explored the apartment with Gosser to verify Swanson wasn't hiding in some closet, or under what few pieces of furniture occupied the place. Only a common living area, kitchen, bedroom, and bathroom required inspection, so they were finished in less than a minute.

"He lived like he might have to up and move at a moment's notice," Gosser assessed aloud, matching Terry's thoughts as they both holstered their firearms.

"Hardly seems like the person who carries out flawless murders, does it?"

Gosser gave a mischievous smirk.

"I know you're good, but that statement's a little outside the box even for you."

Terry inspected the living area around them more carefully, finding empty pizza boxes, Taco Bell wrappers, and empty beer cans. He hardly pictured a criminal mastermind living in a common apartment like some redneck who couldn't cook for himself. Perhaps his assessment of the Sin Killer took shape from the meticulous crime scenes free of trace evidence or DNA, or the media sensationalism Ben Belinski provided. Based on past experience, Terry envisioned a completely different person committing such heinous crimes. Maybe his mind grew disillusioned and he expected the Sin Killer to be something grand like so many serial killers before him. Perhaps killing six to ten people was the only noteworthy thing Daryl Swanson had ever done.

"Now what?" Gosser asked, indicating he wanted Terry to take charge.

"We get a search warrant and tear this place apart. Then we talk to Swanson's employers some more and contact some media outlets. It might be time to go public with our composite sketch unless Erie Wholesale can provide a photograph."

"Hell of a day," Gosser commented. "And to think it was all because the guy finally slipped up."

Terry might have thought of Swanson as too cunning to slip up before laying eyes on the apartment. He hated judging a person based on one-dimensional facts but Swanson was an enigma based on the apartment and crime scenes alone.

"I'll start on the search warrant," Gosser said, holding up his phone as he walked outside the apartment door to reach a friendly judge.

Terry decided he wanted to speak with the folks at Erie Wholesale himself. He wanted no stone left unturned when it came to Swanson's tenure there, including how he worked under an assumed name. If he provided false documentation, that simply added to the list of crimes he had committed since leaving Montana. It would also likely mean he had some help forging identification and documents to become Daryl Johnson.

He saw no business card lying around, meaning Swanson probably took it with him. Too many times internal slips ruined cases on the verge of being busted wide-open. Terry occasionally found himself victimized by such bad luck because the state police were no exception to committing errors. Working with multiple agencies often left individual officers out of the loop, and sometimes they acted without knowing they endangered someone else's investigation.

Terry overheard Gosser request the super remain outside the room, so Terry left the apartment, locking it behind him.

"Please don't let anyone else inside until we return," he instructed the super. "If you see Johnson come back here, please call me immediately at this number."

Terry handed him a card with his cell phone number. He didn't want to risk a dispatcher misinterpreting information or delaying the arrest of Swanson in any way. Based on the apartment's condition, he didn't expect the man to return for anything, because nothing necessary, or damning, appeared to be left behind.

"What did this agent look like?" he asked the super, wanting to check with Gosser and the other local police about agents at the Buffalo office.

As he recalled, about eighty worked in the Buffalo area, which didn't make it easy to narrow down the possibilities.

"Average. Little taller than you, fairly slender, medium hair. He wore a dark suit and he definitely had a piece."

"And he didn't say anything else?"

"No. He kept pressing for me to make sure I gave the card to Johnson though."

Strange, Terry thought, that anyone who knew anything about Swanson actually thought the man would willingly call the police or the FBI. Something about the tale didn't quite add up, but he needed to check with local agents to confirm or deny the validity of the visit.

He gave Gosser a few minutes to brief the sheriff on the latest developments over the phone before they followed the super to the ground floor.

"The sheriff is going to call one of his judge buddies," Gosser stated as they walked outside into the windy afternoon weather. "They golf together, so we should have a search warrant within the hour."

"I trust you can take care of things here?"

"Sure. You going back to the packing place?"

"Yeah. I'm going to call in anyone who can tell me anything about Daryl *Johnson*."

"I'll call my contact in Rochester and see if they found anything new."

Terry nodded before starting for his car, ready to take off the Kevlar vest and return to some form of normal attire. He wondered if Swanson felt the walls closing in, because they certainly were. When his image appeared on news channels across New York and neighboring states, Swanson would have nowhere to hide.

Running for his life was about to take precedence over the hobby of killing complete strangers. Terry still felt uncertain of their conviction chances due to the lack of physical evidence and eyewitness accounts, though his instincts told him Swanson was guilty. Terry stared at the apartment building one last time before climbing into his car in anticipation of some answers.

✳✳✳

Terry quickly discovered Nick Vaughn was capable of answering most of his questions until more of the managers arrived. Though Vaughn left for an early dinner, he readily returned to assist in the investigation. Now seated behind his desk, Vaughn offered Terry a nearby chair before cupping his hands atop the desk.

"I'm still not sure I understand what you think Daryl did," Vaughn asked more than stated.

"We think he may be responsible for a series of murders across the state," Terry decided to reveal, since Swanson's picture was about to hit every television in the tri-state area.

Vaughn's jaw dropped at the news while his eyes completed the stunned picture.

By now the task force was issuing a description of Swanson's vehicle to every police and news agency in the country, along with his registered license plate, though its validity certainly raised some questions. Other members of the group continued to track down a recent photo of Swanson, including one detective a few doors down from Terry who waited patiently for Grace to return. The personnel file in her care likely contained an ID photo, or at least a copy of Swanson's illegal driver's license.

Even Canadian authorities knew to look for Swanson and his vehicle if he dared cross the border. Terry's worst fear was that such a dangerous man had already made his way onto foreign soil and blended in. Of course new regulations made crossing the border more difficult since Homeland Security got involved. Faking a passport wasn't as easy as changing a license plate or paying someone for a fake license. The other option, an enhanced driver's license, was equally difficult to forge.

When the task force was assembled, Terry brought in the FBI for resources and manpower. Though the two agents assisting the group were eventually assigned to other cases, Terry called them occasionally for information and resources. One call to Rod Masterson, a senior agent with the Bureau, started the process of tracing Swanson's mobile phone number and gathering incoming and outgoing call information.

"I can't believe one of my drivers, especially Daryl, could hurt anyone," Vaughn stammered, still stunned.

"This must be difficult," Terry said calmly, "but I need to know what kind of employee Swanson was. Swanson *was* his name, sir."

"The guy was a model employee," Vaughn said after a moment of recovery. "He showed up on time, was quick with his routes, and safe. He logged safe hours on the road. I don't remember him getting a single traffic violation."

Terry jotted down the information Vaughn provided, wondering if Gosser's search warrant provided any additional evidence against Swanson.

"Have you found documentation of Daryl's routes?" he asked.

Vaughn handed him a stack of folders and papers.

"That's a copy of everything he's done since joining the company. It never occurred to me, even when I heard about some of those killings on the news."

Terry blamed himself for not making more of a public spectacle of the murders. His sensitivity for the victims' families and instinctive need to protect vital information from the public may have prevented earlier detection.

"I have to imagine you conduct extensive background checks on your new hires," Terry commented. "Any idea how Swanson slipped through the cracks?"

"You'll have to ask Grace about that. I know we prefer our drivers to have a CDL in case they have to drive the big trucks. He must have faked a lot of documentation and references if he's really who you think he is."

"I'm going to need everything from his personnel file."

"Sure," Vaughn said, jotting himself a reminder since Grace Ellington wasn't back for a second interview yet.

"You don't sit in on the interview process?"

"Sometimes I'm invited, but Grace and the plant managers usually conduct driver interviews."

Terry wanted to know more about Swanson and his personality. Taggart wasn't able to provide much about the man's background or character because he only interviewed him as a murder suspect. Perhaps Vaughn possessed differing knowledge of how Swanson behaved.

"What kind of person was he around the workplace?"

"Fairly typical guy from what I saw," Vaughn answered with a shrug. "He cut up and joked with the guys. I think he went out for beers with them sometimes on Friday nights when they got back from local deliveries."

"Did he ever show violent tendencies, or threaten anyone?"

"No. We have strict policies about that and I'd certainly remember if anyone's well-being was threatened."

"Friends? Girlfriends? Anything he ever wrote down that might be of use?"

"No. Daryl was always professional when he was here, and he kept to himself for the most part. You have to understand, our drivers come in, they drive, they go home. It's not common they even see one another other than Fridays when they run short routes."

Vaughn thought momentarily.

"The drivers have lockers," he volunteered. "I can show you Daryl's if that helps."

"It might."

Terry followed Vaughn through the cool, damp loading areas to the locker rooms where a few of the drivers were changing or packing their travel bags. Unlike the rest of the facility, the locker room looked renovated, with new beige tile covering the floor and a fresh coat of powder blue paint lining the walls. The overhead fluorescent lights illuminated every corner of the room without fail, as though each bulb and ballast had just been installed. A driver stepped from the shower, wearing a white towel around his waist as he eyed Terry suspiciously.

"This is their sanctum," Vaughn explained, apparently catching the glare. "Typically no one else comes back here."

Vaughn excused himself long enough to find bolt cutters that could handle the heavy duty lock on Swanson's locker. Terry caught more penetrating stares while he waited, probably because he was violating the civil rights of one of their own in their eyes. If only they knew, Terry thought. No one ever expected to work side by side with a mass murderer, so the shock element always reared its ugly head when the truth came to light.

"Here we go," Vaughn said when he returned, noticing several pairs of eyes looking their way. "Don't you guys have work to do?"

The drivers, visibly unhappy about disassembling their silent protest, did so slowly and begrudgingly. Vaughn refused to cut the lock until they dispersed, then sliced into the metal with the precision of a practiced burglar.

"Drivers sometimes quit and I'm the lucky bastard who has to gather their stuff," Vaughn commented. "Dirty socks and underwear are my favorite keepers."

Terry couldn't help but chuckle as Vaughn swung the locker door open and stepped aside.

"Let me know if you need anything. I'll keep the wolves at bay."

"Thanks."

Pulling a film canister from his sport coat, Terry popped the top and pulled two rolled latex gloves from inside. Though film was a dying medium, the canisters proved invaluable for holding the pliable gloves. He snapped them over his hands like a doctor about to give a prostate exam and began moving several hung shirts aside within the locker. He found several sheets of paper that turned out to be little more than invoices and receipts related to Erie Wholesale. He dug through several toiletries, a few dirty shirts, and a pair of work gloves until he found a Smith & Wesson .38 revolver.

While it wasn't the type of weapon used in the murders, it might hold some clues regarding the Montana killings or some valuable DNA evidence for later use. The labs determined a .38 semi-automatic was used in the homicides, which used slightly different ammunition.

"Got a bag of some kind?" Terry asked Vaughn, fighting back a grin that came with making serious progress in a homicide case.

***

After half an hour of searching the apartment with investigators from the city and county, Gosser felt frustration set in. Some of the investigators refused to hide their feelings about being called to a simple property search but Gosser wasn't trusting random patrol officers to clinically pick apart the apartment with the thoroughness and organization required.

Of course the forensic people collected hair and fiber samples for future comparison. At the moment the samples were utterly useless because no trace evidence was ever found at the six murder scenes. Sadly, the only way the task force might obtain the necessary samples was through another murder scene if the killer grew careless.

Gosser found himself unable to help very much in the search because his phone kept ringing with inquiries and updates. The sheriff was up to speed on the day's events, following Terry's request to post Swanson's picture on every newspaper and television channel as a person of interest in the case. Terry obtained a quality photo from Erie Wholesale, along with Swanson's cell phone number. The FBI reported the phone hadn't been used in three days, and couldn't be traced by any means. Swanson might very well have disposed of it, wanting to elude the police at the expense of communication.

Finding himself the object of irritated stares and several curse words for directing traffic within the apartment, Gosser silently excused himself and sauntered downstairs for a break. Determined not to return upstairs for at least ten minutes, he stepped outside the front door to light a cigarette, casually leaning against the building's brick facade.

He fielded another phone call from the sheriff, giving him an update on the status of the manhunt. All radio and television stations were broadcasting the make and model of the car and license plate issued to a Daryl Johnson. It seemed Swanson had forged documentation in every conceivable way to assume his new identity, even to the point that he owned a new Social Security number.

With everyone on the task force scrambling to find evidence linking Daryl Swanson to at least six murders, well-informed road officers carried on their search for the car. Gosser suspected Swanson might steal a different vehicle to further distance himself from the law. Swanson was no stranger to changing identities or running from the law. The fact that he left Montana and changed his identity without ever being more than questioned for a crime spoke volumes about his probable guilt.

Turning around to look at himself in the glass beside the front door, Gosser adjusted his tie, thinking he definitely looked like a vagrant. He zipped his jacket to block out the breeze as the sky began to gray and darken as dusk approached. A cold front was moving in that threatened rain and sleet, which did little to raise his spirits.

As he drew on his cigarette once more, Gosser noticed a skinny man wearing a hooded sweatshirt approaching the building, hands stuffed in his front pockets and hood concealing his face. As though overcome with psychic intuition, the detective immediately knew this man was shady in some sense. All of the police cars were parked in an out of sight lot beside the building, none of them with their lights on to alert this man to a police presence.

Without looking up, the man stepped inside the isolated room, tried the door and found it locked, then examined the panel with a button to buzz each room. Gosser took a quick drag from his cigarette, snuffed it in the trash can ashtray, then stepped inside as the mysterious man pushed the button for 229 where an array of police were likely to override the magnetic security door without question. Most of the time they figured one of their own needed to return to the apartment to aid in the search. Gosser's curiosity grew by the second because this man was here to see Swanson about something surely illegal.

Now Gosser's answers were as simple as his colleagues upstairs deactivating the lock and essentially trapping this man between him and a dozen cops one level above.

Of course the detective knew bad luck was the only luck in his life.

"Who is it?" someone on the speaker's other end asked instead of simply letting the stranger into the building.

"It's Carver. You want the shit or not?"

"Who?" the voice returned.

Carver stiffened, obviously knowing his client wasn't the voice, and that he was far too close to the police for his comfort. He also became instantly aware that Gosser was lurking behind him without reason. Gosser reached for his badge and one of Carver's shoulders simultaneously, but the man shrugged him off forcefully and barged his way outside before the detective could snag his sweatshirt. The detective's portable radio fell from his belt due to Carver's forceful resistance.

"Mother fucker!" Gosser muttered, taking chase down the streets of Buffalo. "Stop! Erie County Sheriff's Department!"

Gaffney preached to his detectives to always identify themselves, no matter how redundant or out of place such a statement might sound at the time. As he dashed down the street after Carver, Gosser found no time to call for backup or pull his firearm. Shit, he thought, realizing he didn't even have handcuffs on him. The morning started with a simple body discovery and no predictable epilogue following the event.

In a footrace, Gosser already knew he was going to lose by a country mile, so he kept Carver within eyesight, knowing the younger man would eventually hit a roadblock of some sort. He couldn't afford to lose the suspect, because Carver might lead the task force to Swanson and he didn't even have Carver's full identity or know if that was indeed his real name. As Carver snaked through traffic, Gosser took advantage of the slowing vehicles to cross to the other side. He found himself questioning his own cardiovascular conditioning even as he shortened the distance between himself and the suspect.

Typically, young energetic officers assisted detectives when serving warrants where foot pursuits might occur. Gosser wished an officer, or anyone for that matter, might assist him in slowing Carver's plight.

His heart thumped like a softball trying to escape his chest, and his upper torso in general began to feel like the Green Giant had grabbed hold of him and squeezed. Breathing grew more difficult by the second so he knew he needed to make a move or risk losing his best connection to Swanson.

Though Gosser ran track and played football in high school, and remained in reasonably good shape, he wasn't going to last much longer in a sprint where Carver showed no signs of slowing down. Now almost two car lengths behind the younger man, Gosser pulled his service weapon from his clip-on holster. The holster's safety mechanism made pulling a firearm difficult while standing still, so Gosser's years of experience paid dividends as he freed the weapon, ejected the magazine, then threw the metallic clip at Carver's head.

While his aim produced only a glancing blow to Carver's skull, it provided Gosser with the few seconds he required to catch the man and tackle him from behind. The brunt of his weight landed atop his suspect as Carver crashed with his elbows first onto the hard concrete. Gosser hoped the man wasn't seriously hurt because a hospital trip only delayed interrogating Carver for valuable information.

"Why you hasslin' me, man?" Carver demanded.

"Why aren't you stopping when I identified myself as a police officer?" Gosser huffed between shallow breaths.

"Didn't hear you."

The sassy answer didn't sit well with Gosser, who drove an elbow into his suspect's back, acting as though the move was meant to pin Carver down to satisfy onlookers. Without restraints of any kind, Gosser reached for his magazine, drove it into his service weapon, then pulled out his cell phone to call for backup. Still fighting to catch his breath, the detective prepared himself to do whatever it took to drag information out of Carver.

"You ain't gotta be like that, man."

"I've heard about enough from you," Gosser said as he waited for one of the investigators at the apartment to answer.

He reached around Carver's chest to begin the process of frisking him, a considerably risky move considering he needed to replace the gun to do so. Patting the man from head to toe, Gosser found no weapons, though he pulled a thick envelope from inside Carver's sweatshirt that, when opened, contained several pieces of false identification containing Daryl Swanson's likeness and another new name.

"Looks like you and I are going to have a long talk," Gosser stated, his breathing beginning to slow to a normal rhythm.

CHAPTER 27

Terry dropped everything when word came that Gosser stumbled upon a person of interest related to Swanson and brought him in for questioning. He currently found himself just outside a conference room within the sturdy walls of the Sheriff's Department, adjacent to the Erie County Holding Center. Gosser made it clear he intended to put Carver next door regardless of how cooperative the man proved to be.

Because of the hectic day, news trickled in like a stream born from melting winter snow. Terry found time to call his youngest brother while on the road, discovering that Carmen Loretta Sanchez was, in the killer's eyes, guilty of acquiring unjust riches. After a background check on the woman, Rochester authorities found she was the center of a murder investigation when her husband died. Her lawyer negated all charges and a guilty verdict by discovering some of the evidence didn't properly follow a chain of custody trail.

Family members and friends of her deceased husband had little doubt she was responsible for inducing a heart attack on her unsuspecting husband, though she denied it vehemently. After the trial, she moved halfway across the state, began her own business, and lived without the threat of a microscope looming over her.

Terry leaned against a wall in the hallway just outside of the makeshift interrogation room across from Gosser. Perhaps it was the miserable day outside creeping into the old building's interior, but he thought the fluorescent light overhead made the brown walls around him appear more dismal than usual. The long hours, coupled with yet another five hour drive left him drained of what little energy reserve his body typically put forth in times of need.

"So what do we know about this guy?" Terry asked Gosser as their suspect sweated bullets on the other side of the door.

"He's gone away once for counterfeiting and once for identification theft. This time he's creating fake identifications, so that's strike three."

"Guess he never found the right profession for him, did he?"

"That's one way of putting it. A tree probably died just to print out his list of offenses, which stretch all the way back to junior high."

Terry placed his back against the wall, folding his arms in anticipation of a solid interview. He wanted to arm himself with knowledge before confronting Terrell Carver because Gosser seemed a bit too hot under the collar following the foot pursuit.

"What did you find on him?" he asked.

"Swanson's new life, complete with new name, birthday, you name it."

"Is he technically under arrest?"

Gosser returned a perplexed look.

"I haven't read him his rights if that's what you mean."

"Maybe we should keep it that way. Let him think he has a way out."

"That's not how this works, Terry. You know anything he says won't amount to shit if we don't follow protocol."

"Don't let your ego cloud this, Randy. Just because you had to chase him doesn't mean we need to throw him in prison for life and sacrifice our one chance to find Swanson. This guy isn't going anywhere. He's not going to turn over a new leaf if we cut him loose tonight."

Gosser now crossed his arms, pacing the floor momentarily. He and the sheriff technically had final say because of their jurisdiction, despite Terry's leadership on the task force. Weighing the potential consequences of his actions momentarily, Gosser finally reached a decision.

"Let's put it to the sheriff," he said. "If you can talk him into it we'll do it your way."

Gaffney was already fielding phone calls from the press upstairs, so it took him mere minutes to meet them in the hallway. Both investigators explained the situation to him, though Gosser didn't sell his need to throw Carver in the brig nearly as hard to the sheriff, as though he already knew the battle was lost.

After hearing both arguments, Gaffney likely weighed the media pressure versus the confinement of one career criminal who did little more than deceive people for profit. Considering most of the Sin Killer's work occurred within Erie County lines, his decision proved rather easy.

"Better we stop a serial killer than worry about a piss ant forger. Hear what the piece of shit has to say, verify it, then cut him loose. Spin the deal, Randy, but make sure you squeeze him for everything he's got."

Gosser nodded.

"You got it, Sheriff."

Without another word Gaffney walked away with purpose. Terry appreciated the man handling the press, which allowed him to roam freely between crime scenes.

"Ready?" he asked Gosser.

"Hopefully my swelled head won't get stuck in the door," the detective answered sarcastically, letting Terry know he wasn't happy about the earlier ego comment.

"Then I'll go first to make sure I don't get stuck behind you."

Terry indeed led the way into the room where Carver looked up from the table where he had sat impatiently for nearly half an hour now. Carver, just two years short of his thirtieth birthday, was the son of a black career criminal and an impoverished Caucasian woman who worked two jobs just to feed him, dying one year after he dropped out of high school. Terry couldn't empathize so much as he could recognize the pattern. The path career criminals took wasn't always so different than those of the serial killers Terry pursued. Their means to an end was the almighty dollar instead of the ecstasy of a kill, but what drove them to their lots in life wasn't often very different. Typically one or both parents dropped out of their lives at an early, impressionable age, leaving a void often filled by the wrong crowd or complete isolation.

"You're about to get the deal of a lifetime," Gosser informed Carver, since both investigators knew he loved controlling interviews. "No lawyers, no bullshit. You tell me everything you know about Daryl Swanson, Johnson, Tomlinson, whatever the fuck you want to call him, and don't leave anything out."

Carver shifted his eyes to Terry as though he wanted verification but Terry wasn't about to play nice cop.

"We know what you do," Gosser said, "so there's no need for games, Terrell."

"So what we doin' here then?"

"These can go away," Gosser said, holding up all of the fake identifications made for one Daryl Tomlinson. "I want to know what he wanted and where he was going once he got these."

"Did you do some work for him when he first moved here?" Terry asked before Carver got started.

"A few. Mother fucker already had some of his own shit. He needed a CDL license for some job and a birth certificate from Maine."

"No Social Security card or regular driver's license?" Terry asked suspiciously.

"Already had that shit."

Gosser drew close to Carver so their noses were mere inches apart.

"What did he say to you when you took this job?"

"Said he needed to get out of state quick."

"Where?" Gosser pressed.

"Mother fucker didn't say. Said the police was pressin' him."

Terry looked at Gosser, thinking back to the mysterious agent who conveniently paid him a visit the night before the task force's big break came about. Inquiries within the Erie County Sheriff's Department, local FBI, and Buffalo Police Department returned with zero results, meaning someone was lying or an outsider visited Swanson's apartment building.

"Did he say anything else about why he had to leave, or why the police wanted to question him?" Terry asked.

"You *are* the police," Carver retorted, tilting his head like a thug. "Don't you know?"

"Listen up, asshole," Gosser said, drawing dangerously close to the suspect as though daring Carver to strike him. "You've got one chance to do this right or we can start over with lawyers and jail time."

"No," Carver answered plainly. "Your boy didn't say anything else. Just told me to call him when I finished with my work. I called, but there was no answer, so I went to his crib. That's when you tackled me."

Gosser finally eased back, grinning a bit.

"What number did he call you from?" Terry asked, remembering Swanson's phone listed at Erie Wholesale hadn't been used in three days.

Carver pulled out his own phone, checked the received calls list and wrote down the number when Terry produced some scrap paper and a pen.

"Different number," Terry said. "Looks like a land line prefix."

"Let's go check it," Gosser said, thumbing toward the door.

"What about me?" Carver asked with irritation.

"What about you?" Gosser fired back. "I'm not anywhere close to done with you yet. And you may very well be sticking around until we land Swanson."

Carver glared at both investigators, not daring to speak a rebuttal. Gosser opened the door, holding it for Terry to exit first.

"Hope you know what you're doing," Terry said, plucking his cell phone to have local dispatchers identify the phone number in his hand.

"He needs to sweat a little. Don't worry, my ego's in check."

"I don't get why Swanson would split town without collecting the goods first."

Terry opened the door, standing at the threshold just long enough to ask Carver a question.

"Did he pay you anything up front?"

"Yeah."

"How much?"

"Five-hundred to start and the other half when I delivered."

"When did he approach you about the forgeries?"

"Three days ago."

Terry slammed the door shut.

"Swanson knew how to reach Carver," Terry deduced. "Why didn't he?"

"He was in a hurry," Gosser shrugged.

"But he placed the order three days ago, as though he knew he might need a new life. Why skip town without so much as a phone call to see if Carver was finished?"

"Maybe he did. I can beat it out of him if you like."

"That's your ego talking. Put him away."

Gosser rolled his eyes.

"You're less fun than my ex-wives."

"And wiser. I discovered your character flaws before marrying you."

Terry found a quick dial for local dispatchers, then hit the send button.

"Hey, I don't have that many flaws," Gosser said, playing along, apparently over being called out about his pride.

"Sounds like someone's in denial."

Before Gosser could counter the accusation, Terry was speaking with a dispatcher, ascertaining that the number was indeed a land line from one of the few remaining phone booths in the city.

"Phone booth," he informed Gosser, "on the city's south side."

Gosser leafed through the false identifications, which included a passport, a driver's license for Tennessee and Illinois, and a new CDL, all under the name Daryl Tomlinson.

"With these he could have obtained a work visa in Canada, or gained citizenship there," the detective said.

"He still could. You heard Carver. Swanson can either make this stuff himself, or has other people making more fakes."

Grimacing, Gosser realized the truth that even with Carver they weren't any closer to locating Swanson.

"There's a possibility Swanson may want these," Gosser said, holding up the false identifications again. "I tell Carver we're holding these and filing a report over this little incident, but that I don't plan on doing anything with it so long as he lets us know when Swanson contacts him."

"I don't think he'll ever call."

"Maybe, maybe not. Better to have that insurance policy than nothing, right?"

"Absolutely. Do what you need to. I'm going to see if we have any developments."

Terry started to walk away, then turned for one last verbal jab.

"Try to avoid any foot races through the building, will you?"

"Funny," Gosser replied with a purposely insincere grin. "And I thought *I* was an asshole."

Terry chuckled as he walked away. He couldn't remain intensely focused on the case every second of the day and be expected to retain his own sanity. Besides, he needed Gosser every step of the way, and getting along with the detective meant heckling him a little bit. Some of Gosser's colleagues didn't appreciate the man's past, which caused them to ignore his value to their own agency. Gosser required being kidded with to feel accepted and let his guard down around other officers. Terry wasn't about to alienate anyone who might be of use when it came to catching the Sin Killer.

After checking the tip hotline and speaking with authorities in the Carmen Sanchez murder case, Terry wanted to interview the remainder of the Erie Wholesale employees who had any contact with Swanson. Though it didn't sound like Swanson fraternized with any of them on a regular basis, any detail at all might prove useful in finding the man.

Before he made any moves, he decided it was necessary to call his wife and give her an update. As usual, she showed patience with him, knowing part of his job was to travel and track dangerous people at Duggan's insistence. After a particular incident threatened his ability to carry out his job, Terry found himself on the verge of being pensioned out of the state police. It was Dave Duggan who believed in him and found a way for him to keep his job until Terry's issues passed. Sherri believed Terry was paying back a never-ending debt of gratitude by taking on so many challenging cases, but Terry knew his special talents brought about conclusions more quickly than simply sitting back, waiting for that lucky moment when killers *finally* made a mistake.

Duggan called it his gift, but Terry knew his knowledge of how serial killers worked came from a certain part of his brain that probably didn't function for most people. He could switch from normal thoughts to those of sociopaths and criminals without conscience almost at will. Terry possessed the gift of understanding both worlds. True, he was happily married with three children he loved, but he also understood why serial killers and rapists reached that point in life, not because of textbooks, academies, or weekend seminars. He understood for reasons he never told anyone, because the visions that ran through his mind weren't something everyday ordinary people thought about.

As he called Sherri, he thought of Daryl Swanson's actions, feeling in his gut they didn't parallel the meticulous nature of the Sin Killer.

CHAPTER 28

Armed with a decent night's sleep and a fresh set of clothes, Terry returned to the redone warehouse after phoning Nick Vaughn and Grace Ellington for second interviews. He stepped from the marked car, finding no other vehicles parked outside the facility. Planted beside the vehicle, Terry slowly took in his surroundings with the eyes of a sentry looking for trouble. He didn't know why he felt so defensive, as though someone might be observing him from a distance. With the Sin Killer still on the loose, and the investigation now a very public spectacle, Terry wasn't about to rest easy.

After some urging, Ben Belinski made a personal appearance on television to make Daryl Swanson a known face in the six homicides crossing the state. Labeling him a homicidal maniac didn't seem quite fitting, especially since no one was certain he was armed, so they went with the person of interest moniker instead. Terry was afraid smearing him across the news too much might keep him out of public places, making him more difficult to track.

Nick Vaughn arrived first, driving a newer model pickup truck. Stepping out, he firmly shook Terry's hand before unlocking the front door to let them inside. He deactivated the alarm just inside the door, then turned on enough lights to guide them to the offices.

"I apologize for the lack of heat," Vaughn said, referring to the refrigerator-like temperature inside the building. "The bosses keep the thermostat turned down on the weekends."

"Not a problem. Do you have much trouble with people breaking in?"

Vaughn gave a perplexed look.

"Oh, the alarm. You'd be surprised how many poor and homeless people eyeball a bulk goods facility. We've had a couple of incidents."

Vaughn led Terry down the hallway to his personal office, which the investigator studied more closely this time, considering he wasn't pressing for immediate necessary information. He found the office, like those around it, very well redone considering the building's previous use. The smell of carpet glue lingered in the air and the room felt considerably warmer than the loading areas outside.

"I think you have Swanson's personnel file and his run records," Vaughn said as Terry examined several photographs hung along one wall.

"We do. They were a big help, especially the current photograph we posted on the news. Considering he gave you perfect forgeries, your company couldn't have known who they were hiring."

"But why cover his real identity at all?"

"I'm afraid for the very reason we're tracking him. He was under suspicion for some crimes in Montana. Maybe he thought they would catch up with him."

Terry saw an older color photograph of a man wearing a Buffalo Police Department uniform seated beside a boy in a marked patrol car.

"That you?" he asked Vaughn.

"Me and my dad. He worked for the city police."

"Retired?"

"No," Vaughn shook his head, looking to the floor before meeting Terry's eyes. "He was killed in the line of duty shortly after that picture was taken."

"I'm sorry."

"It was a long time ago, Trooper Levine. He was a great father, and very good at his job. He investigated fires back when Buffalo detectives had an arson squad assisting the fire department."

Terry recalled the squad being disbanded and reassigned sometime before the new millennium. Departments were always changing and reorganizing with new administrations and tax dollar dispersion.

"You come from a long line of lawmen?" Vaughn inquired.

"My grandfather was a sheriff up north. He retired when I was still a kid. He didn't talk much about the job, but I guess the few stories he told kind of intrigued me."

"There were guys on the department who watched over me after Dad died, but I never had the desire to become a cop."

"Looks like you've done fairly well for yourself."

Vaughn shrugged.

"I can't complain. Usually nice and quiet around here until this week."

Terry returned a smile.

"Hopefully we'll be out of your hair by next week."

"Happy to help. Just let me know what you need."

Both men took their respective seats as Terry drew out a pad and pen.

"Tell me all about Daryl Johnson."

***

Terry met with Randy Gosser a few hours later to discuss any developments from the media coverage and the checks on Daryl Swanson's delivery schedule with Erie Wholesale. Sitting in a small café not far from downtown Buffalo, Gosser spread out several sheets across the table for Terry to examine. Gosser had requested a corner booth so they had privacy from snooping eyes and ears. The booth also provided space enough to eat and examine documents, though Terry found the lighting a bit dim for his taste.

"We took into account the travel time and Swanson's scheduled deliveries," Gosser said, thumbing Canton on the map while pulling out the case file from the Mitchell murder. "He had a delivery to Clarkson University in Potsdam late that afternoon. Based on his mileage, Swanson needed to do a layover. The records show he stayed at the Best Western in Canton."

"That doesn't explain how he came into contact with Mitchell, or even knew the man was going to be there."

"No, but that's irrelevant at the moment," Gosser said, waving his hand as though shooing the comment, "because we have him making two trips to Syracuse in both February and March when Allen was thought to have been killed. You said that Hathaway told you it wasn't uncommon for truck drivers to park their trucks in that very lot and stay the night."

Terry looked at receipts from both trips Swanson made to Syracuse under his alias.

"Both of these said he slept in motels."

"Why are you in denial?" Gosser asked in frustration. "He was covering his tracks. This is the Sin Killer you've come to know and love, Terry, at his best."

"This is all fine and dandy, but we need intangible proof to come at this guy when we find him."

Gosser continued, unfazed by Terry's lack of commitment to his hard work and circumstantial evidence.

"We had three murders right around Buffalo and another near Rochester, right? On all four nights when these murders occurred, Swanson had no scheduled runs, or could have easily been back from local deliveries."

"You don't need to convince me, Randy. When we find Swanson, though, we need a smoking gun and I don't think he's dumb enough to keep any incriminating evidence. I'm just looking at the bigger picture when this goes to court. If he gets one of those glory hound, publicity-seeking lawyers, we could look like horses' asses."

Gosser looked deflated, possibly even dejected by the words as his hands fell limply atop the folders he had slaved over for most of the night and into the morning.

"You're doing great work," Terry said, trying to bolster his confidence. "We need every shred of evidence we can get. Armed with enough of this, we might get Swanson to crack when we find him. You're doing exactly what we need by getting this together."

"I know. I just thought all the pieces were falling into place."

"And they are. He can't stay hidden forever. Show me what else you've got."

Gosser shuffled the papers around.

"So we've got him pegged at being in all of those places. The forensics geeks said the Sin Killer did his writing and most of his handiwork left-handed."

"Most?"

"Some was inconclusive. And Swanson is left-handed."

"Anything useful in the apartment?"

"We collected all kinds of DNA samples, but nothing damning like notes or weapons. Got samples of his handwriting, but I doubt it's comparable to bloody finger drawings."

Terry shrugged.

"You never know."

"We also spoke with Tonya LaShomb again. Seems her stint on the morning news created a diva."

"Did her security team let you pass?"

Gosser chuckled.

"Wasn't quite that bad, though she couldn't identify Swanson as the man who attacked her or her boyfriend."

"We're striking out all over."

"That's for sure," Gosser said, his mouth full after taking a bite of a Reuben sandwich.

"That thing stinks, Randy. I'm going to order anchovies and get you back."

"Then you'll have an order of anchovies and puke 'cause I can't stand those things."

Terry picked up his coffee cup.

"I'll just stick with this."

A thought struck him.

"Did Swanson's place have a computer?"

"No. Why?"

"He had to research his victims somewhere."

"Maybe he got a library card."

"That's possible. Maybe he had a laptop he took with him. We should check local library branches and coffee shops to see if anyone recognizes him. Might see if he checked out any biblical materials, too."

Gosser didn't look thrilled about the idea.

"That's a lot of manpower."

"Well, until we get something concrete, we need anything we can use against him. Duggan is going to strand me here again, so I'll pitch in. If Swanson left the state, we aren't going to find him, so we just do what we can until someone does."

"I feel like I'm banging my head against the wall just grasping for anything."

"I know. Me too."

"Maybe he packed up and took everything with him, but I thought for sure we'd find *something* at that apartment."

Terry wondered if they were beating themselves up too badly. Perhaps Swanson was well-organized but never stayed at home. It seemed feasible he took everything important with him at a moment's notice.

"Ever find out who paid Swanson a visit the night before we did?"

Gosser finished swallowing this time before answering.

"No. Never found the fucking business card, either."

"So we have no hard evidence, we don't have Swanson or his car, and we're out of leads."

"Sounds kind of shitty when you put it that way."

"That's because it is shitty, Detective Gosser."

Gosser took another bite from his sandwich, chasing it with a gulp from his Diet Pepsi.

"What did the folks at Erie Wholesale tell you?"

"Nothing new. They thought he was a perfect fit when they hired him, based on his credentials and a solid interview."

"And to think we were looking in all the wrong places for months."

"We underestimated him," Terry said plainly. "Maybe we still are."

Terry continued to wonder exactly how Swanson found his way to Canton at the precise moment Harold James Mitchell was returning from Canada. Knowing Mitchell had a conference in Montreal seemed feasible through the internet. Timing Mitchell's arrival in Canton seemed difficult, though plausible, *if* a person knew he was definitely coming that way to reach Rochester. Terry had taken the liberty of checking routes from upstate New York to Rochester and the route was one of the more efficient ways of getting Mitchell home.

Still, knowing Mitchell's car, his appearance, how to stop him along a state road, and murdering him without calling attention to one's self required lots of planning or luck. Considering the killer left no trace evidence anywhere at the crime scene, even after presumably chasing Mitchell into the grass, the crime seemed too perfect for a man driving a large truck on a layover. Then again, box trucks provided certain advantages to serial killers, like the ability to act stranded and in desperate need of assistance in the middle of the night.

"You look deep in thought," Gosser said.

"What are the details of Swanson's trip to Canton?"

Gosser flipped through the pages and receipts provided by Erie Wholesale.

"He left Saturday morning, April 26, to make five deliveries. According to his log sheet, as verified by signatures and printouts, he made three deliveries before stopping in Potsdam for his last two. Realizing he was exceeding driving limits, he booked a hotel room just outside of Canton for the night."

Terry looked at the hotel and gas receipts, finding they were all just prior to eight in the evening. It made sense that he gassed up, booked the hotel room, then grabbed a bite to eat, but he had to know Mitchell, and had to know the man was returning home that way.

"You're thinking again," Gosser said. "It's scaring me."

"If I want to murder you Randy, and I'm going to lie in wait, I have to know where you are, or what you're driving. And I can't just wait off the side of the road or I lose my chance because it's dark, and I can't see you."

Gosser caught his line of thinking.

"But no one ever reported seeing a box truck that night."

"That's right. No box truck, no hitchhikers, no nothing. So how did Swanson know his victim was coming right to him?"

Gosser rubbed his chin.

"He set him up?"

"We checked phone records and e-mails without any luck."

"What about old-fashioned snail mail?"

Terry snapped his fingers.

"You send the man a letter with something he wants to hear, then jump him before he arrives at the meeting spot."

"Or you designate a spot you know will be dark and secluded. Swanson had to know that area. He drove it dozens, maybe hundreds, of times."

"And the best part is you simply find the letter and take it."

"No such letter at the apartment," Gosser said sourly. "Of course that's not something he's going to leave lying around."

"What about the crampons used to string Cirillo up to the tree?" Terry asked. "I wonder if we can trace any of Swanson's work history. Maybe he was a cable or phone line technician somewhere."

Gosser scoffed at the notion.

"He's like a secret agent. How can we trace a guy with multiple identities?"

"Maybe we can't. He can't have much money, can he? He's going to have to work or start robbing banks before long."

"He only had one bank account that we could trace," Gosser said. "He cleared out a few thousand dollars Friday night."

"Hardly enough to fly to Europe," Terry kidded. "We've got to turn up the pressure and make sure he can't settle anywhere."

Raising a surprised eyebrow, Gosser gave a mischievous grin.

"You thinking about going national?"

"We should have already," Terry admitted. "We need to get the Canadian authorities more involved, too. Composites, descriptions, everything."

Gosser stood and stretched. He gathered his sheets of paper into a nice, neat pile, then left some bills on the table to cover his tab and a tip.

"I'll be back. While you save the world I'm going to step out and burn one."

"Ever thought about quitting?"

"Yeah, but thinking is about as far as I get."

"Well, enjoy yourself out there in the dark, cold, lonely night where people stare at you in passing like you're a vagrant."

Gosser sighed.

"You know we can never truly be friends, right?"

"I've come to terms with that," Terry said with a smile after getting a rise out of the detective. "See you in five minutes."

Shaking his head, Gosser walked away groaning loud enough that Terry heard him.

CHAPTER 29

Terry's frustration mounted after two weeks of no new developments in the Sin Killer homicides. Not only had no one reported seeing Swanson, but no new evidence surfaced linking him, or anyone, to the murders. The deeper the task force looked into the paperwork given to them by Erie Wholesale, the more Swanson appeared directly linked to the six homicides. Terry desperately wanted to see him handcuffed to a table, trapped within a six by six foot interview room like a cornered rat.

Instead of focusing on the homicides, however, Terry found himself closer to home visiting the Upstate Correctional Facility in Malone, nearly an hour from his home. One of his previous cases continued to haunt him, partly because Kevin Alan Kimmerling, an imprisoned serial killer couldn't be executed by state law, but also because of Terry's youngest brother.

It seemed Kenny, in his quest to be closer with God through church and mind, had started writing the man who literally tried to murder his family. Terry never approved of the correspondence, but recently his concern escalated when Kimmerling added Kenny to his approved visitation list and Kenny contemplated paying a visit in person.

After pulling up to the prison and speaking with the appropriate personnel inside, Terry surrendered his weapon and everything in his pockets before following a guard toward a designated room. Ordinarily visitors were placed into rooms where they and the prisoners were lined up in dog runs. Visitation was limited to weekends only with thirty minute intervals. If inmates remained on good behavior, they were not shackled when visitors came.

Considering Terry wasn't on Kimmerling's visitation list, nor would he make such a request, he asked the warden for some special circumstances when visiting the inmate. Kimmerling was between trials, attempting to secure a retrial in hopes of being deemed clinically insane rather than a ruthless murderer.

In truth he was both.

Led down some dim hallways to a well-lit secure room, Terry peered inside to see Kimmerling seated against a wall, free of shackles. The guard opened the door and Kimmerling looked up, not the least bit surprised to see the state trooper visiting him. He wore green Dickies issued to every prisoner at the facility, which in Terry's mind sapped him of the power and influence he once had over unsuspecting citizens.

"You good?" the guard asked Terry, who simply nodded in response.

As Terry stepped inside the room, the solid door locked behind him as the guard stood vigil outside. Before speaking, Terry studied the prisoner, who looked a bit more haggard than he did nearly four years prior at his arrest. Though still a fairly young man, a few etched lines crossed his face in addition to the stubble that came from a few days of not shaving. His hair was also trimmed much closer to the scalp, almost military in nature. The man appeared humbled, but Terry knew from their few encounters in the courtroom that Kimmerling, like most caught serial killers, made every attempt to act empowered.

"Good morning, Trooper Levine," Kimmerling said evenly.

Terry said nothing, simply taking a seat opposite from the convicted killer, staring him in the eye. His aim wasn't intimidation or he would have remained standing. Kimmerling actually owned the situation at hand and knew so. As much as he wanted to keep the conversation short and sweet, then return home to see his wife and children, Terry knew better.

"I'll keep this brief," Terry began. "I want you to completely alienate yourself from my brother."

Kimmerling smiled knowingly.

"He wrote me first, Trooper Levine."

"You didn't need to write back."

"I have little else to do. Why wouldn't I correspond?"

Kimmerling was intelligent and cunning. If Terry slipped up, the man would seize control of the conversation.

"You tried to kill my sister-in-law, my niece, and my nephew," Terry said plainly. "Had my brother not been lying in a hospital bed, you would have abducted and killed him. You have no right to speak to anyone in my family."

Kimmerling crossed his hands atop his lap.

"I understand your position, but your brother wants answers. He wants to forgive me."

"My brother is confused, Kimmerling. You're taking advantage of him for your own benefit."

"I'm doing no such thing. You and I both know my trials are simply a postponement of the inevitable. There's nothing your brother can do for me except show me the way to the Lord."

A slow, methodical smile formed through the man's lips. While Terry wasn't driven to anger, he felt his patience slipping away.

"Do you want answers, Trooper Levine?"

"Not from you, I don't."

"Perhaps you need some. Your brother says he's helping you with a most difficult case. I believe I've seen it on the news."

Terry fought to keep from rolling his eyes. It was no secret he was the face of the task force that continued to search in vain for the Sin Killer, but Kenny had exposed himself along with some dangerous information.

"This isn't some Hannibal Lector visit where I ask you to help me catch the mysterious killer because I'm at my wit's end."

"No, no, of course not. You have everything you need in that mind of yours. You even have your own fantasies, don't you, Trooper Levine?"

Terry felt his face flush red, though not from anger.

From embarrassment.

"That's how you found me, isn't it? You think like me. You think like the Sin Killer, with dreams and scenarios running through your head."

Kimmerling said it so matter-of-factly, like it was etched in stone tablets for the world to read. In prison a man had little else to do except dwell, dream, and think. Study some psychology perhaps to learn one's enemy.

"You don't know the first thing about me," Terry said, denying the words.

In truth, he thought about murder scenarios often, not with a sense of carrying them out, or even waking in the middle of the night with an erection, but he contemplated the intricacies of how to murder others. In truth, human beings were the most dangerous quarry, not because killing them was so difficult, but covering up the crime took skill and intelligence. If someone stabbed a dog or a wild deer, no one really gave it a second thought. Taking a human life, however, required skill on several levels.

"You caught me," Kimmerling continued, "not because you stumbled on evidence or got a lucky tip. Truth be told, you think just like me."

"That's not true," Terry defied him again. "I've never taken a human life."

"Say what you will, but your brother will find out."

"Stay away from him."

"Or what, you'll kill me like you've fantasized about doing a thousand times? Take my neck in your hands. Squeeze it. It feels good, believe me."

Terry shook his head, standing as he knocked on the door. Not only had he failed to keep Kimmerling at bay, but he now felt exposed, like a child caught with a dirty magazine for the first time. He wasn't the same breed as the man before him, but Terry occasionally stooped to similar levels in his thinking to understand what motivated men like Kimmerling.

"Don't worry," Kimmerling said. "I won't tell your brother about any of this. He'll know what you are soon enough."

"There's nothing to know, you son-of-a-bitch. You're where you belong, and I'm out there stopping people just like you. You preying on my brother isn't going to continue, and I'll be damned if I let him visit you."

Kimmerling smiled, saying nothing further.

They both knew Terry couldn't protect his brother forever, especially when he spent half of his time across the state hunting the serial killer of the week. As the door opened, Terry stepped into the dim hallway, his hands trembling slightly from Kimmerling's words. No, he decided, I'm not a monster for thinking about some of the things I do. Religion and the commandment that thou shalt not kill was ever present to keep him from ever really wanting to harm another human being.

He understood serial killers, but he was not one.

Not even close.

CHAPTER 30

Lou Merrill checked the front desk of the Econo Motel as the clock struck two in the morning to ensure no one was checking in or needing assistance before grabbing his old suede jacket from the rack behind the desk. Tossing it over his shoulders as he stuck his arms through the sleeves, the overnight clerk grabbed a pack of cigarettes from his pocket, then stepped outside to light one within view of his desk.

After his departure from the United States Army, Merrill went to work for the hotel chain while he studied for several other jobs. Occupations for someone forty-two years of age weren't abundant, even with his military experience. While his discharge from the military wasn't a blemish on paper, it was a major drawback that would keep him from ever reenlisting or finding another government job.

Leaning his shoulder against one of the faux pillars at the front entrance, Merrill took a deep drag from his cigarette, doubting anyone was going to require his assistance at the early morning hour. He hated his life, working at a small town motel as he waited for something else to come along. Originally from Buffalo, he left the city after his discharge because of the bad publicity dropped at his doorstep. His wife stuck by him, so far, and his family tried to understand the circumstances surrounding his discharge, but even they didn't seem terribly sad that he moved away to start fresh.

Things hadn't truly gone badly until one of his platoon mates brought the incident in question into the limelight by publically accusing Merrill of getting five men in his patrol killed by failing to act due to cowardice in an ambush. While the military skirted the issue entirely by discharging him after a brief internal investigation, several families of the deceased sought to bring about civil charges against Merrill. Despite the judge shooting down their attempts to claim damages against Merrill, the publicity grew too intense for him to stay around Buffalo.

Merrill felt his free hand clench into a fist within his jacket pocket. He absolutely hated his military buddies for turning on him. His life, now a shadow of what he once knew, was basically ruined.

Hearing a beep from his cell phone, he plucked it from his belt to open a text message from one of his friends that turned out to be a forwarded joke. He chuckled, feeling a little better that he wasn't the only one awake in the middle of the night. Taking a final drag from his smoke, he exhaled forcefully toward the ground, then snuffed it in the smoker pole beside him.

About to head inside where warmth awaited him, Merrill looked across the spacious front yard for any activity or approaching vehicles. Military life, particularly in Iraq, taught him to be vigilant of his surroundings at all times. He didn't realistically expect terrorists to dive-bomb a plane into his workplace, but threats came in the form of thieves and graffiti artists several times a year.

His eyes spied something, a lump of some sort, lying in the front yard beneath the only large tree on the premises. Thinking a homeless person might have decided to camp out on the yard, Merrill sauntered out toward the tree. Dew immediately speckled his penny loafers and his socks, getting his feet slightly cold and wet. He cursed under his breath, deciding this homeless person was going to be toted away in handcuffs by the police if he got his wish.

"Hey!" he called when he got closer, realizing the person was covered by some kind of blanket. "Hey, buddy!"

His calls failed to stir the person, who continued to lie on one side, faced away from Merrill as though he didn't hear a thing. Halfway across the yard, the hotel's exterior lights failed to provide much detail for the desk attendant. The overcast sky lingering over most of New York State throughout the weekend prevented any moonlight from illuminating the yard, so he needed to draw closer to see much of anything. Only the light-colored blanket drew his attention in the first place, and now he saw white, almost bleached white shoes on the intruder's feet.

Now only a few feet away, with leaves crunching underfoot, Merrill found more details materializing as he examined the person from head to toe. The blanket appeared sloppily arranged as though to cover something, rather than protect the wearer from the elements. He noticed no movement from the person in the form of shivering, or even breathing. Merrill began to wonder if he might be trampling on a crime scene as his eyes panned toward the feet of the person. Instead of wearing brand new tennis shoes, as Merrill originally thought, the unidentified person wore dark shoes with some kind of shoe coverings on the bottom.

"What the fuck?" Merrill questioned aloud as the person sprang to life, triggering some kind of small device that upended the hotel employee in less than a second.

A strong, thin wire, invisible in the darkness, had wrapped itself around his ankle and pulled him skyward before he could react. He barely let out a yelp as the wire tightened around his foot enough that it broke through his dress sock and dug into his skin, sealing his predicament. Merrill groaned as the pain shot through his foot and blood began pooling toward his head. He found himself just over four feet off the ground, arms dangling, at the mercy of whoever set him up.

"What do you want?" he asked.

No answer.

"I'll give you whatever you want."

No response.

Instead, the figure meticulously reached into the blanket and pulled out an old aluminum baseball bat. Merrill flailed as he realized the distinct possibility of being a live piñata was in his future. As he tried desperately to free himself, he felt the encircled wire dig even deeper into his ankle, creating a bloody trickle that streamed into his khaki pants.

"No, please," he pleaded as the figure slowly circled him, like a lion examining a crippled elk.

Now dizzy from being upside down, spinning, and losing some blood, Merrill tried to look at his attacker's features by looking skyward. The man wore gloves, dark clothing, and even a cloth mask of some sort to conceal his features. After a few agonizing seconds of the man taunting him with mental anguish, Merrill's captor pulled back the bat for a full swing. He reached out, grasping for any part of the man's body to stop him from swinging, only reaching the thick sweatshirt and several layers of shirts beneath it. A thump from the bat forced him to remove his hand as he attempted and failed to swing farther away from the bat.

"Help!" Merrill screamed at the top of his lungs, hoping someone, *anyone*, inside the motel might hear.

He covered his head protectively, intending to sacrifice his hands, but the bat landed with the force of a horse hoof during a stampede against his ribs. Intense pain, accompanied by a cracking sound, was all he knew as he nearly blacked out. Only the pain kept Merrill awake, though he desperately wanted out of this situation by any means necessary. Now feverishly sucking in precious air with at least two broken ribs, Merrill couldn't afford to cry out.

His assailant dropped the bat, though the move appeared deliberate, not like a man having a change of heart about the wrongs in his life. Merrill gasped for breath as the man reached into the blanket, pulling out a long kitchen knife that glistened even in the low lighting. Clutching his ribs with one arm, Merrill desperately tried pulling himself up to free his foot, but even with full health and some flexibility left from his military days, the feat wouldn't have been possible.

"Please," Merrill begged as the man slowly closed in with the knife clutched in his right hand.

As though commanded by the Lord above, the man dropped the knife on the ground. Merrill began breathing a sigh of relief as his eyes followed the blade, not noticing what his assailant produced with the other hand until a large plastic zip tie ascended from his head to his neck. Immediately pulled tight, constricting Merrill's breathing, the tie continued to lock tighter and tighter as he fought to draw breaths for his burning lungs. As his oxygen consumption lowered by the second, he saw red and white stars dancing before him as images of the motel and his attacker grew fuzzy. His extremities began suffering tingling and numbness from oxygen deprivation.

His assailant moved to one side, but Merrill was busy clawing at the plastic tie, unable to free it from his neck. Only a blade could cut through the plastic to save him on time, but the kitchen knife was on the ground.

Merrill carried a pocket knife, but it fell from his pants pocket when he found himself yanked skyward. Nearing a blackout, he saw the darkly-clad stranger reach down for the large blade, then felt the man pull on his hair to expose his neck. Merrill lost consciousness before learning his ultimate fate.

***

By daylight Terry arrived at the crime scene, finding Gosser and several local investigators interviewing motel guests who expected continental breakfast instead of a murder scene when they awoke. Several patrol officers secured the scene at the foot of the drive and around the motel grounds to preserve evidence. Terry suspected they were also in place to keep guests from leaving until the detectives had a chance to talk with each and every one of them.

Terry seriously doubted any of the guests knew about the murder, much less having any part in it. Both investigators were there simply because the murder involved a bloody symbol with numbers. Terry seriously doubted the Sin Killer's name was going to appear in the motel's guest register. Gosser had filled him in on some minor details when he called. The Erie County investigator lived much closer to the crime scene, so he beat Terry by nearly four hours.

"What do we have?" Terry asked when Gosser broke away from the interviews.

"Dead desk clerk. Louis Joseph Merrill, age forty-two. Cameras inside showed him stepping out for a smoke, then he walks in the direction of where he was killed like he spotted something. The only outdoor camera covers the back parking lot, so we have no visual on the killer or what he drove, because no one arrived after our guy stepped outside until two hours later."

"They the ones who found the body?"

"Yeah. Husband couldn't find anyone inside, so he came out here and found the clerk strung up by one foot. Looks like he was strangled by a zip-tie, but his throat was cut slightly to drain some blood for the message."

Terry followed Gosser toward the body, not wanting to contaminate the scene. Again, squeamish with the knife, he thought as the sun lazily hid beyond the horizon. At least the clouds had moved east, so the fear of rain washing away evidence didn't force the technicians to hurry unnecessarily. As they neared the body, Terry noticed his breath against the cold air, wondering how the victim drew his last breath.

Though he took a quick glance at the body, Terry didn't want to focus on it until he knew some details and the technicians finished their jobs.

He thought back to what Kimmerling said, knowing he wasn't a sociopath like that man or the Sin Killer. Terry felt compassion for the families of victims, never finding the blackness in his own soul to actually want to take a life. Though he wasn't as passionate as his brother about religion, he believed in the church and a higher power. So did the Sin Killer, which didn't provide much evidence that Christianity automatically made believers good people.

Gosser checked with the evidence technicians about where they could walk, then led Terry closer to the bloody symbol drawn across the rounded surface of the tree. If not for the tree's smooth bark, the symbol might never have shown up, but Terry suspected the blood shimmered against artificial light making it easy to spot.

Pulling a small notepad and pen from his pockets, Terry squinted in an attempt to read the dried blood against the dark gray tree bark. Gosser handed him a sheet of paper with the illustrated symbol and three numbers on it.

"They had to hold a black light up to it for me to read the thing."

Terry held up the sheet of paper to read the numbers.

46:16:333.

"Our killer seems to have a stiff one for Jeremiah," Gosser commented.

"Maybe Jeremiah had a lot of interesting things to say," Terry replied almost absently as he opened his cell phone to call Kenny.

It took several rings for his brother to answer, and when he finally did, he sounded groggy.

"This is my day off, Terry. The one day I get to sleep in a little."

"Don't give me that. You've got church."

"In two hours."

"Sorry, but I've got another set of numbers for you. It seems our guy has quoted Jeremiah again."

Terry heard a little background noise, suspecting his younger brother was stumbling out of bed to retrieve a writing utensil and paper.

"Go ahead."

Terry repeated the number sequence for his brother, who leafed through a book on the other end of the line. It took several minutes with Kenny grumbling inaudibly as he searched both the Bible and one of his modern translations.

"Basically Egypt is attacked and the soldiers, who fought for the pharaoh, turned and ran like pussies because they didn't have God in their hearts, so they didn't have inspiration to fight. Sounds like those who did stay and fight got slaughtered. That's it in a nutshell."

"Thanks, Ken. You going back to bed?"

"Not now. Might as well cook breakfast and get ready for church. Where are you anyway?"

"Little town called Brockport. Nice little four hour drive if you care to join me."

"I'll pass," Kenny replied with a yawn. "Catch this guy so I can get some sleep, will you?"

Terry chuckled briefly.

"I'll see what I can do. See you later."

"Bye, Terry."

Closing his phone, Terry turned from the bloody symbol to the body, still strung up like a deer during hunting season in someone's yard. The police had provided the courtesy of blocking the view with several tall screens so the guests didn't have to live with the horror of seeing the corpse. Only two sides required the barricade since no one was allowed to enter or leave the property until local authorities decided to let them.

"What kind of cooperation are we getting?" Terry asked, leaning so only Gosser heard him.

"They've been great. They contacted our office right away when they found the blood on the tree. I talked you up, so they'll probably be asking for your fearless leadership when they get done with the interviews."

Terry smirked.

"You're getting back at me for last month, aren't you?"

Gosser feigned surprise.

"I have no idea what you're talking about."

"My wife and I haven't removed you from the Christmas card list yet, Randy. I'm still hoping we can resolve this friendship issue between us."

Finally showing his sense of humor, Gosser played along.

"See this?" he asked, putting up both hands with fingers outstretched and palms facing toward Terry. "This is the wall you've built between us with your negative comments about my character."

"Oh, I was attacking your character?" Terry asked, crouching down close to the body for a closer look as the technicians signaled it was okay.

He saw one large bare spot along the ground where they had literally dug up the grass, roots, dirt and all, because blood and potential trace evidence would have collected in that single patch. Of course they had scoured the rest of the grounds for trace evidence and footprints, coming up empty on the latter thus far.

Bland, foot-sized indentations came from the road with an identical set beside them leading the other way out.

Terry started at the head, seeing where the throat was cut, almost cautiously as though the killer didn't want blood spewing everywhere. The cut was expertly placed along the carotid artery, though barely deep enough to be noticed if the blood were wiped clean along the neck. Because more than a square foot of the sod had been removed from the homicide area, Terry suspected a fairly large pool of blood dripped from Merrill. If that were true, it meant the man's heart hadn't stopped beating before his throat was cut. If Merrill was fortunate, he lost consciousness before the blade slid across his neck and never woke.

Merrill hung by his right foot, gently swinging as the sun's orange and purple fingers crept toward the motel. His eyes remained closed, which indicated he likely had lost consciousness before his actual demise. Along with his arms, his tie dangled toward the ground, giving Terry the impression he might reach out at any given moment. If not for the purplish hue of his fingers and face where blood had pooled in the five hours since his death, he might have simply appeared unconscious.

Terry stood, finding defecation along the front and back of the crotch that came from the release of bowel and bladder contents upon death.

The odor lingered close to the body, dissipating as the morning breeze carried it further away.

"You really think I'd attack your character?" Terry asked Gosser, looking for any signs of struggle along Merrill's waistline and pants.

"You're a curious sort, Trooper Levine. I never really know how to take you."

"I'm just looking out for your best interests, believe me."

Gosser narrowed his eyes a bit in suspicion.

"I had parents for that. How I turned out was my own doing. And I certainly hope you're not listening to speculation about my private life."

Now Terry was intrigued. He heard rumblings about Gosser's life outside of work, though he never put much stock in them. Perhaps the detective's defensiveness meant his closet held some skeletons.

"Your private life is your own, Randy. I don't listen to what people say."

"But they *do* talk."

"Maybe, but why dwell on it?"

Gosser looked to the tree, then returned his gaze to the body instead of meeting Terry's eyes. Perhaps it bothered him that his own people talked about him to complete strangers, which really wasn't the case.

"Anything I heard wasn't directed toward me," he stated, hoping to alleviate the detective's fears. "You know our departments are rumor mills sometimes. People say things on coffee breaks or just outside the station."

"Still, it bothers me that people are so quick to judge."

Terry wondered why the man felt so self-conscious. Being alienated from colleagues happened to officers in every department, but Gosser acted as though they had some kind of damning leverage against him.

"What matters is what we're doing here, Randy. We're a step away from catching this guy and that's a major feather in your cap when we do."

One of the technicians wandered in their vicinity, so Terry waited until he passed to continue.

"I'm not the most liked guy in NYSP, you know. People think I get all kinds of perks because the ADS trained me back in the day. Truth be told, I get shit on, catching cases like these. When I was young I didn't mind the travel, or even the long hours, but now I have my oldest starting to college. It sucks not spending more time with her, but this is what we do. When those other guys are talking shit about you over a beer and getting off the road early to do a traffic report or two, you and I are up to our knees in puke, shit, and blood. Not every cop can handle that, you know."

Gosser sucked in a deep breath, holding it in his chest a moment as he stood and straightened his back.

"So what you're basically saying is we're fucked up but we're good at what we do?"

"In a nutshell. Don't sweat the small stuff, brother. Gaffney thinks you do a fantastic job and that's all that matters. Those other pricks don't want your job anyway."

Ordinarily Terry would have been all business on a crime scene, saving the small talk for later, but Gosser needed a boost. Besides, the scenes all turned out the same when the Sin Killer was involved. No witnesses, no footprints, no DNA, no trace evidence, no surveillance footage.

No nothing.

Terry's eyes went up the wrinkled pant legs of the victim toward the penny loafers, which surprisingly remained on Merrill's feet. He doubted the man had a clue he was about to die when he stepped onto the grassy yard. The Sin Killer planned everything so carefully, so perfectly, that his victims had no idea when their ends were near.

Again Terry wondered if a man on the lam could carry out such perfection. Then again, Swanson proved very efficient at eluding the authorities in multiple states, possibly even countries, for the better part of two weeks. Perhaps his master plan was worked out with victims, locations, and a stash of money that allowed him to carry it out until fruition.

Weighing Swanson's rent versus his income left Terry with the impression the man had enough money for some groceries and utilities, but little beyond that. Unless he worked at some under the table profession that paid him extra, it seemed unlikely Swanson had much money saved back.

"What about this poor sap's wallet?" Terry asked Gosser, who motioned for one of the technicians to join them.

Gosser repeated the inquiry to the young man.

"Found it on the ground, partially covered in blood," the technician answered. "Had no money in it, but the credit cards and ID were there."

"No money in it," Gosser repeated to Terry. "Maybe our guy is running low on cash."

"Could be. He hasn't been one to touch wallets and belongings before."

"Desperation," Gosser said, flashing a smile.

Terry wished he could share the detective's overconfidence that they were mere days, hours, or minutes away from catching Daryl Swanson, but the man was accustomed to life on the run. Terry found it exceptionally strange that the killer wasn't breaking his usual pattern of murder and messages. If he wanted a clean break without being noticed, Swanson might be better suited to kill without leaving messages or any similarities to the previous murders, Terry figured.

He spent the next few minutes circling the body, looking for more evidence. Kneeling down, Terry examined the victim's full head of hair, finding it rather disheveled, guessing the man kept it parted. Perhaps the killer pulled on Merrill's hair for easy access to the throat when the man was unconscious, or pulled the head back to expose the neck for strangulation. Either way, the killer definitely appeared more comfortable with intimate kills, tossing aside the ritual of simply gunning people down.

"So you're the famous Terry Levine?" a female voice asked behind Terry, causing him to turn and rise at the same time.

He found an attractive woman standing beside Gosser with a gun on her hip, dressed in a rather nice blouse and slacks for the early hour.

"Terry, this is Yvonne Jamison. She's with the Monroe County Sheriff's Office."

"Pleasure to meet you," Terry said, shaking her hand, maintaining his professional nature, despite her attractiveness.

Her black, straight hair glistened in the morning sun, reminding him of actresses who portrayed Egyptian women in various movies over the years. Though her skin had no olive tint about it, Yvonne possessed a bronze tan that lasted well after the New York summer weather had diminished.

"I've heard lots about you," she informed him. "I'm surprised you haven't nailed this guy yet."

"He hasn't been very cooperative, as Detective Gosser can attest."

"Sounds that way. The technicians said they found some hair fibers in the grassy area they dug up. Maybe we'll get a break."

Doubtful, Terry thought. He imagined the hair fibers belonged to the victim, based on his find a few minutes prior.

"I can make sure they rush the results when you send them to the state lab," Terry offered.

"Thanks."

"Any luck with the guests?"

Yvonne gave a helpless shrug.

"No one saw or heard anything. Most of them were roomed on the opposite side of the building to cut utilities. The owner showed up, but didn't have much to add. I'm sure Detective Gosser told you the security cameras were a bust."

Terry nodded.

"What did the owner say about tapes from previous days?"

"They keep them for two weeks before reusing them. We're going through them, but the tapes aren't in the best shape and the owner was apparently too cheap to go with discs or a computer hard drive."

"Pakistani," Gosser commented sourly. "They own half this country, but run their businesses on fucking shoestring budgets."

He quickly looked to Yvonne after making the statement.

"Pardon my French."

Yvonne raised an eyebrow, as though stating his language was nothing new to her. Perhaps she didn't like the detective's take on foreign business owners, but she provided no reply.

"Two weeks is about the time Swanson has been on the run," Terry pondered aloud, quickly refocusing on their reason for being there. "If he's on one of those tapes, that's even more damning."

"We have the suspect's photo," Yvonne said. "We'll know if he put in an appearance."

Once again Terry found himself in a holding pattern, wondering when the next clue might surface to prod him along. Waiting for the Sin Killer to make a fatal mistake felt like dog years passing slowly, miserably.

Naturally the police would check local gas stations, teller machines, and anywhere else that might have video footage or potential witnesses.

Terry expected them to turn up nothing as before, though he refused to completely give up hope. Looking to the body of Lou Merrill once more, he vowed to find the man responsible, regardless of how long it took. People made mistakes during their lives, mistakes which could be atoned. He wasn't about to let one man, a murderous vigilante at that, act as judge, jury, and executioner toward such redeemable human beings.

With his image plastered across the news, Swanson couldn't hide forever, especially if he planned to continue his murderous rampage. With the figurative noose tightening, he was bound to make a mistake somewhere.

Soon.

Terry wanted to be the one to interview him. He wanted Taggart with him, partly because he promised the former sheriff that honor, but also because he considered Gosser too much of a hothead to be effective during a long-term interrogation.

His one wish before year's end was to have the Sin Killer in custody with a complete confession so his life could return to normal. Investigations around Canton typically involved simple crimes like burglaries, white-collar theft, and the occasional robbery. Terry wanted to get back to his routine, and the sooner, the better.

CHAPTER 31

Wednesday, October 15
Buffalo, New York

Terry hated the idea of staying in Buffalo again, but this time his presence wasn't required. With Duggan's blessing, he remained a few days to finish paperwork, interview more witnesses, and assist several local departments in wrapping up their contributions for the Sin Killer task force.

He currently found himself seated across from Ben Belinski after the reporter turned writer finished a morning segment in which he profiled the Sin Killer in more detail than before. Terry consulted with Gaffney, finally telling the sheriff he knew Belinski was his nephew, and that the secret was between only them. Relief swept over both of them as a result of the conversation, then Terry helped Belinski mold a television segment that revealed pertinent information to help catch Swanson without giving away key details about the investigation.

"Is it all you hoped it would be?" Terry asked the reporter after ordering a BLT on wheat with potato salad at a local café.

"What's that?" Belinski returned.

"Writing a book on the Sin Killer."

Belinski gave a sheepish smile when he heard the name he himself dubbed the killer.

"I guess the final chapter hasn't been written. Hard to say if anyone will even pick it up when it's all said and done. Maybe it won't have true closure, like Swanson washes up under a pier somewhere."

"That just deepens the intrigue."

Belinski took a thoughtful sip from his Diet Coke.

"I am glad you came clean with my uncle about our arrangement. Maybe we'll speak again by Christmas."

"Truth be told, your broadcasts have really helped."

Belinski didn't appear convinced.

"You haven't caught him yet."

"But we're getting some fairly good tips. We've had Swanson sightings in Vermont and New York."

"No Canada?"

"Not yet. Makes me think he didn't get the documentation he needed to cross the border."

Belinski thought momentarily again.

"It's weird that he went through the trouble of having someone forge new identities and never picked them up. It's almost like he played that guy to take the fall."

"Or mislead us," Terry suggested half-heartedly.

The thought certainly crossed his mind when the task force rushed to contact officials from Canada and surrounding states. Considering Swanson migrated from Montana to New York, there was apparently no limit to his travels. Perhaps the reporter deduced correctly that the Sin Killer might never be caught, or he might die without fanfare like the other suspect in Montana.

Terry also wondered if Taggart felt certain no foul play was involved in the other suspect's death. Taggart said as much when asked, but his personal tragedy kept him from digging for the truth any further. If Swanson orchestrated the other suspect's death to remove suspicion from himself, he truly was more of a mastermind than Terry figured when he searched the man's apartment.

Thinking of the apartment reminded him of something he wanted to give Belinski.

"An early Christmas present," he told the reporter, sliding an encased disc across the table.

"What's this?"

"It's a collection of images that aren't from the case files that should complete your book."

A smile crossed the reporter's face.

"Thanks."

"Thank me when you get the book done, though not *in* the book, please. And don't be using those or showing them to anyone before then."

"Scout's honor."

"You don't strike me as the scout type. And if you break that promise you'll be in the doghouse with me worse than your uncle."

Belinski held up his hands defensively.

"I've learned my lesson."

Their waitress arrived with their food at the very moment Terry's cell phone rang. He looked at the phone screen, recognizing the entry as that of the state police lab from Albany.

"I've got to take this," Terry said, standing to step outside where he could hear without multiple conversations buzzing in his free ear.

He opened the phone as the café door closed behind him. Noontime traffic passed with a peaceful hum as he answered.

"Levine."

"Terry, this is Chrissy Davis at the lab."

Though they had never actually met, Terry and Chrissy had a working phone relationship from his investigations and her analysis skills in the state police lab over the years.

"Hi, Chrissy. I hope you have some good news for me."

"Actually, I have some news you've probably been dying to hear. One of the hair samples found in the blood beneath your motel victim matches a sample you sent us from the apartment."

Terry felt a tingle of jubilation run from the bottom of his spine to his neck. Though it wasn't absolutely conclusive that the hair fibers removed from the apartment belonged to Swanson, the samples Taggart and Lynn Stover had from Montana would surely seal the deal. The pieces finally seemed to be falling into place, figuratively cornering Swanson into a confession when he found himself in shackles.

"That's great news, Chrissy," Terry said, trying to keep a steady voice. "Anything else turn up?"

"There were some microscopic fibers in the victim's fingernails. He might have grabbed his assailant's clothing. We're still trying to determine what they're from, but they're black, so probably a sweatshirt or coat of some kind."

"Very promising."

"Promising, indeed. I know you wanted the DNA match the most, so we got right to it. We should have the rest sorted out within a week."

"Thank you very much for the update and getting to it so quickly."

"You're welcome. Hope you catch this guy, Terry."

"Me, too."

Terry shut his phone before heading inside to his table where Belinski twirled his fork to ensnare some of his chicken fettuccine Alfredo before taking a bite.

"You look happy," the reporter observed, still chewing.

"That was some good news for a change."

"Anything you can share?" Belinski asked, his bright blue eyes widening with a glimmer of anticipation.

"Off the record, let's just say your book may have the ending you're looking for."

CHAPTER 32

Saturday, November 29

Wales, New York

Gary Collins, Jr. felt the sting of the cold autumn wind on his face while conducting a motorcycle escort for the funeral of a former Erie County sheriff who had passed away on Tuesday. The procession left the Tucker Funeral Home in East Aurora, traveling southeast toward Holmes Hill Cemetery near the town of Wales shortly after one in the afternoon. Not an extensive drive in a standard vehicle, the slow-moving procession proved somewhat torturous along the winding county roads on a motorcycle.

A deputy with the Erie County Sheriff's Department, Collins and another deputy led the procession with their Harley-Davidson motorcycles. Several marked and unmarked police vehicles followed the Hearse, but Collins maintained the lead as various police agencies blocked intersections and streets for the motorcade's benefit.

After removing his helmet, he stood behind a group of officers as the prayer and a fairly lengthy eulogy transpired. Several key figures praised the efforts of the deceased former sheriff, though most of them sounded exaggerated to the deputy. Gaffney spoke briefly about the man he openly admitted he met only a few times during the course of his career since the deceased was long since retired.

Collins respected the fact that the former sheriff lived to the age of ninety-four, outliving his wife by almost fifteen years. A tombstone shared their names for years before he finally joined her in the vacant plot beside hers. Now completely etched with their names and information, the tombstone looked complete. Collins watched the entire procession with some apathy, mainly because he never knew, or met the deceased. Families typically decided most of the honors to be bestowed upon their loved ones at police funerals. Apparently this family declined the bells and whistles, because there was no gun salute, no bagpipes, no flag ceremony, and very little other fanfare after the eulogy.

Not until he watched the casket being lowered into the ground, beside that of the man's wife, did Collins begin to get emotional. Now forty-five years old, and married almost twenty-five of those years, he found some disturbing visions creeping into his head if he were ever killed in the line of duty. So final, he thought, being lowered into the damp, cold earth with nothing but earthworms and decay in the future.

His kids were grown, the youngest starting college, the oldest working as a medical assistant, and the middle child in and out of rehab for various drug and alcohol problems. Sure, he lived with a few regrets in life, some in marriage, and a few as a father, but he didn't feel life had passed him by without providing some rewards. He was an accomplished and respected officer within his department, particularly since he possessed the seventh highest seniority at the moment. During the course of three decades he worked on drug task forces, conducted investigations, rode in countless motorcycle escorts for everything from politicians to NFL team buses, and acted as police chief in nearby Akron for four years.

While his resume looked impressive, Collins sacrificed time at home working overtime and second jobs to provide his children with better lives than his own. He planned to retire at age fifty-five and devote much more of his time to Charlene, his wife. If nothing else, the funeral events provided him with reinforcement to carry out that plan.

Collins lingered a moment as the crowd dispersed, many of the gatherers bowing their heads as they headed toward their vehicles. He lowered his head as well, though partly because the brisk, cold wind made his cheeks tingle as though an invisible hand placed a layer of frost upon them.

"You coming?" the other motorcycle officer called, already donning his helmet.

"Go ahead, Bob. I'll see you later."

The man shrugged as he started his Harley.

Collins slowly made his way toward a large tree for shelter from the wind as he watched the grave diggers make their way toward the open plot to seal the casket for good. Maybe Collins felt mortal because he was a few pounds heavier and a bit slower, unable to manhandle suspects like he once had. He worked out, ran on the treadmill, and sometimes swam for an hour at the YMCA, but the years reminded him of human frailty with muscle aches and injuries. Still, he decided, he wasn't ready to go stick a foot in the open grave just yet.

He turned away from the plot and the dozens of tombstones lining the wheat-colored grass behind it. Collins stuffed his hands into the leather duty jacket that barely protected him from the bitterly cold elements. Even his leather riding gloves did little to keep his fingers from numbing.

Placing his helmet over his head, Collins was about to start the motorcycle when his cell phone vibrated inside his jacket pocket. He pulled it out, then opened it to reveal a strange text message that made him wince in confusion the first time he read it.

Be a hero. Look for the intruder at 5630 Shimerville Road.

Collins read the message a few more times, trying to make sense of it. He sighed, realizing Shimerville Road was miles outside of Buffalo, though within his jurisdiction. Already feeling miserable from the weather, he dreaded riding there to find an older couple sitting at home, sipping tea beside their fireplace, with him the butt of a practical joke. Upon further consideration, however, Collins selectively gave out his cell phone number. Only true friends and family members possessed the number, and none of them were cruel enough to send him out there for no reason.

The sender wasn't logged in his contacts, and though the number came from a local 716 area code, he didn't recognize the phone number. He started to call his dispatchers to send a unit to the house, then shut the phone instead. Despite all of his accolades, Collins had never been the one to talk down a crazed hostage taker, rescue a child from drowning, or even save a spouse during a domestic dispute. Some would call his career fortunate, or blessed, for being so dull, but Collins always wanted to accomplish something memorable.

Something they might write on his tombstone when they buried him six feet deep.

Besides, he had an idea who might have sent him the message, and he trusted that person implicitly. Collins saddled himself on the Harley before donning a black balaclava to shield his face from the cold since the need for formality had passed. He looked into the mirror to adjust his helmet, which covered his full head of brown hair. Beneath his nose Collins found his runny nose had formed miniature icicles along the bristly hairs of his thick mustache. He thought about grabbing a handkerchief from the saddlebags, then realized the problem would recur the minute he started riding.

Taking a deep breath, then sniffling back the snotty trickles reaching the edges of his nostrils, Collins aligned his helmet, started the bike, then left the cemetery with very few cars left to slow his departure.

***

Collins tried picturing a house to match the address from the text message the entire ride from the cemetery to Shimerville Road. Once on the road, he recalled several new housing projects occurring down the road for upscale homes. He began seriously doubting the validity of the message, even as he spotted the house about half a mile ahead on his right.

"Wow," he muttered through slightly chattering teeth as he examined the house and the three-car garage sitting caddy corner to it from afar.

Several snowflakes fell from the sky during the lengthy ride to remind him of how cold the weather had turned the past week. He knew rest and relaxation might save him from coming down with a cold or the flu, but even that felt like a long shot remedy at this point. Collins simply wanted to know the truth behind the mysterious message then be on his way.

Reaching the driveway, he parked the motorcycle just off the road, opting to walk almost one-hundred yards to the house. He pulled a handkerchief from his jacket pocket, blew his nose, then wiped his nostrils before replacing the cloth as he walked. The concrete felt exceptionally hard beneath his shined motorcycle boots, which clopped slightly with every step.

Collins stared at the house windows, half expecting someone to peer back at him, possibly wondering why a deputy was approaching the house on foot, like some thief in the night. No eyes ever met his, so he examined the front door, then the back door, finding them both intact. Shaking his head, irritated that his trip was for nothing, he walked to the garage where he peered through one of the five windows along the building's sides.

His caramel brown eyes reflected off the glass, forcing him to remove his helmet and put his nose directly against the glass to see inside. He saw a brand new, top of the line red Dodge truck sitting inside beside a silver Cadillac. While those two items fit perfectly with the residence and property, the 1986 Chevy Impala with faded blue paint and several large scratches did not. Collins remembered a similar vehicle description in the search for Daryl Swanson, the murder suspect who skipped town a few months prior.

While the other two vehicles were carefully backed into the garage for an easy exit, the Impala appeared hastily driven directly inside. A thought struck Collins as he stepped around the back of the garage, finding exactly what he expected. Stowed only inches from the garage walls were two four-wheelers that probably belonged in the garage. Swallowing hard, Collins leaned toward his radio microphone, requesting two more units be dispatched to the address without lights and sirens.

Stepping around the garage toward the back door as quietly as he could, Collins drew his service weapon before trying the doorknob. Finding it locked, he hugged the side of the house, creeping beneath windows as he made his way toward the front. He found that door locked as well, frowning as he pondered his next move. Thanks to his father, he carried a small loaded punch used to puncture car windows for the purpose of removing them. Typically used by firefighters in rescue operations, Collins kept one for that among other reasons.

Returning to the rear door, he pulled the punch from a small pouch on his gun belt after replacing the firearm. He set his helmet on the ground to prevent his vision or hearing from being compromised once he stepped inside. The storm door opened, providing him access to the metal door that contained multiple stained glass window panes. Choosing the pane closest to the lock, Collins touched the punch against the glass, gently touching his other gloved hand against it to prevent it from noisily shattering. As the punch's pointed end created a spider web in the glass it barely made a sound. Collins was able to control the glass as he brushed it inside, reaching inside to turn the deadbolt and lock.

"Oops," he said under his breath. "Looks like a burglary in progress."

Quietly opening the door, he stepped inside then closed it behind him while cautiously examining his surroundings. Drawing his firearm for the second time, he listened for any indications an intruder was on to him. For all he knew, the man might be lying in wait behind a wall, or inside a closet. If he believed for a second the owners of the house were home and safe, he simply would have knocked, but every warning signal his veteran instincts had acquired went off inside his mind.

He immediately spied a security system, which was powered, though not activated. Rural residents didn't leave keys under their doors as they once had, and they typically left their security systems active most of the time.

Considering every vehicle was accounted for, Collins feared the worst. A potential hostage situation was a best case scenario, the home owners being dead and stuffed inside a freezer seemed more likely. Collins checked the kitchen, living room, and common areas along the ground floor rather efficiently. Only the kitchen showed signs of items out of place. A few empty containers and dirty dishes sat on the counter beside the sink. Collins found several family pictures sitting atop the base of a secretary, taking a moment to stare at an image of a couple who appeared just old enough to have the three young grandchildren pictured with them in a nearby framed photograph.

He found a basement door, deciding not to search the downstairs for the time being because escape wasn't going to be easy for anyone hiding below. Collins quietly placed a kitchen chair beneath the doorknob to prevent anyone from backtracking upstairs behind him, then headed toward the access to the second floor.

Dark thoughts crept into the deputy's head as he looked up the carpeted stairway leading to the second story. For some reason he envisioned the older couple, throats slit from ear to ear, lying atop their bed, hands cupped along their stomachs, as though posed for a mortuary showing. Holding his gun in a ready position before him, he stepped sideways up the stairs like a fiddler crab, foot over foot with each step. His nose started running again but he ignored it, keeping his eyes focused on the landing above, waiting for someone to rush out, guns blazing, to keep from being arrested.

Collins heard his leather jacket creak with each movement, though the carpet muffled his steps. With the rest of the house silent, except for the furnace which had just kicked on, each noise might as well have been the trampling of an elephant to an officer trying to sneak up on a fugitive. He didn't have to walk this dangerous path alone with backup only miles away. In minutes, two or three deputies were sure to show up with guns drawn, prepared for the worst.

Though he liked the idea of being the hero for a change, Collins decided to place his life on the line for a more important reason. He didn't want to risk a hostage situation with a possible serial killer, and he didn't want one of his own people getting hurt, or firing unnecessarily at the suspect, if any suspect was indeed present.

Figuring out a way to explain this entire mess, including the anonymous text message, eluded Collins at the moment, so he needed to answer the most basic of questions before proceeding further.

Was there indeed an intruder at this house or were the clues out back red herrings?

He honestly couldn't believe his own impulsive actions, first traveling to the house based on a text message, then actually breaking into the house without the benefit of facts. It felt right, which explained why he found himself creeping up the stairs like a snake stalking an unseen rodent, not knowing if that rodent might actually be an eagle waiting to strike him from above and make him the prey.

Reaching the landing, he peered into the bedroom immediately to his right, finding an empty, made bed and two closets. He checked the room quickly and silently, including the empty space beneath the bed. Now running out of rooms to check, Collins found a new urgency to hurry his search because if someone was in the house, he was going to fight or run once he spied the deputy or the motorcycle outside.

Collins treaded lightly in the guest bathroom beside the bedroom, finding no one behind the shower curtain, so he moved to the next of the two remaining large bedrooms. There, he found a surprise that was both unexpected and most welcome. Taking an afternoon nap on a queen-size bed, like Goldie Locks intruding on the Three Bears, Daryl Swanson was unaware of the deputy training a gun on him. Collins stepped into the room, finding no one else around, keeping a safe distance between himself and the scruffy-looking suspect as he looked for readily visible weapons.

Feeling certain Swanson had no firearms within arm's reach, Collins finally barked a command that jolted the fugitive awake.

"Sheriff's Department! Hands in the air! Keep them where I can see them!"

After being startled, Swanson complied immediately and without hesitation as he blinked feverishly, trying to get a bearing on his surroundings. He remained upright, on his knees, refusing to move from the bed until ordered to do so. Collins kept the gun pointed at him, snatching his handcuffs with his left hand from their leather case. He ordered Swanson onto the floor, cuffed him behind his back, then patted him down from head to toe, all while reading the man his Miranda rights.

"Is there anyone else in the house?" Collins asked once he finished.

"No."

"What about the owners?"

"They're in Florida."

Collins heard the back door open downstairs. His fellow deputies joined him momentarily in the guest bedroom with rather surprised stares. He requested they check the last bedroom thoroughly as he waited with Swanson, who said nothing, as though determined to wait for his court-appointed lawyer. Collins checked under the bed and inside the two closets without letting Swanson out of his sight, before yanking the man to his feet by grabbing his arm.

"I know some people who want to talk to you in a bad way."

CHAPTER 33

Randy Gosser was enjoying his afternoon for two reasons. One, he had the weekend off, and two, he thought he might have found the perfect companion. Not only did she hold down a steady career as a nurse, but she shared many of his likes and fantasies in the bedroom. Though she was vehemently against them conducting an emergency room fantasy, she opposed very little else.

Gosser found himself crying out as the short tentacles of a customized whip cracked against his back once again. Atop his own bed on all fours, dressed only in his underwear, he saw Janice in the corner of his apartment bedroom, sadistic smirk and all, poised to strike again. Older than Gosser by two years, she knew what she wanted after experiencing her own bad marriage. He typically dated younger women, which he now realized might have inadvertently led to his displeasure in the bedroom.

Dark-haired and wicked in her own way, Janice DuBois healed people by day, then picked Gosser apart by night with any number of devises.

But he loved it.

"You've been naughty," Janice said, her voice a smoky purr as she dangled the whip in front of her. "It's time for you to learn a lesson."

"No, please," Gosser said, because she preferred it when he begged for mercy, even though the painful lashes across his back were virtually orgasmic to him.

"You can't escape punishment."

Gosser tensed as the whip crossed his back again, on purpose this time because it brought even more pain, more intensity, than if he relaxed. Their bedroom games, foreplay to some, were the highlight of the experience for him. Gosser felt like he could carry on all afternoon with Janice, order in for dinner, and start with a different fantasy by early evening.

His apartment wasn't conducive to carrying out these kinds of games. Ideally he would buy a house and have one room, or the basement, set up with gadgets and toys so he could give the appearance of an everyday guy while harboring a secret area within the house. Because of child support, however, he barely found himself able to afford the apartment some months, bound by contract to never alter its appearance.

Once opposed to using computers and the internet, Gosser now found himself thankful for its existence. He found Janice through a website chat room created specifically for people like them. With two grown children of her own in their early college years, she found herself free to carry out more of her own hobbies and pastimes.

Strangely, despite the borderline violent nature of their bedroom activities, Janice cared for him vehemently before and after such acts. They talked, finding things in common, and she had urged him to quit smoking without nagging about it. For the sake of his daughter, he wanted to quit, but the stresses of his job kept reeling him like a hooked trout.

Feeling the welts across his back stinging, he anticipated the next crack of the whip when his cell phone rang beside the bed. He wanted to ignore it in the worst way and remain in his pretend world, but the siren ring tone indicated work was calling him for some reason. Other detectives worked the weekends, which meant the call was high priority for him to be summoned, possibly even related to the Sin Killer.

"I have to take this," he said, purposely changing his demeanor so Janice knew he wasn't acting.

She said nothing, though she didn't appear pleased.

"Gosser," he answered.

"Randy, we've got him," the familiar voice of Dave Stephens, another Erie County detective, informed him.

"Got who?"

"Your suspect. The Sin Killer."

"You're shitting me."

"I wouldn't. You're my favorite turd."

"How?"

"Collins got a tip and found him camped out at some house in the county."

Collins and Gosser mixed about like oil and water as far as their backgrounds and lifestyles, but Gaffney didn't place either on a higher pedestal because they both provided him with good press through their individual endeavors.

Gosser began snatching clothes from a nearby chair as he prepared for the inevitable journey to downtown Buffalo. A shower would have felt good to wash off the sweat, and clean the bruises along his back, but Gosser suspected his entire weekend was about to take place inside a small, drab room unless Swanson played the public defender card immediately. He wanted that information before he spoke with Terry Levine. If Swanson was unwilling to speak to authorities, it made little sense for the trooper to risk life and limb rushing to Buffalo.

"What has Swanson said?" Gosser asked.

"Nothing much. He's proclaiming innocence on the murders. Seems willing to talk."

"We'll see about that. I can be there in fifteen minutes, Dave. Don't let Swanson speak to anyone else."

"You got it. Want me to call the sheriff?"

"Please do. I've got my own people to call. I'm sure Gaffney will want to call a press conference."

Gosser hung up, then finished getting dressed, snagging a tie to throw over his lightly wrinkled dress shirt. He didn't plan on any television appearances, since the prisoner wasn't going to be transported anytime soon. Gosser always hated clips of him leading handcuffed prisoners on news segments because he always looked like an angry cop. Maybe he perceived his three seconds of television time differently than some people, but he never felt comfortable with his image.

"Leaving so soon?" Janice inquired as she put down the whip.

"They caught my serial killer."

Her expression changed to moderate surprise.

"Sorry," Gosser added quickly, approaching her to plant a quick kiss on her lips.

Their relationship wasn't built on outward affection, though she accepted the kiss rather well. Checking over his clothing, finding everything in place, Gosser snagged his shoulder holster and gun from a nearby chair before strapping them on.

"I'll be working overtime at the hospital tomorrow if you need me."

"I'll need you," he promised with a sinister grin. "Maybe we can find an empty room there and-"

"No," she said firmly. "Not at work, and no medical fantasies. I don't ask for cop and robber stuff, do I?"

Gosser kissed her again.

"No, you don't. I've got to go, but I want to see you soon."

"You know where to find me. I can show myself out."

"Okay."

With that, Gosser opted to grab a black leather jacket from his coat rack instead of a sport coat. The weather had turned bitterly cold in the overnight while temperatures continued to plummet. Gosser gave Janice one last look, followed by a quick nod before shutting the apartment door behind him. Two weeks into their relationship, he found himself unable to utter the three words that sucked men into relationships like a black hole. Truth be told, he didn't feel that way.

Not yet.

His relationship with Janice felt right, possibly because it remained purely physical. He wasn't ready to explain any new developments to his daughter just yet, or watch the wheels of the rumor mill churn at work. No, at this moment, he was ready to close the Sin Killer case and put it to rest. Plucking his cell phone from his side, Gosser found Terry Levine's name in his phone list and punched the send button.

***

Terry found himself in Buffalo sooner than usual because Duggan arranged for aerial transport with state police helicopters to Syracuse. From there, Gaffney sent Captain Jim Covington from the Erie County Sheriff's Department to fly him the remainder of the way. While en route,

Terry phoned Lynn Stover in Montana to make certain Taggart caught the next available flight to Buffalo.

Unwilling to break a promise to the former sheriff, Terry wanted to see how Swanson reacted when he laid eyes on Taggart. He requested that Gosser let Swanson stew in his juices for awhile as everyone made their way to Buffalo. He hoped and prayed Gosser didn't fly off the handle and begin the interrogation himself. If Swanson clammed up and demanded a lawyer, the investigators would consult with the district attorney and march toward a court date with what evidence they possessed.

If Swanson believed a window existed to explain his way to innocence, he might talk, and he might provide them with more ammunition to use against him in court. Terry considered interviewing suspects his greatest weakness, but he knew exactly how he wanted to approach Swanson. He didn't really *need* anything from the man, which made the process so much easier. Avoiding the cat and mouse game of prodding and pulling for information wasn't necessary, which meant Swanson controlled his own fate through his level of cooperation.

One thing going Swanson's way was that the older couple who owned the house where he stowed away was indeed alive and well in Florida where they had been since the beginning of October. It seemed their son worked at Erie Wholesale with Swanson, and might have inadvertently disclosed his parents' winter plans to Swanson at some point.

What Terry found difficult to believe was how Swanson came to be apprehended. Gosser spoke with the officer who located the fugitive, learning that one of the deputy's former informants came through for him with an unexpected text message. All along, Terry expected an anonymous phone call from someone spotting Swanson at a gas station a state or two away. Discovering him in Erie County expedited the prosecution process, making the lives of the task force members easier.

Saying little during the flight, Terry watched treetops and highways pass below him with little interest. His mind remained steadfast on Swanson and how he wanted to conduct the interview. When the gray and limestone colors of the city came into view, he felt a slight tingle of excitement. He finally saw Niagara Falls in the distance, feeling almost at home as the blue water of the Niagara River rushed with magnificent force, creating white foam along the surface. It looked nothing like the sedentary green algae that formed in swamps in ponds in his home area, creating a stink for those who lived nearby.

"You ready for this?" Covington asked, his voice deep and soothing, perfect for narrating Old West documentaries if he ever wanted to change careers.

"I've been ready," Terry answered from the chopper's rear seat since Covington's copilot occupied the other seat up front. "It's time to give seven families some closure."

"My brother found the first victim back in April, you know."

"I remember reading that in the report. He probably didn't expect it to lead to all of this, did he?"

"Doubt it," Covington replied, preparing to touch down in a field within driving distance of the municipal offices.

Terry spotted a car parked in a driving lane, suspecting Gosser or Gaffney had arranged for someone to drive him the remainder of the trip. He doubted they were going to be as excited about picking up Taggart, but he absolutely wanted the former sheriff present.

It took about a minute for Covington to land the helicopter on the frosted grass, then open the door for Terry to exit.

"Thanks, Jim," Terry virtually yelled so the rotors didn't drown him out. "Take care of yourself."

"You, too. Good luck closing the case."

Terry gave a quick wave before walking over to the marked police car, finding a uniformed deputy inside. He slid into the passenger's seat, ready to begin the process of putting Swanson behind bars for good.

✳✳✳

Instead of conducting the interview downtown, Gosser and Gaffney decided it might be better to keep the press at bay until they finished with Swanson. Recently completed, the Erie County Public Safety Campus served several agencies with dispatchers, evidence and property storage, as well as a forensic analysis lab. It also housed administrators and detectives, including Gosser, on the second floor.

More importantly, the Campus could only be accessed through one sliding gate that required a swipe card. Any number of local police officers from several agencies possessed such cards, but members of the press did not.

When Terry finally saw Gosser in the hallway outside of the interview room, the two investigators shook hands, sharing smiles for the first time in months. Several other detectives and deputies were inside the building, some for security reasons and others simply because they wanted to say they were there when the infamous Sin Killer was humbled. The building was abuzz with cops, while reporters lined up outside the gate to scoop one another with the breaking news Gaffney was about to provide them.

"Finally," Terry said, patting Gosser on the back as the investigator turned toward the room, causing him to yelp in pain. "You okay?"

"I'm fine."

Terry had some genuine concern for his task force colleague, considering November wasn't typically a month for sunburns and Gosser didn't appear especially tan.

"You sure?"

"Yup," Gosser said with a tone that he didn't particularly want to elaborate further.

In his hand he grasped a green folder that Terry suspected held information and images from the crime scenes to help refresh Swanson's memory. Sometimes criminals gave themselves away if they grew excited from viewing the images of their heinous crimes.

Terry shot Gosser a quirky grin, deciding to let the issue of Gosser's pain go, though he began to suspect some of the rumors about the detective might hold water. He decided the timing was perfect to ask for the favor he needed.

"I need something before we get this party started, Randy."

"What's that?"

"One of your people to pick up Taggart at the airport again."

Gosser rolled his eyes with a barely audible sigh.

"You're bringing him here again? I think we have this covered."

"Would you rather have Swanson for seven confirmed murders, or say you caught a serial killer who crossed state lines and barbarically murdered at least eleven victims?"

Terry's words failed to move Gosser.

"I'm not saying I don't care, but can't we handle our end first and bring your buddy in later?"

"We have four families in Montana who need some closure, and that man will never walk right again because he carried out his duties as sheriff. The least we can do is give him the satisfaction of closing this out with us."

Gosser hung his head momentarily, evidently realizing the importance of having Taggart there.

"Fine. I'll get a deputy to pick him up at the airport."

"Good, because he's already on his way."

Gosser exhaled audibly.

"Have I ever mentioned I don't much care for you?" he asked, though breaking down with a weak smile as he did so.

"You've implied it, but this is the first time you've ever come clean with your feelings. It's invigorating, isn't it?"

"It will be when we get inside and get this asshole to confess to every last detail."

"Speaking of that, I don't want you charging him like a bull, Randy. He gets a lawyer and we're done. We both know it. I want him to proclaim his innocence and tell us all. Maybe that way we can get some kind of slipup out of him."

Nodding approvingly, Gosser's expression gave Terry the impression he wanted the case closed, no matter how it happened.

"Let's do this. I promise I won't go off the handle and stick a gun in his mouth."

Terry chuckled, because they both knew Gosser's approach wasn't quite that gruff.

"You take the lead and I'll be the fly on the wall taking notes," Gosser added, holding up a pad and pen.

"You don't have to act like a mime, but this is our one and only chance to wear him down. Look at it as a marathon, not a sprint."

"I get it. This isn't my first rodeo."

Terry placed his hands on Gosser's shoulders, looking him squarely in the eyes.

"I'm sorry. Just been dwelling on the whole thing. Let's go have a chat with Mr. Swanson."

Swanson, who had been shuffled between a holding area at the nearby jail and two different interview rooms at the Campus, looked worn down when the two investigators stepped into the room. Terry immediately recognized that this man was no Kevin Alan Kimmerling. No arrogance appeared in his eyes, no all-knowing smile crossed his lips. Perhaps the man felt some relief from not living on the road, hiding out while assuming new identities to evade the law.

Terry knew Swanson received his Miranda rights from Collins, so he felt no need to read them again, though he wanted to make certain the prisoner understood his position.

"You know why you're here and not in jail, right, Daryl?"

Swanson nodded sourly.

"If it were as simple as breaking and entering, we wouldn't have much to say to you. You also understand that you have a right to an attorney, correct?"

Again he nodded.

"I want you to understand that we have every reason to believe that you've murdered seven people here in New York, and another four back in Montana."

"I ain't done no such thing," Swanson said, some of his Texas drawl still lingering in his voice from living there years prior.

"We have a hair sample from the last crime scene that says differently," Terry countered. "Your choices are simple, Daryl. You can come clean with us, tell us everything, and live out the remainder of your days behind bars. The alternative is lethal injection back in Montana with the families of all your victims watching you breathe your last."

Swanson buried his head in his hands.

"I didn't do it. None of it."

Terry looked to Gosser.

"Maybe we're done here."

"What?" Swanson asked, exasperated. "I can't confess if I didn't do it. I don't know what you think you have on me, but I haven't done a thing."

Gosser stepped forward, giving Terry a nod that indicated he wouldn't overstep his bounds.

"So we're supposed to believe you moved from Montana, where four homicides occurred, to New York, where *another* seven occurred, all in areas you easily had access to? Places your job took you to on the very day these people were murdered?"

Swanson said nothing, simply holding his head in his hands as though his world had crumbled to the ground around him.

"A moment?" Terry asked, leading Gosser to the hallway.

"What's wrong?" Gosser asked, thinking he had acted inappropriately, once they closed the door behind them.

"Nothing. I just want to see how he reacts before we continue."

Terry led the way to a nearby room where the closed-circuit from the interview room's video camera recorded their interrogation. A simple black and white monitor displayed a live feed, which Terry studied momentarily. Half a dozen investigators who had been watching the monitor, ready to provide feedback if inspiration struck them, stepped outside the room for Terry and Gosser. Terry welcomed their input, but this wasn't a case that hinged on breaking the suspect down to the point of a confession because the evidence was stacked against him.

Swanson wasn't gushing to confess, yet he wasn't offering a lineup of alibis either. Considering the man traveled alone for his job, it seemed doubtful eyewitnesses were about to step forward on his behalf. Besides, most of the murders had a wide window of opportunity, too large for Swanson to cover with an alibi here and there.

"Maybe it's time to hit him with everything we have," Terry thought aloud.

"Which is a hair sample if we're talking about hard evidence," Gosser added.

"When did you become Mr. Negativity?"

"About a year after starting this job, but in regards to this case, you said it yourself that it's mostly circumstantial. Surely he knows that."

Terry agreed, but even when a jury threw out ninety-five facts from a pool of one-hundred, there were still five facts that swayed them when they reached a verdict. Between those five theoretical facts and the hair sample, any jury was virtually obligated to find Swanson guilty of murder.

Looking back to the monitor, finding Swanson still wallowing in self-pity for getting caught, Terry decided to change tactics.

"Let's lay it out," he said, nodding toward the folder in Gosser's right hand. "See how he reacts."

When they returned to the room, Gosser flopped the file atop the table so the contents would spill toward Swanson. The man barely glanced at the crime scene photos, which Terry asked the detective to place on top of the stack, as though sickened.

"Don't tell me the sight of your handiwork bothers you," Gosser said before settling into a chair opposite the suspect, letting Terry take charge again.

"I've never seen this, *any* of this, before."

"We've checked with your employer," Terry stated. "You were dispatched to each town where these murders occurred on the day they occurred. When people were killed locally, you were either on short trips or had the day off. One of your hairs was recovered from the latest victim's blood in Brockport. A survivor, whose boyfriend you brutally murdered, reported the killer spoke with a drawl."

Swanson continued to shake his head as Terry spoke, denying everything without speaking a word. Terry shifted a few of the crime scene photos aside until he found one with a bloody symbol from one of the earlier crime scenes.

"Those were drawn by someone left-handed, Daryl. You *are* left-handed. You're a shoe size ten-and-a-half, which is what our technicians believe the imprints at the crime scenes are. After you were caught taking your catnap, our technicians went through your car and found several handguns and a survival knife. I'm betting they'll tell us something when we run some tests on them. Care to save us the trouble?"

"The only gun I own was in my locker at work. I don't own any other guns, or a knife."

Swanson appeared unsure of what else to say, possibly on the verge of breaking down and crying. He nervously licked his lips, then looked to Gosser, as though the quieter detective might have some saving grace for him.

"He's not your friend," Terry said. "There's no good cop, bad cop here. We both want the same thing from you."

Taking a moment to weigh his options, Swanson finally shook his head and spoke.

"I didn't do any of this. If you're not going to believe me, maybe it's time to get me a lawyer."

"You're not giving us anything to contradict the evidence," Gosser explained, much more kindly than Terry expected from the detective.

Gosser pulled a single sheet from the stack that showed a time line of the murders and Swanson's travels, parallel in every instance.

"There. That's you traveling to these towns on the days these people were murdered."

"I'm being framed," Swanson claimed, looking from the sheet to both investigators.

Terry shook his head, losing patience with the suspect.

"No more games, Daryl. You're not handcuffed to that table because we think you did a little B & E with some identity theft on the side. The only way you might be able to spare your life is to come clean with us."

"Okay," Gosser said, waving one hand airily a moment. "Just suppose for a minute someone went through the trouble of killing seven people here for the sole purpose of pinning it on you, what do you say about Montana?"

Swanson couldn't speak for a moment as tears welled in his eyes. Terry wondered if the man's world was finally closing in around himself like a feeder mouse constricted by a pet snake.

"The guy who killed those people died in a car wreck, but the sheriff wouldn't let me alone. That's why I left and started over."

"Then how would anyone here, in New York, know to pin anything on you?" Gosser asked, reaching the culmination of his original question.

Swanson swallowed hard, taking a few seconds to provide the answer.

"I might have said some things at work. Maybe to a few of the guys over some beers."

"So you were bragging that you were a murder suspect and one of them decided to become the next Ted Bundy and pin it on you?" Terry countered.

Gosser wasn't about to give him time to contemplate summoning an attorney.

"What about the fake identifications? If you're so innocent, why were you looking at getting out of town?"

"I saw one of the fliers you were handing out with my picture at a construction site when I stopped to get coffee one day. The foreman threw it in the trash right after your people gave it to him."

"I guess taxpayer dollars do get thrown away," Terry commented. "So you're saying *that* worried you, and not the seven bodies strewn across the state in towns where you had visited?"

"You can't say you didn't know anything about the murders," Gosser added for emphasis.

"I heard about some of them, but people get killed every day. Watching the news ain't one of my hobbies."

Swanson pushed the crime scene photos away from him.

"That's not me. You've got to believe me."

"We don't have to believe anything," Gosser replied sternly. "We have the evidence on our side."

"Then maybe it's time I see an attorney."

"Maybe it is."

CHAPTER 34

Saturday, November 29
Buffalo, New York

Hours dragged on as the court-appointed attorney met with the investigators at Gosser's desk, then asked to meet with his client after receiving the details of Swanson's arrest. Terry judged the man to be about fifty years of age, possibly reduced to public defense after failing to join a firm, or being kicked out of one, because he seemed a bit disgruntled about his job. The lawyer's name, Harold Ramsey, didn't sound familiar, but Terry made certain not to forget it, because Ramsey wasn't going anywhere anytime soon.

Playing the waiting game put Terry on edge, because he wondered if the attorney planned on revealing some kind of sneaky defense, or if Swanson might want to cooperate. Either way, Terry and Gosser collaborated while they waited, deciding where to go and which people to interview, to further solidify their case.

Gaffney satisfied the media with a press conference, stating they had a suspect in custody. He didn't elaborate with details, though they showed Swanson's photograph on every news station again, with his name this time, asking for anyone with additional information to step forward. Several families of the victims called for more details, but Gaffney didn't tell them much more than he said to the media.

Terry walked with Gosser out the front door when the detective decided he wanted a smoke break. As Gosser lit up, Terry looked down the street toward some of Buffalo's oldest standing buildings, now illuminated only by street lamps as snowflakes glistened during their descent to the pavement.

"I'm sick of waiting for that prick," Gosser commented, kicking one foot back against the building as he exhaled gray smoke upward. "What the fuck could they be talking about?"

"Life in prison here versus extradition to Montana, I would think."

The two investigators were the only two people outside at the moment, while a few deputies remained outside the interview room at all times. In such a high profile case, Gaffney wasn't taking any chances with Swanson trying to escape or bring harm to himself.

"Looks like your buddy's here," Gosser commented as an unmarked car pulled into a parking spot below and Taggart hobbled out of the front passenger's seat momentarily.

Dressed much like before, the man sported a light brown Stetson this time, along with a two-tone brown and green western jacket that featured Aztec stitching across the chest and arms. The detective who drove him retrieved a suitcase from the trunk, handed it to Taggart, then waved a goodbye to Gosser and Terry before driving away.

Gosser opened the door for Terry and Taggart after snuffing his cigarette. Terry wanted to offer assistance to the former sheriff with his suitcase, but he knew Taggart didn't like being viewed as a charity case. Instead, he simply led the way inside, then shook hands with him.

"Good to see you, Joe."

"Likewise," Taggart replied as he also shook Gosser's hand. "Where is the son-of-a-bitch at?"

Taggart found a safe spot to stow his suitcase near Gosser's desk, then followed the two investigators to the interview area. Standing in the hallway, looking at the door, the former sheriff sucked in a deep breath.

"I can't believe this moment is finally here."

Terry looked to Gosser.

"Randy, can you let us handle Swanson a moment? Provided his lawyer is ready for us."

"Sure. I'll monitor from the video room."

Neither of the two deputies stationed outside of the interrogation room said a word the entire time, even to Gosser. Terry began to wonder if the detective was indeed disliked by some people within his own ranks. He recalled his own recent rocky relationship with McBride because the man saw the light at the end of the tunnel known as retirement and didn't act as ambitious as he once had.

"Let me go first," Terry said to Taggart. "I want to examine his response when he sees you for the first time."

"Have you gotten anywhere with him?"

"No. He's proclaiming innocence across the board."

Terry knocked on the door to see if the attorney was indeed ready, or if the interview process had reached its end. The lawyer, a thin bald man with a graying brown fringe, stepped outside to join them, briefcase clasped between his hands.

"My client claims you've already condemned and crucified him," Ramsey said with a stiff air about him, standing erect.

"Your client has provided no information to contradict our evidence," Terry responded. "I'll gladly listen to anything pertinent to the case, but so far he has nothing to offer."

"I've been over the charges, Trooper Levine. Your evidence isn't as concrete as you think. Who's to say my client didn't stay at the motel in question, or drop off a delivery there?"

Terry caught a grin creeping across Taggart's face, instantly understanding how the former sheriff regarded lawyers.

"I'm reasonably certain any jury is going to find your client guilty of murder on seven counts based on what we have. But that's just my opinion."

"Then it's a good thing you're not a juror. Luckily for you, my client wishes to speak with you one more time, to shed some light on something you probably didn't consider."

Terry looked to Taggart.

"This ought to be good."

Ramsey opened the door for Terry, who signaled for Taggart to wait momentarily before entering. His read on Swanson's expression was necessary, because a camera didn't always capture details. Nor did it provide an opinion about someone's attitude at the moment the past presented itself.

Terry walked into the room, taking a seat as his eyes locked onto Swanson like some kind of heat-seeking missile. He didn't even look up when Taggart entered last, finding the prisoner's expression go from reasonably indifferent to bitter and hostile within a second. Swanson twisted his lips, saying nothing at first, while his eyes bored into Taggart with an intensity that seemed to blame the former sheriff for all the wrongs in his life.

After a few seconds Swanson realized Terry was observing him, so he sat back, folded his hands on the table, one still restrained by metal cuffs, and looked to Taggart.

"How's the leg, Sheriff?" he asked coldly.

"I reckon it'll be feeling a lot better after today," Taggart answered as he drew the last remaining seat.

"I never feel good about another person's suffering, but your case is an exception."

Ramsey appeared on the verge of stepping in, so Terry cleared his throat.

"I guess no introduction is needed."

"Did you bring him here so he could gloat?" Swanson asked testily. "Sheriff Taggart gets his man, even if he has to frame him."

This time Ramsey did interfere, preventing his client from adding anything incriminating to his random statements.

"My client wants you to check his cell phone records for the nights of the murders."

"We already are," Terry replied. "Any particular reason why?"

"He believes they will prove he could not have been in the areas at the time of the murders."

From what Terry understood about cell phone tracking technology, calls were traceable for years, and pinpointing a powered-up cell phone was easy with cooperation from the service provider or a certain device. Tracking a phone's location on a previous date was possible, as he recalled, though only if the person was making a call at that specific time. Something about the signal bouncing from cell phone towers provided the phone's exact location, though the specifics eluded him.

"How do we know Mr. Swanson was with his cell phone at all times?" Terry countered the lawyer's claim.

"Do you strive to be difficult?" Ramsey asked bluntly. "We're trying to prove my client's innocence and you continue to take the easy path because you don't want to look any further."

"I have nowhere else to look," Terry said, narrowing his eyes as he stared at the lawyer. "This man had nowhere else to look. Do you truly believe it's one big coincidence that your client resided in two states, in two specific areas, where a total of eleven murders occurred?"

Ramsey said nothing as a lump traveled down his throat.

"Unless your client has something of value to add to our investigation, I'm sure the district attorney in Montana will seek the death penalty once we're done with him here."

Swanson continued to eye Taggart with a mix of disdain and suspicion, which worried Terry, though he didn't show his thoughts.

"We will check the phone records, Mr. Ramsey," Terry assured the attorney.

"Thank you."

"Why did you change your pattern?" Taggart asked Swanson bluntly.

"What?"

"You used a knife during three of the murders in Montana, yet you switched to a firearm here. Why the change?"

Ramsey pointed a finger at Taggart, who simply ignored him, continuing to stare at Swanson instead. Terry knew their interviews in Montana couldn't have been pleasant experiences.

"You're harassing my client," Ramsey warned.

"It's okay," Swanson intervened, suddenly transformed from the sullen, defeated man during the original interview to someone who stood his ground. "He's trying to rattle me, like he did when he tried to pin his murders on me in Montana. You're wrong, Sheriff, just like you were before."

"This time the evidence says different, Daryl."

Terry held up a hand before speaking.

"Tell me about the house, Daryl. How did you time all of that?"

"You don't have to answer that," Ramsey warned, though Swanson waved off the notion, knowing they had him dead to rights on breaking and entering.

"It was easy. A guy at work was bitching about his parents leaving for Florida and having to check on the place. I checked it out, spied on them long enough to learn their security code, and waited for them to leave."

Terry referred to a piece of paper.

"You had a few days between skipping out of your apartment and their departure. Where were you those couple of days?"

"I laid low wherever I could. Garages, parks, wherever the cops weren't looking."

"And when you got to the house, what did you do?"

"I holed up for winter. Put the car in the garage and started eating out of their pantry. They had enough canned goods in the basement to last a year."

Terry considered the thought that Swanson might have used his own vehicle, or one of the two parked inside the garage, to travel to Brockport for the last murder. Knowing it was probably a waste of time and manpower because more than a month had passed, he wanted public areas between Buffalo and Brockport checked.

"You never left the house?" Terry pushed, just to see Swanson's reaction.

"Never. I had food and cable TV. Why would I ever leave that?"

"Maybe to slit someone's throat," Taggart offered without humor, leaning toward the suspect.

"Does he really have to be here?" Ramsey questioned irately. "He doesn't even have any authority, does he?"

"He's with me," Terry stated, providing answer enough to justify Taggart's presence. "But we're done unless you have something else to offer."

"Get him out of here," Swanson said, looking toward Taggart.

"I hope they extradite you to Montana so I can watch you fry."

"Fuck you, Taggart. You and your gimpy leg can both go to hell."

Terry watched Taggart clench a fist, then release it. The man certainly possessed self-control enough to watch his words and actions when it counted most.

"I'd like to speak with my client alone," Ramsey insisted.

Terry ushered Taggart toward the door.

"Take your time. We're done with him until trial unless he comes up with something useful to save his skin."

Gosser met them in the hallway, shrugging his shoulders.

"Sorry you came all this way for nothing," he told Taggart.

"Oh, no," Taggart said with a satisfied smile. "I got what I wanted."

"Think Ramsey will let him say anything else?" Gosser asked Terry.

"Probably not. He'll wait until the prosecutors present their case before he does much of anything, I'm sure."

All three stood in the hallway momentarily, collectively breathing a sigh of relief that the case, at least for them, was concluded. The two deputies continued to stand beside the door, ensuring the Sin Killer didn't escape after the collective effort put forth to capture him.

"I'd like to see the rest of the interview if you guys don't care," Taggart asked.

"Shouldn't be a problem," Terry replied.

Gosser shook hands with Taggart, apparently ready to call it a night since little could be accomplished until morning.

"I'll see you two later. We've got some finishing touches to put on this thing the next couple of days, Terry."

Terry nodded in agreement, planning to call his wife with good and bad news shortly.

"You sticking around?" Gosser asked Taggart.

"Probably just the night. Not much I can do to help since you already have all of my old files."

"You and I have a few things to discuss," Terry informed the former lawman.

"I'll give you two your privacy and see you later," Gosser said with an easy grin, excusing himself before heading down the hallway.

Terry looked back to the door behind them, then down the hall where the video room held the taped interview several investigators had already watched unfold live.

"Let's go watch that tape, Joe, then I'm buying you a beer."

✳✳✳

Terry carried out his promise to buy Taggart a beer, though they bypassed the bar scene in favor of chilled convenience store beer so they could order pizza at the hotel once they each booked rooms. With two slabs of pepperoni pizza left in the box between them, Terry shuffled the remainder of the images and paperwork related to the Sin Killer case into a large bound file.

He spent an hour reviewing the files while providing Taggart with details about the past few months since the man last visited Buffalo. They had remained loosely in contact, but Taggart's iffy cell phone coverage at his ranch kept them from carrying on very many live conversations.

"It's about time he paid for *his* sins," Taggart said before taking a sip from his beer. "I really do want to see him fry so those families can have some closure."

"Don't they think it's over with Childress dead?"

"I reckon they do, but they also appreciate the truth."

Against his better judgment, Terry retrieved one of the pizza slices and took a bite before addressing Taggart.

"Why does Swanson hate you so much? That seemed a little deeper than you just questioning him a few times."

"Oh, I spoke to him, but I also followed him with a camera sometimes, talked with friends, family members, and coworkers, and even set up a decoy operation to see if he'd bite."

"Decoy operation?"

"A cute deputy from a neighboring county volunteered to see if Swanson would try and harm her. We dolled her up just the way the killer liked his victims, but he didn't bite. Son-of-a-bitch probably suspected."

Taggart moved from his corner of the bed to a chair beside the television with a considerable limp. He sat down to remove his cowboy boots one by one, wincing as he pulled the one from his bad leg.

"They can never correct that leg for you?" Terry inquired, hinting in a roundabout way that Taggart halfheartedly promised to reveal the story behind his injury.

"It can never be normal, no matter how many pins and artificial parts they put in there. I lost too much bone matter after the accident."

"The accident you kind of promised to talk about when you came back here?"

Taggart returned a sly grin, recalling his words.

"Yeah, I know. You've earned the chance to hear about it. It's no big secret, Terry, but it's just painful to recall the events of that day."

"I didn't mean to dig up bad memories."

"It's not so much what happened to me that hurts. Yeah, it sucks that I'm stuck like this, but someone else was hurt worse than me that day."

Terry watched Taggart, who stared at the floor momentarily in thought, the painful memories evidently pooling in his mind.

"You don't have to tell me, you know."

"Nah. It's okay. It's, you know, a healing thing, like Lynn tells me."

"Therapeutic?"

Taggart snapped his fingers at the correct wording.

"That's what she says. Hell, everyone in my county knows what happened. It's no big secret."

Taggart paused before beginning his woeful tale.

"It was the end of summer a few years back and my dispatcher got a distress call from a farmer almost fifteen minutes from my station. Well, it was early morning and most of my people were either training or dealing with other calls, so I took the call personally and headed that way. My dispatcher said the guy sounded confused or drunk, so I didn't know what I was getting into, but he wasn't the type to screw around. I'm sure you know when it's time to put up hay, these guys keep their heads on straight, especially when there's a waiting buyer."

Terry nodded, recalling his days of helping on the farm. He still helped Pete bale and stack hay from time to time in late summer.

"Anyway, I get out there and at first I can't find the guy. He's not in the field, and he's not in his house. I'm about to leave the property when I hear a tractor running behind his barn, so I head back to check it out."

Taggart drew a heavy breath, pausing a moment. Terry knew even rugged men like Taggart found a breaking point in their careers if a devastating call crossed their paths.

"Bill, the farmer, was pinned beneath his own hay baler, and it wasn't a pretty sight. He was in and out of consciousness, muttering things I couldn't understand. A few of the baler's spokes had penetrated his lower stomach, basically pinning him under it. There wasn't any way to reverse the rotation of the spokes without hurting him, so I called for medics and more backup to see if we could pry it loose. There he was, his cell phone right next to his hand, but he couldn't ask for help when he called."

"That's terrible," Terry said, genuinely feeling for Taggart and the victim.

"For safety, I stuck a pry bar in front of the spinning mechanism just in case. The PTO wasn't running, so I figured the baler wasn't going to start again. I ain't the brightest guy in the world, but I knew he was bleeding out quick enough that he was going to die if I didn't get him out of there in a hurry. I grabbed the pry bar and started trying to force the rake back far enough to pull him out of there. By myself it was a bitch to move it much at all, but I had to get Bill out of there."

Terry saw emotion creep into Taggart's face, his blue eyes staring ahead as though he could see the gruesome scene in perfect clarity all over again.

"Problem was, I made the same mistake he did by trusting the PTO was shut down. I fought that thing for what seemed like forever before it finally inched back enough that I could pull him out a few inches. Terry, his legs and his stomach were punctured by those pins so badly. What I've been told is that a flaw in the design kicked in the PTO when I pulled the rake backwards, so instead of freeing Bill, the baler kicked on and sucked him further in, taking my right leg with it."

"Jesus, Joe."

"Yeah, well that finished off any chance Bill had of surviving, and broke my leg in about a dozen places when it twisted my muscles and tendons. There I sat with Bill, a man I virtually killed by my actions, for ten long minutes in agony before help arrived. The only thing that kept me from being sucked under there was his body preventing the rake from churning. That bastard of a rake kept grinding and churning, wanting to chew me up like some demented machine from a Stephen King book for those ten minutes. It kept starting and stopping, like it was taunting me. I spent every second thinking that thing was about to kick loose and grind me up."

"My God, Joe. Now I know why you don't like talking about it."

Taggart looked from the floor up to Terry, a bit misty eyed.

"I know Bill's death wasn't really my fault, but I ain't totally innocent. If I had just waited for help to arrive he might have made it."

"You did what you had to, what any of us would do."

"You say that, the medics said that, and even the court system that awarded me several million dollars in damages said that, but it doesn't help me sleep any better some nights. There are mornings where I wake up from dreams where Bill is staring at me in a death trance, even though I never saw his eyes."

"We all have those dreams," Terry assured him.

Taggart painfully moved his injured leg to a different position. Terry wondered if the blood flow was affected by the injury, making it less comfortable in certain stances.

"You know, I found ol' Bill because I heard his tractor running, but when I got back there, I forgot all about it. If I'd been smart enough to shut her down, things might have turned out different. From what I heard, Bill got a great deal on the tractor, and now I know why."

From personal experience, Terry knew how rescuers sometimes got caught up in the moment and forgot about their personal safety. Being a hero was great, but dead heroes didn't get to enjoy their accolades.

"I owe you a debt of gratitude for getting me off my farm, Terry," Taggart said sincerely. "The last few years I've holed up, positive I'm the world's biggest failure. You got me off my ass and doing something useful again. I know I wasn't much help to you, but it felt good to be along for the ride."

"You're welcome, Sheriff. And for the record, your contribution was necessary. Without you, Swanson might have gone about killing for years."

"Glad I could help."

Terry was puzzled about one thing relating to Taggart's story.

"Why only the one leg?"

"The right leg got caught up in the spokes and yanked into the rake," Taggart answered rather casually. "The other leg was in a divot when it happened. I just kept it close to me so it didn't get sucked in."

"That must have hurt like a mother."

Taggart absently rubbed a hand down his right thigh.

"It did, but the fear of being killed kept me from thinkin' on it too much. Plus I was in and out of shock."

Terry finished off his third beer of the night. He seldom drank more than one or two, usually saving such occasions for celebrations or gatherings. Tonight was a celebration with a man he respected in a few different ways. While some people regarded him as small town and small time, or a cripple, Terry saw beyond those superficial assumptions. The man brought perspective to a stalled investigation and ultimately helped them find Daryl Swanson.

"Here's to Daryl Swanson," Terry said, raising his empty beer bottle. "May he be ass-raped behind bars before he rots and dies."

"Here, here," Taggart said, tapping the bottle with his own.

CHAPTER 35

Terry passed up breakfast with Gosser to visit Erie Wholesale, and Grace Ellington in particular. Grace had called the Sheriff's Department stating she had gathered the last of the receipts and vouchers from Swanson's travels during the year he worked for the corporation. Since no one else jumped from their seats to retrieve them, Terry volunteered because he wanted to speak with a few of the employees. Gosser and his people had conducted most of the supplemental interviews and character statements. Though Terry considered them adequate, he wanted to hear a few things personally from Grace and Vaughn in particular.

Even as he walked through the back entrance, he still felt bad for Taggart. Despite acquiring riches from his accident, he still seemed miserable. Money didn't equate happiness, especially not to a sheriff who lost use of one leg while trying to save another human being. Taggart struck him as the type of man who wanted to spend all of his free time tilling the land, riding horses, and occasionally catching fish. Having a bum leg took a lot of the fun out of those and other activities.

An inch of snow covered the ground in the Buffalo area, but Terry didn't feel much of a climate change when he stepped inside from the freezing temperatures. Compared to his initial weekend visit, he found the place abuzz with activity on a Monday morning. Forklifts were busy loading box trucks and tractor trailers inside, while half a dozen trucks were departing from the warehouse when Terry stepped from his car.

Ignoring the looks a few of the workers shot his way, Terry marched toward Grace Ellington's office, finding the gray-haired bookkeeper behind her desk. Her door was closed, but he saw her working busily through the partially tilted shades, stacking and arranging files at her desk. He gave the door a quick rap, then stepped inside.

"Good morning," she said pleasantly.

Her petite glasses, which rested on the central part of her nose, completed the look of a librarian grandmother from the Victorian era. Though she wore contemporary business casual attire, Terry thought her one of the most sincere and forthright people he had ever met. If she indeed had children and grandchildren they probably cherished her. Though she was beyond retirement age, she kept herself busy, and her mind sharp as a tack.

"Hello, Ms. Ellington," he said almost shyly, like an elementary school student meeting his new teacher.

Grace plopped a box atop her desk with an exaggerated air of exhaustion.

"I found every last receipt and voucher after searching through every cabinet. They were scattered everywhere because they came back from the tax people in disarray."

"That's understandable. We appreciate the effort."

"We have a few hundred people on the payroll, and I'm not always savvy with the computer. I apologize."

"No need," Terry said emphatically. "Really."

"Where's that red-headed partner of yours?"

"Detective Gosser? He's working some other angles at the moment."

"Such a pleasant young man. And very handsome, too."

Terry provided a smile, thinking of what fun he'd have relaying those sentiments to the "handsome" detective later. He wondered what Gosser's pleasant side looked like, never seeing the detective anywhere close to euphoric during their time together.

"These are yours," Grace said, nodding toward the box, confirming what Terry already suspected.

"I know the detectives covered everything with you and Mr. Vaughn, but I was wondering if I might ask you both a few additional questions for my own benefit."

"Nick is out, but I'll help however I can."

Terry pulled out his notebook and trusty pen.

"Is he out sick?"

"Oh, no," Grace said with an easy smile. "That boy is *never* sick. He's out on a delivery."

"A delivery? I thought he was a supervisor."

"Of course he is, but he sometimes delivers if people call in sick, or the load isn't put in a truck quite right. It's a hectic job, but he seems to like it."

"Bet his wife isn't too thrilled."

"He doesn't have a wife, Mr. Levine. Dates occasionally, but Nick doesn't seem the type to settle down."

Terry stood with his pen hovering over his pad, finding nothing noteworthy to write, because his mind kept returning to the idea that Vaughn carried out the same work as his drivers.

"Please have a seat, Mr. Levine," Grace offered. "No sense standing there."

"Thank you."

Terry asked her a few basic questions about Swanson, carrying out his original agenda without any staggering discoveries. No one he spoke to seemed to think Swanson was the type of guy who could execute perfect murders. One, he didn't seem violent, withdrawn, or socially backwards to anyone, and most people didn't regard him as a very intelligent person. Swanson possessed some street smarts, obviously, but didn't seem to have intellectual prowess enough to devise traps or track down potential victims with the internet.

Putting down his notebook and pen, Terry casually slipped back into conversation about Nick Vaughn, trying to keep Grace from thinking he was probing.

"So Nick's father was a cop?"

"Yes, and a very good one," Grace said with a thin smile that stated she knew the man by more than just reputation. "I knew Raymond very well through his sister, and the church for that matter."

Terry couldn't recall the name Ray Vaughn through any previous associations, though he only worked around the Buffalo area for several years. Even then, most of his work was nearly thirty minutes east at the

Batavia barracks. He seldom ventured into Buffalo unless local agencies requested him. While no police turf war kept county, city, and state agencies apart, each department had adequate resources to handle most anything on their own.

"Nick said his father died in the line of duty?" Terry asked, hoping for more details.

"Yes," Grace answered heavily. "Right in front of Nick when he was just a boy."

Terry fought to keep his eyes from growing to the size of cup saucers. He wanted to believe the dark areas where his mind continued to stray were a figment of his imagination, but pieces of this new puzzle kept falling into his lap. Perhaps the jigsaw puzzle the task force spent the last eight months solving was completed with some incorrect shapes.

"His mother fell apart after that, leaving poor Nick to grow up fending for himself," Grace continued. "He graduated, joined the military for a few years, then came back here looking for a job. Even with his military background, he couldn't land anything, so I got him on here as a driver."

She smiled warmly, thinking of the man she likely considered an adopted son.

"He excelled, of course, and got promoted about five years ago to the spot where he is now."

Terry's mind raced for questions, delicately-worded questions, to ask next.

"Did he ever mend his relationship with his mother?"

"She fell apart, like I said. Fell away from the church, started drinking heavily, and eventually died alone. It was just a few years ago, but poor Nick just didn't know what to do. I helped him plan the services and burial. Only a few people attended, but the people here at work really chipped in."

Terry kept reminding himself to act casually as he asked a few more questions he desperately wanted answers to.

"Did Nick ever try out for any police departments? You know, try to be like the old man?"

Grace laughed easily.

"I don't think he wanted any part of what his father did after witnessing the murder. It was a terrible day when that happened. I think he was only nine or ten years of age. Did you know they wrote a book about Ray Vaughn and his partner? They were police detectives who investigated arson fires, and someone wrote a children's book about them."

"Oh, really?"

"Yes. Maybe they'll write a book about you, now that you've nabbed an infamous serial killer."

Terry wondered if the book regarding the Sin Killer truly was closed. He tried putting such negative, virtually insane thoughts out of his head. Even the notion of investigating a police officer's offspring raised eyebrows and shut doors within police organizations. Friendly inquiries quickly led to internal rumors and the alienation of the inquiring officer soon after word got around.

He hated his mind wandering to such lengths when the simple truth seemed to be laid at his feet all along. Perhaps the simplicity of the case was the problem. For months the Sin Killer proved elusive, almost flawless in his crimes, then in October he suddenly made one little mistake on an open lawn? And one simple hair at that. DNA typically didn't come in a singular form from Terry's experience, not in the great outdoors anyway.

Too perfect, he figured, like the case came in doses perfect for investigators to handle until the guilty party chose to end the game.

"You remember the name of the book by chance?" he asked Grace, acting as natural and curious as possible without giving away his true motive.

"Something about a day in the life of an arson investigator or detective, or something like that," she said, struggling to recall the exact title. "Oh, my. It was printed just a month or two before Ray was killed. I think Nick keeps a copy in his desk, possibly for inspiration."

Grace gave a warm smile, but Terry's mind tracked a bit differently, thinking the inspiration spawned a vigilante serial killer who couldn't cut it as a cop. My God, he thought, knowing the can of worms that came with reopening a closed investigation, even casually.

A cop's son at that.

Still, he wasn't about to see an innocent person fry for the crimes of someone else, if that indeed proved to be the case. He thought back to some of the knickknacks on Vaughn's wall the day they spoke in the fall, remembering an old child's baseball mitt hanging from a thin nail on one wall. The mitt went on the right hand, which implied the wearer threw left-handed. Terry wanted to slap himself across the face for not realizing some of the signs earlier. If Vaughn was indeed left-handed, or ambidextrous in any capacity, he could have carried out the murders. The man was certainly intelligent enough to speak with a drawl to imitate Swanson's accent during one of the murders where a victim was conveniently left alive and untouched.

"Sorry to get so far off track," Terry said apologetically, ready to move along and check on a few new ideas.

"It's quite all right, Mr. Levine. I'm sure Nick would be thrilled that we're speaking of his father like this."

I'm sure, Terry thought sarcastically.

"Are any of your drivers still here that I might speak with?" he inquired.

"They come and go. You might catch a few in the locker room if you step back there."

Terry never liked flashing his badge for the sake of asking questions about coworkers, but sometimes the job demanded it. Grace wasn't going to lead him by the hand to the men's locker room, so he started for the door.

"I'll be back for the box. If you don't mind, I need to speak with a couple of the drivers."

"Be my guest. I'll let the plant manager know you're back there."

"Thank you."

***

When Terry walked into the locker room this time, he found the few present drivers fully clothed. He doubted any of them had reason to shower so early on a Monday morning, so he approached two of them who were talking at a locker, one of whom he recognized from his first visit.

"Hate to interrupt you guys, but I need to ask a few questions about Daryl Swanson," Terry said, quickly flashing his badge.

"Don't you mean Daryl Johnson?" one asked with a confused expression.

"I suppose I do. Look, I just really want to know if he ever made reference to his life in Montana."

Both gave shrugs, neither wanting to answer first.

"He talked about Montana and Texas every so often," the taller of the two replied.

"Did he ever brag about some of his exploits in Montana?"

"Well, he said he was a murder suspect. He was trying to be big shit, but we blew it off. Guess it was true, huh?"

Terry decided to bypass responding to the question, because he wasn't so certain and it was unprofessional to state opinions.

"When and where did he say this?"

"A couple of times," the second driver answered. "He'd say it here sometimes, but one time we all went out on a Friday night and he said some sheriff out there was hounding him. He gave the whole story about some other guy committing murders and the sheriff trying to pin it on him."

"That all he said?"

"No. He said the other dude died and the murders stopped."

"Man, to think we worked with him all this time," the other added. "He could've targeted any one of us or our families."

Terry wondered how they could be so uneducated about the case, considering Belinski went public with his findings and the news coverage extended across the country. Finding out a colleague might be guilty of mass murder shook any average person to the core. Perhaps they didn't want to know the full truth, so they distanced themselves from the news and rumors.

"Is it true?" the first of the two asked. "Did he really kill all of those people?"

"I'm not at liberty to say," Terry answered neutrally. "It's still an ongoing investigation."

"But you arrested him, right? You wouldn't do that without knowing it was him."

Terry held up his hands.

"You'll just have to watch the news. We're still sorting everything out."

A few questions remained, but Terry didn't want to be bombarded with their inquiries. He needed to end the interview or take charge over voluntary witnesses, which he hated doing.

"Look, guys, I just want to know one last thing. Did either of you ever consider Daryl capable of murder?"

Both took a few seconds to form their answers.

"He's kind of a goof. When he talked about that stuff in Montana we didn't think much of it."

"When I heard he was arrested, it just struck me as impossible," the other driver said. "He tried so hard to fit in around here like it was a new start for him. I guess maybe we just didn't see the signs."

"Did he ever hang out with any of you guys outside of work?"

"Nah," the taller man answered. "We all have families and he didn't."

"Some of us grabbed a beer with him sometimes, but we all come and go at all hours, so that kind of thing don't happen much."

Terry thought a moment as he jotted the word "goof" down on his pad.

"When you say he was a goof, what did you mean?" he asked the driver who made the statement.

"Daryl was always forgetting things, or screwing up his paperwork. We have to keep logs just like anyone else and Vaughn was always on him about filling in his times and mileage."

"Don't get us wrong," the other driver chimed in. "Daryl's a smart guy, but he didn't always seem organized."

Deciding to go in a different direction, Terry wanted to know a bit about Vaughn.

"Is it common for Vaughn to go on the road himself?"

"Not really. He only covers if one of us is sick and the rest of us aren't going near a certain delivery area."

"Does he badger you guys about your books?"

"Not really," the taller driver answered. "I work under him, but Dan here doesn't."

"Did he pick on Daryl more than any other driver?"

Now Terry received some questioning stares, indicating they recognized his different line of questioning.

"He stayed on Daryl more, because Daryl didn't always do his job."

Terry flipped his notebook closed.

"Thanks for your time, fellas."

"You won't need us in court or anything, will you?"

"We shouldn't. Still, what you told me does help."

Terry gave them a friendly wave before heading toward the door. Considering the new developments, he suspected his afternoon plans were changing from wrapping up one case to opening another entirely new one.

CHAPTER 36

Monday, December 1
Buffalo, New York

Terry considered asking Belinski to meet him for lunch, but what he wanted to ask the reporter couldn't wait. Instead, he asked the aspiring novelist to meet him at Central Library in downtown Buffalo because he planned on needing computer access. Besides, he hoped against all odds a copy of the book about Nick Vaughn's father might still be in their system.

He checked their online card catalog, finding nothing under the title Grace Ellington gave him, even after trying some variations. After a few subject search failures, he turned to the general internet, trying a few keywords there. He finally found a subject line that appealed to him after typing in Raymond Vaughn's name.

The book, entitled *A Day in the Life of Fire Cops*, appeared in a few site references, which satisfied Terry. For a book printed thirty years prior, in an age where books came and went by the day because of online information, he felt fortunate to find anything about it. Terry returned to the card catalog as Belinski approached him from the side.

"What's the emergency?" the reporter asked.

Terry called him at the very moment Belinski was loading his clothes and equipment for a workout session. He said very little about why they needed to meet, though he stressed the importance of them meeting right away.

"I'm looking for a kids' book."

"And you required my services for that?"

Terry decided to string him along a little further.

"I know you do lots of research, so I figured you could help me locate it faster."

Belinski, suspecting he was being played, refused to show irritation, simply waiting for Terry to play his hand.

"I really am looking for a book," Terry finally said as his eyes scanned the search results.

He felt an excited tingle as the catalog located two copies within the library system. Unfortunately the Erie County library network contained nearly forty branches, so Terry predicted bad fortune with the books being signed out, or located in other branches.

"Why the hell are you looking for *that* book?" Belinski asked with an air of familiarity in his voice.

"You know it?"

"Sure. Read it when I was a kid."

"I want to know if it mentions Ray Vaughn's partner by name."

"Why?"

"Because he may be able to tell me some things about Vaughn's son. And the book may give me some background information itself."

Belinski folded his arms, looking from the screen to Terry.

"I know this isn't what you called me about. What gives?"

"Let me locate this book and I'll tell you everything."

Terry scrolled down the internet page, discovering one of the copies resided in the Alden branch, while the other was reportedly only a floor away from them sitting on a shelf.

"Why the sudden concern about all of this?" Belinski asked as they took an elevator to the children's book section. "Aren't you supposed to be wrapping up the case so I can write my future award-winning book?"

"Your book may be flawed as things stand," Terry replied as the elevator doors opened.

"Come again?"

"I'm having some doubts about Swanson being guilty, which is why I need your help."

"Please tell me you're kidding," Belinski said, his face draining of all color.

Terry continued marching toward the correct section, refusing to answer just yet. He found the section, then began skimming through the author names until he found Brian Painter, the man who wrote the book in question. Painter had only two titles on the shelf, but one of them was indeed the book Terry needed to examine.

"It's a done deal," Belinski persisted, his tone verging on desperation. "Everything points to Swanson. How can you possibly doubt he's your man?"

"I'm not sure, but I'm working on a hunch," Terry said as they walked to a nearby table. "If there's even a possibility I'm right, that's why I need you, and not a local cop, helping me."

Terry flipped the book open, finding a picture book of Ray Vaughn and his partner from the Buffalo Police Department as they carried out their daily duties. It showed pictures of them investigating a fire scene, interviewing suspects, going to court, speaking with witnesses, and finally arresting a suspect.

While Terry recognized the progression of an investigation, he felt the book depicted a rather full day for any detective. Skimming the wording for pertinent information, Terry flipped the pages with purpose.

"What are you looking for?" Belinski asked impatiently.

"Shush a minute, would you?"

Belinski walked away in a huff, giving Terry a moment's peace as the investigator finally reached the book's credits on the second to the last page.

"Holy shit," he muttered, drawing Belinski toward him once more.

"What is it?"

"This could be worse than I thought, Ben. Ray Vaughn's partner was Gary Collins."

"So?"

"The guy who found Swanson on an alleged tip has the same name, so he's probably the man's son. And the man I think may have set up Swanson is the younger Vaughn."

"Holy fuck, Terry. I'm lost."

Terry closed the book heavily upon itself.

"Let's go grab lunch and I'll explain everything to you."

"Something tells me I'm going to need a strong drink, too."

"I'm betting you will."

∗∗∗

After finding a nearby Italian restaurant Belinski recommended, Terry explained the entire situation to the reporter as they waited for appetizers, then their meals. He left out no detail, including how he worried all along that Swanson didn't seem to fit the mold. Music played softly in the background as Terry found only a few couples and businessmen seated near them. Light-colored wood and mahogany trim blended nicely with a mix of artificial lighting and natural sunlight to make diners forget about the miserably cold conditions outside for awhile.

When Terry's tale concluded, Belinski bit off part of a seasoned bread stick, then washed it down with some of the lager he ordered with his meal.

"I can already guess where this is going," he said, getting serious. "You want me to investigate this on the lowdown to see if you're right, before you go blowing eight months of work on a hunch. About right?"

"Pretty much. I'm not going to leave you hanging, because I've got a friend in Batavia who can help me check some things without getting us in hot water."

"What do you want me to do?"

"I need to dig into Vaughn's past. My thought all along was that your Sin Killer took a vigilante approach to his murders. Vaughn's dad was murdered right before his eyes, working as a cop. I need to know what happened there. You've got connections in the police department, don't you?"

"Sure, but not many who can remember that far back."

"Do what you can. I'm going to talk with Collins' parents if they're still alive. Either Collins is an unwitting pawn in this, or he could be part of it. The killer had ideas of how police procedure worked, which really worries me."

"What about Swanson?" Belinski questioned. "Has he suggested someone set him up?"

"He doesn't seem to know much. If he knows anything, he's not saying."

"What would Vaughn's motivation be? And why wait this long?"

Terry found himself with a mouthful of salad, forced to chew and swallow before answering.

"Sometimes these people can carry out fantasies for years before committing the acts themselves. I think in Vaughn's case, he might have thought he was doing a public service by killing these people, justified because he saw them as bad and corrupted. That's what never fit with me, Ben. The murders in Montana grew more violent and personal in succession. Killers don't regress in their methods as they grow more comfortable. They expand their fantasies and experiment with new ideas."

"In Montana, wasn't the first victim murdered with a gun, then the rest with knives?"

"Yes, each progressively more violent. These murders grew more personal as time went, but the killer seemed almost squeamish with a knife in the Cirillo murder. Even with the motel clerk the knife was used almost surgically to simply extract blood. And this doesn't go beyond these walls, understand?"

"Yeah, yeah, I got it. It's bad enough my uncle has disowned me, so I'm not talking."

"He hasn't disowned you. I smoothed things over for you a little bit."

Belinski still appeared uneasy.

"That may be the least of my worries if I start poking around about Vaughn."

"You worried about him getting to you?"

"I was a reserve cop, remember?" the reporter replied with a bit more confidence. "And I still carry a gun."

"You better grow eyes in the back of your head, too. I'm sure your buddy considers the money you'll be making from naming him a sin of some sort."

Belinski didn't appear to like the statement one bit.

"He has to change his M.O., doesn't he?"

"I would think so, unless he wants to foil a complete frame job of Swanson. The problem I foresee is now Vaughn has no restrictions."

"You're talking about this like it's a foregone conclusion he *is* the killer."

"With every passing second I feel more strongly about it."

Belinski chomped into a new bread stick.

"Proving it is an entirely different matter."

A female server brought their meals to them, along with an additional requested beer for Belinski. Terry thanked her, then thought of his next dilemma.

"We have to move fast, Ben. My time here is limited because I'm supposed to be wrapping up the Swanson case. If they find out I'm doing this instead, they'll yank my ass back to my barracks in a heartbeat."

"Most of our archives are computerized, but it still takes time," Belinski replied, twirling his fork into the edge of his pasta. "I can probably get some help from the interns, but I'm only good for Vaughn's background."

"I was hoping you might tail him," Terry suggested.

"What?" Belinski asked, almost coming out of his seat. "And see if he leads me to a treasure trove of corpses? No thanks."

"What kind of investigative reporter are you? In title only?"

"That's not fair, and that's *not* the point. Following him around isn't going to be easy. I'm a public figure, you know."

"No offense, but I'm not sure one or two television appearances a week will have groupies hounding you for autographs."

Belinski took a long swig from the beer bottle. He then looked around him, as though searching for anyone in the vicinity who knew him to prove his point. Finding no takers, he returned his attention to Terry.

"What you're asking is highly unethical."

"You want the complete story? The true story?" Terry pushed.

"Of course."

"We spend two days on this. If it's a dead end, we both move on. You write your book as-is and I work with the district attorney to put Swanson away forever. However, if we find Vaughn is possibly involved, I will bring in my person and start debunking my own investigation."

With a look that indicated he still wasn't completely sold on the idea, Belinski weighed it over by fidgeting with his fork.

"Two days," Terry insisted. "You can surely spare two days and give up a little sleep."

"Fine. Two days."

Terry knew two days barely gave him enough time to get started, considering his contact list began and ended with the man across from him. Of course, he didn't need to prove Vaughn's guilt or innocence by

Wednesday evening. Simply giving himself an assurance one way or the other was enough to let him sleep at night. Truth be told, he wanted to be wrong, wanted the investigation to be over, and wanted to be home with his wife and kids conducting normal investigations.

Slapping the task force in the face with the news the entire investigation led them to the wrong person only served to embarrass some of the investigators, leaders, and politicians now driving to see Daryl Swanson convicted.

Conducting his own investigation placed Terry on dangerous ground with local investigators, his own department, and certainly Nick Vaughn if his theory proved accurate.

"You want me to suck up to my uncle and ask about Collins?" Belinski volunteered.

"I'll handle that. Collins is one of your uncle's favorites, and his involvement in this may be strictly accidental. I should know one way or another within a few hours."

"Good luck."

"You too. And be careful, reserve cop or not."

CHAPTER 37

Terry discovered his old patron information was long gone from the Erie County library database because they had switched software. The move, whether cost-efficient or for ease of use, deleted any users not actively signing out materials during the past two years, which included him. After a brief talk with the director, Terry legally borrowed the book copy until he found a way to procure his own, because he wanted to know every detail about Ray Vaughn and the senior Gary Collins.

As he pulled in front of a single-story house with newer white vinyl siding and a detached garage, he contemplated one final time how to handle the interview. Going in with guns blazing, informing the man his son might be part of a major murder conspiracy felt like laying it on a little thick. His only other angle seemed to be inquiring about Vaughn, which felt dangerous because he didn't want Vaughn knowing anything about his inquiries.

Walking up to the house, he still couldn't finalize a reason for wanting to talk to the retired Buffalo cop that sounded good. He saw no car in the driveway, so his chances were half and half that Collins was actually home. Looking to his watch, he found two hours had already passed since his lunch with Belinski, meaning the two day doomsday clock continued to tick away.

To discover if Vaughn harbored psychotic tendencies, however, Terry needed to start at the beginning. He knocked on the front door, hoping he possessed the skills to pull off at least a partial deception on a noted detective. In his left hand, he clasped the copy of the children's book from the library.

He waited almost a minute, hearing no one inside. Tapping his foot nervously on the ground, Terry began to turn away when the door opened behind him, startling him. Turning around, he found Gary Collins standing in the doorway wearing blue jeans and a denim button-up shirt. Still recognizable from the book images thirty years later, Collins' once brown hair and mustache remained, though they were now completely grayed. Terry suspected the man had to be in his early seventies, though his condition appeared anything except deteriorated.

"Can I help you?" Collins asked, eyeing Terry's sidearm and the badge clipped to his belt.

"Terry Levine, State Police."

Both men shook hands, though Collins continued to shoot him a suspicious stare.

"I was wondering if I could ask you a few questions about your old partner and your book," Terry said, holding up the copy. "Nothing official, I promise."

Collins smirked, giving the impression he still wasn't convinced.

"I'm retired," he said. "Don't have nothing else to do, so come on in."

Terry followed him inside the well-kept home. Based on the plain decor, he suspected Collins lived alone, possibly divorced or a widower. His research provided him with an address for the man and little else.

The front door led directly into the living room where a fireplace mantle contained images of Collins when he was an active officer and detective, several family photos, and one of his son in uniform with a departmental Harley-Davidson. One of the images showed Collins with his wife, which answered Terry's question without him asking.

"Margie passed away four years ago," Collins said, noticing Terry's accidental attention to the photographs. "The kids took it badly."

Collins displayed little emotional response to his wife's death, which left Terry wondering about the man's psychological makeup.

"I met your son during the course of the Sin Killer investigation," Terry revealed.

"I'm proud of him for finding that son-of-a-bitch. Gary was never much of an investigator, but that's something he can tell his grandchildren someday."

Terry suspected the younger Collins simply never chose the route of investigations, opting instead for his motorcycle and traffic enforcement duties. He began to think the man before him was going to be a tough nut to crack, especially without getting to the heart of the matter.

"Have a seat," Collins offered, breaking the ice a bit. "I really don't think you're here for an autograph, or to ask me about my fifteen minutes of fame."

"No," Terry admitted readily, "though some of it ties in with your book."

"For the record, I didn't want any part of that book, but Ray talked me into it. I really didn't want my name in the credits, but he snuck that one past me, too."

Terry grinned, knowing how partners sometimes worked around one another, occasionally screwing up while thinking they were doing some good.

"Can you tell me about Ray?"

Collins drew a thoughtful breath.

"Ray was the kind of guy who changed the mood of a room when he walked in. Probably the most charismatic guy I ever met, and damn good at his job, too. Those book people came here wanting to get some of the guys on patrol, but they met him and decided they wanted a ham like him in their story."

Collins abruptly walked to the kitchen, then opened his refrigerator.

"Soda? Beer?" he offered.

"No, thank you."

Returning with a cold beer, Collins popped the top before continuing.

"He was great at his job, too. We busted all kinds of thugs, and Ray usually got confessions through his charm alone. It got to the point that arson for profit was too scary for anyone to try because they knew we'd find 'em. People brought in outsiders and we busted them, too."

"What about his home life?"

"Ray was an excellent father and husband. I've never seen a man so loyal to his family. Nick was his only child and he loved that boy. I take it you heard about what happened to Ray."

"I know he died in front of Nick."

"That was a terrible day," Collins said, showing a glimmer of emotion for the first time. "Poor Nick was more than devastated. We became his second family over the years, going to his high school events and helping him with school."

"What about his mother?"

"She kind of fell apart after Ray died. Couldn't really take care of herself, much less Nick, so we unofficially adopted him. My youngest son was about his age, so they ran around together."

"What about Gary?"

"Nick looked up to him like a big brother. He's the reason Nick joined the military because he wanted to join the force afterwards."

Collins suddenly changed his expression, as though realizing he'd been rambling without questioning Terry's real motivations in the least.

"What's all of this about?"

"It's really about Nick. It's his employee we just arrested for the Sin Killer murders."

"So I heard."

Terry wondered if he dared come out and speak with the truth or continue to tapdance around the truth.

"Did Nick ever have psychological damage resulting from his father's death?" he decided to ask.

"What are you getting at?"

Collins suddenly drew a flabbergasted expression.

"Are you implying what I think you are?"

Only one direction remained in Terry's line of questioning.

"Tell me, straight up, that you have no doubt Nick is capable of violence against another human being."

Turning red, Collins drew in a breath and held it, refusing to provide an answer.

"I think you better leave."

Without argument, Terry stood and walked toward the door. He suspected the cat was out of the bag, damaging his two day window within the first few hours of launching his personal investigation.

"Here's my card," Terry said, handing it to Collins, who made it a point to follow him to the door.

"I doubt we'll be speaking again."

"The fact that you didn't even ask me how Nick could be involved in this worries me. If you have a change of heart, feel free to call me."

Collins still looked incensed.

"That boy is like a son to me."

"Every criminal is someone's son, Mr. Collins. That doesn't make the things they do any more right."

Terry turned and walked away without asking Collins to keep their conversation to himself. He figured the retiree would either ruin his chances of discovering the truth by tipping Nick Vaughn about his inquiry, or he might actually call once he calmed down.

He walked halfway to his car, then stopped to turn around for one last look at the house. The front door had slammed closed almost immediately after he stepped outside. Though he waited a few seconds, nothing happened, so Terry walked to his car hoping Belinski fared better on his end.

***

Belinski set his team of unpaid and underpaid interns to discreetly digging up information about Ray Vaughn's career and death, as well as the exploits of his son. Though he stuck around to assist in the search for a few hours, he eventually grabbed an early dinner at a drive-thru, then parked his car outside of Nick Vaughn's Tonawanda apartment building. He wondered why a supervisor making good pay rented instead of buying a house.

Perhaps he wanted to make himself more difficult to track.

"You may be smart, Nick, but I'm just a little smarter," Belinski said to himself as he thumbed through some of the newspaper clipping printouts his interns had found.

Now just after five o'clock, Vaughn had been home less than half an hour. Belinski watched the man walk into the building, which consisted of only two levels and probably four sizeable apartments. No lights switched on in the two front apartments, so Belinski narrowed it down to the two in back. Setting down the paperwork, he stepped from his car, zipping his leather jacket in the process as light snow fell all around him.

He walked to the front of the building, looking at the mailboxes, discovering Vaughn lived in Apartment 4. Stepping around back, Belinski peered around the corner to discover which apartment now had lights on as dusk overtook the area. Not wanting to attract attention as a prowler, he returned to the front and the warmth of his car just in time to see Vaughn step out front. Fearing the man knew something, Belinski hunkered down in his seat, watching the man walk briskly to his truck before driving away.

Left with the decision to follow or try his luck with the apartment, Belinski decided to pursue him because Vaughn's apartment was virtually inaccessible. The front door remained locked at all times, and a second story apartment required militaristic skill to reach from the outside. Belinski possessed neither the tools, nor the physical attributes to climb a building from the outside.

He did a U-turn in the street, pursuing Vaughn from a safe distance.

As he drove, Belinski contemplated ways of getting closer to Vaughn without the man knowing of the investigation. When Vaughn stopped at a red light a half a block ahead of him, the reporter suddenly thought of the perfect way. It involved him making himself a potential target later, because he figured Vaughn would love nothing more than to be a witness account in the novel he was penning.

Following the man posed a major risk, because Vaughn could conceivably see his car now, and later when Belinski introduced himself. Nearly an inch of snow covered the area, with flakes still shimmering in the light as they fell. It didn't take the reporter long to discover that Vaughn was likely returning to his workplace for some reason. Belinski considered it the perfect place to approach Vaughn because it was somewhat public, and safe. It also avoided Vaughn questioning how the reporter knew his home address if Belinski never visited him there.

People tended to dislike being visited at their houses unannounced, particularly by reporters.

Typically Belinski maintained his composure regardless of the situation, but as he watched Vaughn pull into the parking lot, a bundle of nerves knotted up within his stomach. Finding five other cars in the lot, he decided to pull inside once Vaughn entered the building. After taking several deep breaths, he opened the car door, trying to perfect the work of fiction he was about to feed Vaughn. His stomach continued to tighten, as though two hands took hold of it and wrung it like a wet towel.

"Settle down," he told himself as he walked toward the back entrance, reading an overhead post that announced only employees were allowed access.

Cautiously, he stepped inside, looking around for the closest available employee. Several forklifts were facing out from a corner, as though they might come to life with their headlight beams flaring like a bull's nostrils to pursue him. Finding no one nearby, but hearing the hum of motorized equipment around the bend, he stepped in that direction. He had only taken a handful of steps when a voice reached him from down a hallway.

"Can I help you?"

Belinski turned to find Vaughn exiting an office. Fighting to maintain his composure and not look surprised, the reporter walked toward him. In the back of his mind, he wondered if a knife or gun might end his life any second. The hallway was dim, with everyone gone for the day, though Vaughn didn't seem to recognize him.

"I'm trying to find Nick Vaughn," Belinski said, putting forth the calmest, collected countenance possible.

"You've found him," Vaughn said suspiciously, holding a few files in one hand.

Belinski cleared his throat.

"My name is Ben Belinski. I work with the local newspaper and do a crime stoppers show on the news sometimes."

"Oh, I recognize you," Vaughn said, warming up a bit as he flashed a smile. "You do the investigative reporting, don't you?"

Of all the people to recognize me, Belinski thought sarcastically, the one man who probably wants to kill me for making money by naming him.

"How can I help you?"

"I'm doing a book on the whole Sin Killer incident from start to finish," Belinski explained rather easily, since this was about the only truthful thing he planned on saying. "I was wondering if I might set up an interview with you, since you were Swanson's supervisor here."

"How did you know that?" Vaughn asked, suspicion creeping into his voice again.

"I've been working with Terry Levine and Randy Gosser the past few months."

"Really?"

"Really. I was one of the two people who cracked the codes left by the killer."

Stupid, Belinski thought as soon as he said the words. Might as well just wrap a cord around your neck and hand the ends to him.

"Codes, huh? I don't remember hearing anything about that."

"Wasn't made public," Belinski said with a dismissive, quick statement, wishing he could quit verbally digging his own grave. "Anyway, I'm glad I found you. Are you interested in speaking to me about Swanson and his time here?"

"I don't have a problem with that," Vaughn answered casually, though Belinski could tell the man was very interested in sitting down with the reporter, possibly to gain insight on his own malicious deeds.

"Have you got a few minutes to swap contact information?"

"Sure. Let me get back into my office."

Vaughn inserted a key into the door as an idea came to Belinski.

"Got a restroom around here I can use real quick?"

"Sure. Just down the hall on the right."

"Thanks."

Belinski started down the hall, then called Tim Schultz, one of the interns at the newspaper. He didn't consider Schultz as reliable as some of the young women when it came to getting things accomplished, but he needed a male voice to call him back to fulfill the plan he prayed didn't get him killed.

A few minutes later, he returned to Vaughn's office, finding the man filling out some forms behind his desk. Remaining wary, but trying to avoid acting so, Belinski stepped into the office, taking a seat across from the supervisor.

"Here's my card," Belinski offered, pushing it across the desk. "I'd love to talk whenever you can spare an hour or so."

"You're not even waiting until Daryl's convicted?" Vaughn asked. "What if he isn't found guilty?"

"From what I hear, they're going to seek the death penalty when he's extradited to Montana, Mr. Vaughn. It sounds like they have an airtight case against the guy."

"It's too bad," Vaughn said, shaking his head. "Daryl was a great employee. I never would have thought it."

Liar, Belinski thought, understanding why Terry Levine felt so strongly that this man devised Swanson's incarceration.

Virtually on cue, Belinski's phone rang at his side. He plucked it from his belt to read the Caller ID, seeing it was his intern. Giving a grimace, he looked to Vaughn.

"Sorry. I've *got* to take this. I'll be just a second."

"Take your time," Vaughn said, putting forth a friendly smile.

Belinski felt certain he had the man hook, line, and sinker at this point. It was time for his next strategic move in human chess.

"Hello," he answered.

Schultz talked loudly enough that Vaughn could hear it was a man's voice, as Belinski requested. He spoke momentarily, while Belinski pretended to listen intently.

"You're kidding," Belinski said momentarily as he bolted to his feet, hoping he deserved an Oscar for his performance. "Tomorrow? Why not tonight?"

Again Schultz filled the conversation with aimless dialogue so Vaughn could hear murmurs from a male voice.

"Oh, I see. No, that's fine. Tomorrow it is."

Belinski replaced his phone, putting forth a quizzical look toward a slightly perplexed Vaughn.

"That was Randy Gosser," Belinski lied. "Says they found something interesting tonight from one of the old crime scenes that might point to someone else."

"That's interesting," Vaughn replied, though flatly. "Why would he call to tell you that?"

"They may want me to go public with it tomorrow if it pans out. Hey, sometimes it pays to be well-connected with media outlets."

"Sounds like it."

"Maybe your buddy isn't guilty after all," Belinski offered, trying to act happy for the supervisor.

Vaughn said nothing, struggling to keep from showing any reaction at all while Belinski studied him like a cartographer might look for stray lines on a map. He chose to use Gosser's name because he didn't want to risk linking himself and Terry Levine in any way.

At least not yet.

"Bugs me that he didn't want to meet tonight, but he says he needed to go over a few things to make sure," Belinski added, shaking his head. "Oh, sorry about all of this. Didn't mean to throw it in your lap."

Vaughn jotted something on a business card with his right hand, started to hand it to Belinski, then took it back to jot something additional with his left hand. The casual slip might have eluded some people, but not the astute reporter.

"Here's my phone number and e-mail," Vaughn offered, as though trying to hurry the reporter along. "Sounds like you may not need to talk to me with this new information."

He's fishing, Belinski figured.

"Yeah, well I doubt this new development will change anything. I'll probably give you a call in a day or two."

"Thanks," Vaughn said, holding up the reporter's business card.

Belinski gave a brief wave before showing himself out. His plan worked, and he felt certain Levine was on the right track. With Vaughn nervous about the potential new lead that didn't exist, he might slip up and give himself away for real.

Every good book had at least one twist to it, and Belinski relished the idea of writing about this one.

CHAPTER 38

Monday, December 1

Tonawanda, New York

Randy Gosser felt on top of the world as he retrieved his Glock 27 from beneath his car seat. He took up a bag of groceries bought at a neighborhood store, then strolled from the parking lot of his apartment complex to the front of the building. Though not upscale by any means, the building and three others just like it lined the block, housing folks who made honest wages and didn't want the burdens of crime and gangs.

Most of his neighbors knew he worked for a police department and felt more secure with him around. They even overlooked the noise he and Janice sometimes made in his apartment, though he tried to maintain a respectable image by shielding them from his activities.

After a night of nothing except dinner with his girlfriend during her lunch break at the hospital, he felt he might come around to the idea of a conventional relationship.

In some aspects, maybe.

Tucking the spare firearm into his backside to free up one hand, Gosser punched in the door code to gain access to the building before jogging the stairs to the second floor. Each floor contained four apartments, his being the last on the right. As he walked the new, but cheap carpeting toward his door, Gosser contemplated his good fortune the past few days. Not only was his relationship working out, but he restored the faith of others in his abilities by helping nab the Sin Killer. Not many detectives ever worked a truly high profile case that books and documentaries were made of, but now he was part of that elite group.

Digging for his keys, Gosser thought of how good it felt to be out and about without wearing a tie and slacks. For once he enjoyed the comfort of blue jeans and a button-up shirt, which still burdened him because t-shirts were so much easier to don. For Janice, however, he wanted to make a good impression with her coworkers. He felt certain they already gossiped about the new couple behind Janice's back, but he didn't care. Tolerance went a long way for Gosser at the workplace, because even the newest of rookie deputies eventually heard from someone about his indiscretions.

Gosser stepped inside, set the sack of groceries on the table, then removed his jacket to hang it behind the door. Only then did he notice the heat running within his apartment, and a cold chill emanating from somewhere. He sometimes left the main window open a crack if he smoked, or to let some fresher air inside. Often when he left for the night, or for work in the morning, he turned his thermostat down, so he turned it up to seventy-two degrees now.

Still, something didn't feel quite right because the chill hung in the air like a storm cloud that couldn't move on or cut loose with rain. He looked around his apartment suspiciously, seeing nothing overturned or out of place. Only then did his eyes shift toward the room darkening curtain covering his main window. On those nights when Gosser found himself out all night for cases, or other reasons, he liked to sleep peacefully when his head hit the pillow. Transforming the apartment into a daytime cave did just that for him.

Before his hand could even brush aside the curtain for a look, he noticed the right side flapping from a sudden breeze that indicated it was open more than just a crack.

"Shit," he muttered, instinctively reaching for the firearm nestled against his back.

Before he could take the necessary step backwards to look around, he saw something to his right from the corner of his eye. Gosser turned, gun still not fully drawn, to see the blurry image of a ski mask and dark clothing. He saw little else, because a fist was already coming directly toward his face, connecting with his nose within the same blink that he spotted it.

A pop, followed by a brilliant white flash, sent Gosser reeling as he backed into the kitchen counter and slumped to the floor in intense pain. His nose was broken and he heard heavy footsteps running out of his apartment as his consciousness wavered. Propped on his hands and knees, Gosser reached for his firearm as blood gushed from his nose, the red droplets immediately swallowed by the dark carpeting beneath him.

Unsteady as he regained his footing, Gosser stumbled toward the door in pursuit, holding his firearm in a ready position. As he reached the hallway he heard the apartment's entrance door slam shut, meaning he was hopelessly behind his attacker. Refusing to give up, to let a person who invaded his personal space get away cleanly, Gosser darted down the stairs, bleeding the entire way. He felt the droplets soak into his shirt, strangely warm and cold against his skin simultaneously. Almost falling twice during his descent, Gosser saw one of the apartment doors open to reveal one of his fellow residents with a shocked look across her face.

If he appeared half as dizzy and disoriented as he felt, Gosser understood the frightened look crossing his neighbor's face. Undaunted, he pushed through the main door, looking both ways down the street. He saw no one except a few people casually opening car doors or entering their own apartments. His attacker had undoubtedly run down an alley or ducked behind some cover along the streets.

Either way, Gosser had reached the end of his physical threshold, falling to one knee as he struggled to maintain consciousness. The gushing blood from his nose, coupled with the immediate swelling, diminished his ability to breathe. He knew of stories where people with broken noses fell unconscious to the floor and the bones were forced into portions of their brain, killing them instantly. He didn't particularly want his girlfriend to see him in this condition, though the thought of her viewing him on a slab seemed less appealing.

He stabilized himself on one knee, looking to the one neighbor who dared follow him outside. The man worked for the sanitation department as a sorter during the week, though Gosser couldn't recall his name.

"Can you call an ambulance or give me a lift to the hospital?" he asked before his pride got the better of him.

"Sure."

Gosser looked down at his light-colored shirt, finding it saturated in blood. Cursing under his breath because the shirt was less than a week old, Gosser sat directly on the cold, snowy sidewalk holding his gun. He needed to lock his apartment before leaving, and double-check that his windows were locked at all times for future reference.

"You okay?" the neighbor asked before making a call or fetching his car keys.

"Never better," Gosser answered sarcastically.

The neighbor realized the stupidity of his own question, heading inside and returning with an old towel. He handed it to the detective who immediately placed it against his nose, wincing as the pressure brought about more pain.

"No offense," the neighbor said, "but if I'm going to drive you to the hospital I don't need you bleeding all over my car."

"None taken," Gosser replied, his personal high from earlier plummeting faster than a brick discarded from an airplane.

Only now did he begin to wonder why someone took such great risk breaking into his apartment when he owned little of value and had no known enemies. He only knew he wanted this horrific night to end because he literally didn't want to show his face to anyone, including his colleagues.

Though his nose stung badly at the moment, he knew the morning was going to bring about an appearance similar to those of mug shots following violent altercations. Willing himself to his feet, Gosser pressed the towel to his nose, determined to make it upstairs to secure his apartment before the next chapter of his ordeal unfolded.

CHAPTER 39

Terry started his morning with a cup of coffee as he examined his list of remaining leads to check regarding his new hypothesis. From his hotel room directly across from the Erie County Sheriff's Department, he used the land line to phone Lucy Wheaton, the secretary who worked under Harold James Mitchell.

When he first considered the idea that the killer requested Mitchell to meet him in Canton, possibly by conventional mail, Terry phoned her with a request to check all incoming calls and letters a month or two previous to his Canada trip. He conceived the killer could have read Mitchell's public speaking schedule online and plotted the pastor's demise almost immediately. The fact the murder did not occur across the border indicated the killer's awareness of customs and security measures at the border gates.

It also suggested he intended to keep his crimes within New York State to throw off investigators and delay FBI involvement. While the FBI was always a willing and helpful resource for investigators at the state and local level, their involvement didn't become automatic until related crimes crossed state lines.

"Pastor Franklin's office," a female voice answered after a single ring.

As Terry recalled, it took less than two weeks for Mitchell's church to appoint a new lead pastor. Out of respect for the deceased, most churches waited a month or more before even considering replacing such a figurehead, but Mitchell was reportedly on his way out, and not voluntarily.

"Lucy Wheaton, please."

"Speaking."

"Lucy, this is Terry Levine from the New York State Police."

"I remember you. How can I help you, sir?"

Terry looked at his list of items to check, making certain he covered everything he needed to with Lucy.

"I was just following up on the items I talked to you about a few weeks back."

"Um, I found the records you requested and forwarded them to your office in Canton."

Terry's status in Canton might as well have read "visitor" with him residing in Buffalo throughout much of the case. Most times his commander and his sergeant were excellent about forwarding information to him, but they had cases of their own. Considering the Sin Killer case was all but closed, they might have sat on information or overlooked it altogether. Strangely, Terry never saw it in his box during the few days he spent at home between trips to Erie County.

"The information never reached me," he said vaguely. "Do you have it handy?"

"Sure," Lucy said, beginning to shuffle papers.

She took a minute or so locating the information before returning to the line.

"Pastor Mitchell usually disposed of his mail in a shredder, so any letters he received he either filed or recycled. He received so many letters from corporations and individuals, I can't say I remember anything that stood out. I typically didn't open his mail unless it dealt with finances."

"Okay, thanks."

"There was one call that I remember," Lucy said, offering some hope that she might yet salvage his dwindling hopes of linking Vaughn to the murders. "He received a call from someone in the Buffalo area asking when he would be returning from his Montreal speech a few weeks before he left. That wasn't unusual, but the person asked if the pastor was driving or flying, which alarmed me a bit."

"As well it should have. Did this person leave a name or number?"

"No, but after several civil suits, Pastor Mitchell had me jot down information about every phone call we received in a log book. This particular call came from a company in Tonawanda called Erie Wholesale Shipping on April 11th which was a Friday."

"Do you have the time it came in?"

"It was 2:32 p.m."

She read him the phone number, which he jotted down, finding it highly familiar.

"Does that help?" she inquired.

"I think it just might," Terry tried to assure her. "Thank you for your time."

"You're welcome. I hope this helps you put away the creep who did this. A lot of people didn't like Pastor Mitchell, but he wasn't a bad man."

Just greedy, Terry thought.

"Every little bit helps, Lucy. Thanks again."

Terry hung up the phone before looking to his list, realizing he needed to contact Grace Ellington at the very number Lucy had just given him. With the change of a single digit at the end, he reached her office directly on the second ring.

"Grace," she answered smoothly.

"Good morning, Grace. This is Terry Levine."

"Good to hear from you, Terry," she said, obviously comfortable using his first name, which he didn't mind in the least. "Have you gotten me a date with Detective Gosser yet?"

"No," Terry chuckled. "I'm still working on that. I was wondering if I could trouble you for one more favor."

"Certainly."

"For court purposes, I need a copy of Nick's work hours during the time he was Daryl Swanson's supervisor. He's going to be a key witness when it comes to testimony."

Terry surprised himself with his ability to lie so smoothly, but when it came to doing a greater good, he lost no sleep over such actions.

"I can probably have them in an hour or two. Those are computerized these days, so it'll take me longer to itemize them than anything."

"Thank you. I can drop by before I head to lunch."

Terry wasn't sure about finding time to eat lunch the way things were unfolding. He would certainly take time to pick up copies of the days and hours Nick Vaughn worked.

Finishing his coffee, Terry picked a tie from the three he brought from home, then threw on a sport coat before crossing the street. Readily recognized by everyone inside the Erie County Sheriff's Department, he made it past an administrative assistant to the elevator. A moment later he was shown to Gaffney's office on the second floor when a secretary said the sheriff wanted to speak with him.

"Paul," Terry said when he walked into the large room, shaking Gaffney's hand.

"Terry, good to see you. Have a seat."

Instead of seating himself behind his large desk, Gaffney sat beside Terry along one side of the conference table taking up part of his mammoth office.

"What's going on, Paul?"

"Gosser was assaulted last night at his apartment."

"What?"

"A masked man attacked him after sneaking in through the window when Randy got home from a date."

"Is he okay?"

"He won't be here the few days. I just wanted to let you know because I know the two of you were wrapping things up this week."

Shit, Terry thought. Gosser was capable of tying loose ends by himself, but without his assistance, Terry might find himself caught between preparing for a trial he didn't want to see happen, or following what he considered to be the truth. He needed to speak with Gosser, regardless of the detective's condition, to see what paperwork and witness accounts remained.

Gaffney seemed to sense his hesitation, though the sheriff inaccurately deduced the reason for Terry's silence.

"I can give you someone else if the workload is too much," Gaffney offered.

"Thanks, Paul. I'll have to let you know."

Giving him a concerned look, the sheriff seemed to sense Terry's anxiety. For everyone else, closing the Sin Killer case provided a sigh of relief. Terry knew his actions and emotions conveyed a different story because his acting prowess had limits.

Terry also wondered if the senior Gary Collins told anyone about their weekend conversation. He felt the weight of his own two-day clock pushing down on him like a thumb might squash a bug.

"You okay?" the sheriff asked.

"Yeah. Just ready to go home I guess."

"That nephew of mine been badgering you?"

"No," Terry answered with a smile. "Ben's the least of my problems."

"Look, if there's anything you need, and I mean *anything*, just let me know."

"Thanks again."

Now Gaffney gave him a reassuring look.

"That's twice you've come down here and gotten the job done."

"And both times I've had lots of help, so thank *you*, Paul."

"If you ever want to quit that part-time job of yours and come work down here, just let me know."

Terry chuckled.

"Any more moves will probably result in my second bachelorhood, but thanks just the same."

Unexpectedly, his phone rang at his side. When Terry looked, he found his younger brother calling him during the middle of his workday. Pete seldom phoned other than weekends, meaning this might be an important call.

"I've got to take this, Paul. I'll call you later when I check some things."

Gaffney simply nodded as Terry left the office to answer his phone.

"What's up?" Terry asked when he opened the phone.

"Kenny went to see Kimmerling yesterday."

"Jesus," Terry muttered as he walked past the sheriff's assistants. "Can't you talk some sense into him?"

"No. I thought you had this talk with him."

"I did, but he doesn't listen to me. Did he skip church to drive out there?"

"No, but he skipped out on Mom and Dad. When I called, I finally got the truth out of him."

"Look, I can't do a thing about it from here."

"You still in Buffalo?"

"Yeah, for a couple more days."

"Might as well buy a fucking house out there."

Terry watched the elevator doors close behind him, pushing the button for the ground floor. The idea of his youngest brother paling around with a serial killer in any fashion upset him, but Pete was in a better position to talk some sense into their brother.

"What does he want out of this?" Pete asked. "He won't give me an answer."

"I think he wants understanding. He might even want to forgive Kimmerling, but that guy is bad news."

"Well, duh."

"I'm not talking about his murders. He can get inside Kenny's head, maybe even turn Ken against us."

"No way."

"Keep an eye on him, Pete. Get whatever you can out of him. Go in there for lunch, after you're off work, whatever it takes. I don't want Kenny around the guy because Kimmerling is going to say whatever Kenny wants to hear."

Stepping out from the elevator doors as they opened, Terry found the sun shining outside the glass entrance door. He walked outside without much thought, finding the weather far more frigid than it appeared.

"I'll watch him," Pete promised. "Cantcha do somethin' ta stop his visitation rights?"

"It's a free country, and Kenny's on Kimmerling's approved list, so probably not."

Terry heard a beep that indicated another incoming call on his phone.

"I've gotta go, Pete. Another call coming in."

"Talk to ya later."

"Later," Terry said as he pushed a button to answer the incoming call from Belinski. "What do you have, Ben?"

"I just heard something about Gosser getting beat up. That true?"

"Yeah. Your uncle just said something about him getting attacked in his apartment last night."

"Oh fuck."

"What do you mean, 'Oh fuck'?"

"I have good news and bad news. Where do you want to meet up?"

"I'm outside your uncle's building. How soon can you be here?"

"Five minutes."

***

When Belinski pulled up in his BMW a few minutes later, Terry wondered if Gaffney was spying on them from above. He hated feeling so paranoid, especially considering his new investigation was founded on the best of intentions. Accepting a ride from Belinski certainly wasn't a crime, or reason to suspect him of anything nefarious.

"What's going on?" Terry asked immediately upon shutting the door and fastening his seatbelt.

"Yesterday I went to talk to Nick Vaughn."

"What?" Terry yelled loud enough that his voice drowned out the radio.

"Don't get worked up. I didn't go at him."

Belinski pulled away from the curb, above the speed limit within seconds as he headed toward the freeway.

"I approached him about being interviewed in my book and he agreed to it."

"What's this have to do with Gosser?"

"Nothing. It's what I did to set Vaughn up that might have gotten Gosser smacked around."

Terry watched as Belinski merged with traffic, weaving in and out of lanes well above the speed limit.

"You always drive with a desire to kill yourself?"

"This is the big city, not some country bumpkin roads. You either drive to get somewhere or you get trampled."

"At the risk of distracting you and getting us both killed, please explain to me how you set Vaughn on the warpath."

Belinski passed another car, then settled into the right lane.

"I told him Gosser called me with information that they might have evidence pointing to someone else committing the murders."

"Goddamn it, Ben! Why didn't you toss him my name?"

"I couldn't risk him putting it together that you and I were working together on this."

Belinski passed another car before zipping into the right lane as he signaled for an upcoming exit.

"You could have gotten Randy killed!"

Terry wasn't going to disguise his emotion. He hated the idea that Gosser was placed in danger because of their secret investigation. Using the detective as an unwitting pawn did not sit well with him.

"I didn't ask Vaughn to go over there and pummel him. When I put that information out there, I was gauging his reaction, nothing more."

Still fuming over the reporter's bold move, Terry considered the fact that he gave Belinski freedom to work on his own. If he chose to put a red herring in play, Terry certainly would have put himself in danger and no one else.

"Are you going to get over this so we can plot our next move?" Belinski asked as he took the exit just north of Buffalo.

"This partnership may be dissolving after your latest stunt. I have to bring Gosser into this now."

"He's a hothead," Belinski complained. "The first thing he'll do is go after Vaughn."

"No he won't. This saves me going outside of the task force for help."

Belinski found a nearby parking lot where he settled the BMW into a marked space.

"So let me get this straight, Ben. What exactly did Vaughn do?"

"I assume he went looking for evidence he thought Gosser had against him. He can't go breaking into my uncle's building, so he hoped Gosser took something home with him. From what I heard, Gosser got home after going out, noticed something wasn't right in his apartment, then got sucker punched."

"A punch kept him out of work?"

"Guess it broke his nose. They said he lost a lot of blood and almost lost consciousness a couple times."

Between Gosser's injuries, Kenny's relationship with a serial killer, and the Sin Killer case still unsettled, Terry felt his head swimming with responsibility he didn't want. Yesterday, he might have considered the possibility his theory was flawed and his instincts failed him for a change. With the attack on Gosser, and Vaughn's timecards only an hour away from proving or disproving another of his theories, Terry needed to see this case to its end before solving his other problems.

Putting things into perspective, Terry decided he needed to examine Vaughn's work times before moving forward.

"Take me to Erie Wholesale," he told Belinski.

"Vaughn might see us together."

"No he won't, because you're going to drop me off and drive around the block until I call you. I'm picking up records that will indicate if we have any prayer of putting Vaughn away."

Belinski put his car into gear, speeding toward the closest main road that put them on the path to Tonawanda.

***

Terry found the process of retrieving the records painless because Grace had them printed. She handed them over after Terry made small talk with her, careful to avoid bringing up Gosser or Vaughn during their conversation. The last thing he needed was to slip up and reveal that he knew anything about the events of the previous night.

Once he took possession of the paperwork, Terry made his way toward the exit, careful to avoid contact with Vaughn or his office. Instead, he phoned Belinski as he reached the exit, instructing the reporter to pick him up just outside of the visitor entrance. Carrying the clasped envelope like precious cargo, Terry slid into the passenger's seat a moment later. He undid the metal prongs faster than a kid tearing into a birthday present, then yanked the papers from the brown sheath.

"What exactly are you looking for?" Belinski asked.

"It's a bit of a long shot, and may not prove anything," Terry said, his finger guiding him through the dates until he reached the one in question.

"Vaughn worked Sunday April 27, Ben. The day Mitchell was killed near my hometown."

"So?"

"It's a five-hour drive from here to Canton. Vaughn clocked out shortly after noon, and according to this, he normally works a full day unless he works Saturday or Sunday. He didn't work that weekend."

Belinski kept his eyes on the road, trying to wrap his mind around the information.

"Not exactly the nail in Vaughn's coffin, my friend."

"But it's a start. Some credit card receipts, cell phone records, or eye witness accounts could place him traveling to Canton."

"Don't most of those items require the search warrant you're so desperately trying to obtain?"

"Are you always such a buzz kill?"

"I'm a realist. There's a difference. What about the other dates and places?"

Terry shuffled through the work times.

"Except for the murder in Syracuse, they all happened around here, so times aren't necessarily relevant. We don't know when the biker was killed in Syracuse, or exactly when he disappeared, so there's nothing concrete on that front."

"I might have an idea," Belinski said as an idea came to him. "Tonya LaShomb got a glance at the killer's eyes, right?"

"Okay."

"She said the man who locked her in the trunk has distinctly blue eyes, like Vaughn. Swanson has brownish hazel eyes."

"I'm sure a judge will jump when he hears that conclusive evidence."

"Now who's being pessimistic?"

Terry knew every shred of evidence that possibly linked Vaughn to the murders needed to surface before he requested a search warrant. His first battle was obtaining the warrant, the second being the grave possibility Vaughn already knew he was under the microscope. If he disposed of any remaining evidence that tied him to the murders, all would be lost. Talking to Collins put Terry's hopes in jeopardy, but his next step might crush them completely.

"Where to now?" Belinski asked.

"I have to talk to Gosser, and that'll probably go better without you present."

"You're going to tell him everything, aren't you?"

Terry remained silent a moment, letting the reporter stew in his juices.

"He doesn't like you anyway, so me telling him you tried to get him killed won't change much."

"Oh, thanks. Sounds like you're going to smooth things over so I don't have to live in fear of being pulled over or shot each morning."

"I'll be sure to explain how you didn't mean to get him disfigured."

"Thanks. I'll just shut up now and enjoy my few remaining days of life."

Terry shuffled through the paperwork, finding the information Lucy Wheaton provided him about the mysterious phone call. He found the information she provided over the phone, then looked up Vaughn's time sheet for the day in question, finding the man was indeed at Erie Wholesale the entire day.

"What are you looking for?" Belinski asked.

"Almost got it," Terry replied vaguely.

Belinski sighed as Terry looked through Daryl Swanson's log books, since drivers didn't exactly clock in for work. They were paid by the mile, more like traditional truckers, which suited Terry for the purposes of his search. He examined the departure time, several receipts, including a confirmed overnight stay in Vermont, and the mid-afternoon Saturday return time.

"I think I have something."

"Something good?"

"Something solid. I can prove that the person who called Pastor Mitchell's office two weeks before his death, from Erie Wholesale no less, was *not* Swanson."

Belinski drew a mischievous grin, looking his way.

"That mean you don't have to talk to Gosser?"

"Hardly. You're not getting off the hook that easily. I need him onboard before telling the task force about this because our deadline is almost over."

Belinski grumbled to himself, continuing to drive toward Terry's hotel.

CHAPTER 40

Terry knocked on the detective's door an hour later, receiving no answer during his first attempt. He persisted, calling out Gosser's name during his second attempt, knowing the detective's car sat in the adjacent parking lot.

"What?" Gosser asked through the door in a nasally voice without opening it.

"We need to talk."

"This isn't a good time."

"You're going to want to hear what I have to say, believe me."

Gosser groaned as he opened the door, presenting a face that looked worse than most domestic dispute beatings in Terry's experience. His eyes were both blackened, particularly beneath the eyes, his nose swollen in shades of black and purple, topped with a white bandage that crossed the bridge of his nose like a bow atop a present.

"No laughing," Gosser warned as Terry stepped inside.

"There's nothing funny about what happened to you, Randy. And I'm here because I know exactly who did it."

Gosser said nothing, studying Terry instead as though awaiting some kind of punch line to a practical joke.

"Have a seat," Gosser offered, waving his arm toward the kitchen table which contained only three chairs.

Sitting across from Gosser, Terry understood why the man called in sick. Gosser wasn't too ill to carry out his duties, but a man who worked in the public required a conventional appearance. The way he looked conveyed the impression he participated in bar brawls instead of solving crimes.

"Does it hurt?" Terry asked, receiving a sour look for an answer.

"Did you come here to poke fun at me or give me some good news?"

"I have some excellent news for you, but you're not going to like part of it."

"And what part is that?" Gosser asked, painfully twitching his nose, though it didn't improve his speech.

"We just put the wrong man in jail for the Sin Killer crimes."

Instead of looking surprised, Gosser resigned himself to the fact he somehow knew such a development was coming. Terry spent almost fifteen minutes explaining why Swanson never felt like a perfect fit for him, then went into how he first suspected Vaughn might be setting up his employee to take a fall. He skipped over the part about how he knew Vaughn broke into the detective's apartment.

"But why set up Swanson?"

"Opportunity. I think Vaughn found out Swanson was a person of interest in the Montana murders and decided to carry out his own need to kill, albeit in a vigilante style."

Gosser looked thoughtfully at the ceiling a moment.

"I have to admit most of what you said makes sense, but if Vaughn is really the psycho maniac you make him out to be, he's not going to stop killing just because Swanson's behind bars."

"I know."

Now Gosser's expression darkened as he realized the dire consequences of not acting on the information.

"What do we do next?"

"We have to talk to your buddy Collins."

Gosser rolled his eyes.

"Gary already hates me. It might work out better if you do the interview."

"Could he be involved in this? He and Vaughn have a long history."

"How long?"

"I talked to Collins' dad the other day. Their family practically raised Vaughn after his father was killed."

The last piece of information did little to make Gosser come around to the idea of approaching Collins.

"Collins and I are kind of the sheriff's golden boys," he revealed. "I'm kind of the bad boy and he's the squeaky clean father of three. We've never gotten along very well, and what we do at work couldn't be much more opposite. Do I think he's capable of cold-blooded murder?"

Gosser looked Terry squarely in the eyes.

"No."

"That's good to know, but I have to talk to him just the same."

"What exactly do you need me for?"

"Like it or not, I'm going to have to take these findings to the task force and request a search warrant for Vaughn's home and workplace. I need you to help me sell it, so I'm not on the edge of a cliff by myself."

"I trust you, Terry," Gosser said earnestly. "I always have. You know I'll go to bat for you."

"I appreciate that. You can't do anything rash, like go after Vaughn."

"I have a temper. I'm not stupid. When this all plays out and he gets sentenced to life in prison, I'll have the last laugh and I'll look the prick right in the eye."

Terry looked around the apartment, seeing nothing that looked out of place.

"Tell me what happened here last night."

"How about you tell me why Vaughn was here in the first place?"

"After you relive your traumatic event. You're not going to be happy when I tell you what I know."

Openly unhappy about having to share first, Gosser told Terry about unlocking his apartment, putting down the groceries, hanging up his jacket, then sensing something wasn't right. He talked about the cheap shot from the intruder, his pride more injured than his nose.

While he spoke, Terry spied several looks around the apartment, surprised to find the detective kept his place so neat and tidy. Based on rumors about Gosser, he expected to find machinery with restraining devices in every corner. Instead, he found a bleakly furnished living space with only a few pictures of Gosser's daughter and one of himself during his early days as a uniformed deputy. While Gosser probably didn't receive many visitors, he maintained the illusion he lived a conventional existence for the outside world.

"So he got in through your window?" Terry inquired once Gosser finished.

"Apparently. I'm not sure how, because there wasn't a rope or ladder sitting outside."

"He covered his tracks because he didn't know how long you'd be gone."

"Yeah, I figured that much out on my own. Now how about you spill the beans on why Vaughn singled me out when he supposedly doesn't know he's a suspect?"

In his attempt to spin the tale in a positive light on Belinski's behalf, Terry succeeded only in raising Gosser's ire. By the end, Gosser had clenched and unclenched his fists no less than a dozen times.

"I could kill that little son-of-a-bitch."

"That probably wouldn't be a good career move. He's related to the sheriff."

"Figures," Gosser said, still steamed. "Maybe I could make it look like an accident."

Terry laughed briefly, though the weight of his problems lingered in his mind.

"He didn't mean to send Vaughn after you. He was trying to protect the fact that he and I were working together."

"You could have trusted me over that fucker."

"I have no trust issues with you, Randy. I needed Belinski's set of skills, and a reporter's resources to help me make sure I was right."

Terry rubbed his head in frustration momentarily, knowing his next move potentially ruined his case against Vaughn if he timed it incorrectly. Questioning the younger Collins without having the search warrant ready, or at least in the works, possibly provided Vaughn an opportunity to clean house and discard any remaining evidence. Terry clung to the belief that the elder Collins truly believed Vaughn might be capable of the heinous murders, thus keeping quiet about their discussion.

"I know you're hurting, Randy," he finally said, "but I need to move forward with a search warrant on Vaughn before he gets wind of what I'm doing. I want your blessing, and your help, to focus on Vaughn instead of wrapping up the case against Swanson."

"We have to tell Gaffney. I can't go behind his back and spring this on him later."

"I know. We'll go with Belinski and tell him everything tomorrow, after you've had some time to cool off."

"Then tomorrow won't be soon enough."

"It'll have to be. I'm getting my paperwork in order so we can request the search warrant tomorrow morning right before I talk to your buddy."

Gosser grumbled at the thought of Collins being called his buddy.

"Tomorrow is going to be a long day, isn't it?"

"Probably, so buckle up."

CHAPTER 41

"You want to do what?" Gaffney questioned, even after Terry, Belinski, and Gosser had done their best to explain why the man in custody probably wasn't guilty of more than minor offenses.

All three sat around the conference table within the sheriff's office, though Gosser appeared as fidgety as a kid waiting for the school day to end.

"I want a search warrant for Vaughn's workplace and apartment," Terry said without faltering one bit.

"He's the son of a decorated police detective, and a model working citizen," Gaffney countered. "This is going to open up a can of worms you don't want."

"So you're okay with the wrong man going to prison for seven, maybe eleven murders?" Belinski asked his uncle.

Because the impending meeting with the sheriff left Gosser a bundle of nerves, the detective had remained quiet and restrained all morning, even when he and Belinski met face to face outside of the sheriff's second floor office.

"I'm not convinced any of you are on the right track," Gaffney said, picking up a file from the table and flapping it for all of them to see. "Your lab results came back. One of the guns found in Swanson's vehicle matched two of the crime scenes and the knife had remnants of Cirillo's blood on it."

Terry suspected nothing less, based on the fact he believed Vaughn completely set up Swanson to take the fall.

"He planted the hair fiber, Paul. He planted the guns and knife, too."

"Then how do you explain four unsolved murders in Montana where Swanson used to live?"

"Swanson wasn't the only suspect, but he bragged about being a suspect at Erie Wholesale. Vaughn used the opportunity to frame him for the murders he committed."

Gaffney didn't appear convinced. As a former state police trooper, investigator, and commander, his experience told him the most obvious answer usually proved accurate.

"If you get a search warrant, what do you expect to find?"

"Based on what you just said, there may still be murder weapons left to find. We never found the pole cleats or the cord used to strangle the hotel clerk, or the .22 silenced pistol used to kill Paulson."

"He could have thrown them away," Gaffney countered.

"And Vaughn could throw them away if we don't act today. I've already spoken with Ray Vaughn's old partner and he didn't exactly speak highly of young Nick."

"You could at least look at this from the angle that maybe Swanson had an accomplice," Belinski suggested.

"And *you* are still on my shit list, dear nephew."

"Mine too," Gosser uttered his first words since entering the room, his nose showing some improvement over the black and purple mess from the previous day.

"Are you on board with this, Randy?" Gaffney finally asked, unable to produce more objections.

"Yes, Sheriff."

"There are some things that point directly to Vaughn," Terry said before Gosser could change his mind about challenging Gaffney. "Like a call made to Harold James Mitchell's office from Erie Wholesale two weeks before his death that couldn't have been placed by Swanson."

"A call doesn't exactly prove much."

"He's ambidextrous," Belinski chimed in. "He also scheduled all of Swanson's deliveries, usually only a day or two beforehand. Certainly no more than a week ahead of time, so how could Swanson have known he would encounter Pastor Mitchell in April, much less an exact date?"

"That does lessen the chance of it being coincidence, doesn't it?" Gaffney concurred. "But a lot of this is still circumstantial."

"So is a lot of the case against Swanson," Terry countered. "Until that hair fiber conveniently appeared at the last crime scene, we didn't have jack shit on the killer. Which brings me to my next point. I need to talk to Collins while we get the search warrant underway."

"Collins?" Gaffney asked with a suspicious stare.

"His family practically raised Nick Vaughn. Conveniently, he was the one who got the anonymous tip about Swanson's hiding place."

"You can't be serious. Gary would never have anything to do with any of this."

Terry folded his arms, sitting back.

"I want *him* to tell me that."

Disturbed by the new revelations, especially concerning his own deputy, Gaffney thoughtfully rubbed his chin, deciding his next move.

"Okay. We run this search warrant under the assumption Vaughn might have assisted Swanson somehow. Otherwise no judge is probably going to go for it."

Gaffney looked directly at Terry.

"I want to be there when you talk to Gary. He's one of the best I've got, so I need to know."

"Fine," Terry said, "but I don't want you sticking up for him like some kind of union rep. I'm going to ask some tough questions."

"Okay," Gaffney agreed. "Get me a list of everything you three have and I'll take it to Howard Edelman. He's the most friendly judge when it comes to weaker cases, and I doubt he has any ties to the Vaughn family."

Terry knew very little about the judge except that he wasn't a Buffalo native. He ran on the platform that he was from the upstate area, capable of bringing change to the city while eliminating corruption. He won his first term, then his second, after convincing voters and police alike he deterred crime through his convictions and the sentences that followed.

"Here's what we have," Terry said, handing a full inventory of evidence against Vaughn to the sheriff.

Gaffney leafed through it, apparently satisfied.

"I'll draw up the paperwork and submit it to Edelman. I can have Gary up here within the hour."

Terry nodded, knowing it pained the sheriff to see Gosser pummeled by their new suspect, then discovering his other favorite deputy might be involved with a murderer.

No one bolted from the table, though each of the four men looked equally anxious to depart for different reasons. Feeling content to let Gaffney, or one of his people, draw up paperwork, Terry decided to step outside with Gosser and Belinski to prevent any disputes stemming from their unresolved issues.

Instead, he found Gosser extending the olive branch.

"I owe you many thanks for getting this resolved," he told the reporter.

"You mean that?"

"My broken nose doesn't appreciate how you went about it, but we wouldn't have known for certain if he hadn't made such a dumb move."

Terry noticed some of the staff outside of Gaffney's office trying to look away, though everything the three men said was within earshot.

"Maybe we should take this outside," he suggested, nodding toward the elevator.

One elevator ride later, they walked outside to the brisk December morning where an overcast sky blanketed the city. Gosser reached for some chewing gum instead of a cigarette, despite the pressure all of them felt regarding Vaughn. Even Belinski had something to lose if the search warrant turned up no hard evidence.

Namely his life.

"You want a go at Collins?" Terry kidded Gosser, trying to break the tension a bit.

"No thanks. He hates me as it is."

"Hate is a strong word."

"Yeah, well I don't fit into his picture perfect Norman Rockwell world, so he doesn't much care for me."

Terry didn't want to pry into Gosser's private life, so he decided to change the subject.

"I appreciate everything you've both done, and for sticking with me up there."

"You're welcome," Belinski said. "Thanks for tossing me a bone, too."

"Better get ready to add a couple chapters to your masterpiece."

Gosser looked at them both suspiciously.

"You getting any kickbacks from this little project?" he asked Terry.

"Hardly. My reward will be seeing Vaughn locked up for what he's done."

"It's too bad your buddy from Montana never solved his end of it," Gosser said. "Might have made our job a little easier."

"Vaughn was destined to kill in some form, no matter what. The fact Swanson presented the opportunity to mask his crimes may have brought this about sooner than later, but people were going to die at his hands eventually. I don't think Joe had a prayer of solving that case. He did well to narrow it down to two suspects."

"Either way, we're all going to be targets if this search warrant doesn't work," Belinski noted. "Vaughn will know."

All three stood silently a moment as a civilian brushed past them to get inside, unaware of the dire conversation she passed through. Terry thumbed toward the door, knowing he needed to ready himself to interview Collins.

"Much as I hate to, I've got to get back upstairs. I'll talk to both of you later."

Both men gave brief gestures before turning to find their vehicles. Terry felt all alone, against the police agency he'd teamed with the past eight months, Nick Vaughn, and the legend of Ray Vaughn.

"Forgive me," he said, looking skyward in case the senior Vaughn was looking down upon him.

***

Gaffney quickly got the search warrant information gathered and sent to Edelman for approval through one of his other detectives involved with the task force. The investigator had strict orders to call if there were any hang-ups or requests from the judge. Occasionally they asked for additional information or requested documentation of the search warrant. The sheriff assured Terry his past working relationship with Edelman was sure to get the warrant issued without a problem.

"You have people you want on this thing when it goes down?" Gaffney asked almost five minutes after Terry returned to his office.

"I want Lee Harris and anyone else from the task force who's available, including Gosser. I'm not dragging a bunch of strangers into this when we can toss his apartment and office in no time flat."

"Does Vaughn own any other properties?"

"I checked. He doesn't have properties, but he banks at two locations. One of the locations has a safe deposit box in his name."

"Do you really expect to find something convincing?"

"I don't know," Terry replied. "I'm worried Collins' dad might talk to Collins or Vaughn about this. One word and Vaughn is going to dump everything, if he hasn't already."

Gaffney stood from the swiveling office chair beside the conference table, pacing the floor momentarily. He, like Terry, seemed to understand that everything hinged on them finding something of relevance at one of the locations. Failure meant the task force being crucified by the media for going on a witch hunt against the son of a local legend.

"I really don't see Gary having anything to do with this."

"Vaughn had a lot of people fooled," Terry replied. "Collins was like a big brother to him, so maybe the whole family never saw beyond his facade."

"Maybe," Gaffney grumbled. "Is there a chance Vaughn worked with Swanson on this?"

"Slim to none," Terry replied. "I have documents that say they were in different places at the same time on several occasions."

"How could we have been so wrong about this?"

"What you mean to say is how could I have been so wrong about this. To be honest, Swanson never fit for me, but that's where the clues led us. Good detectives follow the clues, right?"

"Right, but you're better than anyone I've ever met, Terry. I suspect you're better than Ray Vaughn, too, which might piss off his son."

"He can be pissed all he wants once he's behind bars."

"You know if we don't find anything the guy might walk."

"And an innocent man may die in Montana. Bad as that may be, I'm more worried about what Vaughn will do if he remains free."

Gaffney sighed with a worrisome look.

"If this doesn't work, not only will we look like the bad guys, but Vaughn will be off-limits."

"That's a chance we have to take. Either way I'll be able to sleep at night."

Not afforded the luxury of an elaborate discussion or the insight Terry shared with Gosser and Belinski, Gaffney didn't appear entirely sold on Vaughn's involvement. Terry hoped the talk with Collins might shed more light on Vaughn's ultimate plan.

When the deputy walked in a few minutes later, he swallowed hard with an uncertain look about why the sheriff and a state police investigator wanted to see him. Instead of wearing his motorcycle gear, Collins wore the standard black uniform, complete with the Stetson style hat he held and a nylon jacket complete with his department's emblems and patches. He didn't appear quite as intimidating without the helmet, and in fact seemed sheepish about being called upstairs while on duty.

"Come in, Gary," Gaffney said, offering the deputy a seat at the conference table which Collins reluctantly took. "I take it you've met Terry Levine."

"Sure."

"He has a few questions for you."

"What kind of questions?" Collins asked skeptically, turning his attention to Terry.

Terry spoke with the deputy briefly about Swanson's apprehension, trying to detect any differences between Collins' oral recollection and his original written statement. No glaring discrepancies could be pinpointed, so he moved on to his true purpose for calling the interview.

"I've been through your written statement several times," Terry said, holding it up for display purposes briefly. "From this, there's only one thing I want to know, and that's who tipped you off about Swanson."

"As my statement says, I received a text message from one of my informants saying I should check out a break-in at that address."

"Who was the informant?"

"I'm not sure. The number wasn't listed in my phone."

"No, it wasn't," Terry said, holding up another sheet of paper. "It came from a disposable cell phone that had one-hundred minutes and five free text messages to send or receive. Since the buyer paid cash, we have no way of knowing exactly who bought the thing, but I do know one of those five messages came your way. I still think you have an idea who sent that to you or you wouldn't have ridden your Harley all the way out there to check."

Collins grew more agitated by the second. He gave the sheriff, who stood to the side, several glances as though asking for assistance, but Gaffney stood firm. Like most of the deputies who worked under Gaffney, he showed complete respect for the sheriff, even when being grilled by an outsider.

"What is this about?" Collins asked, fighting back additional words. "I brought Swanson in. He's off the streets. What does any of this matter?"

Terry bit his lip a moment, deciding how to proceed with the deputy. Already knowing he wanted to participate in the search warrant process, he decided to stop fishing.

"What is your relationship to Nick Vaughn?"

Collins reacted with a confused look too quickly to be anything except genuine or a professional liar. Based on the Collins everyone spoke highly about, Terry doubted he could be the latter.

"I know Nick. My family practically raised him after his father died."

"Is it possible Nick sent you that text message the morning of November 29th?"

Collins adjusted his seated position, not answering immediately.

"I don't know how Nick could know where Swanson was hiding."

"Sure he could. He was Swanson's boss. Maybe he put two and two together and wanted to throw his surrogate big brother a hand."

Shaking his head, Collins looked again toward the sheriff but Gaffney remained silent.

"I don't know who sent the text, and I don't appreciate you treating me like a goddamn street thug. If you're going to come at me, ask me what you want to and quit playing games."

"Fine," Terry said, rising from his chair to stare down at the deputy. "I think your buddy was involved in the Sin Killer slayings and I'm not entirely convinced you didn't have something to do with it."

"That's ridiculous!"

"Is it? Vaughn oversees all of his drivers, including Swanson, and makes their schedules. It's a strange coincidence that one of your *informants* happened to know exactly where Swanson was staying and knew that you were free to check it out in uniform on your scheduled day off."

Collins fumed, though he said nothing.

"Just tell us what you know, Gary," Gaffney finally ordered more than requested.

"Nick has police instincts because he was around my dad and me growing up. I wouldn't doubt it if he sent me that text, or if he somehow knew where Swanson was hiding. Nick is no killer though."

"Do you trust any of your informants as much as you do your pal?"

"No, of course not."

"I'm betting you wouldn't have gone over there and made your way into the house on just any old random text."

"I didn't enter the house until I saw the suspect's car in the garage," Collins reiterated. "If you're so sure Nick committed these murders, why are you hounding me instead of arresting him?"

"That may be coming shortly. I'm only going to ask this next question once, Deputy Collins. Do you personally have any involvement in the Sin Killer murders?"

"No," Collins answered firmly. "And Nick Vaughn has nothing to do with them, either. I don't know where you came up with this bullshit theory, but I won't have any part of it."

"I'm not asking you to."

Terry knew within half an hour teams were going to converge on everything they knew of that Vaughn owned. Even if Collins called to give his friend a warning, Vaughn would be caught trying to dispose of evidence, providing Terry with exactly what he wanted.

"Does Vaughn rent any storage places or other apartments that you know about?" Terry asked Collins to gather any additional search locations and test where the deputy's loyalties resided.

"No," Collins said with a hint of defeat in his voice, indicating he placed duty before friendship. "None that I know of."

"Let's start calling everyone," Terry suggested to Gaffney. "I'm going to start with Harris and Gosser. We can split into two teams and have one person check the safe deposit box."

"Did Gosser come up with this whole idea?" Collins asked, bolting from the chair, using his last line of defense to protect Vaughn.

"No. I did. I know he's a family friend and you two grew up together, but he's not the man you think he is. If I had more time to explain what we have against him, you might come around to our way of thinking."

"I'm not so sure about that."

"And I hope for your sake you aren't involved in any of this."

Terry understood Collins' loyalty to his friend, ill-placed as it might have been. Perhaps when the search warrant turned up some useful evidence against Vaughn the deputy's opinion would sway toward that of his colleagues. He seemed quick to blame Gosser for the witch hunt, which led Terry to believe the two possessed more history than either cared to share.

Somewhere, somehow, Vaughn slipped up during one of his murders, or during the planning stages of a murder. Terry only needed one solid piece of evidence to tie Vaughn to his malicious acts of murder, then the headlines could state the truth in every newspaper and newscast.

First, he needed to assemble his task force, and quickly, so he opened his cell phone to begin calling everyone he knew, including an old friend from the state police he hoped might be free to assist him.

CHAPTER 42

When Terry Levine requested Randy Gosser be part of the search warrant party, the detective considered it natural that he would assist in every way, despite his injuries. Terry said he would head up the search at Erie Wholesale because he wanted Vaughn to know he was the one responsible. After several minutes of arguing over the phone, Gosser convinced the trooper to let him be the one overseeing the man's office.

Personally, Gosser wanted to see the look on Vaughn's face when his office was ransacked for evidence. He also wanted the man to squirm when he learned Gosser knew exactly who his attacker was from Monday night. Though Gosser wasn't allowed to say anything to the man, except lawful statements while they searched his office, that didn't mean the detective couldn't shoot piercing stares his way.

Though he considered the office search the more mundane of the two primary searches, Gosser prayed something turned up so he could slap his handcuffs over Vaughn's wrists. Modern policing discouraged roughing up suspects as urban police had a decade or two prior, but Gosser wanted to make an exception when the time came.

A city police detective waited outside with two officers and a forensic technician for word to search Vaughn's truck once the warrant was presented. The group knew to look for hair fibers, blood, or any trace of the weapons used in each of the seven homicides.

Gosser walked with Lee Harris and two detectives from the Buffalo Police Department who assisted the task force when asked. The group met with the plant manager to explain their presence, then marched their way toward Nick Vaughn's office. Harris did the honors of presenting their copy of the search warrant to Vaughn and explaining that he was suspected of collaborating with Daryl Swanson on statewide murders.

Vaughn acted flabbergasted, though it quickly passed when the investigators refused to hear his verbal complaints.

Gosser passed on the opportunity to serve the warrant since he still sounded like a nasally cartoon character with his nose swollen and bruised. He immediately stared at Vaughn, who continued to give him uneasy glances, though the man refused to show fear or discomfort, as though he knew this might be coming and he already had it beaten.

Gosser's one regret was that he couldn't barge into Vaughn's apartment uninvited as Terry Levine and the other crew were certainly doing at this very moment. A feeling of violation still crept into the reaches of his mind. Gosser now understood the trepidation and uneasiness victims of theft and burglary felt. All of his life, Gosser considered himself fortunate to never be victimized in such a way. Perhaps his status as a cop, or his good sense in choosing secure housing kept him from being targeted by criminals, but Nick Vaughn was no common criminal.

"You care to explain this to me?" Vaughn asked Harris, trying to ignore Gosser as though the two had never met.

Technically speaking, they hadn't officially met, so Vaughn played his role perfectly.

"Sir, if you don't wait outside, I can have you restrained," Harris replied.

Vaughn threw his hands up, then walked toward the door.

"This is entirely ludicrous. I've done nothing wrong, so you're not going to find anything."

Based on previous results, Gosser believed the last part of Vaughn's statement, which worried the detective, though it didn't stop him from providing menacing looks in Vaughn's direction.

Gosser joined in the search, helping rummage through desk drawers, the filing cabinet, and even looking behind and inside family heirlooms. Since janitors and other personnel likely had access to Vaughn's office, it seemed doubtful he would hide anything damning at work. The gold-mine, if one existed, resided within his apartment, his sanctuary where he could dream of his vigilant acts, then plan them thoroughly.

Wondering how the other group fared, Gosser glanced up once again to give Vaughn a piece of his mind when he found the man staring back this time. His provided a smug look, just short of a smirk, as though he knew the groups were destined to find nothing. Even more than that, his eyes bored into Gosser, as though to let the detective know the score was Vaughn two, Gosser zero.

A strange tingle went up his spine as Gosser returned to the search, suddenly feeling somewhat uneasy. He hoped so arrogant an individual was careless enough to slip up somewhere, and hopefully Terry and the others found a crucial piece of evidence that condemned this heartless bastard to life in prison.

***

Terry finally decided to call Duggan because he didn't want the state police brass caught unaware if evidence against Vaughn turned up and the media got wind of the story. Though a bit surprised at the turn of events, Duggan supported Terry and the decision to conduct the search. Terry went on to ask if he could borrow Anita Soriano from the Batavia barracks, receiving immediate approval, though Duggan informed him her last name was now Soriano-Jordan because she had finally married.

When she pulled up to Vaughn's apartment, Terry couldn't help but smile at one of his favorite coworkers from his old assignment. Anita stepped from her unmarked car, looking him up and down before the two bypassed handshakes and opted for a quick hug, despite a few task force members looking their way.

"You haven't changed a bit," Anita said, still examining him. "You still have lousy taste in ties, I see."

"There isn't much need for more than one or two in the North Country. What were you thinking, getting married? You said you'd never tie the knot."

"Got tired of waiting for you to get divorced and come back down here."

Terry grinned, missing the playful banter they shared when they worked cases together. Relocating had its perks, but Terry always found himself leaving great people behind.

Conceived by a Dominican Republic father who played minor league baseball for three years and a black waitress mother, Anita knew what having little in life meant. She fought and clawed for a position with the state police in the recruit class that preceded Terry's. Fluent in French and Spanish, Anita made herself necessary in numerous instances because she served as an interpreter for French-Canadians or the growing number of Hispanic residents occupying areas of New York.

One of the byproducts of being deprived during her childhood was self-indulgence in lifestyle and food. Terry noticed Anita's weight loss since their last encounter, wondering if she had finally decided to market herself to settle down.

"My husband is a pilot, so thank God he's gone half the time or I'd go crazy," she revealed. "It works out well, because when he's home, I'm usually on-call and gone half the night."

Terry led the way toward the front door where the apartment manager stood with a key, impatiently tapping his foot.

"So what have you got, Terry?" Anita inquired as Terry held the door for her to enter first. "I thought you already had someone in custody for this."

"We do, but we might have followed the wrong breadcrumb trail."

"And this guy?"

"The supervisor of the guy we arrested," Terry said as they followed the manager upstairs. "I think this guy set Swanson up for a variety of reasons. Swanson never really fit the profile, but everything just pointed to him. This guy has motive and the means to pull it off."

"And deflect blame."

"Yeah. That too."

When the door opened, Terry found Vaughn's apartment as tidy as his workplace, which told him about the man's anal retentive habits. Excessively organized and tidy, Vaughn fit the Sin Killer profile far more accurately than Swanson. With Gosser occupying Vaughn at Erie Wholesale, Terry was free to conduct the search thoroughly, without interference.

"You all know what we're looking for," Terry stated once everyone stepped inside. "We need anything tying Vaughn to the murders. Josh, can you check his computer?"

The civilian computer technician borrowed from BPD nodded affirmatively, then made his way toward the home computer in one corner. Terry stuck with Anita while a detective from BPD, and another from Erie County, took opposite ends of the apartment to begin their search.

"Tell me what you think," Terry asked of Anita.

With a background in criminal psychology, she knew how a variety of criminals thought regarding their crimes and their lives. She sized up the apartment rather quickly, having never met Vaughn, which allowed her to develop an unbiased assessment.

"Look carefully through his paperwork," she suggested. "Someone like this probably isn't going to keep anything from his crimes around here. It's almost like this apartment provides an alias, or alter ego if you will, to keep that side of him from the rest of the world."

Terry joined in the search, careful to examine every document thoroughly, hoping to find some kind of secret storage facility, or a piece of land Vaughn owned that wasn't publicly listed. He worked around the computer technician at the desk, finding mostly bills and old newspaper clippings. All of the articles pertained to his father, everything from the man's heroics to his tragic death. A few photographs of a younger Nick Vaughn and his father, usually in uniform or dressed up, were stacked beneath the yellowed articles. Only one family photo with Vaughn's mother could be found, with no images or mention of her anywhere else in the desk.

Vaughn worshiped his father, but not so much his mother. Perhaps her weakness in the wake of Ray Vaughn's death, turning to drugs and alcohol, pitted her son against her. Few people, including his surrogate family, probably knew the real truth, and neither father nor son Collins was providing much assistance.

Sparsely decorated, the apartment showed little pizzazz. Without the benefit of paintings, family pictures, or any other artwork, it looked more like a guest room than a residence.

"It's like he eats and sleeps here," Anita said as she opened a kitchen cupboard with standard food, "but he lives somewhere else."

"Maybe inside his mind," Terry figured aloud, closing the last of the desk drawers. "Finding anything, Josh?"

"Oddly enough, he didn't password protect his computer," the technician answered. "I'm not finding any files out of the ordinary in here, but I haven't even touched on the internet search information yet."

"Keep at it. We'll take the computer if we have to."

Terry turned to Anita as they headed toward the bedroom where one of the detectives continued to rummage through several shoeboxes of photos and scrap pieces of paper.

"Look at this," Anita said, her attention captured by a collection of videos and books lining every inch of a bookcase. "All of this is information about police investigations, particularly murders."

Terry found entire documentary box sets about police conducting murder investigations throughout the country. Most of the books revolved around true serial killer sprees, or the investigations of long-term cases that included multiple victims. Though certainly not a crime, it appeared Vaughn had an interest, if not a fascination, regarding investigations. An intricate knowledge of investigative workings would certainly give an edge to anyone planning to commit homicides, again confirming Terry's theory.

"Any other vibes?" he asked Anita.

"He's trapped within a world, either from his past, or conjured up within his mind. To the world he looks perfect, lives a normal life, but he's really isolated. Probably never had a girlfriend, and if he dates, it's for show. No woman lets an apartment look this bland for long, so he probably hasn't had a long-term relationship."

"You're picking all of this up from a quick look around his apartment?" the city detective asked without looking up from the box as he continued to sift through paperwork.

"That, and what I know of the murders," Anita answered. "This man isn't done, Terry. He *can't* be done killing people, even if he gets away with what he's done so far."

She drew a perplexed look, searching for the right words.

"This is where he lives, but I don't think it's his temple."

"His temple?" the detective asked, still hunched over the box.

Anita ignored his comment, still looking to Terry.

"It's like here he is his father's good boy, but there's somewhere where he can be his true self. He might keep his weapons there, maybe even souvenirs from his victims."

"I don't think he took anything from the victims," Terry noted.

"No, but that doesn't mean he didn't record the events themselves."

"Well, I'm not finding anything useful," the detective said, shutting the last box before shoving it into the closet.

The Erie County detective approached them.

"No weapons, and no incriminating paperwork in the drawers," he reported. "Found tax records and some old birthday cards, but that's about it."

"What's left to check?" Terry asked.

"Just the computer."

"I want you guys to double-check if Vaughn's parents might have left him property that's still in their names. This place is too sterile. There has to be something we've missed."

"Bank records didn't show payments for any property, storage, or extra apartments," one of the detectives noted.

"But we still have the bank box," Terry said, deeply suspecting his search warrant was little more than a brick wall at the end of this investigative avenue. "Can you two help Josh pack up the computer while we check out the bank?"

Both nodded.

"Let's see if this is strike three," Terry said as he and Anita prepared to step outside to the cold, windy day.

***

After the ordeal of getting the bank manager to assist them in locating and opening Vaughn's bank box with the assistance of a locksmith, Terry hung his head in complete disappointment. Inside the box were several pieces of jewelry, life insurance forms, some cash, and a variety of stocks. No smoking gun or condemning evidence like trinkets taken from the murder sites presented itself.

Standing inside a secured room within one of Buffalo's largest banks, Terry suddenly felt overcome by hopelessness because a murderer was slipping through the law's grasp. They still had the computers at his apartment and workplace, and several items left to check, such as his cell phone use and locations during the confirmed murder dates. If Vaughn made a call during his travels to murder someone, his location could be triangulated by the cell phone towers that bounced the signals while he talked.

"I don't know what to tell you," Anita said as they stood in the room, disappointment lingering overhead like a storm cloud. "I don't doubt this is your killer, but he seems awfully prepared for this."

Surrounded by gold, brown, and silver coloration that glimmered beneath artificial lighting, Terry sighed as he found the case slipping away. He still possessed circumstantial evidence against Vaughn, but nowhere near enough to convince the district attorney to press charges against the man. Even under the pretense that Vaughn conspired with Swanson, they had no physical evidence against him. By planting DNA evidence at a crime scene, then the guns and knife inside Swanson's car before contacting Collins, Vaughn virtually ensured his immunity from prosecution.

"You were lucky to even figure this out, Terry," Anita said. "No one else did."

"Lot of good it did. Short of a miracle, he's going to remain free to kill again."

"I'm sorry I wasn't more help."

"I appreciate you coming. You validated my thoughts, which is a big help."

"What are you going to do?"

"What *can* I do? I live five hours away, so I can't even track his movements. He's going to get away with this and no one will stop him."

Despite being in a vault, Terry heard his cell phone ring, so he stepped onto the bank floor to answer it.

"Levine."

"Terry, it's Gosser. We turned up empty at Erie Wholesale, but we took his computer."

"Same here."

"What about the bank vault?"

"Zilch. We may be screwed."

Gosser remained silent a moment.

"He had a look, Terry, like he knew this was coming and he was totally prepared for it. Kind of a cocky attitude about the whole thing once we got started."

"Did you say anything to him?"

"No. Harris did the talking. I just shot him some dirty looks."

"Is he still there?"

"Yeah."

"See if Gaffney will put a tail on him for the evening. Maybe he has some stuff stashed somewhere and he'll go for it."

"I'll call him. You really think Vaughn might do that?"

"Probably not, but we're running out of chances. Keep me posted."

"Will do."

Terry clipped his phone to his belt, ready to leave the bank. He wasn't accustomed to defeat, so he wasn't certain what he might do if Vaughn escaped cleanly. Kimmerling pegged him incorrectly because Terry wasn't capable of cold-blooded murder. Therefore, a vigilante killing of Vaughn wasn't his nature, nor was he willing to stoop to that level.

Somewhere, somehow, Vaughn left a damning clue behind. Blossoming serial killers often made mistakes, and he certainly kept some kind of memorabilia for his pleasure. Reliving their crimes becomes crucial to tide them over until the next opportunity presented itself. The fact that Vaughn didn't keep newspaper clippings in his home or work desk surprised Terry. Most killers loved hearing about their exploits, especially when it came to outwitting the police.

Of course Vaughn believed himself to be righteous in his actions. He likely felt he was assisting the police and all crime fighters, and if that theory proved accurate, Vaughn might feel scorned by the police who had the audacity to implicate him.

"What are you thinking?" Anita asked as they walked past the bank manager, thanking him quickly for his assistance.

"I'm thinking I've failed seven murder victims and their families."

"It's not over yet."

"No, but we're hanging by a thread. Vaughn knows how cell phones work, so I doubt he was stupid enough to call anyone when he traveled."

When they stepped outside, an awkward moment passed between them.

"Is there anything else I can do?" Anita asked.

"No. I'm sorry for dragging you into this, but I needed to see a familiar face, and to hear that I was on the right track."

"You're quite welcome," Anita replied, giving him a hug. "Call me if there's anything else I can do."

"I will. You take care of yourself and that husband of yours."

Anita returned a weak smile before turning toward her car for the return trip to Batavia. Like Terry, she was accustomed to closing major cases without fail.

As he turned toward his own vehicle, a thought crossed his mind. If Vaughn grew up around the Collins family, perhaps they owned a summer resort, or some kind of lodge outside of the city, or even the county. If he possessed a key and unlimited access, perhaps Vaughn hid his secrets there. With no one from the family cooperating, because of their faith in Vaughn, Terry could not pursue his thought. And because they were not named in the search warrant, he couldn't check their bank records or their properties.

What frustrated him most about the case was being one step away from conclusively fingering Vaughn for the murders and the misplaced trust of two men possibly making all the difference.

Opening his car door, Terry prepared for the waiting game ahead. He doubted Vaughn would trust Belinski after the search warrant, and putting the reporter's life in danger wasn't a viable option. Either way, Terry's time in Buffalo neared an end, so he planned on calling his wife to let her know their holiday plans were on track.

Starting his departmental car, Terry pondered how to handle the bad news he felt certain was coming his way. He didn't want Nick Vaughn to be the albatross he toted the rest of his career, yet he felt powerless to stop the man within the confines of the laws and ethics he swore to uphold.

For the first time in a long time, he didn't know where to go or what task to work on next. Holing up and hiding from the world sounded good, but Terry wasn't ashamed of his work, even when he failed. Deciding he didn't want to face anyone until answers came his way, he started the car, then drove toward his hotel.

CHAPTER 43

Terry considered the final task force meeting a bittersweet experience, minus the sweet. Standing before Gaffney, Gosser, Lee Harris, and a handful of other investigators, he delivered the news that Vaughn's computers turned up nothing incriminating and his cell phone records, and checks with his provider, failed to place him near the murder sites. Vaughn likely avoided incriminating himself by never making calls in transit, or leaving his phone behind altogether.

Standing at the head of Gaffney's conference table, he found disappointed looks across the faces of everyone in the room. None of them believed the search warrant was issued in error, or that Swanson carried out any of the murders. Terry presented a strong case, from their point-of-view, that incriminated Vaughn beyond a doubt.

Their failure to discover any evidence at three different locations only served to affirm the beliefs of the Collins family that Vaughn was like another son and an angel for all intents and purposes.

"There isn't much I can tell all of you that we haven't already covered," Terry said. "We know who's responsible for the Sin Killer murders, but we don't have proof. Daryl Swanson is probably going to do life for nothing more than identity theft and breaking into someone's house."

"Making things worse," Gaffney stated as he looked around the table from his seat, "Vaughn has hired a lawyer who made sure to tell us any further investigation against his client was grounds for a civil suit. He said his client would let the misunderstanding behind the search warrant go, but he didn't want to be a target because it might disgrace his father's good name."

"He's doing a bang-up job of that himself," Gosser added testily.

Terry looked outside as the sun tried to peek around several gray clouds unsuccessfully. It provided a mock appearance of warmth, like Terry's mind felt knowing he found the Sin Killer only to watch him slip away.

"I want to thank all of you for working so hard on this," Terry said earnestly, looking everyone in the eyes. "This isn't what we wanted, I know, but I'm absolutely positive Vaughn can't stop killing now that he's gotten a taste of blood. It's up to you guys to keep tabs on him when you get the chance and think of him every time you have an unsolved homicide."

Gaffney stood.

"We want to thank you for coming down here and spending so much time heading this thing up. After what we did, I doubt Vaughn's coworkers will look at him the same again. He's going to slip up, or someone will rat him out."

"Let's hope so. If there's anything I can do for any of you, I'm only a phone call away."

Everyone at the table stood to shake hands with Terry, wishing him a safe journey home. The only thing he wanted more than his regular life at home was knowing Nick Vaughn would somehow pay for the sins he committed while playing God. No man deserved the titles of judge, jury, and executioner under man or God's laws because man wasn't always correct in his assessments.

Gosser took the elevator down with Terry purposely.

"I really thought Collins would come around," Terry said wishfully.

"Father or son?"

"Father. I don't think your buddy knows exactly what Vaughn is, but I think his dad is hiding something."

"Would a sworn officer, retired or not, really assist a murderer?" Gosser questioned as though his own faith were shaken.

"Probably not," Terry replied as the doors opened, revealing the first floor to the investigators. "I think he's going to put two and two together, but I was hoping he'd do it before I left for home."

Gosser stood before a collage of every photographed sheriff who'd ever held office in Erie County, including former United States President Grover Cleveland. Terry wondered how their predecessors might have handled Vaughn in the old days. It didn't much matter, because while the present situation reeked of deception by several people, Terry found no other options.

"I'm going to feel like shit if this goes to trial and they want me on the stand," Gosser confessed.

"They won't want me, Randy, because I'll probably be more help to the defense."

Several investigators walked past them to the brisk outdoors, returning to their jobs. Because some of them merely brushed against the case without seeing every murder firsthand, or understanding the development of Vaughn's bloodlust, they might easily move on and focus on other cases.

Not Terry.

"Don't worry," Gosser assured him. "I'll be taking up a new hobby so Mr. Vaughn doesn't get lonely. I still owe him one."

"You be careful, Randy. The last thing I need is to be coming back here for your funeral."

"It's a little harder to take me out when I see it coming. Believe it or not, I can be discreet."

"I *don't* believe it, but I'll feel better knowing Vaughn can't rest easy."

Gosser grinned as he extended his hand.

"It's been great working with you."

Terry firmly shook hands, because he respected Gosser as a detective and a person, despite the vicious rumors.

"You're a hell of an investigator, Randy. Don't let anyone tell you otherwise."

"I appreciate that, Terry, but you did all the hard work."

"I took some good guesses but you did all the legwork."

"All for nothing," Gosser said with a deflated tone that lasted only a few seconds. "What are you going to do with yourself, Trooper Levine?"

"I've got one last appointment with a reporter, then I'm heading home. You be careful, Randy, and call me if you need anything."

"Will do."

Terry gave a nod before walking out of the Erie County Sheriff's Department for what might have been the last time. He never wanted to return unless he got to confront Nick Vaughn behind bars, or to serve the warrant that put the man there. Because his efforts turned up nothing concrete against Vaughn, all local departments would have to abide by a hands-off policy regarding him, or risk harassment issues.

Walking to his car, Terry hoped Gosser played it safe when monitoring Vaughn because the man obviously knew the detective. His worries extended to the victims and families lying in a path of destruction when Vaughn felt safe to take lives once again. Terry plucked his phone away from his belt, opening it to call Belinski for their final meeting.

***

A growing desire to be home as soon as possible overcame Terry, so he opted to meet Belinski at a coffee shop on the east side of Buffalo. From there, hitting the state highways for the start of his trip home would be a cinch. With luck, he could be waiting at the house when his kids came home from school and Sherri from work.

Although he liked Belinski the more he got to know him, Terry didn't want to spend the day with the man. He wanted to enjoy his own house instead of a hotel and wash Buffalo from his skin with a long, hot shower.

"I'm sorry things didn't work out," the reporter said as they occupied comfortable chairs beside the window.

"Me too. I have to admit I'm used to winning."

Terry took a long sip of coffee, staring outside at the inch of white snow lingering along the curbs and grassy patches like a bad rash. He felt fortunate the weather report didn't call for additional snowfall or drifting during his drive home.

The coffee shop, by comparison, felt rather roomy. Tables and chairs lined the main lobby so people could set up laptop computers and browse the internet. Several other chairs, strategically placed near magazine racks, provided views of the city where friends could chat or eat the overpriced pastries and bagels.

"You called this meeting," Belinski noted. "I thought you'd want to be getting home instead of hanging out with me."

"I need to know something, Ben."

"What's that?" Belinski asked curiously before taking a long swallow from his own coffee cup.

"How does the book end?"

"The book isn't finished yet," Belinski answered cautiously, suspecting Terry was fishing for a particular answer.

He was right.

"For now it ends with Swanson being taken into custody followed by whatever verdict a jury decides."

"Even though you know better?"

"That's what second editions are for, my friend."

"So you're willing to ignore facts as readily as the prosecutor's office?"

Belinski shifted his eyes toward the city beyond the window.

"I'm not a cop, Terry."

"You were. And you think like one."

"Thinking like one might get me killed if I pursue this any further."

Terry shrugged.

"I'm not asking you to stalk the man, Ben. Maybe you could dig a little deeper into his past, put together a dossier of sorts for me."

"I thought this case was closed, Trooper Levine," the reporter replied slyly.

"You know, you and Vaughn aren't that much different," Terry said, receiving a roll of Belinski's eyes in return. "You both come from police families, you both have local notoriety, and you both tested for police jobs. And though you both failed, it was for different reasons."

"I'm sure my uncle gladly told you about my life's history, but how could you possibly learn about Vaughn?"

"Friends in Albany," Terry said, holding up an opened envelope with a sheet of paper inside. "He tested twice for my department. The first time he was eliminated after the interview, but the second time they passed him and he failed the psych exam."

"Failed how?"

"Failed miserably. I can't and won't use this because in the scheme of things it doesn't mean shit, but it might down the road."

Belinski took a small bite from the blueberry muffin he bought with his coffee.

"You still haven't gotten to why we're even sitting here," he noted.

Terry cleared his throat.

"I want to know if you're in this for the right reasons or just the big payday, Ben."

"At the risk of sounding conceited, I'm not exactly hurting for money, Terry. Like you, I guess I just like getting to the bottom of things."

"Then you're not entirely like Vaughn."

"Not at all, actually."

Terry wanted to hear that clear separation before continuing their conversation. Belinski showed disdain for Vaughn, because he knew the truth, and Terry believed that ultimately the man would print the truth if Vaughn were caught and convicted. Perhaps, just perhaps, he might be game to help bring the man to justice in his own way. Reporters possessed access points with the same general public that tended to slam doors in the faces of well-meaning police officers.

"How long before the book is done?" Terry inquired, receiving a suspicious look from the reporter.

"I'm still sorting out the research and gathering items. It could be months."

"I heard you had a publisher already lined up."

"Damn, you *are* good. If I were Nick Vaughn I'd be worried."

"That was actually a lucky guess on my part, but if you have someone lined up that means you'll be working double time to get it finished."

"I suppose," Belinski said before sipping his coffee again.

"Then maybe you'll want these for reference," Terry said, sliding a thin packet of papers toward the reporter along the end table between them.

"What are they?"

"My personal notes, censored where necessary, but complete nonetheless, regarding this entire case."

A very subtle, cautious grin crossed the reporter's face.

"Including Vaughn?"

"Especially Vaughn. Can I count on you to help me finish that part of the story?"

"Yes," Belinski answered without hesitation. "I know the bastard is guilty as much as you do. I can probably dig up some more stuff on him."

"Good, because you're the only hope at this point. Your uncle and I have been taken out of the game."

"Thank you."

"You're welcome."

"Hey, is the stuff from Albany in here?"

"Yes, but that didn't come from me, or Albany," Terry replied adamantly. "You know how to treat that information, right?"

"Of course."

"Good, because being on your uncle's shit list is nothing compared to being on mine. I expect to hear from you regularly, and I definitely want to see a rough draft of that thing before your publisher butchers it."

Belinski looked relieved, yet burdened at the same time.

"Can I give your brother credit for deciphering the bloody symbols?"

"You did just as much as he did."

"I know, but I'm getting the glory and the paycheck from writing the book. It's the least I can do."

"I appreciate that, and I think Kenny would, too. He probably needs a pick-me-up in his life right now."

Belinski waited a few seconds before asking his next question.

"Think he'd talk to me?"

"I'm sure he would. Kenny's nothing like me, so he's not jaded against reporters."

"Funny. I was actually referring to his incident a couple years ago. Thought maybe he'd clam up when it came to serial killers."

"No, he really doesn't. In fact, he's been visiting the man who almost killed his family."

"Wow," Belinski said for lack of better wording. "The same guy who admitted he wanted to kill Ken?"

"The same. And the more I push him to stay away from Kimmerling, the more he goes there. He's on a religious forgiveness kick and it worries me, because God knows what that psychopath is filling Kenny's head with, especially about me."

"Sorry to hear that," Belinski said, uncomfortably shifting his weight in the chair.

"Maybe talking to you would give him a fresh perspective about what these guys are all about."

"Didn't I read that Kimmerling was up for an appeal soon? Could he be using your brother to his advantage?"

"I don't see how. Ken's not a material witness, and hopefully Kimmerling won't be in a spot where he can use character witnesses. To be honest, I don't care if the son-of-a-bitch gets transferred or rots away in Malone. I just don't want some crazy loophole to put him in minimum security or a mental facility."

"Maybe we can drop him and Vaughn off on some desert island."

"We can always dream, can't we?"

Both men had run out of conversation, and Terry saw little need to prolong his trip home. He stood to say farewell to Belinski, then return to the one place that still provided him with strength and some measure of peace. This time, however, his mind was sure to wander during the five hours he spent on the road. Normally he could reflect on a job well-done, but this time he wanted to think up a way, any way, to keep Nick Vaughn from harming more New Yorkers.

After a goodbye and a handshake, Terry stepped into the cold, thinking how falsely warm the sunny weather looked from inside. Much like Vaughn, Mother Nature sometimes deceived people without a care in the world.

CHAPTER 44

After returning to his hometown in December, Terry attempted to live a normal life again. He acted the part, eating dinner with his family, watching his son's basketball games and his younger daughter's cheerleading sessions. Britney, his oldest child, returned home occasionally on weekends from her freshman year at college. He tried to analyze her behavior without being overbearing, concerned that she might get experimental with boys, drugs, and alcohol, no longer inhibited by home life.

With two children still at home, he didn't exactly feel any empty nest syndrome yet, though he felt old with a child in college. It didn't seem that long ago that he was a rookie state trooper fresh off his marriage and honeymoon with Sherri. Nearly twenty years with the state police had come and gone with numerous highs and lows.

Terry struggled during his first few weeks at home to put Buffalo and Nick Vaughn behind him. Somehow the man evaded every part of the search warrant, phone records and all, which placed the blame squarely on Daryl Swanson. It seemed every time Terry began to move on and fall into his normal routine someone called with an update, or the news mentioned the case or the impending trial.

Today he found himself outside on a sunny day, just above the freezing mark, returning fire after some snowballs hit him in the side. The culprit, his ten-year-old son, giggled and laughed as he playfully dodged several packed white chunks. Thankfully, Corbin had yet to reach his rebellious teenage years, though he still felt certain he wanted to follow in Terry's footsteps. Surrounded by love and support his entire life, Corbin endured only minimal setbacks during his childhood. Terry and his wife put no restrictions on their children, except that they expected them to attend college. Telling them otherwise meant selling them short before they even reached their high school years.

"You missed, Dad!" Corbin yelled as they both packed snowballs in the front yard, ready to continue their playful battle.

Of course Terry had missed when he threw hard, not wanting to injure his son. As Corbin dared to draw a bit closer, however, he lobbed a snowball with half power that smacked his son in the chest where he was protected by no less than four layers of clothing.

"Got you that time!"

Corbin threw and missed, then missed again as Terry dodged them successfully each time. He playfully dove behind the snow fort he and Corbin had built a month prior during a wet snowfall that made packing snow rather easy. Occasionally sunlight reduced its stature, or bitter cold temperatures turned it to solid chunks of ice, but the fort remained steadfast and ready for impromptu snowball fights.

Rounding the corner, his son threw a snowball that hit him squarely in the shoulder before he could regain his footing. Terry scrambled to his feet as Corbin reached for more snow, wrapping his arms around his son's waist and hoisting him into the air and over his shoulder as he ran around the yard. When he finally found a soft mound of snow, he performed a wrestling type throw on his son at half speed to cushion the impact. As expected, Corbin giggled when he hit the snow pile, springing immediately to his feet to wage more snowy war.

From the corner of his eye, Terry spied Sherri at the front door holding the cordless phone, which always meant someone wanted him. During the past few months, calls related to his job, namely the Sin Killer case, brought nothing except bad news. It seemed Belinski threw himself into his book writing, rather than seeking the truth about Vaughn, because he typically avoided calls and e-mails from Terry. Despite orders from the state police brass and everyone who oversaw the task force to cease any investigation of Nick Vaughn, Gosser made the man his new hobby.

Perhaps out of spite for his broken nose, or a sense of justice that paralleled Terry's, Gosser monitored Vaughn's activities both on and off the clock until early February when Vaughn's attorney went to the sheriff with video proof that Gosser had conducted surveillance on his client. The video showed Gosser, in his personal vehicle, outside of Vaughn's residence simply waiting and watching.

Because he wasn't on the county's time, Gaffney let him off with a written warning and the threat of an unpaid leave if such behavior continued. While Gaffney wasn't on Vaughn's side, he couldn't risk public attention that might cause Vaughn's lawyer to take legal action against the department while Swanson sat in a jail cell awaiting trial.

Sometimes justice was blind and deaf Terry thought as he climbed the three stairs to his porch to get the phone from his wife.

Terry believed Vaughn reported Gosser, rather than targeting him for two reasons. One, killing an officer of the law was likely taboo for a man who pictured himself a vigilante, and secondly, harming Gosser would draw unwanted attention to himself while destroying his flawless credibility.

"Hello?" Terry answered after receiving the phone.

"Terry, this is Gary Collins. We spoke a few months back."

"I seem to recall you ordering me out of your house."

"Yeah, well, a few things have changed."

Terry stepped inside, finding the kitchen almost dark because he was snowblind from the winter wonderland outside. His eyes began to adjust as he removed his jacket, then headed toward the den where he kept an office full of his own files and books.

"How exactly have things changed?" Terry asked, taking a seat behind his desk.

"We have a camp around the Adirondacks. Whenever we went camping as a family, Nick went with us. I just went over there to clean up and check on the place. I found a little box in the wood pile behind the camp."

"Oh?"

"Don't get too excited," Collins said. "The box had some newspaper articles, but no trinkets. Nothing that would tie anyone to any murders."

"So you're basically calling me to tell me I was right?"

"I suppose. And for what it's worth, I'm sorry."

"Sorry doesn't help the man rotting away in a jail cell for seven murders he didn't commit. What does your son think?"

Collins sighed.

"He's not sold. I didn't even tell him about what I found because he's stubborn as a mule on the subject."

"Kind of like his old man."

"Yeah. Kind of."

"Look, I can't do anything further with the investigation, Mr. Collins. We've been ordered to stay away from Nick short of him holding up a bank."

"I know. Maybe you can't tail him, or ask him questions, but he'll trust me. Maybe I can get something useful out of him. If he has that box at the camp, maybe he has some other items lying around somewhere."

"Maybe," Terry said, swiveling in his office chair a bit to look out the window at the snow-covered field beside his house. "I won't hold my breath, because he's beaten us at every turn."

"I understand. Maybe I can bring him into the family fold again. It can't hurt."

"Seven people would disagree."

"Yeah, well I'll be careful."

Terry stood, noticing his son walking in from the cold outdoors as Sherri helped him remove his layers of clothing. He couldn't fathom inviting such a dangerous individual as Vaughn into his life and near his family. Terry couldn't help but wonder where Collins took his family on weekend retreats. The precious family memories were surely wasted on the man's surrogate son, but such a place might harbor dark secrets to this day.

"Take care of yourself, Mr. Collins."

"You do the same, and I'll be in touch."

Placing the phone on its charging cradle, Terry found a slight glimmer of hope that he might still arrest Nick Vaughn one day. Unfortunately, circumstantial evidence wasn't enough to complete his quest, but if anyone could provide concrete proof, that person was Gary Collins, Sr.

CHAPTER 45

Joe Taggart felt certain the scenic view around him was perfect for a postcard or computer screen saver. Two and a half hours north of the area he called home, Flathead Lake didn't have a bad view because it was surrounded by the greenest of grasses and the most beautiful of trees during the summer, with some of the cleanest water a tourist could ever hope to see. Even the few incorporated areas where cabins and restaurants existed fit right in, because tourism forced ownership to keep them appealing at all times.

One of the largest lakes in the country, Flathead seemed to span forever at thirty miles long by sixteen miles wide. Such a vast body of water tended to hide some dark secrets.

While Teton County remained windy as always, this particular part of the state was nestled in a valley where calm breezes were sometimes hard to come by. Taggart stood beside Lynn as the lake's water caressed the shore and piers around them like a mother might gently comb a child's hair. The ebb and flow barely made a sound, as though mourning the loss it returned to the surface world from its depths.

"It's a shame," Lynn commented, "but it will be closure for her family."

"Yup."

Taggart wasn't feeling up to conversation at the moment. The instant Kelli Martin's body was discovered by a restaurant worker beside the shore, local authorities were summoned. Flathead County authorities discovered the identity of the body right away, so they phoned Lynn, who in turn picked up Taggart instead of trying to reach him by phone.

Strangely, the discovery provided closure for Taggart as well, though it meant he made a grave error in Buffalo when he pointed the finger at Daryl Swanson. Part of the reason Donnie Childress always remained the prime suspect, ahead of Swanson, was the fact that he dated Kelli Martin steadily until a month or so before she disappeared. Childress consistently denied anything to do with her disappearance, but without a body, witnesses, or trace evidence, Taggart found himself helpless to pursue the man.

By the time he arrived with Lynn, the body and area had been examined by authorities for nearly four hours. She was wrapped heavily in a black tarp of some sort, and based on the hole along one end, it appeared whatever weight was initially used to hold her body at the bottom of the lake finally tore through, allowing her body to surface after nearly three years underwater.

The timing almost seemed like a miracle from above.

Surrounded by pines and a variety of other trees, the restaurant boasted delicious seafood and steak platters, looking something like a New England eatery. Rounded tables with permanent seating bolted around them remained in the elements. A simple cleaning and some new patio umbrellas, and they would be ready for the summer tourism season. Snow mounds dotted the hilly grasses beside the building where plows had deposited their loads over the winter. Most days in April had reached forty degrees, but some shady and built up areas were slow to surrender their winter fortresses.

Like some kind of scented car freshener, the spring air smelled of pines and the new floral life sprouting around the lake's vast acreage. Taggart found the clean air similar to that at his ranch because mountains overlooked both areas. It was the kind of air they named candles after, like "Mountain Pine" or "Spring Bouquet" with decorative labels.

Despite this otherwise perfect postcard scene, the wildlife around the lake remained strangely quiet, as though in observance for the deceased. Virtually every critter known to North Americans resided in the state of Montana, so for birds, raccoons, frogs, deer, and every other mammal to suddenly take a vow of silence seemed a bit odd to Taggart.

He stood beside Lynn, looking at the restaurant, which had closed for the day, then to the body. Pale as a ghost, poor Kelli appeared very much intact, her eyes half open as they were the moment she lost her battle with a suspected killer. Though tattered, most of her clothing covered her body, indicating the killer disposed of her rather quickly instead of trying to discard evidence first.

Legends about Flathead Lake keeping its dead spread throughout the state, though most of them were absolutely true. Pockets of the lake nearly three-hundred feet deep made for good fishing, but their extremely cold temperatures kept bodies from surfacing for years, even decades. Taggart knew of several instances where drowning victims from the 1950s surfaced after the new millennium when summer warmth touched the pockets enough to free the corpses from their icy graves.

Fortunately, the fresh water's cold nature preserved the bodies exceptionally well, which left the former sheriff optimistic about finding clues in this instance.

Perhaps Childress knew of the tales as well, purposely tossing her into the deepest reaches of the lake with added weight. At least he's burning in hell, Taggart thought.

"There's some skin under her fingernails," one of the local deputies informed Lynn and Taggart. "If we're lucky, it might still work for DNA analysis."

"We certainly have a suspect to match it with," Taggart said.

He remembered the cuts and scrapes on Childress' hands, which the man dismissed as work on the farm. Now armed with the skin under Kelli's nails, coupled with the scratches and bruises along her arms and neck, Taggart wished he could have done something more. Granted, the bastard got his in the car crash, hopefully burning alive and suffering before he died, but this wasn't the closure the former sheriff wanted for Kelli's family.

Even if the skin proved too far deteriorated for analysis, Taggart felt certain Kelli's disappearance and murder were solved. Only one thing remained, and while he still had a cell phone signal, he found Terry Levine in his list of five contacts and called the state trooper.

"Levine."

"Terry, this is Joe Taggart from Montana."

"What an unexpected pleasure, Sheriff."

"I'm retired, remember? But I'm calling with some interesting news."

"Oh?"

"Daryl Swanson didn't commit the murders here. We just found Childress' first victim at the edge of a lake."

"I figured Swanson was innocent," Levine said after only a few seconds of soaking in the information, "because he didn't commit the murders here either."

Now Taggart was taken aback. He hadn't spoken with the trooper, or anyone else on the task force, since leaving Buffalo. Simply taking it for granted they would provide a courtesy call if anything turned up, he left them to their investigation.

"What happened?"

"We arrested Swanson only to find out his boss set him up for murder," Levine explained. "The problem is we don't have enough evidence on the boss to even arrest him, so Swanson is going to take the fall."

"Shitty luck seems to follow that boy."

"Yeah, well it's not over quite yet. Can I count on you to come rough this guy up for a confession when the time comes?"

"Sure," Taggart said with a chuckle, turning away from the group so no one thought he was expressing anything except remorse for poor Kelli. "Why didn't you call me with any updates?"

"You're a tough man to reach. Besides, nothing ever officially changed around here. They're going to prosecute Swanson and find him guilty because the prosecutor wants a feather in his cap."

"Damn shame when politics affect justice."

"In this case justice is affecting justice because the rules and a noteworthy attorney are keeping me from throwing the right man in jail."

Taggart understood all too well from his own situation.

"They're going to test the body for DNA, but they think it's fifty-fifty on that front."

"Keep me posted," Levine replied.

"You getting along with those cowboy brothers of yours?"

"With one of them. The other seems to believe an inmate's words over mine these days."

"That's never good."

"No, but it's life. Pete and I can knock some sense into him later. How are you doing?"

"Just threw my name in for the Olympic trials," Taggart said with his own brand of dry humor.

"Sprinting events or the whole decathlon?"

"You know, they do have games for us impaired folk."

"But I'm betting a wealthy recluse such as yourself couldn't be bothered with such rubbish. Besides, they'd never be able to contact you short of the Pony Express."

"That's true," Taggart chuckled. "I'm doing okay. Ain't looking forward to telling this girl's family she's been underwater the better part of three years."

"That's not your job, Joe. You're retired."

"Yeah, I know," Taggart said with a feeling of remorse because his career truly, officially ended with the closing of this case. "Those people depended on me to find out what happened to their daughter, Terry. Took me three years, but I finally got it done. I'll be damned if I let some stranger break the news to them."

"I understand. Take care of yourself, Joe, and don't be a stranger."

"I won't. I'll send the Pony Express your way sometime."

Now Terry laughed briefly.

"You do that. Thanks again for everything, Joe."

"Anytime. You take care of yourself, city slicker."

"You too."

Taggart put his phone back as the ambulance personnel loaded the body for transport to the morgue where the coroner's office would begin their investigation. Although he felt bad for Kelli Martin's family, he took comfort in knowing he and Lynn Stover were bound to be married within the year.

He had yet to propose, but the ring stayed hidden in a drawer at his house until the moment felt right. Taggart knew Lynn would say yes, because she hinted at marriage every other time they saw one another. She damned well better say yes, he thought, turning to her as the ambulance doors closed behind the black body bag Kelli and her tarp resided within.

"You know what I have to do," Taggart informed her.

She smiled gently as she nodded.

"You don't have to do it alone."

"I know," he replied.

He never wanted to live life alone again. She was his companion in every way, so he wanted to make it official and take her hand in marriage. For the moment, he simply took her hand as they walked toward her marked truck, unconcerned with how badly he limped, or what strangers thought of him.

Why care at all? he pondered. I'm retired.

CHAPTER 46

Terry returned to the Buffalo area briefly to speak with the district attorney about the impending case against Swanson. Strangely, the court hearings were moving far more swiftly than most murder cases, as though the prosecutor knew his case might be poisoned if he didn't hurry it along.

If he hadn't initially felt that way, he certainly did following his conversation with Terry. In no uncertain terms, Terry conveyed his belief that Swanson was completely innocent and another individual was responsible.

"The same individual you conducted a raid against when you found no useful evidence?" the man countered.

More stubborn than a mule, the prosecutor didn't want to hear anything about the case unless it incriminated Swanson. Terry basically ended their conversation by stating the prosecution team didn't want to call him to the stand because the truth might damn their case.

"Don't worry about that," the district attorney assured him.

Fuming, but already knowing from previous discussions that the prosecution wasn't going to budge, Terry considered the irony if the defense team called him to the stand. He didn't plan on volunteering his services, because in no way did he want to reveal anything about his mounting case against Vaughn. With Belinski finally feeding him juicy bits about the budding serial killer's past, Terry compiled his own psychological profile of the real Sin Killer.

Despite his previous reprimand, Gosser sometimes called him with updates because the man detested using e-mail or text messaging for some reason. Terry wondered if Gosser was an extremist who believed technology was going to take over the world and eradicate mankind during their lifetime. So far, Vaughn had remained close to home, without calling attention to himself. Granted, Gosser only checked on the man periodically, but none of the dozen or so unsolved murders in New York State pointed his way.

Soon, Terry thought, he'll have to kill again. The man was likely boiling over with the urge to kill, likely satiating himself with whatever memories or hidden trinkets he took from his previous murders. He still possessed the perfect cover with which to travel the state and commit homicides, now free from police harassment.

Before he even left for Buffalo, Terry knew the meeting with the prosecutor wasn't going to fare well. It could easily have taken place over the phone, but Terry had an ulterior motive for driving five hours southwest of his hometown. Already within Tonawanda town limits, he drove his borrowed unmarked car to Erie Wholesale, then parked at the neighboring business, ensuring he was in plain view of Vaughn's truck.

Checking his watch, he figured only fifteen minutes or so remained before the man walked out from his daily shift. Terry wondered if the Erie Wholesale employees suspected Vaughn of anything, or they rallied around him with love and support. The thought of anyone embracing the sadistic bastard irked Terry, but even he had fallen for the man's cons at one time.

Vaughn worshiped his murdered father, placing Ray Vaughn on a pedestal as the greatest investigator who ever lived. Terry wondered if the deceased detective would have pegged his own son as a killer before seven lives were lost.

He doubted it.

Having a book, a children's book at that, done about oneself did not make the subject any better at his or her job. Still, Nick Vaughn knew how not to get caught. His father likely had something to do with that, in some bizarre kind of way.

When the workers finally began filing out, Terry watched carefully for Vaughn, not seeing the man exit with the laborers. He suspected management might take longer to leave for the night because their salary contracts demanded it, or perhaps they attended meetings. He patiently waited, tapping his feet occasionally, listening to the radio, and checking the dashboard clock until it read 5:24 p.m.

At that moment, Terry stepped from the car as he looked to the overcast sky. Perfect, he thought. No shadows, no doubts about why I'm here or who I am. He spotted Nick Vaughn exiting the building at long last, prompting him to reach for his gun and shift the entire holster toward the front. As the man crossed the parking lot, Terry wanted him to see the gun and know exactly who came all that way to see him. Terry then leaned against the front of the hood, feet planted firmly in the ground as he crossed his arms. Like a sentry, he remained perfectly still, his blue eyes burning into Vaughn until the man finally made eye contact and stopped just short of his truck to return the stare.

It took Vaughn a moment to recognize Terry, who refused to blink or look away. He wasn't trying to act tough or put on a show, but Terry wanted to send a message that he knew exactly who, and what Vaughn had become. Vaughn stood beside the car momentarily, breathing casually as his chest rose and fell.

Seconds passed, though time seemed to stand still as Terry waited for a response.

Any response.

A chewing gum wrapper blew through the parking lot like a tumbleweed in a western movie during a tense stare down. While Terry's objective wasn't a justified shooting, he supposed it might serve as a fitting end to the case.

Vaughn finally gave a little, knowing smirk which he held only a second or two, before proceeding to unlock and enter his truck.

Even as Vaughn backed up and left the parking lot, Terry followed the car's movement. He knew the killer understood their silent conversation well enough. The smirk proved Terry correct, though he worried that he, and everyone on the task force, were powerless to stop Vaughn until he got sloppy.

Someday, Terry thought as he opened his car door. Though the case was beyond his control, he wanted Vaughn to know he wasn't overlooked by authorities. Hopefully the move might prompt the killer to carry out some rash action that got him caught sooner than later. Living five hours away, Terry doubted he would ever be the man to slap the cuffs on Vaughn when the time came, but he felt certain Vaughn was going to kill again, and get himself caught eventually.

Nick Vaughn wasn't going to elude him forever, but Terry needed to save his youngest brother from a predatory serial killer before Kenny bought into everything Kimmerling said. He already had some ideas about how to get the old Kenny back. He needed Pete's help, but he figured between them things would work out just fine.

Then back to Vaughn, who likely saw Terry as a threat to his father, the supposed greatest detective of all time. Terry shook his head as he grunted to himself about the vanity filling Vaughn's mind. The more he got to know the man through Gosser's and Belinski's updates, the less Terry liked the challenge ahead of investigators. For the time being, Terry had accomplished what he wanted to, letting Vaughn know his crimes weren't being overlooked by everyone. Someone, somewhere, would always know exactly how he tarnished his father's good name by breaking the laws Ray Vaughn took an oath to uphold.

"But first things first," Terry said as he started the car for the return trip home, ready to put his family first and not let the lunatics of the world consume him.

If the weather permitted, perhaps he would dig his boots out of the closet and ride horseback with his brothers over the weekend. Terry knew he couldn't stop every criminal who crossed his path, but like Joe Taggart, maybe he needed to take life at face value to appreciate his family and the simple things he took for granted.

Win or lose, there was always going to be a new challenge ahead of him. Though his family members sometimes had their differences, they were never going to leave his side. Their loyalty made the five hour drive ahead of him a bit more tolerable, reassuring him that no matter where he traveled, he always went home in the end.

Terry knew his job provided closure to the families of so many victims, and the victims themselves.

And for that simple reason, Terry wouldn't contemplate leaving his position anytime soon.

CHAPTER 47

Friday, July 3

The Adirondacks

Gary Collins, Sr. parked his old pickup truck at the foot of the campsite where his family had spent dozens of nights surrounded by nature. The land was privately owned, leased to numerous individuals who enjoyed hunting, fishing, hiking, and other outdoor activities. A simple building served as the camp, complete with bunks, a wood-burning stove, a few furnishings, and some shelves for storage.

No electricity or running water could be found for miles, which meant despite staying inside a solid building, the family roughed it whenever they visited the camp. Even the outhouse about twenty feet from the main building required manual maintenance whenever the stench became too much to tolerate. Cell phones were useless so deep in the woods, and the kids sometimes looked lost without the internet until the family began group activities.

Collins stepped from his reliable 1983 Chevy truck to find wood stacked at the foot of the camp building, and another small stack, covered with a blue tarp, nearby. Entirely untended, the plant life came about knee high around the entire camp. A fire pit, still containing charred wood, sat on the side opposite the outhouse, where his kids, and now the grandchildren, roasted marshmallows and hotdogs over the fire.

As much as Collins cherished the memories made with his family, he came to the camp with a grave mission on his mind. After finding the little box in one of the woodpiles, he figured his surrogate son might have hidden other objects at the camp, feeling confident no one would disturb them before he returned.

He walked to the woodpile, ensuring the little box still rested where he had replaced it during his last trip to the site. Regrettably, his children all had different plans for the Independence Day weekend that didn't include camping, which was just as well considering the negative connotation linked to the camp for Collins. He found the box, opened it to find the newspaper clippings and a tie clip inside. The clip hadn't been there before, which sent his mind on a journey through the seven homicides the police believed Vaughn might have committed. He made a mental note to ask Terry Levine or one of the task force members if any trinkets were taken from any of the victims.

Collins touched nothing inside the box, opting to leave any forensic evidence intact, now that he felt differently about his old partner's son. Replacing the lid, Collins hid the box in the woodpile exactly the way he initially found it.

Though retired, Collins felt his investigative juices kick in, telling him the box's contents might be just the beginning of the hidden trinkets at the camp. Armed with a metal detector and some determination, Collins decided to unlock the cabin and step inside for a search of the building. He dreaded the thought of scouring the grounds for evidence that may be anywhere around the campsite, or not exist in the first place.

Using a combination of oil lamps, candles, and a flashlight, Collins searched the dark interior within half an hour, finding nothing. Every adult in the family, including Vaughn, possessed a key to the building, so Collins considered the search necessary. Groaning to himself after turning up nothing, he locked the door and returned outside, scooping up the metal detector.

He spent the next hour circling the camp's buildings, sweat dripping down his chest and back, while mosquitoes and horse flies took turns biting his exposed arms and neck. Hot and miserable, Collins refused to give up as he began looking for paths leading away from the camp that might indicate a familiar trail Vaughn used to hide items where only he might know to locate them during future visits.

Endless possibilities surrounded him, but Collins decided to head toward the trickling stream that ran less than one-hundred yards from the camp. A guaranteed present landmark throughout the year, the stream also provided adequate hiding spots with a few hollow trees and stumps lying atop the ground. Some family members hiked to the stream, then followed it to a pond where they fished for dinner.

He walked the slightly treaded path toward the stream, carefully swinging the metal detector from side to side. It remained so silent that he checked the power lights from time to time to make certain it hadn't shut down. Chirping birds and the squeaks of small mammals were the only noises that filled the air until Collins drew closer to the stream, which provided the steady sound of running water just over a small hill. He trudged up the hill, still being dive-bombed by local insects. Collins jumped a bit when the metal detector blared as it skimmed over the top of a large rock to his right.

Collecting himself as he stood only halfway up the hill, the retired detective moved around the rock, fully expecting a false reading from the detector in the form of empty beer cans or some coins. When he searched behind the rock, he discovered it wasn't a rock at all, but rather a prop of some sort that looked exactly like a gray rock, complete with grooves and bumps. Just over a foot around, the rock felt plastic to the touch as Collins searched for an access point. After feeling it up and down a moment, he attempted to lift it off the ground, finding the feat rather easy.

Hearing a rattle from within the false rock, Collins set it down, looking for a way to reach inside without destroying the prop. He already felt stupid for covering it in his fingerprints, but he found a small hatch along the back held in place by two clasps that matched the coloration of the rock. He undid the clasps before looking inside to find a firearm of some sort. Tall, thick trees obscured the daylight, and he forgot to bring a flashlight, so Collins held up the rock for a better look, finding what appeared to be a perfect match for the only firearm not found in Daryl Swanson's vehicle by authorities.

His heart skipped a beat, because now Collins knew without a doubt Vaughn was harboring a dark secret that would have devastated his father. Setting the rock beside him, Collins dropped to his knees, simply sitting on the ground momentarily, realizing the most difficult decision of his life lie before him. Realistically, it wasn't a decision at all, because he knew Vaughn needed to be brought to justice, even if he never planned to kill again. Emotionally drained, Collins hated the idea of turning in a member of his own family. Even though Vaughn wasn't his own bloodline, everyone in the Collins family treated him no differently than they did their own kin.

"Jesus," Collins muttered, realizing innocent people may have been placed in grave danger because he didn't act on Terry Levine's information sooner.

To the best of his knowledge, no unsolved homicides occurred after Swanson was taken into custody, but Vaughn could have changed his style, hidden the bodies instead, or stopped killing for an undetermined length of time.

After pulling himself together, Collins sealed the fake rock, put it on the side of the path where he found it, then stumbled back toward the camp. He wanted to leave the evidence, every bit of it, exactly where it was currently placed, because he wanted the authorities to return with him and collect it. For all he knew, there might be more evidence yet to be unearthed.

Feeling partly responsible for what Vaughn turned out to be, Collins felt a tear trickle down his cheek by the time he reached the clearing. His attempts to connect with Vaughn hadn't proven very successful, as though the young man knew he was prying for information.

As a retiree, Collins possessed no arrest powers, and taking any evidence to authorities would undermine a potential court case because the defense could simply contest that he planted the evidence, or somehow tampered with it. Collins now needed to convince his son of the truth, and keep it within the family to avoid a media circus. Regardless of how he handled Vaughn's arrest in the end, it needed to happen officially and swiftly.

He owed the families of seven victims the truth. Collins wasn't going to take such a dark secret to his grave without bringing the truth to light. When he partnered with Ray Vaughn, they never kept information from one another, and in his heart, Collins knew his partner wouldn't put himself, or his own son, above the law.

Collins took one last look at the camp, determined to finish what the task force had started and put the last mystery in his life to rest.